D1512850

New York Times bestselling author **Rosemary Rogers** has written over twenty historical and contemporary romances. Dubbed "the queen of historical romance," she is best known for her passionate and sensual characters, and her Steve-and-Ginny series is a classic with fans. Born in Ceylon, Rosemary now lives in Connecticut.

JEWEL OF MY HEART

Rosemary Rogers

*MILLS & BOON and MILLS & BOON with the Rose Device
are registered trademarks of the publisher.*

*First published in Great Britain 2007
by Harlequin Mills & Boon Limited,
Eton House, 18-24 Paradise Road, Richmond, Surrey TW9 1SR*

© Rosemary Rogers 2004

ISBN: 978 0 263 85538 8

037-0807

*Printed and bound in Spain
by Litografia Rosés S.A., Barcelona*

JEWEL OF MY HEART

To my granddaughter,
with all my love

Book One
London

1

London, England
Boxwood Manor
September 1888

"Madison," Lady Westcott shrieked. "Madison Ann Westcott, unlock this door at once!"

Ignoring her mother, Madison concentrated, the tip of her tongue held between her teeth, as she drew her horse-hair paintbrush through the red ochre on the palette in her hand. With a broad, confident gesture, she stroked the color over the canvas in a sweeping, dark curve that was the man's shoulder.

She gazed up at the model, then back at her painting, and smiled, at last satisfied. She'd been laboring for two days on the hue of the male model's ebony skin, and, at last, she felt she had it.

"Madison, what are you doing in there? Unlock this door at once or I'll have Edward remove the hinges again," Lady Westcott threatened.

Cundo's intense, black-eyed gaze shifted past Madison to the secured double paneled walnut doors, but he did not move a muscle. "Honorable Miss, perhaps—" he began in a deep, melodious rumble.

"She'll admit defeat and withdraw, Cundo. She always does." Madison touched the streak of muscle on the black man's shoulder in her painting, shading it a bit more. "Do you need to relax a moment?" she asked, her gaze darting in his direction again. "Because, heaven knows I do. We've been at this for hours."

"Madison, I won't stand for this behavior any longer, do you hear me?" There was a knock on the door, then a bang, which was quite out of character for her mother. "Your aunt has arrived and I demand that you come out of there! I insist that you go to your room, have Aubrey bathe you and then dress you fittingly, and that you come to the drawing room without delay."

Madison wiped her brush down the front of the white floor-length smock she wore over her nightdress, smearing paint but cleaning the bristles quite efficiently. Though it was near to four in the afternoon, she hadn't yet found time to dress. Not that she cared, but if her mother found her way into the studio, there would be hell to pay. All the more reason why she could not, presently, leave the studio.

"Tell Lady Moran I'm working," she called over her shoulder in the direction of the locked double doors. "Perhaps I'll see her tomorrow when she's rested from her journey."

Madison was, in fact, anxious to welcome the aunt she'd never met but had heard romantic tales of. But Lady Moran hadn't been due in until tomorrow, and an artist had to work when the muse bid, didn't she?

The doorknobs rattled one more time and then were silent. Her mother had capitulated and gone away, just as Madison had predicted.

"Please, Cundo," Madison said, setting her palette and brush on a small table beside her easel. "Let go of those frightful chains and come have some fruit juice with me." She waved to the only person she'd seen face-to-face in three days. When she was at work, she preferred not to be disturbed in any way, even for necessities. She'd commanded the servants to pass meager meals and liquid refreshment through a window that opened into the garden. "Truly, I won't take no for an answer."

Reluctantly the man released the heavy, rusted chains wrapped around his wrists and let them fall to the floor, then stepped gracefully off the pedestal where Madison had him posed in front of a dark drape of fabric.

"It's freshly squeezed orange from our orangery," she cajoled, pouring two glasses. "I know you'll like it."

"C'mon, jus' like that?" the young housemaid from next door whispered. "She brought that creature in?"

Aubrey, Madison's personal maid, patted the young girl's hand. "Shh, Lettie. Else the miss will 'ear us and roast us both." She indicated the ebony-skinned man with a dip of her dimpled chin. "Sneaked 'im in, she did. Was barely dawn when she come in through the back servants' quarters door. I been tellin' yer fer months she in't got no decency."

The two young maids lay on their bellies beneath a table at the far side of the art studio, concealed by a large canvas drop cloth and stacks of Aubrey's mistress's canvases.

Lettie stared at the viscount's only daughter in astonishment. "Lady Westcott got ter be shocked."

"Garn!" Aubrey whispered harshly. "I daresay the lady don't know her daughter got a naked African in the studio! Poor Lady Westcott, she'd fall over dead if she knew."

Pushing back one corner of the drape that hid them, Lettie studied the powerfully built black man with fascination as he strode across the studio. She licked her dry lips. "'E ain't naked. 'E got that nappy thing goin' 'cross 'is possibles."

"Garn, everything but!" Aubrey swore, eyeing the young man's muscular buttocks as he turned to accept a glass of juice from her mistress. "I told yer it would be well worth yers five pence to see 'im up-close like."

"Scand'lous. And 'er 'bout to be introduced to 'ciety." Lettie shook her mobcap-covered head.

"Hmm," Aubrey snorted. "Maybe she *is* and maybe she ain't."

Lettie's milky-blue eyes widened even further. "No! Do tell."

"That's why Lady Westcott's in such a tear. Not only has the young miss been livin' day and night in this studio, but she say she ain't attendin' her comin'-out ball come Saturday a fortnight."

"No," Lettie breathed.

"Would I lie ter yer, Lettuce Hogg?" Aubrey demanded in a heated whisper.

"'Course not."

"'Course not," Aubrey repeated. "Miss Madison say she ain't bein' introduced ter proper 'ciety, and she ain't marryin'."

"What *is* she doin'?"

"She say she's goin' to Paris ter paint with some man. Somebody called *Master.*" Aubrey lifted one shoulder. "Now, Miss Madison's comin'-out gown arrived yesterday," she continued. "The most beautiful gown yer ever seen in yer life. Fer two hours Lady Westcott tried to carrot 'er daughter out of 'ere. 'Course, she didn't know what was keepin' 'er." She nodded deliberately in the direction of the African.

Lettie gazed over her shoulder in the direction of the open window they'd climbed through to secretly gain entrance into the studio. "Why didn't Lady Westcott—"

Aubrey frowned, silencing her companion with a squeeze to her plump arm. "Yer don't think Lady Westcott would stoop to climbin' through windows?"

"'Course not," Lettie breathed.

"'Course not," Aubrey repeated, eyeing her mistress, who was now in conversation with the black man. "And if Miss Madison don't go to 'er comin'-out ball, you know wot that means."

Lettie's jaw hung slack. "'Nother year with nary a marriage proposal, and she already bein' twenty-one."

"And—"

"And?" Lettie begged.

"And Lady Westcott'll not be marrying Viscount Kendal, I'll warrant yer that."

"Viscount Kendal? Fetch my stars, the buzzin' is true?" Lettie scratched her armpit. "They gettin' married."

"Nothin' 'fficial yet." Aubrey hooked her thumb in the general direction of the main house. "Lady Westcott's got ter get rid of that sack a trouble first. Viscount Kendal's already made it plain. 'Eard 'im say so myself. *While I'm quite fond of yer,*" she mimicked haughtily, *"I'll have no part of that 'oyden, Madam."*

Lettie stared at Madison again.

"Worse, I 'spect," Aubrey went on, quite full of herself. "Now the auntie from the islands is 'ere to Boxwood

Manor a good day early. The late viscount's half sister, yer know. Widered long ago, stinkin' rich and as 'culiar as they come, they say. And 'ere the young miss is locked up with 'er African brute."

"We had no idea at Barton Place." Lettie pressed her chubby hand to her flushed cheek. "And to think we only livin' a stone's throw 'way. What Lady Barton would think, if she knew."

"Yer better not tell." Aubrey jabbed her companion with her elbow.

Lettie gave a loud squeak of surprise and both young women, realizing what they had done, recoiled.

"We best go 'fore we're caught," Aubrey mouthed silently.

The maids rose on their hands and knees and attempted to turn around beneath the table so they could crawl out. But in the close quarters, with their yards of starched underskirts beneath their black uniforms, they found their escape more difficult to execute than their entrance had been.

"Ouch," Aubrey groaned, yanking her ruffled petticoat out from beneath her companion's knee. "Garn, Lettie, yer cow, let me out first." She ducked her head beneath the canvas, poised to dart out, when a hand clamped over her ankle.

Aubrey squeaked in fright as the hand jerked her backward, forcing her down on her face, then dragged her out from beneath the table, knocking canvases over in every direction.

"So I've found my mole," Madison Westcott flared. "Didn't I tell you, Cundo, that I thought my mother might have a mole, spying on me?"

Aubrey turned onto her back to stare up in horror. "Miss… Miss Madison. Yer know I would never—"

"And your accomplice," Madison beckoned. "Come, come, or I'll be in after you, too," she warned.

Lettie, clutching her mobcap until it nearly covered her eyes, stuck her head out from beneath the table. "Miss Madison," she whispered, her voice trembling with fear. "Yer…yer lookin' fine today."

When Madison realized that one of the servants had sneaked in through the window she'd left ajar, she'd fully intended to ferret them out and release them from service at once. She could not have disloyal staff serving her. She would not.

But somehow what the maid, no more than fifteen, said, struck her funny. Madison tipped back her head and laughed. "What a fatuous thing to say." She rubbed at the paint she knew smeared the end of her nose. She could smell it. "I look dreadful."

"N-not, dreadful, Miss Madison." Lettie found her voice as well as her feet. "Dressed in that there sheet, 'air a'tumble and paint on yer face, yer prettier than Miss Fanny Barton any day the month."

Madison couldn't resist a smile. Her mother was constantly comparing the neighbor, Fanny, to her. Though two years her junior, Fanny had come out two years ago, landed seven marriage proposals and was engaged to be wed this fall to one of the most eligible bachelors in all of London. Rich and titled. Of course, Fanny had a face like a hyena, the temperament to match, and the brain of a split pea, so Madison was actually quite happy for her.

"What are you doing under my table?" Madison asked, shifting her gaze to her personal maid. "Are you tattling to my mother?"

"Garn! Certainly not, Miss Madison." Aubrey drew herself up to stand at attention before the best employer one could ever have. "I was jest tellin' Lettie 'ere 'ow beautiful your paintings was and she wanted to see fer herself."

"Liar," Madison accused.

Aubrey's face puckered as if she were about to burst into tears.

"You're not here to see my paintings, you're here to see my model." She stepped aside. "Well, see him if you must. But let me introduce you properly. Cundo," she called. "I've someone here who would like to make your acquaintance."

As the black man, nude but for a loincloth, strode toward them, Lettie squeaked and lifted her apron to cover her eyes. Aubrey looked down, embarrassed.

"Lady Moran," Lady Westcott cooed, slipping back into the plush drawing room and tucking her hands behind her back. "I apologize profusely, but my Madison is still not quite ready."

Lady Kendra Moran watched with fascination as her sister-in-law's mouth remained frozen in a smile as she spoke, her lips barely seeming to move. A truly extraordinary feat, in Kendra's eyes.

"But you know how young girls can be," Lady Westcott continued. There was a brittle, artificial laugh. "Always taking one more moment to primp."

"Young girl?" Kendra snorted, rising to her feet and stretching her hands over her head to ease her aching muscles. The sea journey from Jamaica had been long and bone tiring. "By Hindi's gold teeth, Alba, at twenty-one she can't very well be categorized as a young girl, now can she?"

Kendra glanced at her traveling companion and closest neighbor in Jamaica. "You know this fickle town, Carlton. Twenty-one years old and unmarried, and gossips begin to insist the woman has a third eye in her forehead or madness in her brain."

Lady Westcott made a little sucking sound as she inhaled. "L-Lord Thomblin, might I offer you another refreshment, sir?"

"Most certainly not, thank you." Lord Thomblin offered Alba his most handsome smile as he leaned back in a horsehair wing chair and propped one ankle on his knee. "But might I take this moment to say that your home is truly a delight."

"Well, thank you, Lord Thomblin." Alba giggled as if she were the unmarried maiden in the household. "Please feel free to walk in our gardens." She indicated the open French doors that led onto a stone patio and beyond it to the formal gardens of Boxwood Manor.

Kendra watched with amusement as her sister-in-law's gaze shifted to Jefford Harris, who stood with his back to them as he studied a bookshelf containing a row of volumes that had once belonged to Kendra's brother. Even from here, she could see his scowl. He despised afternoon tea, ladies' parlors and nonsensical chatter that Englishwomen so often engaged in.

"And you, too, sir... Mr. Harris."

"Jefford," he grunted, not bothering to look at Alba.

Kendra could tell by his tone that he had already passed judgment on her deceased half brother's wife and it was neither favorable nor flattering. Heavens, she wished now she'd insisted he remain in Jamaica where he belonged.

Bringing her arms down to complete her stretch, Kendra turned to Alba. "Shall we go to her, then?" she asked, realizing she was as bored as Jefford.

The smile, frozen on Alba's pinched face, grew tauter. She clutched her thin hands. "Go to her?"

"Yes, go to her." Kendra swept her arms grandly. "Nothing encourages a woman to dress faster than visitors to her chambers." She glanced over her shoulder as she breezed out the door. "Gentlemen?"

"I believe I'll take Lady Westcott up on her offer and walk in the gardens," Lord Thomblin said, rising.

"Jefford?"

A rare volume cradled in one hand, he never glanced her way. "Pass."

Kendra rolled her eyes as she swept down the wide, portrait-lined passageway. "Ignore his ill humor, Alba. He was born on a rising moon. It can't be helped."

Her sister-in-law hurried in her wake. "Lady Moran—"

"Please, Alba, you know I was never a standpat for titles. You must call me Kendra."

"Kendra," she said breathlessly. "Really, I think we should wait for Madison. I'm quite certain she will be—"

"Where is she? Upstairs?" Kendra halted in the massive front hall, taking in the familiar sight. "My, it looks no different than it did when I lived here as a child more than fifty years ago!" She studied the sets of armor flanking the massive walnut entry door, still poised with raised weapons, standing guard. The old swords and scabbards that lined the walls and spoked the ceiling were still gathering dust. "Still smells of lemon-polished walnut and long-dead relatives," she mused.

"P-pardon?" Alba stammered, patting her mouth with a lace handkerchief.

"Memories, Alba, too many memories. Now, where is this daughter of yours?" Kendra reached out to grab her shoulder. "Are you feeling all right?"

"Yes, yes, quite fine, thank you." Alba fluttered the

handkerchief, obviously, despite her protest, quite beside herself. "Actually…actually Madison could still be in the studio."

"Excellent. I should like to see her work. Harrison wrote several times over the years of her remarkable talent, but I assumed it was all hot air expressed by a proud father." Kendra crossed the broad, Italian-tiled entrance hall and took a familiar passageway. "I'm so pleased Madison has been able to make use of Papa's studio. You know, Papa fancied himself quite an artist, but he truly was without talent."

"My heavens" was all Alba managed.

Kendra found the studio doors in the far end of the long passageway, just where she remembered them. Before she even reached out to tap on the door, she smelled the thick, cloying scent of oil paints and was bombarded with fond memories.

"I got them tools you wanted me to fetch, Lady Westcott," announced a balding middle-aged man in a work apron, as he approached. He set down a toolbox beside the studio door. "Won't take but a minute to get them hinges off now that I got the hang of it."

Kendra drew back her hand and looked to her sister-in-law. "We are removing the doors rather than simply walking through them?"

Lady Westcott's frozen smile returned.

"Is my niece inside?"

Alba nodded. "She won't come out," she whispered.

"Is she ill?"

"I…I don't believe so. She…she says she's working."

"Is that all?" Kendra shook her head. "Just like Papa. Do you know he once sequestered himself in here for nearly two months? He produced some of the most dreadful paintings I believe I have ever seen." She rapped firmly on the door. "I certainly hope she's more talented than he was."

"Go away," responded a strong, young female voice from inside.

Alba looked to Kendra. "She's been under a great deal of strain, with her coming-out ball."

Kendra rapped harder.

"Mother! If you do not cease that distracting noise, I'll not be out for a week."

"Madison Ann Westcott," Kendra called. "Open this door at once, or I'll take the hinges off myself." She took a breath, her tone softening. "Now, be a good puss and let me in before your mother faints right here in the corridor."

Behind the door, Kendra heard voices. A woman squealed, but it didn't sound like Madison. And she could have sworn she heard the rumble of a male voice. Something fell, making a loud crashing sound.

"Is everything all right in there, dear?" Kendra called.

"Lady Moran," Madison sang. There was more movement. Whispering. "You…you're early."

"It's Aunt Kendra, please, dear. And what possibly makes you think I can control the winds of the seven seas? The ship docked early, but I hadn't realized I needed an appointment to see my favorite niece."

"I'm your only niece," Madison called cheerfully. Then she spoke more quietly to someone else with her in the room.

"Come, come," Kendra called impatiently. "Open the doors now."

The doorknob jiggled from the inside, and then the lock turned and one of the double doors swung open.

"Aunt Kendra, so good to meet you at last."

A young woman who could be no one but her half

brother's child rushed forward, and Kendra opened her arms, surprised by the emotion that suddenly overwhelmed her.

"Go, Edward, go," Lady Westcott ordered, shooing the servant with the tools.

Kendra closed her arms around her tall, willowy niece and squeezed her tightly. "Heavens, but aren't you a sight for weary eyes," she muttered, embarrassed by her reaction.

Madison stepped back, smiling. She was probably the most beautiful young woman Kendra had ever laid eyes upon. Certainly prettier than she herself had been, even in her early years. But Madison had her golden hair, and her eyes, a most mesmerizing shade of blue-green. Kendra's father's eyes.

"Run up and change, Madison," Alba ordered quickly. "We can wait for you in the drawing room."

"We'll do no such thing. I think she's just lovely the way she is," Kendra said, sweeping her gaze over her niece.

The young woman was dressed in an absurd outfit that Kendra might have worn herself, a thin white smock that only fell to her ankles, without any undergarments beneath at all, it appeared, save for a thin sleeping gown. The smock was covered with splotches of paint, as colorful as a rainbow. On her feet, she wore some sort of heavy mules like the Dutch wore…and her hair! It was twisted on her head with a brightly colored scarf to tumble in a tangled waterfall of the most beautiful golden color God could create.

"I want to see your work. May I?" Kendra asked, poking her head into the studio. She took note that not another soul was to be seen, but the windows that flanked the far wall were all thrown open, revealing the walled garden Boxwood Manor was renowned for.

It took Madison a moment to acclimate herself, and the look on her mother's face right now was truly without price.

At first impression, her aunt Kendra was nothing like what she had expected…she was better. Madison caught both doors with her paint-stained hands, blocking her aunt's entrance as she glanced over her shoulder in the direction of the open window the two maids had just escorted Cundo through. The chains he had held still lay on the floor; there had been no time to hide them.

"I…you're certainly welcome to see my work," Madison said, trying to think fast. Thank heaven she'd had the forethought to cover her half-completed portrait of Cundo. "Perhaps it would be better if I dressed first, as Mother suggested. I could bring a piece of my artwork to the drawing room for you to see," Madison said sweetly, trying to stall for time.

Aunt Kendra, dressed in a brightly colored caftanlike gown with a white silk turban on her head, craned her neck, trying to see into the studio. "I think that would be most advisable," Madison's mother said, seeming to wilt against the wall.

"Nonsense." Aunt Kendra pushed Madison's hands down. "Alba, there's no need for you to see Madison's work. I know you've seen it all a thousand times before. Why don't your retire to your chambers to rest and we'll see you at dinner."

"I—"

"I'll not take no for an answer." Kendra waggled a finger. "I know you must be exhausted with all the plans for Madison's coming-out ball and then me barging in like this, with my entourage."

"I believe I could lie down for a moment," Lady West-cott said weakly. "It has been a frightfully long week."

Madison turned to her aunt as her mother took her leave, looping her arm through Kendra's. "An entourage? Now, really. Whoever have you brought with you?"

"You know, servants, a good friend of mine, a neighbor, Lord Thomblin and—"

"You've brought servants? Are any of them Jamaican?" Madison asked excitedly. "I should give anything to be able to paint one of them."

Shouts and loud barking suddenly erupted in the garden. "Oh, no, Cundo," Madison exclaimed. Releasing her aunt's arm she ran for the window. Just as she reached the great glass panes, one swung open and Cundo, escorted by a man Madison had never laid eyes on in her life, leaped through the window. Two bloodhounds were hot on their heels, barking and snarling in a frenzy.

Cundo leaned over, breathing heavily, a thickly corded forearm bleeding profusely.

"Damnation, my brother's dogs, Cundo, I'm sorry." Madison went down on one knee in front of her model and tried to check the extent of the dog bite.

"You little twit," the stranger bellowed, turning on Madison. "You could have killed this man!"

2

Still holding Cundo's arm, Madison turned on the stranger, whom she might have considered handsome, in an exotic way, if he hadn't been frowning so. He was very tall and broad-shouldered with dark hair worn slightly longer than was fashionable. His skin was a most unusual sun-kissed color, and he had eyes that were a piercing black. He wore conservative gray trousers and a matching gray jacket, but the fabric was of the finest any tailor in London had to offer. Who was this man and where had he come from?

"I beg your pardon, sir," Madison cried indignantly. "And who might you be, climbing in my window?"

"What did you think you were doing, sending this man sneaking out of the house through the garden?" the stranger demanded. "Those dogs could have torn him limb from limb."

"Jefford," Lady Moran cut in. "No harm has been done—"

"You know this…this abominable man?" Madison

turned to her aunt, her cheeks burning with a mixture of embarrassment and anger.

"Not only do I know him…" Aunt Kendra sighed. "But I fear I'm the one responsible for toting him here." She indicated Madison, and then the stranger with a raised, bejeweled hand. "The Honorable Madison Westcott, Jefford Harris."

"Honorable Miss, I am not hurt," Cundo said, rising to his feet. "Please, the dogs have been called. I must go before someone else sees me."

"You'll do no such thing." Madison tried to examine his wounded arm again. "This should be cleansed and bandaged. A dog bite can fester so easily."

"This man was your guest and you sent him through that garden knowing that dogs—"

"Mr. Harris!" Madison interrupted, furious that an outsider, her aunt's guest or not, would dare take such a tone with her. "This man was serving as a model to me, and when my mother came to the door saying she and Aunt Kendra were coming in, I thought it wise—"

"You were afraid of the consequences of being caught here alone with him, so you selfishly sacrificed him, *his life,* for your own well-being," Mr. Harris went on.

"Certainly not!" Madison rose to her full height and planted both hands on her hips, unintimidated by the fact that, though she was tall for a woman, he still towered over her. "I had no idea my brother's dogs were free in the garden. They are never permitted to run loose, and my maid was supposed to escort Cundo to the street behind the property."

Aubrey burst into studio and slid to a halt only feet from the others, her mobcap akimbo, the hem of her dress covered with leaves and debris. "Oh, Miss Madison, 'e's 'ere!" she declared. "Thank the Virgin! I didn't know what ter do. Lord Westcott's dogs done—"

"Aubrey," Madison snapped. "I don't want to hear your excuses right now. Run for some clean bandages for Cundo's arm."

"Honorable Miss, please," Cundo insisted in his fluid voice. "It is nothing. I will go."

He stepped toward the window, but Madison grabbed his arm. "If you are adamant, but not that way." She glanced at her personal maid. "Aubrey, please escort Cundo out the front door."

"Honorable Miss, it is not necessary that you—"

"Thank you, Cundo, for sitting for the portrait." She grasped his hand in both of hers and squeezed it. "I think it might be one of my best yet. Should I need you, I can find you in the same place, can't I? There at the wharf?"

He nodded, walking toward the door. "Thank you, Honorable Miss."

Madison turned back to Mr. Harris, glaring. "You should not speak, sir, of what you know nothing about."

"I think, my dear, I already know quite a bit about you." He walked away, his chuckle dry and without humor. "Titled London family, and a spoiled, obstinate, young woman who can think of no one but herself and her own diversions, even at the risk of others' lives." He glanced over his shoulder. "I'll be in my room, Kendra, should you need me."

"How dare you…how insolent…" Madison huffed, starting after him, but Aunt Kendra caught her hand and stopped her.

"Let him go, Madison, dear. It's not you. He's been grouchy like this since we set foot in London."

Madison stood beside her aunt and watched the broad back disappear down the corridor. "If that is not the most conceited, hubristic, vulgar man I have ever encountered."

Aunt Kendra chuckled, slipping her arm around Madison's slender waist. "There, there, Madison dear. Now, smooth your ruffled feathers. No harm done. I'll have no brawls on my first day back at Boxwood Manor. Now come, show me the painting of that exquisite man."

Madison slipped on her pearl earring as she waited at the top of the stair landing for Aunt Kendra. The two had spent a delightful hour together looking at and discussing Madison's artwork, and she already felt as if she'd known Lady Moran her whole life, loved her her whole life. Finally, at her aunt's suggestion, they had retired to their bedchambers to dress for dinner, where they could continue their conversation. Madison had not intended to dine with her mother and aunt this evening, especially when she learned that Mr. Harris would be joining them, but Aunt Kendra had a way about her that was hard to resist. Before Madison realized what she had done, she had not only agreed to attend the evening meal, but to dress in a manner suitable to her mother. No paint smock, no tangled hair and appropriate undergarments and shoes.

Madison could barely contain herself. Aunt Kendra was the most exciting person she had ever encountered. She was bright, articulate, well-traveled, and most important, she didn't seem to give a tart about what anyone thought about her. Aunt Kendra seemed to understand Madison's desire, her *need* to be a real artist, not just a lady who dabbled in painting while awaiting a suitable marriage. Madison hadn't yet mentioned it to her aunt, but she was hoping that perhaps she could help her convince her mother that a year in Paris, to study under one of the masters, really wasn't an unreasonable request.

"I'm coming," Aunt Kendra trilled, gliding down the hall, her exotic gown stitched of layers of bright fabric fluttering behind her. Tonight she wore a gold turban on her head, embellished with a circlet broach of glittering sapphires and diamonds.

"You look lovely tonight, my dear, quite the young lady." Aunt Kendra took Madison's hand. "Come, come, take a turn and let me see."

Madison had chosen one of her favorite dinner dresses, a peacock-blue cashmere that was princess-shaped with a trained skirt and deep pleating, trimmed with pale green satin. It had tight elbow sleeves and the bodice was open in a V with a frill of lisse. She wore her hair pulled back into a gleaming chignon.

"Thank you," she said, turning on her aunt's hand as if they were dance partners. "Mother feared the fabric was too bright for a woman of my *advanced* age, but I like it."

"Your age? Heaven's stars!" Aunt Kendra chuckled.

"You laugh now. Wait until she corners you alone in the drawing room tonight." Madison offered Aunt Kendra her arm to escort her down the long, curving staircase to the first floor. "She's insane with worry because I'm not yet wed, and fears I'll be an old maid like my cousin Roselyn." She cut dancing blue-green eyes at her aunt. "Truthfully, I don't think she's so much worried about my welfare as she wants to get rid of me so she can marry that old windbag Lord Kendal and be assured of a pension and as many sugar tarts as she can eat."

"Now, now." Aunt Kendra patted Madison's hand. "I know your mother finds life difficult without your father. She is doing the best she can, and society dictates—"

"Oh, posh! I don't care what society thinks," Madison declared passionately. "All I care about is my painting." At the bottom of the stairs she released her aunt's arm and spun around, arms flung out, head tipped back. "I want to be like you, Aunt Kendra. I want to travel to foreign lands, I want to see things I've never seen before, paint people of all races. Through their faces, their pain, I can tell their story." She stood still for a moment, waiting for the entrance hall to cease spinning. "What do I need a husband for? You haven't had one in nearly thirty years!"

Aunt Kendra folded her arms in front of her and smiled a smile that seemed a little sad to Madison. "Ah, to be young again and so full of such noble ideals. Now, come." She motioned to Madison. "Let's join the others in the dining room before they send out a hunting party for us," she whispered, "or the dogs."

When they reached the dining room, Lady Westcott's guests were just beginning to take their seats around the massive oval fruitwood dining table laden with silver and china. Madison's brother, Viscount Albert Westcott, was already seated at the head of the table and was pouring dinner wine for himself. He didn't like his sister any better than she liked him, and Madison dismissed him without a second glance. As far as her brother was concerned, little sisters were never meant to be seen or heard, only married off as quickly and quietly as possible.

Mr. Harris walked over to them, nodded to Madison and offered his arm to escort Aunt Kendra to the table. Madison shifted her gaze to the final guest. This had to be Lord Thomblin, whom her aunt had briefly mentioned, a grand nephew of her late husband. As she examined the man, who appeared to be in his mid-thirties, with interest, he met her gaze.

"This must be the Honorable Madison Westcott," he said, crossing the dining room at once.

She curtsied but did not lower her gaze as women her age were instructed to do. "Pleased to make your acquaintance, sir." She offered her gloved hand and he accepted it, half bowing as he pressed his lips to the thin cotton fabric.

Lord Thomblin was utterly charming and rather handsome, as well. A tall, slim man, he wore his blond hair short, his face shaven save for a very fashionable curling mustache. She noted that his clothing, blue-and-black-striped trousers and a matching blue jacket, was quite exquisite.

He offered his arm to escort her to the table. "I must say, Miss Westcott, the day has been long, waiting to meet you, but a wait well worth the final outcome."

Madison felt her cheeks grow warm as she slipped into the chair he offered her. "My aunt tells me that you own a plantation in Jamaica. However did an English gentleman such as yourself find himself in the islands?"

"A long story, Miss Westcott." He met her gaze, something few gentlemen her own age dared more than once. "One I hope there will be time to share before my return to Kingston."

Madison smiled, utterly infatuated. She should have known her aunt would keep company with such an entertaining gentleman. "I look forward to it," she whispered as her brother came to his feet, a wineglass in hand.

"A toast," Albert announced, his voice already slurred. "To my charming aunt, Lady Moran, and her homecoming."

The other two men rose and everyone at the table lifted their glasses in salute. Once the men were seated again, the

servants wheeled in the dinner wagon they used to transport food from the dumbwaiter to the table, and Madison's
mother began questioning Lord Thomblin on the fashion
of English women on the Jamaican plantations.

Soup tureens were placed on the center of the table and
servants ladled steaming bowls of fish and corn chowder.
When the bowls were cleared away, the first course was
served: roast pig, jugged hare and smaller dishes of stewed
carp and pupton of pigeon. Madison toyed with her food,
pushing it around her plate with her fork until the dishes
were cleared away and the second course was served. She
barely touched the dishes of lamb's fry, apricot fritters,
sturgeon and fried sole as the conversation concerning
fashion dragged on.

Madison's attention started to drift as she listened to
Lord Thomblin graciously answer all of her mother's inane
questions. As she nibbled on a forkful of fried sole, her
gaze shifted from one diner to the next, doing what artists
did best, observe.

Her brother, Albert, spoke to no one as he tore into a
slice of sturgeon nearly the size of his dinner plate. He al-
ternated between stuffing fish into his mouth and washing
it down with great gulps of wine. His wife, Catherine, immense with their first child and seated to his right, continually attempted unsuccessfully to blot his greasy chin with
her linen napkin.

Madison's mother flitted her hands, smiling and making what she conceived as clever remarks as she conversed
with Lord Thomblin. She barely touched her meal, which
was not unusual when there were guests for dinner. Later,
Madison knew, she would take a meal in the privacy of her
bedchamber.

Madison's attention shifted to her aunt, who was talking in a hushed tone to Mr. Harris, seated beside her, on the end. She seemed nonplussed by his angry tone of voice as she savored each morsel of the meal she placed in her mouth.

Madison reached for her glass of watered wine, and though she didn't want to look at the dark-haired man across the table, she couldn't help herself. She shifted her gaze, telling herself it was mere boredom that made her look, but there was something about him, about his exotic appearance, his total disregard for politeness, that fascinated her.

He'd said not a word to her since she came to dinner, which was rude beyond words, considering that he was a guest of the Westcott family. Not that she wanted him to speak to her after he had treated her so rudely earlier in the studio.

While looking at some paintings, Madison had asked her aunt what relation Mr. Harris had to her. Was he, too, a neighbor, traveling on business? Aunt Kendra's response had been vague. Apparently Mr. Harris, *dear Jefford,* as she called him, ran her plantation in Jamaica. But Madison had the feeling this Jefford was not just an overseer of Aunt Kendra's plantation, Windward Bay. He was more. Aunt Kendra just wouldn't say how.

Madison suddenly realized that she'd been caught staring. That insufferable man was looking right at her, his mouth turned up at one side in an arrogant smile of…what, amusement? Derision?

Lady Westcott was still going on about English fashion in other parts of the world with Lord Thomblin, and now Aunt Kendra and Catherine had joined in. As Madison looked away from Mr. Harris in embarrassment, she nearly groaned aloud and fluttered her napkin to fan herself. She'd read a great many essays on what hell might be like; her guess was that this was it. A boring conversation at a dinner table that never went anywhere, and a rude, irritable man staring at her.

I have to get out of here, Madison thought. The room was too warm, the beef overdone…or perhaps underdone? She reached for her wineglass, maneuvering it to tip it toward her.

The glass hit the table perfectly. "Oh, dear," Madison cried as wine splashed everywhere, droplets hitting her bodice.

"My dear," Lady Westcott cried. "Martha!"

One of the maids scurried toward Madison as she rose from her chair, blotting at her bodice. She hoped she hadn't ruined the gown; she truly did like it, but sometimes sacrifices had to be made.

"I don't know why she doesn't eat in the nursery," Albert grumbled over the rim of his wineglass.

"I'm so sorry," Madison apologized as Martha attempted to help her blot the wine that had made large red splotches on the peacock-blue fabric of her gown. "If you'll excuse me," she announced to her mother, as well as their guests, "I'll have to change."

Lord Thomblin and Mr. Harris both half rose from the table as Madison hastily walked from the dining room.

She was nearly undressed by the time Aubrey knocked and entered the bedchamber. "Sorry it took me so long, Miss. Martha did jest fetch me."

Madison knew it was more likely Aubrey had been occupied flirting with Albert's manservant or one of the other men who served the family. The young woman was apparently quite popular with the men. She understood that her personal maid had more than one male *friend* outside the gates of Boxwood Manor, as well.

Madison turned for Aubrey to unfasten the last button of the gown.

"Will you be redressing and returning to the dining room, miss?"

"Certainly not," Madison groaned. "Just get me something comfortable. The green silk dressing gown will be fine." She glanced out the window that opened into the gardens. "There's a lovely moon out tonight. I think I'll sketch it over the ruins once it fully rises."

"Yer goin' out in your dressing gown, miss?" she asked, handing it to her mistress.

Madison stepped out of a ruffled petticoat. "Not until everyone else is in bed."

"As yer wish, miss." Aubrey gathered the soiled gown and the petticoat in her arms and began to pick up the discarded stockings and shoes Madison had shed.

"I can finish from here," Madison told her maid. "Could you take the blue gown to the laundress and see if there's anything that can be done to save it?"

Left alone in peace, Madison stretched out on her four-poster bed draped with a ruffled blue hydrangea floral cover that matched the drapes. A book of poetry in her lap, she gazed at the wallpaper walls that were lined with several of her favorite paintings. There was a watercolor of the Thames and a sketch of the cook making piecrust, but her favorite was the oil painting of her father, who stared down at her now, a Scottish cap perched on his head and his nose slightly reddened by good Scotch.

Nodding her head in respect to him, she rolled onto her side and opened the book to wait for the house to quiet down and everyone to retire.

Jefford followed a stone path through the lush garden, away from the house. He was restless this evening, and though he had already removed his cumbersome English trousers and jacket and slipped into a silk dressing robe, he knew better than to even attempt to retire yet. He would only toss and turn and worry about what was happening at home on Windward Bay—and think about Chantal, how much he missed her.

London was not what he expected. It was worse. The noise, the stench, the endless, pointless chatter. How had he forgotten so easily? His head was near to splitting, and he hadn't been here a full day yet. Kendra was only intending on remaining in England a month or so, just long enough to attend this ridiculous coming-out ball for her niece, and look into another matter, but he seriously questioned whether he could survive even a fortnight of this.

Who was he kidding? For Kendra, he would do anything.

Jefford followed the stone path, through hollyhocks and boxwood, around a hedgerow, and spotted the glow of a cigar, smelling the tobacco on the cooling evening breeze. It was Thomblin.

He almost turned back, realizing he wasn't in the mood for him tonight, but then he saw why the viscount was there in the dark and strode up beside him.

"Evening, Harris," Lord Thomblin said, drawing in on the thick cigar. "A smoke?"

Jefford shook his head, following the line of Thomblin's vision. Fifty feet ahead, deeper in the garden, sat a figure dressed in a shimmer of pale green before a massive Roman pillar set amid a pile of carefully placed rubble. Moonlight streamed down over the marble ruins, faintly illuminating the long golden hair of the young woman who was obviously unaware of being watched.

Had Jefford not known he was in an English garden, he would have thought he stood at the base of the Colosseum in Rome. But this was not Rome and the ethereal figure was not a Roman goddess, but the lovely, spoiled Miss Madison Westcott.

"Pleasant enough people, the Westcotts," Thomblin murmured, tapping ashes on the stone path beneath their feet.

"I suppose."

Both men continued to study Madison.

"An acceptable diversion while we are here," Thomblin murmured, nodding toward Madison.

"I thought you would be gone by now," Jefford muttered. "Surely the finest of London's streets awaits you, my lord."

Thomblin did not take the bait. Three years earlier, when he'd come to Jamaica from India, he'd learned rather quickly to stay out of Jefford's way if he wanted to continue to reap the rewards of his great-aunt's good name. He knew well that Jefford disliked him, but knew also that Kendra insisted she could never turn him away, not when Lord Moran had been so good to her.

"I was waiting until it was a little later," Thomblin murmured. "I'm just now on my way out."

"Be sure to return before dawn. I doubt Kendra wants to have to explain your absences."

"You worry too much, Harris. You should relax more." He glanced over his shoulder. "Would you care to go with me? I assure you, I can get you admitted into any place that interests you. Any place you fancy."

Jefford scowled. Thomblin and his lusts sickened him. "Just see that you are discreet."

"Always." Still watching the young woman, Lord Thomblin dropped the half-smoked cigar on a flagstone and crushed it with his polished shoe. "I thought I might say good-night to her."

"Leave her alone," Jefford ground out, "or you will regret the day you set foot in London again."

Thomblin chuckled as he walked away. "Ah, Jefford, you are such a dull boy. Whatever are we to do with you?"

Madison drew the charcoal across her sketch pad, eyeing the marble column in the moonlight. With charcoal, it was all about light and dark and the depth of the shadows. She had always struggled with this medium, but discovered it oftentimes resulted in some of her best work. Somehow, in the simplicity of the black-and-white sketch came emotion that could not be relayed by color.

She deftly added shading, a little additional depth here and…she froze at a sound behind her. She was accustomed to the night sounds of the garden, but what she had heard behind her was not the wind. It was not a branch scraping against the stone wall, or an errant rabbit sending tiny pebbles flying as it hopped out from beneath a bush.

It was a footstep.

Madison rose and spun around, cradling her sketch pad to her breasts. Not three feet behind the bench she had sat on stood Mr. Harris.

"I'm sorry," he said quietly. "I didn't mean to frighten you."

"Frighten me?" she managed, her heart pounding.

The man was practically unclothed. He wore only a burgundy silk robe tied at his waist to fall to his corded, muscular calves. His feet were bare.

"W-whatever makes you think you frightened me? And what in heaven's name are you doing out here at this time of the night, in that…that state of undress?" she demanded, pressing her lips together, taking a step back.

He chuckled, moving a step closer, around the stone bench. "I could ask you the same thing."

Realizing he was looking at the V of her bare skin revealed where her dressing gown gaped, she grasped the fabric and pulled it taut, covering herself.

Madison had never been a prude like her mother, but this man made her extremely uncomfortable. She had very little experience with men and even less dealing with sexuality, her own, or another's, but she could feel an energy crackling in the cool night air that was both exciting and disturbing at the same time. It was not just the way Mr. Harris looked at her with those dark eyes, but the way he made her feel. Here in the dark, in the moonlight, only half dressed, her entire body seemed to quiver.

"I was sketching the ruins." She slid a bare foot back.

"I can see that." He took another step closer. "They are very impressive," he said, not looking up at the great column. "May I see your sketch?"

"Papa had them shipped from Rome, and no, you may not." She clutched the sketch pad tightly. "It…it's not complete, Mr. Harris."

"Jefford." He was close enough now for her to see the dark pools in the centers of his eyes. Mesmerizing pools.

She licked her upper lip. Her mouth was dry. Her breath came in short little pants. This man had her utterly out of sorts and she had no idea why. "I beg your pardon?"

"Jefford. You can call me Jefford."

She drew herself up haughtily, realizing she was a little afraid of this mysterious, dark-eyed, dark-haired man. "I think not, sir. And you certainly may not address me by my Christian name. It's utterly inappropriate," she said, looking him up and down. "Especially considering the present circumstances, sir!"

He chuckled, and to her shock reached out and caught a wayward lock of blond hair that had slipped from her chignon.

"You truly have no idea how attractive you are, have you, Madison? How dangerous you could be to a man…"

Her eyes widened as his deep voice seemed to reach the very core of her being. So close, she could see a tiny scar at the corner of his lips.

She couldn't stop looking at his mouth, and of its own accordance, her own began to tremble.

He still held her gaze and she swayed, suddenly dizzy. She felt his hand brush the small of her back….

His touch jolted her. "Sir!" she cried indignantly, pulling back. "If you think I have any intention of allowing you to kiss me, you are mistaken!"

3

"Kiss you? Madison…my girl, you flatter yourself without warrant."

Of all the responses she could have expected, disdain was not one of them. "How dare you! Who do you think you are speaking to?" She took another step back, filled with anger and indignation, her blue-green eyes narrowing to slits. She grasped the long skirt of her dressing gown and turned, dropping her sketch pad as she ran for the house.

"Madison, wait," Jefford called after her.

Madison ran and she didn't stop until she reached the drawing room door and then slipped into the house and hurried to her room, closing the door behind her. She flung herself on her bed, face into her pillow. She was shaking all over, angry and mortified by her presumption that he had meant to kiss her, angry that he was not more of a gentleman.

Damnation! She would have to put up with him for at least another month.

* * *

Jefford turned up the gas lamp beside his bed and sat down on the edge of the feather tick. He held Madison's sketch pad in both hands and studied the half-completed drawing of the Roman ruin in the garden. He knew very little of art, but enough to know what was good and what was not, and this was good. Quite good, to his surprise. When they had arrived at Boxwood Manor earlier in the day and he had heard Lady Westcott's explanation that her daughter was presently occupied in her art studio, he had assumed Madison was just another spoiled young English-woman, passing the hours toying with a brush and paints while she waited to become engaged, to be married, to have children.

Jefford wasn't wrong often, but he realized he was wrong this time as he carefully studied the captivating shades of light and dark that brought the pillar to life. But there was more to the sketch, he realized with fascination. He could see…no, *feel,* the heartache of the Romans as the empire had fallen. He could almost taste their tears. How extraordinary a talent for such a young, unworthy woman…

There was a tap on the door and he rose. Opening the sketch pad, he propped it on the bedside table so the lamplight fell across the drawing, then walked to the door and eased it open. "I was beginning to think you weren't coming."

Aubrey, dressed only in a thin white sleeping gown, slipped through the door and leaned against it to close it. "Garn, and I was thinkin' yer'd never ask me up," she murmured, reaching out to tug on the tie of his dressing robe.

The silk fabric fell away and Jefford pushed all thoughts of Madison Westcott out of his head as he reached out for the attractive domestic. He pulled her against him and felt his desire spring up, hot, urgent.

Maybe this was what he needed to sleep, a little release, he thought, as he pressed his mouth to the hollow between her breasts.

Lord Thomblin stepped out of the hired hansom and into a feeble circle of light cast by the gas lamp overhead. A damp mist had settled over the city, muffling the grating of carriage wheels, the barking of dogs and the splash of God-knew-what in the open sewers. The stench, however, had not changed since he was last in London and he brought a scented handkerchief to his nose.

"Ye want I should wait?" the driver asked, staring at coins in his dirty hand.

Lord Thomblin shook his head as he walked away. Behind him, he heard the clip of hooves and the jingle of harnesses as the hansom pulled away. The dark, damp night air was punctuated by the shriek of intoxicated female laughter coming through the open windows above. Yes, he had found the right street.

The square lay only a narrow alley behind a busy street, but it was a different world. Here were the crowded tenements that reeked of middens, crumbling mortar and despair. Here lay the brothels, pawnbrokers and sweatshops of London. Here waited an evening of sensual entertainment for any gentleman with a sense of adventure and coin in his pocket. The hairs on the nape of his neck prickled, and he felt the all-too-familiar rush of raw anticipation. Lord Thomblin glanced over his shoulder and spotted the constable on the corner smoking his pipe. If he saw Thomblin, he gave no indication. It was not his job to police the wealthy men who entered the lane, only to keep the pickpockets off them.

As Lord Thomblin hurried up the cobblestone foot-path, he passed a dark archway and heard a woman's voice. She beckoned him from the darkness, murmuring under her breath as she opened her cloak to reveal her sagging, pale breasts. Ignoring her, he walked on. He was almost there now, Jack Pendleton's place. Whenever he came to London, he made it his first stop. Jack knew how gentlemen such as himself liked to be treated. Knew their *tastes*.

A mangy dog scuttled by and Lord Thomblin delivered a vicious kick to the animal's ribs. The verminous creature gave a yip of pain and fled. He hated dogs; were it up to him, he would order them all clubbed to death and served up as gruel to the lazy dregs in the city's workhouses. He ducked into a short alley off the street and climbed a rotting and fetid staircase. At the top, he tapped on the door.

A man with sour breath and a pointed face like a rat from the alley below opened the door a crack and peered out. "Yeah?"

Thomblin casually offered a coin between his thumb and forefinger, but when the doorkeeper reached for it, he held tight. "The best room you have."

"Aye, capt'n."

"And no lice, mind you," he warned.

The door squeaked open, and he stepped into the pale light as the doorkeeper took his cloak.

"Ye come to the right place, capt'n. I'll warrant ye that."

Thomblin smiled. It was good to be home.

After allowing herself a brief time to lie in bed and mull over the incident that had just taken place, Madison had fully intended to get up, pack a few personal items and retreat to her studio. There she intended to remain a month, a year, it made no difference, until Jefford Harris boarded that ship bound for Jamaica and out of her life forever.

She must have fallen asleep, though, because one moment she was envisioning her brother ordering Jefford Harris to leave Boxwood Manor, the next thing she knew, someone was banging keenly at her bedchamber door.

"Madison! Madison, don't tell me you're one of those lazy chits who sleeps until noon," Aunt Kendra declared from the hall.

Madison sat up in bed as the older woman barreled into her bedroom.

"Good. You're awake. But is that what you're wearing to go?" She lifted a brow that had been plucked and painted.

Madison ran her hand over her rumpled dressing gown, the same one she had worn to the garden last night, and then apparently slept in. "What I'm wearing to go where?" She rubbed the sleep from her eyes, trying to figure out what her aunt was doing here and what she wanted of her.

"Shopping, of course." Aunt Kendra hustled across the room to pull open the flowered drapes.

Madison flinched as the bright morning light filled the semidark chamber. "I'm not going shopping."

"At the risk of sounding like you-know-who—" Aunt Kendra pointed down the hall in the direction of Lady Westcott's bedchamber "—I'm not certain what you have on now would be wise to wear in public."

Aunt Kendra patted her rather conservative chignon and for the first time Madison realized the older woman's hair was a delightful golden red.

"Look at me." Lady Moran tugged on her flounced skirt. "Even I am dressed like a proper Englishwoman of quality today." She opened Madison's chifforobe. "So what shall it be?" She pulled out a gray walking gown, wrinkled her nose, pushed it back in and reached for another.

"Aunt Kendra, I'm not going shopping," Madison laughed, trying to smooth her bed-tangled hair as she pushed off the bed. "I'm going to my studio, where I may well reside for some days to come."

"Don't be a coward, Madison. It is utterly unbecoming of the Westcott name. Here, wear this peach. It's quite pretty," she trilled, pulling a morning gown from the large chifforobe and shaking it to dislodge any wrinkles.

"A coward?" Madison stiffened. "Whatever do you mean?"

Aunt Kendra tossed the dress on the unmade bed, moved to the chest of drawers and began to pulling out lacy undergarments. "You know just what I mean."

Madison lowered her arms to her sides, her hands in such tight fists that her fingernails cut into the soft flesh of her palms. Surely Jefford had not been so uncouth…so loutish as to have told Aunt Kendra what had happened in the garden last night?

"It's Jefford." Aunt Kendra tossed a pair of crocheted drawers, stockings and a corset cover on the bed. "I know he can be intimidating when he sets his mind to it, but really, he can be just as easily swayed as any man. Ignore him." She wrinkled her rice-powdered nose. "He hates that."

Madison stared, still unable to catch her breath. "You mean he didn't tell you—"

"Tell me what?" Aunt Kendra tossed a bustled petticoat to Madison and started for the door. "He didn't come to your room last night, did he?"

"Certainly not! Aunt Kendra!" Madison clutched the petticoat to her breasts as if to protect herself from the man.

"Good. Now, join me for breakfast in twenty minutes. We are going shopping to buy some things every woman needs once she is presented to society." Aunt Kendra slipped out the door, a whirlwind of jewels and perfume.

"But I'm not going to my coming-out ball!" Madison shouted from the doorway. "I'm not being presented to anyone!"

"Poppycock!" The older woman fluttered her hand as she walked down the hallway. "Hurry now," she called. "If we don't sneak out before your lady mother is out of bed, we'll be forced to invite her along and won't that be great fun?"

Madison stared down the hallway for a moment, not knowing what to do. She had never met a woman—anyone, for that matter—so forceful in such a nonchalant way.

She closed the door, then gazed at the pile of clothing. She didn't want to go shopping. She most certainly did not want to attend the blasted ball in which she was supposed to be the guest of honor. Least of all did she want to go to breakfast and chance running into Jefford.

But this was her house, she thought angrily. What right did he have to keep her from having breakfast in her own home? What right did he have to keep her from spending as much time as possible with Aunt Kendra, whom she already adored even though she'd known her less than a day?

Jaw set, Madison slipped out of the wrinkled dressing gown and went in search of a clean chemise. *No* right. That insufferable rogue had no right at all!

In fifteen minutes, Madison was dressed, her morning ablutions complete, and she glided into the lavish dining room, her head held high, a sketchbook tucked under her arm. She made a habit of carrying one with her at all times, never knowing when a certain angle of light or facial expression of a servant might catch her eye.

A meal had been set out under covered dishes on the buffet for the diners to serve themselves at their leisure, and Aunt Kendra was already seated in the same place she had taken her dinner the evening before.

As Madison entered the room, a splash of pale lavender, out of place on the dining table, caught her eye. Upon closer inspection, she realized it was a freshly cut flower on her plate. She almost smiled. So, Mr. Jefford Harris was trying to apologize, was he?

She walked around the table to her chair, set down her sketch pad and picked up the exquisite orchid. If he thought it would be this easy to win her over after his intolerable behavior last night, she would just have to prove to him that he was wrong. She would snap his gift of apology in half and toss it in the kitchen scrap heap where it belonged.

But the flower was so lovely, so unusual, that the artistic eye in Madison couldn't resist lifting it for closer inspection.

"Ah, rare beauty for another rare beauty."

She looked up at Lord Thomblin, who stood in the dining room archway, looking exceptionally handsome this morning in a well-tailored navy pin-striped suit. His hair was combed fetchingly to one side and his mustache was obviously freshly waxed.

Madison smiled shyly and lowered her gaze, brushing her fingertips over the delicate leaves of the flower. "Lord Thomblin, what a delightful gift. I have never seen an orchid this color." She glanced up. "Wherever did you get it?"

"Carlton, we would love to stay and discuss where you

would find such a rare flower this time of morning," Lady Moran declared, sliding her dining chair back noisily. "But we're off for a day of ladies' shopping and we haven't the time such a conversation would warrant." She dabbed at her lips with her napkin. "Unless you care to escort us?"

Lord Thomblin cleared his throat and half bowed. "I would, of course, be delighted to escort you, Lady Moran, and Miss Westcott, but unfortunately I have an appointment with one of my bankers this morning."

"Pity." Aunt Kendra brushed by. "I've already sent for the carriage, Madison. Come, dear."

"Yes, of course, Lady Moran." Madison grabbed her sketch pad and hurried after her aunt, the orchid still clutched in her hand. As she passed Lord Thomblin, who stepped back to allow her through, she nodded her thanks again.

At the front hall, Aunt Kendra plucked the orchid from Madison's hand and held it out to one of the housemaids. "Put this in water and leave it in the studio. I should suspect Miss Westcott will wish to paint it, sketch it, *something,*" she said, accepting the parasol, gloves and wide-brimmed hat Malia, her personal maid offered.

Aubrey was there, too, waiting with Madison's straw boater, her parasol and reticule large enough for her ever-present sketch pad.

"Really, Aunt Kendra," Madison said as they walked out the front door. "Aren't we being rude to leave Lord Thomblin in such a rush?"

"I don't want you fretting over Lord Thomblin," Lady Moran said, allowing a footman to assist her into the carriage. "There's more to a man than the cut of his suit. Now, climb up here beside me." She patted the carriage seat. "And explain to me this nonsense about you not attending your own coming-out ball. I came all the way from Jamaica, young lady, to see your coming out and I have no intention of missing it!"

Madison shared a wonderful day with her indomitable aunt and had even agreed to allow her to purchase, among other things, two new gowns and a charming cameo for her. Her favorite acquisition of the day, however, was an antique paint box they'd found in a tiny shop tucked away off Fleet Street.

That evening, Madison arrived for the dinner hour dressed in a new pale green silk gown of the latest Paris *Harper's Bazar* fashion to find Jefford Harris absent. He had left a message for Lady Westcott and her son saying he had met old friends and would be dining out with them. Madison doubted it was true, but that was certainly of no concern of hers. The evening would be far more pleasant without him.

At the candlelit dining table, Madison was again seated beside Lord Thomblin, and they carried on a delightful conversation throughout the meal. As they dined on a ragout of breast of veal, broiled leg of lamb with cauliflower and a rich marrow pudding, she revealed to him her dream to go to Paris. He divulged that he had been to Paris many times and had actually lived there once, and then entertained her with fascinating stories of places he had been and people he had encountered. As the evening wore on, she found herself utterly infatuated with the handsome gentleman, partially because he seemed enchanted by her. She was beginning to realize that not all men were the tiresome louts her brother was.

All too soon, dinner was over and everyone prepared to move from the dining room to the drawing room, including an additional guest, Viscount Kendal. Lord Thomblin assisted Madison from her chair and offered his elbow, but Lady Westcott approached. "Sir, if you would pardon my daughter and me for just a moment?"

He smiled, releasing Madison's arm. "Most certainly, Lady Westcott." He bowed and then followed the others out of the dining room.

"Mother," Madison seethed. "Lord Thomblin was going to escort me to the drawing room. What is it that cannot wait?"

"Lady Moran tells me that you have reconsidered your position on attending your coming-out ball," she said sweetly, fiddling with the new cameo Madison wore on a bit of lace around her neck.

"Ah, so that's why Viscount Kendal was invited to join us for dinner at the last moment! Mother," Madison said, smiling. "Once again you're thinking toward your own future. Do you seriously think the night I'm presented to society men will be lining up with offers of matrimony?"

"I just wanted you to know how pleased I am," her mother continued in a simper. "Your father would be pleased also."

Madison pushed her mother's hand aside and readjusted the cameo the way she had placed it. "Papa would understand. It's not that I want to go," she explained, still watching in the direction Carlton had gone.

She knew it was entirely inappropriate to think of him by his Christian name, having only known him two days, but the impression he'd made was so remarkable and his personality so pleasing that she felt their acquaintance had been much longer. "I was only thinking that it would be a pity that Aunt Kendra and Lord Thomblin came so far to attend the ball and then it didn't take place."

"I know you're nervous about your formal introduction to society, dear. All young women are, but—"

"Mother, I'm not nervous." Madison turned her full attention to Lady Westcott, realizing that her mother was not going to let her get away until they discussed her debut once again. "You know I don't like balls, I don't like dancing, and I certainly don't like the idea of being put on display!"

"Goodness." Lady Westcott laughed lightly. "What lady doesn't like to dance?"

"My consent is not unconditional, though. Did Aunt Kendra tell you about my request?"

"Yes, that you'd like one of your paintings unveiled publicly at the ball." Lady Westcott removed a perfumed lace handkerchief from her sleeve and patted her forehead. "Such an event would be highly irregular."

"'Original' is what I would call it," Aunt Kendra said, returning to the dining room. Tonight she was wearing a pale pink chiffon dress that made her look as if she were floating. On any other woman her age, the gown would have been preposterous, but Madison thought it was lovely on her.

"After all, why do we have these things, anyway? It's just as Madison said." Lady Moran gestured with a heavily ringed hand. "To put our young women on exhibit, of course. To show off the goods, see if we can get any takers."

"Lady Moran!" Madison's mother choked. "What an indelicate way to—"

"Well, it's the truth," Aunt Kendra interrupted, adjusting the elaborate pearl bracelets she wore. "So if we're putting our Madison on display, why not show what she's got? She may not like to dance, but her talent is quite amazing.

I should think there would be many a young man interested in having a wife so gifted," she enticed.

"Do you think so?" Lady Westcott was suddenly rapt with interest.

Aunt Kendra glanced discreetly at Madison and nodded. While taking tea in a hotel earlier that afternoon, they had bargained. With Madison attending the coming ball, the older woman insisted, her family got what they wanted. If Madison was permitted to make public one of her paintings, she, in turn, would get something *she* wanted. The idea of being able to display one of her works before the more than two hundred guests who had been invited was an opportunity Madison couldn't resist. Like any artist, she yearned to share her paintings, her messages, with the world.

Lady Westcott tugged thoughtfully at an earbob. "I suppose we would make the social column with such an unusual event," she mused.

"I'm quite certain you would, my dear. The Westcott family would be the talk of the town for days, and anyone who did not receive an invitation to the ball will be sorely peeved." Lady Moran slipped her arms around both Madison and Lady Westcott's waists. "Now come, let's go to the drawing room and play some games. By now poor Catherine should be just about done with that dreadful piece of music she's trying to play and I do so love games!"

Jefford assisted Kendra into the hansom and then climbed in after her, closing the door. He took a seat across from her and settled his gaze on her.

Kendra set her parasol aside and adjusted the wide ribbons of her bonnet. The day was yet early and the house was quiet; she doubted anyone but a few servants knew they had left. The hansom lunged forward and she grasped a leather strap, closing her eyes for a moment to steel herself against the motion.

The hansom found smoother ground and Kendra opened her eyes. "Stop looking at me like that!" she snapped.

"Like what?"

"You know what." She eyed him sternly.

He opened his arms in innocence. "I've said nothing."

"You don't have to."

He leaned back, stretching his arm out along the upholstered leather seat. "I only thought that you intended to rest a little while we were here. Do some of the things English-women are supposed to do, like take tea and tour gardens, perhaps even sleep in late and have breakfast served to you in bed."

Kendra gave a snort of laughter. "Have you ever, in your life, recalled my sleeping in late or having breakfast served to me in bed?"

He couldn't resist a smirk. "Only when you had company in your bed to share a late breakfast with."

She lifted her parasol and poked him with it. "Madison is right. You must be one of the most vulgar men on God's green earth."

He lifted a dark eyebrow, curious. "She said that, did she?"

Kendra met his gaze with those green eyes he so loved. "She did. She thinks you're the rudest, most unmannered, boorish man in London, presently."

"Well, I think she's a spoiled, headstrong little girl who would not last a moment in the jungles of Jamaica."

Kendra nodded thoughtfully. "But she is rather beautiful, don't you think?"

He shrugged. His jacket was tight and uncomfortable and he longed for the clothes he had left home in Jamaica. "In a childish way, I suppose."

"Poppycock. She's one of the most lovely women in England and you know it."

"England is not the world, my dear," he said, gazing out the window at the passing scenery of marble mansions, stone walls and well-groomed trees.

"You can't fool me," Kendra teased, leaning forward a little on the seat. "I know you've noticed her beauty, and her wit as well. I guessed as much from how storming mad she was with you the other night over some incident that apparently took place."

Without moving, he glanced at her. "And what incident was that?"

"I've no idea. She's not a tattle." Kendra sat back again, obviously pleased with herself. "She's quite bright and independent—"

"Giving no regard for others—" he cut in.

"If I didn't know better, Jefford, I'd think you were smitten."

"A man my age is not *smitten* with anyone," he growled. "And if I were to take notice of a suitable beauty, it would not be a green girl without an ounce of altruism to her name."

"Jefford, you're not getting any younger. Have you thought any more of marriage?" She smiled, a hint of cunning in her raspy voice.

"Marriage," he snorted. "Damn it, Kendra. What need have I for another woman? I have Chantal. I have you. Twice as many women as any man needs."

"But you need to have a wife," Kendra insisted.

"Why is that?" Jefford demanded. While they spoke, the

hansom swayed as it turned onto another street, bringing them closer to their destination. Wooden apothecary, chemist and surgeon signs swung from posts before their storefronts.

"Children, of course," Kendra cried, gesturing enthusiastically with both hands. "A son. A way to perpetuate your name."

"What makes you think I would want a child?" He averted his gaze. "What makes you think I would bring another human being into this appalling world we live in? The poverty, the anguish—"

"Your child would not be born into poverty or anguish, Jefford," she said gently. "Your child would be born at Windward Bay, surrounded by those who would love him to the end of his days. Born to a father who would sacrifice his own life for his well-being."

"Life on Windward Bay is not what it once was, Kendra, and you know it." Passion filled his voice. "With the workers' riots, we could go home to ashes."

She rolled her eyes. "You always did have a flair for the dramatic, Jefford. I should have sent you to the London stage instead of Oxford."

"How is it that our conversations always turn to the subject of me, hmm?" He leaned forward, taking her hand, rubbing it between his. "This trip is about you, not me. I agreed to come to London not to attend some ridiculous girl's coming-out ball. I came for you."

She smiled tenderly, holding his gaze. "All I want, all I *ever* wanted, was for you to be happy, dear."

"I think that, perhaps, some of us were never meant to be happy," he answered truthfully.

"And I think you are wrong. Very wrong."

4

"I should never have agreed to this," Madison groaned as Aunt Kendra tugged on the bodice of her ball gown and Aubrey fussed with the silk flowers adorning her elaborate coiffure.

Already the sound of a Chabrier waltz was filtering through the open window of her bedchamber from the garden below. Because of the number of guests invited, and the blessing of still balmy weather, Lady Westcott had agreed to Aunt Kendra's suggestion of allowing the ball to "spill" into the gardens.

While the entire house would still be used for ladies' retiring rooms, a cloakroom and rooms to serve refreshment, the garden had been transformed into an outdoor ballroom. A dancing platform had been hastily constructed and flower arbors brought in, laden with roses and lilacs imported from Holland. With the addition of twinkling candlelight after dark, Lady Moran insisted that Madison's coming out would be the finest London had seen in Queen Victoria's time.

"There's no need to be nervous about this ball," Aunt Kendra insisted. "Smile, dance when you're asked, don't drink too much champagne, no matter how often a gentleman offers it to you, and everyone will fall in love with you just as I have, my sweet."

Madison couldn't resist a laugh. As long as she didn't get intoxicated, the ball would be a success. Leave it to Aunt Kendra to put everything in perspective.

The two weeks Lady Moran had been in London had passed so quickly that Madison could hardly believe it, and the notion that she would be gone in another month was difficult to accept. There were ever so many things Madison wanted to discuss with her: literature, art, music, travel. There wouldn't possibly be time. What little she had learned of Jamaica and its people, struggling to establish a new economy no longer reliant on slavery, fascinated Madison. She wanted to know so much more!

"I'm not nervous about the ball or whether people will like me," Madison confessed, shooing Aubrey away. The picking and prodding at her hair and clothes was driving her mad. "I don't give a fig whether or not people like me. I am who I am." She leaned in front of the mirror and rubbed at an errant speck on the end of her nose. "It's my work. What if it's not well received? What if they don't like it? An artist needs an audience!"

Aunt Kendra, dressed in a lovely ocean-blue gown of draped chiffon, walked toward the door. Tonight with her striking red hair twisted atop her head and the glittering diamond and sapphire jewels on her neck, she appeared a decade younger than Madison knew she had to be.

"Is it your best work, my dear?" Aunt Kendra asked solemnly.

Madison thought of the still life she planned to display.

Painted in a classic manner, it consisted of a small table, and on it, a bowl of exotic fruit and the rare orchid Lord Thomblin had given her. She had painted the fruit bowl earlier in the year, but the piece had been missing something, and the orchid in a delicate glass-blown vase had completed the canvas. It was very good, but...

"Madison! Is it your best work?"

Madison pressed her rose-petal-stained lips together. She had chosen the painting for its appropriateness, not necessarily because it was her best work. Portraits were what she did best because of the emotion she was able to emote through them. "Probably not," she said softly.

"Because?"

"Because I was trying to choose something appropriate for the evening. Something..." She frowned. "Something acceptable."

The room was quiet for a moment except for the sound of the music below in the garden as Kendra met Madison's gaze. "I cannot tell you what to do, dear. You're far too old for that."

"But if you were me?"

"I would display my best. I would offer myself entirely." Aunt Kendra smiled slyly. "Who knows, one of the art connoisseurs I invited just might be interested in putting a word in the ear of an appropriate gallery. You never know, my dear. The ball you have tried so hard to avoid may result in the consignment of some of your work."

"Aunt Kendra! Mother said you had invited guests, but I had no idea." She clutched her hands together, overcome by nerves. "I can't possibly display a bowl of fruit! Any artist with half an eye can paint fruit!"

"Do what your heart leads you to do, dear. Sometimes it's not the right moment to step aside from the crowd." Her aunt kissed her cheek. "But whatever you decide, make haste because you'll be expected downstairs momentarily."

Madison stood for a moment in the center of her bedchamber, dressed in her exquisite sage-green and ecru striped silk taffeta ball gown, frozen in indecision. Aubrey buzzed around her like a little black-and-white bee, picking up discarded packages and returning brushes and combs to their proper place.

The music, the scent of the potted gardenias Aunt Kendra had ordered and the hushed voices of the men and women who had come to welcome her into their world floated through the open window. This entire evening was devoted to her, yet she felt as though she had no real part in it.

Suddenly, Madison spun around. "Aubrey, I need you to get me down the servants' staircase to my studio without being seen. Can you do that?"

"'Course, miss. You think we domestics don't move round this house unseen?" She winked and curled her finger. "Just follow me and we'll be near invisible."

"There you are," Lady Westcott cried, rushing down the silk-wallpapered corridor on the second floor. "I sent one of the maids up to knock on your door a few moments ago and she said there was no answer."

"I must not have heard," Madison said sweetly, walking beside her mother as she slid her hands into her elbow-length white silk gloves.

"Well, no harm done. You're ready now." She patted her upper lip with a lace handkerchief. "Allow me go down ahead of you so that Viscount Kendal and I can watch your entrance. I'll send Albert to escort you down." She took one look at her daughter, as if she wanted to say something, then hurried ahead.

Madison wanted to protest; she didn't need Albert of all people to escort her down her own staircase. But she let her mother go. Taking into consideration what she had just done, it was the least she could do for her mother who she knew meant well.

Madison waited several minutes in the shadows of the hallway, then several more, but her brother did not come for her. Just when she had made the decision to descend the grand staircase alone, Lord Thomblin appeared at the top of the landing looking most fetching in white tie and tails.

"I've come to do the honor of escorting you to your coming out, Miss Westcott, if it would so please you."

She wrapped her gloved hand around his arm, gazing up into his pale blue eyes. "I would be honored, sir."

Then, taking a deep breath, she started down the stairs on Lord Thomblin's arm. When they were halfway down, an authoritative male voice announced, "the Honorable Madison Elizabeth Westcott," and suddenly she was surrounded by the sound of ladies and gentlemen clapping.

At the bottom of the grand staircase, she dropped a deep curtsy to her mother and Lord Kendal, then kissed her mother's cheek and joined the receiving line, smiling and accepting congratulations.

For more than an hour, Madison kept the smile etched on her face, making polite conversation with the guests until she felt numb. At last, when her mother excused her from the receiving line, she went in search of Lord Thomblin. He had asked that he be permitted the first dance that she was available for. Though she didn't care much for dancing, the chance to allow Lord Thomblin to place his arm around her was quite intriguing.

Thinking she heard his voice in the parlor, Madison cut

down a small hallway with the intention of using the moment alone to gather her wits, but the second she turned the corner, she saw Jefford Harris.

There he was, alone in the hallway, leaning casually against the wall, a glass with a small amount of amber liquor in his hand. Scotch. Her father's favorite.

Madison was tempted to turn around and go the other way. She and Mr. Harris had barely spoken in the past two weeks, and then only polite, cool conversation in the presence of others. They disliked each other and neither saw any reason to pretend otherwise.

But she thought about what Aunt Kendra had said about the Westcotts not being cowards. To turn and run with her bustle between her legs would be cowardly. Instead, she glided toward him, her gaze locked with his, her mouth pursed in a manner she knew men found attractive.

"You look quite lovely this evening, Miss Westcott."

His words were complimentary, yet his tone was mocking.

She drew herself up, raising her chin a notch. "Imbibing too much Scotch too early in the evening, sir?"

"This?" He chuckled. "I haven't had nearly enough."

"Enough to what?"

"Get me through this tedious evening, of course."

Madison could feel her anger burn on her cheeks. "Tedious? How dare you! You that you are not here for my benefit, sir, and there is no one who would keep you from walking out that door." She pointed toward the front of the house.

He lifted the glass to his lips and took a sip, his movement unhurried and agonizingly annoying. "No, I am not here for your benefit, Madison. I'm here for Kendra."

Madison set her jaw. "You are arrogant, sir, and rude.

Here for Aunt Kendra. May I ask, sir, just what your relationship is to my aunt?"

"You may not." He lifted the glass as if in toast to her. "Enjoy your big night."

He was gone before she could form an appropriate retort.

"Miss Westcott, there you are," Lord Thomblin called from behind.

She spun around, smiling again.

"I was afraid you were hiding to prevent having to dance with a clod such as myself," he intoned, keeping a gentlemanly distance.

Her laughter was genuine as she accepted his arm he offered. "Certainly not, Lord Thomblin." She gazed up into his eyes in quite a forward gesture. "In fact, I was looking for you."

His gaze swept over her and she bathed in his approval. He obviously thought she was beautiful, witty and talented. She feared she was falling in love....

Overheated and dizzy with excitement of the evening and Lord Thomblin's attention, Madison allowed him to lead her off the dance floor and into the drawing room for some refreshment.

"Have some French champagne," Lord Thomblin murmured in her ear. He didn't touch her, but his mouth was close enough that she could feel his warm breath on her skin. In public, on the dance floor, he had behaved like the true gentleman he was, but alone in the drawing room, Madison realized he was crossing the line just a bit, enough to be exhilarating, without being dangerous.

She lowered her lashes, beginning to understand how young women could sometimes behave so foolishly in the presence of men. Lord Thomblin made her giddy with the sound of his voice and his brash compliments to her appearance. Simply having his body so near to hers made her pulse race. She'd had no idea that this was how men sometimes affected women.

"No, I had better not have the champagne," Madison said, lifting her gloved hand as she remembered Aunt Kendra's warning. She was already capricious enough; she didn't need to add alcohol to the chemistry of what had become a magical evening.

"What?" he teased, his voice taking a husky tone. "Did your mother warn you not to have champagne or a man might draw you into the darkness…." He slipped his arm around her waist and pulled her into the corner of the room where a painted screen had been placed to conceal a serving table piled with dirty dishes. They were completely hidden from any passersby. "And…"

"And what?" she breathed, glancing up at him.

"And," he whispered, pressing his hand to the small of her back and leaning over her.

Madison closed her eyes.

"Thomblin," a male voice barked. "Where are you? Madison! They're waiting for you in the garden."

Madison's eyes flew open. Damnation! Had Jefford Harris come to London just to infuriate her?

The spell was broken as Lord Thomblin released her.

"What do we do?" she whispered, in a panic. She couldn't be caught behind the Chinese screen with his lordship. Not tonight of all nights. To be caught unsupervised with a man who was not a family member would be scandalous.

He closed his hand over her arm, taking immediate charge of the situation. "Compose yourself and walk out. You were simply setting aside a broken glass to prevent your guests from using it."

She nodded furiously. She could hear Mr. Harris bellowing for her in another room now. "And what will you do?" she whispered.

"I'll wait a reasonable time and then slip out, perhaps to the room set aside for gentlemen's cigars. No one will notice, I assure you."

She nodded again, her heart pounding, her mouth dry.

"You had better go now," he urged gently.

Madison took a deep breath and walked out from behind the screen as if nothing was amiss.

"There you are!" Mr. Harris called impatiently, entering the drawing room. "Kendra is looking everywhere for you. They're ready for you." He looked at her face and scowled. "Have you been with Thomblin?"

She shook her head, fearing that if she spoke, he would hear her deceit in her voice.

"I thought you were warned to stay away from Thomblin?" Harris said under his breath.

Once again, he spoke to her as if she were a child, and what truly angered her was that he made her feel as if she was. "It's none of your business where I have been or with whom, sir!" she hissed.

"Thank God we're leaving soon. Now, come on." He grabbed her none too gently by the elbow and steered her across the drawing room toward the French doors that led into the garden. "Kendra wants to do this unveiling and everyone is waiting for you."

As they entered the perfumed garden that twinkled with candlelight and stars, the crowd of guests parted to let them pass. Everyone was smiling, murmuring. Such an unusual event at a coming-out ball was already causing great interest.

Halfway across the garden, Madison began to have second thoughts. "Oh, heavens," she whispered, swaying a little as she took a stumbling step.

Mr. Harris tightened his hold on her arm. "Hell, don't tell me you're going to faint."

She glanced up at him, keeping a smile on her face for the sake of everyone watching. "I don't faint," she spat under her breath.

"Good."

"And here she is, my dear niece, Miss Madison Westcott," Aunt Kendra announced grandly as Mr. Harris handed her off.

Madison turned to face the crowd of two hundred esteemed guests. There were men there of Parliament, titled ladies and gentlemen…and art lovers…perhaps even talented artists. She bit down on the inside of her lip, forcing herself to calm down.

"As many of you know, my dear late brother's daughter Madison is not only a beauty, a scholar in many disciplines, but she is also an artist."

There was a ripple of gentle, well-mannered applause.

"And so tonight, the Westcott family would like not only to introduce you to this talented young lady, but to introduce you to her work. This is highly unusual, I know, but once you see this painting, you will realize why we could not longer keep it to ourselves." Lady Moran caught the corner of the black silk that covered the canvas that was six feet tall by four feet wide. "So without further ado—"

Madison heard the swish of fabric and turned her head from the canvas being unveiled, to gaze out at the guests. She loved to see others' reactions to art. It was so telling of whether or not an artist had accomplished what he or she had set out to do.

Mouths fell open. Painted, plucked and bushy eyebrows

arched. The guests gasped, groaned. Some turned away, covering their eyes with gloved hands or fans.

Madison's smile fell.

She heard her mother cry out and then a great commotion. Lady Westcott had fainted.

The sounds of the crowd, along with their facial expressions, moved from shock, to distaste, to contempt.

A lump rose in Madison's throat as she slowly turned to look behind her, beyond her mother crumpled on the flagstone, to the canvas that had been revealed.

It was, indeed, her best work. In the self-portrait, she stood reflected in a full-length gilded mirror, her turquoise gaze fixed on the observer, her long blond hair falling over her shoulders to her tiny waist. Nude.

5

Madison felt an arm slip around her waist and the warmth of a body close to hers.

Lord Thomblin...*Carlton,* had come to her rescue.

"Madison, *chérie,* I think we need to get you out of here."

Still floating in that ethereal sensation that time was standing still, Madison turned slowly to him. "Carl—"

To her astonishment, it was not Lord Thomblin holding her gently in his arms; it was Mr. Harris.

He tugged at her waist, trying to lead her away. "Madison, we have to get you out of here."

"They didn't like my portrait," she whispered, tears suddenly welling in her eyes.

"Oh, I'd say there were some who found it quite appealing," he teased.

She took a faltering step, feeling weak-kneed. "It was my best," she whispered, staring into his eyes, willing him to understand. "I gave them my best."

He leaned down and whispered in her ear. "But you were naked, *chérie.*"

"It's art," she protested. "True art. Michelangelo and Rubens, their nudes are displayed prominently."

His face was so near that his nose almost touched hers. "I'm not sure that London is quite ready for such highly developed thinking."

"Jefford, please, get her out of here," Aunt Kendra called from behind them where she was trying to assist Lady Westcott.

"Madison, *chérie*," Mr. Harris whispered again, trying to shield her from the guests. "Walk with me."

Madison wanted to run from the garden, but her limbs wouldn't obey.

Mr. Harris took one last look at her and then swept her into his arms.

She slipped her arms around his neck and buried her face in the lapel of his coat. He smelled good, faintly of tobacco and Scotch, but mostly of maleness. In his arms, she felt safe.

She closed her eyes as he carried her, his stride, long and confident. She vaguely heard the sounds of the guests as they began to take their leave. Everyone was talking at once as carriages were called and wraps were located. Albert was bellowing drunkenly at his mother, something about the ruination of the family. Catherine was crying loudly. Aunt Kendra was shouting orders.

"Where are you taking me?" Madison managed, realizing they had not gone into the house but deeper into the garden.

"Your studio."

"But how—"

"Do you want to go through the house, through all those people?"

She shook her head, burying her face into his coat again, now damp with her tears.

"I didn't think so." He stepped high over something, still holding her securely in his arms as if she weighed nothing. "I was in your studio earlier. The windows were open. As we are both aware, one can step in and out of them."

"You were in my studio?" she asked, lifting her head from his shoulder to look at him. It was so dark in the side garden, where the brick of the house loomed high above them, that she couldn't really see his face. She could only feel those dark eyes gazing down at her. It was unnerving.

"Your work is quite good. I did not get a chance to see it when last I was here."

"You had no right!" she snapped.

He stepped through the open windows of the studio, into the room that was dimly lit by a kerosene lamp.

"I have to give credit where it is due. Your portrait of the African was extraordinary." She could feel the rumble of his voice through his chest. "I could sense the agony of those chains, the agony of the chains of his ancestors."

The emotion in Mr. Harris's voice was penetrating.

Madison trembled, suddenly needing to put distance between them. The scent of the oil paints, the canvas stretched over fragrant newly cut frames steadied her. "Please put me down," she said, pressing her palms to his broad chest.

"Can you stand?"

"Of course I can stand."

He lowered her to her feet and she stood upright triumphantly for a moment. Then swayed.

He caught her in his arms. "Easy. Sit down." He helped her to a brocade upholstered chair that was too frayed for the main house. Madison had found it in the attic and had a servant carry it down for her.

"I'm all right," she said, pushing his arms away once she felt the support of the old chair.

"Of course you are. Will be, at least." He thrust his hand into his coat and pulled out a silver flask. "Take a sip of this."

He thrust it under her nose and the strong scent of Scotch assailed her nostrils.

She pushed his hand away. "I don't want that."

"You might not want it, but you sure as hell need it."

"Sir, I know nothing of your Jamaica, but your language is really quite unacceptable in polite society here."

He forced the flask into her hand. "So that makes two of us unacceptable in *polite society* here, now, doesn't it?"

Realizing the truth of his words, fearing the ramifications, Madison tipped the flask to her lips. Cool liquid hit her tongue; the taste was biting. Numbing. She coughed and took another sip.

"Easy there." Mr. Harris covered her hand with his, taking the Scotch from her. "I get you drunk, and Albert will toss us both out on the street."

Madison pressed her hand to her mouth, her lips burning from the drink.

"Jefford! Jefford, are you in there?" An abrupt knock sounded at the door.

He walked toward the door. "Yes."

Aunt Kendra opened the door and poked her head in. "Is Madison there with you?"

"She's right here."

"Good." Aunt Kendra bobbed her head. "Keep her here until everyone is gone and then get her up to her room. Albert needs to sober up before we deal with this." She shifted her gaze to Madison still seated on the chair. "Are you all right, lovey?"

Madison nodded, trying to be brave, though the sight of her aunt's friendly face made her want to begin crying again.

"Good. Now, try not to worry. I feel terrible that I've gotten you into such a stew, but I promise, I'll think of something." She smiled bittersweetly. "Let Jefford take care of you." She backed out of the door. "Lock this," she called.

Aunt Kendra's footsteps died away as Mr. Harris locked the door and turned back to face Madison. "You should sit another moment."

"I don't want to sit." Madison rose to her feet, steadying herself with the back of her chair. Her mouth was a little numb, but she felt better again.

He removed his jacket and tossed it over an easel. "Madison—"

"You can go." She yanked the flowers from her hair and threw them down on the tiled floor. "I'm quite fine, really."

"I can't go. I told Kendra I would stay here until it was safe for you to go upstairs."

He stopped in front of her. She didn't know what made her do it, but she lifted her chin and looked into his eyes. Again, he was close enough that she could feel his breath on her face. Her intention had been to order him from the room, but when his gaze met hers, she found she couldn't tear away. There was something about the depth of the dark pools that held her mesmerized. Suddenly, her pulse was racing.

"Madison," he murmured. "I—" He stopped short, glanced away, then back at her. "Ah, hell," he muttered, and then he grabbed her around the waist and pulled her roughly against him.

Madison made a little sound that was more a rush of air than a cry for help as he lowered his mouth to hers, crushing her lips.

She flung her arms around his neck and kissed him

back as the room spun, swam. She squeezed her eyes shut, lost in the feel of his hard body pressed to hers, to the sensation of his mouth, and the taste of him. She'd had no idea this was what a kiss could be so…primal.

Not until she was breathless and was forced to hold on to him to prevent crumbling to the floor, did he finally release her.

"Oh," Madison cried, letting go of him, stumbling back as the realization of what she had just done washed over her.

"Madison, I'm sorry."

She wiped at her mouth with the back of her hand, as if there was some way to wipe away his searing kiss. She stared angrily at him, tempted to slap his face, but afraid to. "You should not have done that," she spat, as angry with herself as with him.

He hung his head, running his fingers through his thick, dark hair. "You're right, I shouldn't have. Again, I apologize."

Easing around him cautiously, Madison made for the door. "I should warn you now, Mr. Harris, that you would be wise not to lay your desires on me. Someone else is already the object of my affection. Lord Thomblin—"

"Lord Thomblin," he cut in angrily, lifting his head to look at her again. "Madison, you must stay away from him. As for my falling in love with you, you need not worry. You are probably the last woman on earth I would lay my affection upon."

Madison opened her mouth to retort. When she realized, once again, he had left her with nothing to say, she unlocked the door, pulled it open and ran.

"Is everyone here?" Albert asked, standing in the drawing room doorway.

They were all there, Madison's mother, her sister-in-law, Aunt Kendra and, for some unthinkable reason, Mr. Harris. Thankfully, Lord Thomblin had not been invited to the family meeting and he was out making arrangements to have some items he had purchased delivered to the docks for his return to Jamaica.

"Good," Albert said, rubbing his hands together. "Then let's get started. I called this assembly, as you know, because of the incident that took place last night at the ball which was to be Madison's official coming out." He eyed her accusingly, looking at her for the first time since last night.

Madison was tempted to stick her tongue out at him. She knew it was an adolescent response, but he made her so livid that she wished she could spit. She knew he was going to profess to be concerned with her reputation, but the truth was, he was only concerned about his own. He cared less whether the world thought his sister was the Virgin Mother or a Fleet Street whore, so long as their opinion of her did not affect their opinion of him.

"It is my hope," Albert continued pompously, "that we will be able to conceive a way to smooth over this regrettable incident as quickly and as efficiently as possible."

"Our family name will be ruined by this scandal," Lady Westcott cried, throwing up her hands. "I'll never be invited to another tea or poetry reading. Lord Kendal—" She broke off with a sob as Catherine handed her a dry handkerchief.

Madison rolled her eyes at her mother's dramatics and slid down farther on the horsehair settee, flipping open the sketch pad on her lap.

Aunt Kendra, beside her, slid her hand onto Madison's knee to settle her. "Perhaps it's not as bad as you perceive," she said hopefully.

"In truth, it is probably worse, Lady Moran," Albert re-
torted. "This morning when I walked for my paper, I cannot tell how many people stopped to tell me how sorry they
were that this potentially devastating incident has befallen
us. By dinnertime, everyone who is anyone will know that
my sister has bared her naked body before all of London."

Madison shot off the settee, throwing her sketch pad
down. "I beg your pardon, sir, but I did not *bare* myself to
anyone." She could have sworn she heard a chuckle from
Mr. Harris, who was watching the scene between her and
her brother with amusement. She chose to ignore him. To
acknowledge him would force her to consider the kiss they
had shared the previous night and she couldn't possibly do
that right now. "I simply displayed a self-portrait," she
said. "All artists paint self-portraits!"

"Sit down, Madison, sit down at once or you will leave
this room," Albert snapped, pointing his finger as if she
were one of his disobedient hounds.

"How dare you suggest I had behaved improperly by dis-
playing that painting," she spat. "And even if I did, how
could that be any more improper than you cheating on
your—"

"Madison!" She felt Aunt Kendra's hand in hers and a
slight tug. "Sit down!" she urged. She lowered her voice.
"Stay quiet and trust me."

"I think, Albert, that you have blown this entirely out of
proportion," Aunt Kendra declared. "However, if you think
it would help to remove Madison from London for a time,
just until this dies down or some other society scandal takes
precedent, I should like to offer a suggestion."

"I should think you would, considering the fact that
none of this would have happened had you not come here
in the first place," Lady Westcott burst out.

"Mother!" Madison cried.

Aunt Kendra whirled, her eyes widening with indignation. "How dare you, Alba?"

"Well, it's true," Lady Westcott simpered, turning her attention to her son. "This wouldn't have happened if *she* hadn't encouraged Madison, if she hadn't made such a fuss over her painting. My daughter never had any intention of showing any of her canvases to anyone until *she* came along. Dabbling in art was merely a young girl's way to pass time."

"Mother!" Madison turned to her. "How can you be so rude to Lady Moran? Do you know so little of your own daughter?"

"What do you propose, Lady Moran? Paris is out of the question. Despite my distaste for the French, I would not set this hoyden upon them."

"My proposal," Aunt Kendra announced, rising regally to her feet, "is that I cut my trip short, departing at once, and take Madison with me to Jamaica."

"Absolutely not," Mr. Harris fired from where he sat.

"Jefford, please," Kendra said, continuing to address Albert. "She can come to Jamaica with me. We have several wealthy English gentlemen in need of a proper wife, and there are very few unwed Englishwomen to be had. Who knows, one of them might find a hoyden artist acceptable as a wife." She raised an arm and posed. "Surely word of the scandal will never reach Kingston."

"And if we find she is unmarriageable in Jamaica, as well?" Albert intoned.

Madison's eyes gleamed; her heart began to hammer as she clutched her sketchbook to her chest. To travel to Jamaica? To live with Aunt Kendra? Good heavens! Last night had been a blessing in disguise. A gift from God.

Kendra shrugged matter-of-factly. "We'll cross that ocean when we come to it. She can return to London, I suppose. Surely in a year or two everyone will have forgotten this silly incident."

"Kendra," Mr. Harris said striding toward her, his face stony. "You cannot be serious. There is no place at Windward Bay for that child."

"Not now," Kendra said softly.

Mr. Harris gave Aunt Kendra a look that would have reduced most women to tears. She stood her ground, and after a moment he swore under his breath in an odd language, and strode out of the room.

"You...you're not serious," Lady Westcott said, dabbing at her eyes with her handkerchief. "You would take her off my hands?"

"Father left her only a meager inheritance," Albert warned.

Kendra motioned with one hand as if Viscount Westcott was a bothersome bottle fly. "Keep her inheritance. Should she wed, you may send it to furnish her trousseau."

Albert looked to Lady Westcott questioningly.

Madison gripped her hands so tightly in her lap that it pained her. Please, she mouthed silently. Please, God, if you're there, grant me this one wish.

"I think a change of scenery would be wise for Madison." Lady Westcott eyed her daughter. "Perhaps after a year in the jungle, in the heat without the refinement of the life she has grown accustomed to here, she will think better of her actions."

Madison could not control herself any longer and popped off the settee. "I can go to Jamaica, then?"

Kendra shot her a warning glance over her shoulder and Madison lowered her gaze, clasping her hands. "I mean, if it's what you wish, Mother, I will, of course, obey you."

"Fine. It's settled." Albert turned on his heels. "And the sooner she's out of here, the better, I think." He snapped his fingers as he started down the corridor. "Catherine."

The young woman, clumsy with child, came quickly out of her seat. "Coming, dearest," she cried as she hurried after him.

Madison pressed her lips tightly together as she turned to Aunt Kendra. "Should I pack, Aunt Kendra?"

"Most assuredly. I will send a list to your chamber of the clothing and personal necessities you will require."

"And my paints and canvases?"

"Pack what materials you have, and I will order more supplies to be sent to the ship. There are no such fripperies in Jamaica, dear."

"Oh, thank you, Aunt Kendra." Madison threw her arms around her aunt and gave her a quick hug, then spun around and dipped a curtsy to her mother. "I'll start at once," she declared, already on her way out the door.

"There you are," Kendra called, walking out onto the garden patio. It was a dark, cloudless night, and though the rain has ceased, the air still had the feel of inclement weather. She hugged herself for warmth. "I thought perhaps you had sailed without me."

Jefford scowled and turned to her. "You shouldn't be out here without your wrap. You heard what the physician said." He slipped out of his wool jacket and placed it around her shoulders. "Of course you've heard what they all said—physicians in Milan, Paris and London. You listen to no one, do you?"

"Now, now." She slid her arm through his and patted his hand. "You are just out of sorts because you didn't get your way on this issue with my niece."

"It is not about getting my way." His voice cut through the darkness. "It's about that young woman's safety. Does her family have any idea how dangerous the political climate in Jamaica is right now? Do they know nothing of the workers' rebellions?"

"Alba knows little beyond what happens on this street," Kendra declared impatiently. "So what? The girl is still better off with me at Windward Bay than here where they will marry her off to the first clout willing to take her off their hands. The wrong man could ruin her talent. Ruin her spirit."

"Right now I'd like to take her spirit and—"

Kendra laughed aloud. "Jefford, dear, I haven't heard you so passionate in years."

"You're not going to be swayed on this issue, are you?" he asked, ignoring her comment and her insinuation.

"I am not."

"Not even knowing that she is infatuated with Thomblin?"

"He's only toying with her." She leaned against him and pressed her cheek to his sleeve. "A mere diversion while he's here. He has no genuine interest in her."

"You would hope to sweet Jesus not."

Kendra turned to look up at him. "Jefford, for me. Will you let this be my one last adventure? Will you do it for me?"

Against his will, Jefford felt himself soften. He could never deny Kendra anything, not ever…and she knew it. "Do you really think you can marry her off?"

"There's a good chance, as beautiful and bright as she is. George Rutherford, perhaps?" She lifted a brow questioningly.

He scowled and glanced away. He still could not believe he had made such an error in judgment the previous night. How could he have been so stupid as to have kissed Madison? How could he have been so stupid as to allow his lust to overrule his sensibilities? Not since he'd been a young man had he made such a mistake. And now she would be returning to Windward Bay with them. It was a nightmare he feared he'd not awake from.

"Say you are with me on this," Kendra prodded. "Tell me you'll keep an eye on Thomblin, keep him and Madison apart. Tell me you will protect her once we have reached home, as you've protected me all these years."

Jefford turned to face her, taking her by her thinning shoulders. "If it's truly what you wish."

"It is."

He leaned over slowly and brushed his lips against her cheek. "To bed with you now," he murmured. "Tomorrow will be a long day, as will the day after. The tides look good to sail in three days."

"Thank you," she said, looking up at him, her jewel-green eyes filling with tears. "Your loyalty to me will not go unrewarded on earth or in heaven."

"Go to bed, you foolish woman." He released her. "You're babbling now."

Kendra started for the door, then turned back. "Aren't you coming in?"

He shook his head. "It will be hours before I can sleep again." He turned away from the house, looking up into the dark sky. Against his will, images of Madison and her kissable mouth invaded his thoughts. Her innocence struck him in a way he had not been touched in far too long and it made him uneasy. "I think it will be a lifetime before I sleep again," he muttered.

6

"I don't know what to do with her," Kendra fretted, grasping the railing as the clipper ship rolled. "It's been almost a week since we set sail from London, and while the ocean has been rough at times, the weather has not been entirely uncooperative. I just don't understand why she's so ill."

"Not every woman takes to the sea as well you do," Jefford responded dryly. "Nor does every woman take to each new experience the way you do."

"I think she needs to get up and move around a bit. Get some fresh air. Down there in that tiny cabin, it's suffocating. She doesn't eat, she barely even drinks the water I bring her. She says she can't sleep, either." She glanced up at Jefford. "I'm very concerned."

"No one has ever died from seasickness in a week's time," he said drolly, gazing out over the rolling blue-green waves.

The journey home on the *Alicia Mae* was already taking longer than the trip to London had taken, and Jefford was restless, anxious to get home and to his duties on the plantation, back to Chantal. He feared his idle time in London had made him soft, made him dwell on thoughts of Madison because he had nothing else to do to occupy his time. He knew, however, that once he returned to Windward Bay, this fixation with Kendra's niece would pass.

"Would you please look in on her?" Kendra rested her hand on his bare forearm.

Jefford had been helping a couple of the ship riggers hoist a square sail and had rolled up the sleeves of his open-necked cotton shirt. He'd forgone the jacket the moment he'd stepped off the London dock onto the ship's deck. The crew of the *Alicia Mae* was large enough to sail, but one of the leaders of the ship riggers had taken pity on him and his boredom and had offered to give him some lessons on the rigging of the old clipper ship. Jefford had some experience sailing smaller barks used to ship merchandise in the islands, but this was a new experience, and he appreciated the opportunity to keep his hands and mind busy.

"Just look in on her?" Kendra asked. "You're probably right. She's not as ill as she seems. She's young and young women are prone to exaggeration, but—"

"Fine, I'll go, but send Maha," he grumbled, pressing both hands on the polished wooden rail and leaning over to breathe deeply of the salt air.

"I'll send her right now. Perhaps if you could just get Madison up out of bed…" Kendra hurried across the deck, the long skirt of her bright green caftan flapping in the breeze. "Maha could change the sheets and bring some water and a towel for her to bathe."

Jefford scowled at the thought of having to go below and look in on Madison. He was no one's nursemaid. Damn, why didn't Kendra ask Thomblin? He was the one Madison was smitten with; he'd certainly paid plenty of attention to her when they were at Boxwood Manor. Jefford knew very well that Thomblin would not be interested in the young woman's health, nor would he want the man near Madison, particularly in her state of vulnerability, but it galled him all the same.

A high-pitched sound below in the water caught Jefford's attention and he gazed down, then out, smiling at the sight of three dolphins swimming beside the ship in a perfect V. They dove and resurfaced again and again, giving the impression that they were overjoyed by the appearance of the ship. He watched them another minute and then reluctantly turned away.

"I might as well get this over with," he muttered.

He crossed to the aft hatch and slid down the ladder to the corridor one level below deck. Following the narrow passageway, he passed Kendra's cabin and saw Maha waiting at the end of the dim, stuffy hall that was barely wide enough for him walk without turning his shoulders.

The clipper ship had been built in the 1850s to carry cargo, not passengers, but the owner of the *Alicia Mae,* realizing that the life of the clipper was dying with the arrival of the iron barks and steamers, had been smart enough to add several private staterooms. The sailing ship, sporting four masts and fifteen thousand square yards of canvas, now crossed from the Caribbean to London regularly, serving wealthy Englishmen living far from home in the islands of Jamaica, the Caymans and Haiti.

"Did you knock?" he asked the middle-aged, Indian-born maid, Maha. Her husband was one of Jefford's overseers and had remained behind in Jamaica, and Jefford knew she was as anxious to return to Windward Bay as he was.

"She says I am to go away," Maha answered.

Jefford reached over Maha's shoulder and knocked impatiently. When there was no immediate response, he knocked again.

"Please, Maha" came a weak voice. "Go away."

The frailty in Madison's voice startled him.

"Madison, it's Jefford," he said, resting his hand on the doorknob. "I'm coming in."

"No," she cried faintly.

"Madison—" He thrust the door open and was immediately assailed by the heat and foul smell of the tiny cabin. One look at her pale, drawn face, and he felt guilty for not having listened to Kendra days ago when she said she was concerned that Madison was not finding her sea legs.

"Open that window," Jefford ordered Maha. "Then get that dirty slop bucket out of here." He tried to breathe through his mouth, rather than his nose. "You're going to need a wash bucket and something to wipe down the bed and the floor. Get help if you need to." He ducked his head to sit down on the edge of the bunk built into the curve of the hull.

Tangled in a dirty blanket, a sketchbook clutched to her chest, Madison rolled away from him. "Go away. I don't want anyone to see me like this," she half sobbed.

"Don't be silly. You're ill." He turned to the maid, who was already out of the cabin. "Maha, on second thought, could you bring me a basin of cool water and a clean cloth first? And something she can change into. One of Kendra's caftan things, perhaps." He gestured. "Something that will cover her so I can take her up on deck."

"Yes, *sahib*." She nodded and hurried away.

Jefford turned back to Madison and grabbed the dirty blanket that covered her.

"No," she groaned, holding on to it, still hiding her face.

"Madison, this is filthy and damp. Your linens need to be changed and you need to get up and get some fresh air."

"I can't," she moaned. "I'm dying."

"Hardly." He brushed his hand over the blond hair plastered to her head. "But you'll feel better if you get up and get something in your stomach."

"No." When she released the blanket to clutch her abdomen, he took the opportunity to snatch it away from her.

She cried out in protest and tried to shrink beneath the folds of her soiled, pale blue sleeping gown.

He tossed the blanket through the open doorway into the corridor and grasped the hem of the nightgown and pulled it down to cover her bare calves. "Madison, *chérie,*" he said tenderly, laying his hand on her hip. "It could be as long as two weeks before we see Jamaica. You cannot go without food or water another two weeks." He reached up and brushed the hair that stuck to her cheek off her face. "Another two weeks really could kill you."

"I want to die," she whispered through cracked, dry lips.

"No, you don't. You want to get up and walk on the deck with me and have something to eat and drink, because there are some wonderful places I want to take you when we reach Jamaica. Places you will want to paint. Waterfalls, beaches. You must see the workers at the day's end carrying their lunch sacks on their backs, walking in from the sugarcane fields or the coffee groves, singing. You'll want to paint them, *chérie,* I promise you."

She sniffed. "It sounds beautiful."

"More beautiful than you can imagine." Jefford heard footsteps and turned to see Maha appear in the doorway with a washbasin, a towel and a bright garment of emerald green thrown over her arm. He looked back to his patient. "Now, Madison, I'm going to step out and let Maha bathe you."

"No." She grasped the lumpy pillow beneath her head and tried to cover her face it with it. "Just leave me."

He rose, keeping his head low to prevent striking it on the overhead beam. "Either Maha is going to bathe you or I am. It's your choice."

Madison hesitated. "Maha."

"Good." He rubbed her shoulder that was so thin it concerned him. How could she have lost so much weight in just a week's time? "Now, I'm going to step out and give you privacy, but I'll wait right outside the door."

She didn't answer and he walked to the doorway. "If you could bathe her and help her into that thing," he told Maha, "I'll take her up on deck and you can give this cabin a good cleaning."

"I will clean good, Mr. Jefford."

He smiled. "You're a fine woman, Maha."

She smiled back. "No, Mr. Jefford. I have known you most of your life. It is you who are a fine man. You are big and loud and you stomp, but we all know what is in your heart."

"Well, just don't tell anyone, all right?" he teased. Then he stepped out of the cabin, closed the door and leaned against the wall to wait. Twenty minutes later, the door opened.

"She is ready."

Jefford stuck his head through the doorway to see Madison sitting up on the edge of the bed. She was bathed, her face freshly washed and her hair pulled back in a ribbon. The gown was far too large on her, but it covered well for propriety's sake.

"You ready to go above deck and get some fresh air?" he asked.

She hung her head, pressing her hand to her forehead. "I'm dizzy."

"You'll be all right."

"I'm not decent. I have no—no corset. I cannot go in public—"

"Nonsense. You're dehydrated. Once we get up above, I'll get you something to drink, something you can stomach."

She swayed a little and he took a quick step forward to catch her. "Come on, Madison. Let's see some of that spirit I encountered in the garden that night when you were sketching. Remember?" He gently helped her to her feet and she leaned against him, too weak to stand on her own. "You know," he said softly in her ear. "I have a confession to make. You dropped your sketch pad that night in the garden and I kept it."

She looked up. "Whatever for?"

He shrugged. "It was very good."

"I don't think I can walk," she murmured.

"Try."

She slid one foot forward, then the other, then swayed and fell against him again. The feel of her hand on his chest sent a ripple of pleasure through him and he had to fight it, putting a distance, mentally, between them. "What if I carry you up, and we try again once we're above?"

She nodded and he lifted her into his arms.

"Wait," Madison cried, stretching out her arm. "I need a sketch pad. And a pencil. There."

He groaned impatiently, but carried her back to the bedside to collect the items, then ducked out of the cabin. Taking care with his footing, he carried her up the ladder. Once on the deck, she pressed her face into his chest to avoid the bright light. He tried to think about all the work waiting for him at home, rather than the touch of this woman in his arms and the feel of her breath on his chest.

"Bright, isn't it?"

"I don't want anyone to see me like this," she moaned. "Lord Thomblin—"

"It's all right," he soothed, annoyed at the mention of his neighbor. "I know a place near the lifeboats that's secluded. No one will even know we're there and there's a place to sit."

He crossed the deck with Madison in his arms, for the most part unnoticed. The crew was busy with their ship's duties and Thomblin and Kendra were nowhere to be seen. "Here we are, my own private place," he said, walking around one of the lifeboats and cutting between several casks lashed to the deck. "There's a nice pile of lashing here to sit on." He leaned over and eased her out of his arms, setting her down on the coil of thick rope.

Madison covered her face with her sketchbook for a moment, using it as a shield against the bright sun, then slowly lowered it, easing her eyes open. "The cool air feels good," she said shakily.

He squatted beside her. "I told you it would."

She lifted her head to gaze over the side of the ship. "The water is pretty today." She pressed her cracked lips together. "I'm a little thirsty."

"I was hoping so." He stood. "Will you be all right here alone for a moment?"

She reached up and grabbed his hand and he had to force himself not to flinch. He had vowed to stay away from Madison. She was not the kind of woman he wanted to become involved with. She was too headstrong, too self-centered. He would not have a marriage based on nothing but lust.

"I'll be right back," he told her, and pulled away.

Madison heard Jefford's footsteps die away on the deck as she set her sketch pad down and lowered her head for a moment, swallowing hard. She was dizzy and her stomach was queasy, but she did feel better.

Several minutes passed before he returned. "Here you are," he said, squatting beside her, pushing a cool tin cup into her hand.

"What is it?" she asked.

"Try it."

Madison lifted the cup to her lips and took a tentative sip. The liquid was cool and sweet and so delicious that she took several greedy gulps.

"Easy there, not too fast." He closed his hand over the cup, taking it from her.

"Whatever is it?" she asked, wetting her lips.

He half smirked. "Hummingbird food."

"What?" she laughed.

He reached up with his finger to catch a drip at the corner of her mouth. "It's what we feed the hummingbirds in our garden at Windward Bay. Water, sugar, a little fresh juice squeezed from fresh fruit."

"Hummingbird food?" She laughed again. "Give that to me."

"I have something to show you if you think you can stand." Jefford passed her the tin cup and came to his feet, offering his hand.

Madison tipped the cup, finishing its contents, and reached up to accept his aid. Her legs wobbled a bit as she rose, but she really did feel much better. The warmth of the sun and the cool ocean breeze felt so good on her prickly skin.

"What is it?" she asked.

He pointed and she followed the line of his finger. "Oh," she breathed. "Dolphins."

"They've been following us for a while. I saw them earlier."

Moving slowly, Madison released Jefford's arm and took a step toward the rail. She rested her forearms on the polished wood and leaned on the edge. "They're so beautiful," she breathed.

"Makes you think maybe there really is a God in heaven, doesn't it?" he said quietly, coming to stand beside her.

Madison watched the dolphins glide through the blue green water. After a moment, she turned to Jefford. "Thank you," she whispered.

He met her gaze, his dark eyes intent, and then he looked out over the water again.

He didn't respond to her thanks, but for once his impoliteness didn't matter. For a moment she studied his profile: the line of his jaw, the length and breadth of his nose, his skin a rich suntanned hue that did not divulge his ancestry but gave him an air of mystery.

Just who was this man?

Catching her looking at him, he smiled, and she looked away. "Could you pass me my sketch pad?" she asked, pointing to where she'd left it on the deck. "I must draw the dolphins before they're gone."

Two days later, Madison was well enough to dress with Maha's aid and walk the *Alicia Mae*'s deck unescorted. Once she was on her feet, Jefford did not come to her cabin again, and when she saw him on the deck, dressed much like the crew, working as if he were one of them, he barely acknowledged her presence.

Not that she cared.

"Miss Westcott, how good to see you," Lord Thomblin said, approaching Madison where she stood at the stern, hoping for another glimpse of the dolphins she had seen with Jefford.

"Good afternoon, sir," she responded, tucking her sketch pad under her arm and offering a curtsy.

He bowed gracefully and came to stand beside her. Dressed in a pale yellow jacket and trousers with a straw boater on his head, he looked like any London gentleman out for a stroll in Hyde Park. "I understand you've been feeling under the weather. It's good to see you out again. I do hope you'll be joining us for dinner this evening. Meals have been so dull without you."

He smiled down at her and she self-consciously fiddled with her bonnet. "Actually, I do think I will join you this evening. I'm feeling quite a bit better. Found my sea legs, at last, according to Aunt Kendra." She gave a little laugh.

Out of the corner of her eye, Madison saw Jefford approaching. He wore trousers cut off at the knees and a tattered shirt that clung to his torso, outlining every ripple of corded muscle. The wind blew his long, dark hair loose and free.

"Madison, Kendra's looking for you," Jefford grunted, walking past her, a coil of rope on his shoulder. "On the forward deck."

Thomblin cleared his throat and stepped back. "I'll see you this evening, then?"

"I look forward to it, sir," she said, curtsying and walking away, annoyed with Jefford. Hadn't he been able to see that she and Lord Thomblin were having a conversation?

She found her aunt on the bow of the boat, seated on a small crate, her eyes closed, her face tilted upward to the sun, her red hair loose and blowing over her shoulders.

"You were looking for me?"

"What's that?" Kendra asked, opening her eyes.

"Jefford said you were looking for me." Madison didn't know when she had gone from Mr. Harris to Jefford in her mind, but it did seem rather silly not to call him by his Christian name considering the familiarity they had shared when she was ill.

"Oh, yes, of course. Come sit with me." She pointed to a pile of crates. "Pull up a chair, dear."

Madison hesitated for a moment. She didn't want to sit and chat with Aunt Kendra, she wanted to flirt with Lord Thomblin, but she couldn't very well go back and find him now, could she?

With a sigh, she grabbed a crate and dragged it over beside her aunt. "What are you doing?" she asked, grasping her skirts and sitting down with her sketch pad on her lap. While on board ship, she had decided to go without some of the layers of underclothing she normally wore. A bustle or a cage petticoat seemed impractical considering the wind and the fact that she had to climb up and down a ladder to move from her cabin to the upper deck.

"Getting some sun." Kendra slid a map across the deck toward her. "We'll be home soon. You see, we've crossed the Atlantic, sailing southwest."

Madison picked up the faded map and rested it on her lap on her sketch pad to study it.

"Here is your geography lesson for the day, my dear, so listen carefully." Aunt Kendra waggled her finger. "The islands of the Caribbean look like stepping-stones stretching in an arc from the western end of Venezuela in South America to the peninsula of Florida in North America. The islands are divided into two groups—the

Greater Antilles form the northern part of the arc and include four large islands, Cuba, Hispaniola, Jamaica and Puerto Rico."

In fascination, Madison followed along the map with her finger. "Yes, I see."

"At the eastern end of the arc, we have the smaller islands that together form the Lesser Antilles. These include the West Indian islands of St. Kitts, Antigua, Barbados, Trinidad, Tobago." The older woman waved her hand. "And so forth. The body of water bounded by these islands and the northern coast of South America is the Caribbean Sea. Almost at the center of the Caribbean Sea, Jamaica lies ninety miles south of Cuba and one hundred miles west of Haiti."

"I hadn't realized we would be so close to South America," Madison observed.

"Yes, well, it is believed that the Arawak Indians first settled the island of Jamaica, paddling dugout canoes from South America. The Spaniards settled there at some point, then the English. Many say that the true history of Jamaica did not begin until slavery was outlawed in the 1830s. Since then, we have been struggling to make our way in the world, struggling to live side by side with such a mixture of cultures. Madison, dear, are you listening?"

"Yes, yes, of course." She stared at the map on her lap. "How much longer until we land? I can't wait to see the jungles you've described."

"A week, give or take." Lady Moran frowned. "Do take off your bonnet, dear. You could use a little sun."

"Mother says I'll get freckled if I don't wear my bonnet." Madison obediently untied the ribbons and removed it.

"What does she know of its healing properties? Now,

close your eyes and lift your face to the sun's warmth."
Kendra did so. "Isn't it just lovely? Makes one feel years
younger."

Madison closed her eyes and imitated her aunt, having
to admit the sun did feel good.

"Well, Madison, tell me, what do you think of Jefford?"

Madison's eyes flew open and she turned to her aunt.
"What do I think of him?" She opened her pad on her lap
to begin sketching the map of the Caribbean Islands so that
she could study it better on her own, later.

"Yes, what do you think of him? Isn't he handsome?"

"I...suppose some might think so," she said carefully.

"And he's quite bright. For a man, at least. I should think
he would make a good catch, in the area of matrimony,
don't you?"

Madison studied her aunt. Despite the slight wrinkles
around her eyes and mouth, she was still quite lovely. And
very rich. "Aunt Kendra!" she said, suddenly full of concern for the older woman. "Has Mr. Harris intimated that
he is interested in marrying you? Because if he has, I think
you would do well to take care. A man his age, without title
or money to speak of, might think to better himself
through—"

Kendra's laughter halted Madison in midsentence and
she studied her aunt for a minute in shocked silence. "Aunt
Kendra, I'm serious. Surely you don't think this would be
the first time a man would try to take advantage of a
woman to gain wealth. You said yourself that Windward
Bay consists of thousands of acres—"

"Madison, love..." Kendra was still chuckling as she
opened her eyes, turning to her niece. "I was asking if *you*
thought he was attractive. If you found yourself attracted
to him."

"Me?" Madison touched her bosom with her pencil. "No. No, of course not."

"You wouldn't even *consider* marrying him?"

Madison rose from the crate. "Cer-certainly not," she huffed. "You know how I feel about him. How…how he treated me in my own home—"

"There, there, do calm down." Aunt Kendra grabbed Madison's hand. "Don't get your drawers in a twist. I was only asking."

"Aunt Kendra, exactly what is your relationship to Jefford Harris?" she asked, even more confused now than before. "Who is he to you?"

"Sit down. Sit down." The older woman tugged on Madison's hand, still laughing. "Our relationship would be hard to explain, dear."

Madison sat on the crate again, listening.

"He is my friend, my business partner. So many things," she said, closing her eyes again and lifting her chin skyward. "Now, tell me, I saw you had set a canvas up in your cabin. What are you painting?"

Madison opened her mouth to say she was not yet satisfied with her aunt's explanation of Jefford, but then, knowing it would be pointless, she sighed in surrender. "I thought I would paint the sea," she said closing her eyes and lifting her face toward the warmth of the sun. "And the dolphins. I do hope they come again."

As Madison stepped back to study her painting of the crystal blue-green water lapping the side of the sailing ship, she absently wiped her brush tip with a rag. The boat was swaying rhythmically beneath her, but now that she was used to it, she found it somehow soothing, especially when she was working.

Behind her, she heard a tap on the door. "I said, no supper, Maha. Thank you, really, but I'm working," she called without taking her trained eye from the painting. The shading needed something….

The knob turned. The door opened.

"I said I'm working. I don't have time—"

"Madison."

She spun around, startled. Jefford ducked his head and entered the cabin without waiting for her invitation.

"I brought you something to eat," he said, brushing past her to set a small wooden tray on her hastily made bed.

The tiny room seemed, at once, to be filled with his presence, so filled with it that she could barely find her tongue. He was so close that she could have reached out and touched him; she could smell the scent of his freshly washed hair pulled back in a neat queue and his clean clothing, dried in the sun on the ship's stern on the mast lines.

Madison drew herself up to her full height, shaken, telling herself that she was simply annoyed that he would barge in this way, take over her cabin as though he had some rights here. "I sent word that I wouldn't be attending the evening meal in the captain's cabin because I was working." She slapped the brush down on the ledge of the easel, trying to move back from him so as not to brush against him. He seemed taller beneath this low ceiling, broader at the shoulder. "I asked that I not be disturbed," she said, in a voice that revealed some of the unease that prickled beneath her skin and brought back memories of the kiss in her studio that she preferred to forget.

He flashed a charming smile and lifted a silver lid on the tray to reveal a platter of fresh bread, crackers and fruit. "You'll be sick again if you don't eat. You still don't have your full strength back yet and we'll be arriving in Jamaica—"

The ship pitched suddenly and Madison thrust out both hands to catch the easel with her precious artwork as it swayed. At the same instant, Jefford put out his arms to steady her.

"Oh!" Madison cried, unable to keep her footing. Jefford pulled her against him, while steadying the easel with one hand, preventing it from crashing to the floor.

As the ship rocked back, the floor leveled and the easel landed on its legs again. Madison found herself gazing up into Jefford's eyes, her palms pressed against his chest, momentarily mesmerized by the nearness of him, by his overwhelming maleness.

"I—"

Jefford swooped down over her, covering her mouth with his, and Madison parted her lips to cry out in protest, but no sound escaped. She tried to struggle, but to no avail; he had crushed her in his arms, trapped her mouth with his, leaving her no way to escape.

She squeezed her eyes shut, her knees threatening to buckle. She couldn't breathe, couldn't think. Against her will, a sensation of pleasure curled deep in the pit of her stomach and began to radiate outward. She felt light-headed, as if she were going to faint. She couldn't stop him; what was even more frightening was that she feared she didn't want to. "Please," she muttered against his bruising mouth.

He released her so suddenly that she nearly lost her balance. "I'm sorry," he grunted, heading for the door. "I swore—" He halted in the doorway, meeting her gaze, brushing his mouth with the back of his hand.

Madison was breathing hard, staring at him, wanting to fling some accusation at him.

"I'm sorry," he repeated. "It won't happen again."

Madison sank down on the bunk, staring at his broad back as he walked through the doorway. "It certainly will not," she managed softly, brushing her fingertips across her lips. "It would be…impossible," she whispered. Unbidden, a single tear welled in the corner of her eye and spilled down her cheek. "Unthinkable."

Book Two
Jamaica

7

Kingston, Jamaica
November 1888

"There it is, my dear, Kingston." Lady Moran swept her arm grandly, taking in the harbor crowded with myriad ships and small watercraft, some anchored, others jockeying for a position at the teeming docks.

Beyond the wharf, stacked against verdant hills beneath a cloudless azure sky, lay the town Madison had dreamed of for weeks. As the crew members bustled around her, coiling thick tarred ropes on the deck and lowering sails, she stared, mesmerized by the unfamiliar scene.

"Disappointed?" Kendra smiled.

"Never! But how will I ever capture the essence on canvas?" Madison exclaimed joyously, staring at the patchwork of ramshackle wooden buildings teetering on the water's edge.

"Come along, dear. We've much to do before disembarking," Lady Moran informed her charge as she turned back toward the main cabins.

Madison clutched the ship's rail, devouring the color and sweep of the harbor, taking in the cries of seabirds, the shouts of sailors and the groan of the *Alicia Mae*'s timbers as the captain eased the vessel closer to mooring.

"Madison!"

Reluctantly, Madison tore herself from the vision of paradise and hurried after her aunt.

Two hours later, an impatient Madison stepped off the gangplank onto the hectic dock and was at once overwhelmed by the scent of the lush tropical forest. The capital city stretched out before her, but she could smell the abundant vegetation with its sago palms, massive ferns and wild orchids that surrounded them. The afternoon air was hot and humid and hummed with insects.

"Come along," Kendra ordered, pushing through the crowd of dark-skinned natives, her bright orange caftan flapping in the hot breeze.

Clutching the canvas of the painting she had been working on to her chest, Madison fell into step behind her aunt, overwhelmed by the heat and the crush of chattering men and women with crates and baskets on their shoulders and heads and the scents of fish, overripe bananas and what could only be hot gingerbread. The women were brightly garbed in colorful dresses that only fell halfway between their knees and their ankles to reveal dirty, bare feet. Their hair was bound up in rectangles of bright cloth, in much the same way that Lady Moran wore hers.

Madison turned her head to watch a woman, a squawking chicken carried under each arm, strut by barefoot in little more than a fragment of yellow fabric tied around her midsection for a dress and a very fashionable English walking bonnet on her head.

"Lord Thomblin sent word ahead earlier to Windward Bay that we've arrived. There should be someone here to fetch us," Aunt Kendra said over her shoulder. "Heavens, but it's nice to be home."

A silver coin flashed in the air and two naked boys dashed past Madison, followed by a barking terrier and one girl-child in striped green-and-white pantaloons. All four plunged off the dock into the water and bobbed up as merrily as dolphins—the leader's happy smile flashing in his ebony face as he waved the coin over his head. A portly captain with olive skin and chin whiskers laughed and showered the adventurers with a handful of shining pennies. Aunt Kendra paid no more attention to the children than she did to the shaven-headed Indian with the ring through his nose or to the loose goat nibbling at her caftan.

"Shouldn't we wait on the dock?" Madison wondered aloud. She wasn't used to people pressing so close to her. In England ladies and gentlemen, even servants, were careful to remain in their own space and not invade another's. Here everyone was brushing again her, bumping into her. "Jefford said he would be back for us."

"Oh, pish!" Aunt Kendra pushed forward, through the crowd, seemingly unaffected by the throng of natives. "We've no need of an escort, have we, Maha?" she asked her maid, who was bringing up the rear, carrying her mistress's parasol. "I can find my own carriage, I'll warrant you that."

Still holding on dearly to her painting wrapped in sailcloth for protection, Madison attempted to keep up with her aunt while taking in the sights and sounds around her.

Kingston's dock was as busy as London's. As far as the eye could see, ships were being loaded and unloaded. Horse-and-mule-drawn wagons full of supplies clogged the muddy street that ran along the dock. And there were people everywhere, people of every shade of skin known to God—not just Jamaicans and Englishmen, but Haitians, Chinese, Indians and other nationalities she couldn't identify.

A tall Jamaican woman hawking fragrant roasted meat thrust a long skewer under Madison's nose and she shook her head. Another cracked open a green coconut, revealing a fragrant milky water inside, and offered it to her, but she was too intent on preventing herself from becoming hopelessly lost in the crowd.

Madison caught the scent of a strange, burning odor and turned her head to stare at an elderly Jamaican man with white hair, smoking something that appeared to be a fat homemade cigar wrapped in leaves. "What—"

"Ganja." Aunt Kendra looped her arm through Madison's, hustling her on. "Some call it Indian hemp. Used for *medicinal* purposes by many Englishmen here." She raised her eyebrows. "But not in my household."

Madison could tell that her aunt disapproved and she wanted to ask exactly what this Indian hemp did *medicinally,* but Lady Moran was waving wildly, almost trotting now. "There they are. Do you see? The carriage with the green fringe. That's ours. Oh, Punta!" she called.

A dark-skinned man dressed all in white, wearing a red hat, was seated on the driver's bench of the carriage. He stood and waved, grinning. "Miss Kendra, it is good to see the big wide ocean did not swallow you up," he called, a rollicking cadence to his speech.

As they approached the carriage, Madison's gaze

strayed to a wagon parked behind it. She spotted Jefford striding toward the wagon and was shocked to see a young, dark-skinned woman dressed much like Aunt Kendra hurl herself out of the back of the wagon and into his arms.

Madison's mouth went dry.

"Madison, dear, what are you gawking at?" Aunt Kendra demanded, allowing Punta to help her into the carriage. Her gaze shifted to the wagon behind them. "Oh, that's his Chantal, dear. No need to worry your pretty head over her. Now, do get in. It appears we're about to have another rain shower."

Madison passed her painting up to Aunt Kendra and then allowed the man, Punta, to help her onto the seat beside her aunt. On closer inspection, she could see that Punta's skin tone was not the same as the other islanders and that his accent was very different. She did not have a great deal of experience with foreigners, but she suspected he was not of the West Indies, but from India.

The wagon was quickly loaded with crates and parcels, carried from the ship, and the two vehicles soon rolled off down King Street. As they made their way through the rambling town of storefronts and homes with verandas open to the street, Madison stared straight ahead, purposely not looking back to see Jefford driving the wagon, *his Chantal* on the buckboard seat beside him.

"Kingston is a charming town, of course," Aunt Kendra announced as light rain began to pitter-pat on the canvas awning over their heads. "To the northeast are the Blue Mountains." She pointed. "The most beautiful ridge of mountains in the world, I do believe. But Windward Bay lies to the west, nestled on the water between Kingston and Port Royal, which was once a pirate town," she confided, her eyes sparkling with mischief.

"Are there pirates there now?" Madison questioned. One night at dinner hour, the captain of the *Alicia Mae* had entertained them with tales of piracy in the Caribbean and Madison was both fascinated and horrified by the subject.

Aunt Kendra patted her arm. "Only a few, dear, and they're old and without most of their teeth, so don't worry." She then leaned over the carriage seat to speak to Punta. "Was I missed at Windward Bay?"

"Not at all, Miss Kendra. Your servants have run wild about the house, letting the chickens and goats in the kitchen, wearing your clothing, sleeping in your bed and drinking your bottles of wine."

Aunt Kendra laughed, patting him on the shoulder as if it were the greatest joke. Madison was fascinated by her aunt's relationship with her servants. The older woman was surrounded by people who ran at her beck and call, and yet they all seemed more like good friends than mistress and maid or driver.

The carriage left the town of Kingston behind and followed a rutted path west through the rolling hills. They passed ramshackle huts nestled in thick greenery and open fields that Punta pointed out as coffee or sugarcane. They also passed men, women and children on the road, on their way to and from the capital city. Everyone seemed so friendly, so content. Women waved, men tipped their hats, some real, others imaginary, and children ran after the wagon, laughing and trying to catch a ride.

After nearly an hour's journey, Aunt Kendra opened her arms wide, her smile broad. "Look around you, love, and all you see is Windward Bay," she announced proudly.

Madison had been observing the flourishing jungle that surrounded them for some time, watching the colorful birds that flitted through the palms and the snakes that slithered along the path. Suddenly, she pulled a deep breath. So this was to be her home, at least for the next year, perhaps for her lifetime?

The path began to widen and she noticed beds of orchids that had obviously been cultivated, growing on both sides of the road. "Oh, how lovely," she murmured.

"My orchids. They are exquisite, aren't they? I have forty-seven species growing in the vicinity of the house. Many native, but some collected from as far away as China. I seem to have a way with them. Carlton is so envious, he's green," Kendra explained with delight, patting Madison's knee.

"Lord Thomblin grows orchids? How interesting a diversion for a man. You said he was a neighbor. How far does he live from Windward Bay?" Carlton had left the ship immediately once it had docked, insisting he had urgent matters to attend, but promised Madison he would see her soon.

"Farther west, along the coast, but there's no need to concern yourself with Lord Thomblin, dear. There will be plenty to do at Windward Bay to occupy your time." Aunt Kendra turned in her seat again. "And here we are, home at last."

The carriage followed a lazy bend in the road and a great plantation house such as Madison had never imagined lay before her, a crisp white stone-and-plaster oasis in the middle of the emerald jungle.

"Aunt Kendra, it's…stunning," Madison murmured, at a loss as to what to say. She had understood that Lady Moran, sadly a widow at nineteen years of age, had been left well off by her husband, Lord Moran, but Madison's mother had never hinted that Aunt Kendra was this wealthy.

Madison grasped the back of the seat and half rose, craning her neck. She caught a glimpse of a second-story veranda that ran the full length of the house, lined with pots of lush ferns and flowering vines. The sprawling, multi-winged house was two stories in some places, only one in others, and had massive floor-to-ceiling windows with shutters thrown wide open, with frothy white curtains billowing in the warm breeze. There were little alcoves, stone benches and more verandas, and flowers and plants everywhere, seeming to sprout right from the foundation.

Dogs barked from behind a pink stone wall and Aunt Kendra stood up, even before the carriage came to a complete stop. "Home," she breathed, her eyes glimmering with moisture. "Just as I left it."

Punta climbed down from the wagon, offering his hand to his mistress.

"You are my jewel, Punta. I knew I could trust you to keep all safe under my roof."

Madison stood at the carriage trying to take in the expanse of Windward Bay's great house. Servants spilled from the doors and archways to greet their mistress. Two little girls in bright-colored dresses waved from the main balcony.

Madison glanced behind the carriage to see Jefford leap down from the driver's seat of the wagon and lift the young woman, Chantal, to the ground. She was shocked by his show of familiarity with the young woman, in plain sight of others. Madison watched as they walked side by side around the house and disappeared through an archway woven with bright pink flowers.

"Madison, I know you must be fatigued, love," Aunt Kendra called, offering her hand. "Come let me show you to your chambers. I have the perfect room around front for you with a large study that will work flawlessly for your new studio."

"This is the back of the house?" Madison accepted her aunt's hand, staring again, in awe.

"The front faces the bay, of course, dear. Now come and let me introduce you to our staff. I already know who will make a perfect personal maid for you," Aunt Kendra assured her. "Sashi is a lovely young woman, just your age and also far from home. You'll get along splendidly."

Madison walked out onto the balcony that ran the full length of her chambers, leaned on the iron railing trellised with pink trumpeting vines and inhaled the floral scent of the evening air.

The series of rooms Aunt Kendra had given her were more than she could have hoped for. The bedchamber, studio and small room for her maid were situated on the second story and nestled in the northwest corner. The wraparound balcony, furnished with comfortable chairs, tables and an abundance of potted plants, could be reached from her studio or her bedroom. Half the balcony faced the open lawn that ran down to the turquoise waves and white sand of the bay, while the side balcony opened into gardens and the jungle. Surrounded by palm trees and giant ferns, Madison reached out and grabbed a leaf, imagining this was what it would be like to live in a tree house. All around her she could hear insect song and the flutter of branches and leaves.

"Miss Madison," Sashi called, stepping out onto the balcony. "Miss Kendra sent word that dinner would be in one hour."

Madison turned around and smiled. As her aunt had promised, Sashi was warm and friendly and had immediately made her feel right at home. She was from India, Madison had learned, and had come to Jamaica alone at fifteen years of age after the death of her family in a typhoid epidemic. She had been working for Lady Moran ever since and called Windward Bay her home. Sashi was a tiny, strikingly beautiful young woman who wore an unusual garb—to Madison—called a sari. Her black hair was pulled back in an elaborate chignon.

"Thank you."

"I have laid out a gown Miss Kendra sent up for you— a gift," she said, clasping her hands in obvious approval. "When you are ready, I will help you dress."

Madison leaned on the white-painted rail again, unable to inhale enough of the scent of the jungle or to tear her eyes from the overwhelming sight of it as darkness settled in. "I'll be ready in just a few more minutes," she called over her shoulder.

"Miss Kendra wishes me to move my things to the small room beside yours, so I can be near, if you have need of me."

"That will be fine, Sashi. Do it now, if you like. I'll call you when I'm ready to dress." When Sashi was gone, Madison turned her attention to her surroundings again. Torches had been lit along the edge of the garden to illuminate its splendid disorganization. Unlike those at Boxwood Manor where every plant, every leaf had been placed just so, Aunt Kendra's garden had a magnificent fluidity about it. Flower beds overflowed onto paths. Trees grew against old stone walls. There were places where variegated, leafy vines had grown quite out of control, running along fences, benches, even birdbaths, seeming to tie the entire garden together. And everywhere there were flittering rainbows of iridescent blue and green birds, some no larger than her thumb.

Madison was thankful Aunt Kendra had thought to provide her with a room suitable to be a studio, but here on the covered veranda, she knew, would be where she would do her best work. They were already moving into the rainy season, and she realized there would be days when monsoon rains would keep her inside, but barring inclement weather, this was where she intended to work.

She turned to glance at the easel she'd already set up against the whitewashed stone wall of the house. She had propped the canvas she had carried from the ship on it, and covered it with the drape. The painting was frustrating her, and she was hoping that now that she was feeling better, it would come more easily.

She was painting a portrait of the man she had fallen in love with. She'd begun by brushing in a backdrop of swirls of color, and then started on the face. The strange thing was that while she had Lord Thomblin's face fixed in her mind, it would not take form on the canvas. She knew the handsome turn of his mouth, his aristocrat nose, his thick lashes and blue eyes as well as she knew her own features, and yet, she could not paint him.

Madison turned back to the garden and saw Jefford appear through a gate that led to another part of the house. He seemed to be going out of his way to ignore her and she was angry with him, maybe even a little hurt. She had thought they were getting along so well for that day or two. She even thought that perhaps he liked her, but now he was back to his old peevish self again, even more infuriating.

As Madison turned away, she heard the murmur of a feminine voice and, against her better judgment, leaned farther over the rail to get a closer look.

Jefford and the woman, Chantal, walked along a white stone-slab path, talking. She stopped to pluck a bright flower and tucked it behind her ear. Then she turned to Jefford, a playful, teasing look on her face. He reached out with one hand and slid it over her shoulder, around her neck, gazing into her eyes.

Madison felt herself grow flushed. Damn him to hell! Did the man have no decency? From what she had learned of the house on her brief tour earlier, practically every room opened onto one of the many verandas and the garden. Anyone could see them.

Chantal tipped her head back, baring her slender throat to him, and Jefford pressed his mouth to her willing flesh.

Madison gasped, remembering Jefford's kiss that night in her studio at home, the feel of his mouth against hers, the taste of him. She remembered the pressure of his hand on the small of her back and the way she had instinctively wanted to move toward him, to press her body to his, just the way Chantal was doing now.

Madison lifted her hand to the place on her throat where Jefford had kissed Chantal. How dare he? she thought angrily. How dare he take advantage of Aunt Kendra, the way he obviously was, and then have the indecency to carry on in the garden with that…that loose woman!

She pressed her lips together, staring down at them as her ire grew more heated. Now they were kissing mouth to mouth and Jefford had lowered his hand to cup her buttocks through the thin fabric of the loose gown she wore.

Damn him, Madison thought suddenly, if he didn't know how licentious and objectionable his behavior was, perhaps someone needed to tell him!

She turned away from the railing and strode into her bedchamber. "I'll be right back, Sashi," she called through the doorway that led to the maid's room. "Then I'll dress for dinner."

"Of course, miss," Sashi called as she spread an intricate embroidered coverlet on her sleeping couch.

Madison pushed out her door and followed the long corridor in the direction she thought her aunt had brought her. She passed door after door, hallway after hallway, not really sure at all where she was. The house was an enormous maze of rooms and alcoves, but she was determined to find the stairs. At last she found a flight that led not just below, but directly outside into the garden.

Her feet found the flat, smooth stone of a path and she emerged between two trees with stunted trunks and leaves half as long as she was tall. The path diverged in two directions and she tried to get her bearings in the semidarkness. Ahead, she saw torch light. A few steps in that direction and she spotted a statue of an elephant she recognized as the one she had seen from her veranda. She passed a pool of fat goldfish the size of her palm and followed the turn in the path. The warm, humid air was filled with insect and frog sounds and it felt as if the sky was about to open up with rain again, but she would not be deterred.

Then she saw them, Jefford and Chantal wrapped in each other's arms, illicit lovers. "Pardon me, Jefford," Madison said loudly, walking right up to them. "May I speak with you?"

He lifted his head, and to her amazement, there was a look of amusement on his face, rather than anger. She would have preferred his hostility. When he looked at her the way he did now, he made her question herself, and she didn't care for that feeling, not one bit.

"Could it wait?" he asked, amusement in his tone, as well. "As you can see, I'm a bit occupied." He made no move to release the woman from his arms.

"I would prefer now," Madison snapped.

One arm still around Jefford's neck, the sloe-eyed Chantal looked Madison up and down disdainfully.

Jefford glanced at the woman in his arms, then at Madison. "If it can't wait, I suppose—"

"It cannot." She eyed Chantal with equal contempt.

Jefford leaned over and whispered something in Chantal's ear. Madison could barely contain her impatience.

Chantal whispered something in return, then sashayed away.

"Now, what is it, Madison?" Jefford demanded. "It's almost dinnertime. You should probably dress. If you're late for one of Kendra's dinners, you're liable to be the one put on the spit."

"Just who do you think you are?" Madison demanded, planting one hand on her hip.

He raised a dark eyebrow. "Pardon?"

"Who do you think you are, behaving this way in a public garden?"

He chuckled. "This is not a—"

"It most certainly is public. Anyone in the house can see you out here cavorting with that…that *woman!* Now, I don't know exactly what your responsibilities are here, Mr. Harris, but I think it's high time you are put in your place. This is my aunt Kendra's home and I will not continue to allow you to take advantage of her the way you have obviously done in the past."

"Madison—"

"I don't know what your intention was when you wheedled your way into my aunt's life, into her home, but I think it's time to take a step a back. Windward Bay is my aunt's home, it's her property and it is time you stop taking liberties with her money and her servants."

"Madison, damn it. Will you listen? There's one major flaw with your little diatribe."

"Don't start with me, Jefford Harris!" Her blue eyes flashed angrily. "Don't think that because I am a woman I will not—"

"Madison, it's mine."

She blinked. "What did you say?"

He folded his arms over his chest, his gaze meeting hers, his dark eyes unreadable in the dim torchlight. "Windward Bay doesn't belong to Kendra. It belongs to me."

8

"How can you…what do you mean, it's yours?" Madison flared.

"I mean I own it. Almost a thousand acres here along the bay—" he pointed "—and then a parcel larger than this in the Blue Mountains where we grow coffee."

Madison's hands fell to her side. Was she too late? Had this scoundrel already swindled her aunt out of her property? No wonder Lady Moran had been unwilling to reveal his relationship to her; she was humiliated by what she had allowed him to do to her.

Madison took a step closer to Jefford, her ire rising again. "My aunt received this land as part of her inheritance when her husband died, and you think you can somehow defraud it out of her? Well, I have information for you, sir. She is no longer alone, a helpless elderly woman left to—"

"Madison." Jefford held up his hand, chuckling. "Please stop. I don't want you to embarrass yourself any further."

"Embarrass myself! It's you who should be embarrassed. To take advantage of a woman as good-hearted as—"

"Madison—" he touched her sleeve "—Windward Bay belongs to me because it is *my* inheritance."

"*Your* inheritance?"

"From my mother who passed the deed to me several years ago."

"Your m—" Madison cut herself off, suddenly realizing what he was trying to say. "No…" she whispered, glancing down.

"I'm Kendra's son."

Madison wanted to argue that it wasn't true, that he was lying to her, but she knew he wasn't. She knew by the way he was smiling so smugly. She grasped her skirts in both hands, mortified she could have made such a mistake, angry he had allowed it to go on so long. "Well, I—" She stopped, then started again. "You should have—"

"Yes?"

She gave a loud groan of frustration. "Excuse me, but I have to get ready for supper or I'm going to be late."

"I told you that," he called after her, still chuckling. "See you then."

Flushed and perspiring, Madison hurried down the corridor in the direction of her rooms. Jefford didn't carry the Moran name…and if he wasn't the son of her aunt's late husband… The word *bastard* rose in her mind and she pushed it away. Illegitimate? Jefford must be Aunt Kendra's son out of wedlock. Madison was stunned, both by the ramifications of such a realization and the feeling of having been shut out of such an enormous part of Aunt Kendra's life. Even if her aunt was concerned with the stigma of having an illegitimate son, why hadn't she at least told her the truth?

Madison pressed her hand to the cool wall to keep her balance. She was confused and upset and now she was overheated, and most likely lost in the sprawling house that had seemed so magical only minutes ago.

To her relief, she bumped into Maha in one of the upstairs hallways that she thought ran in the direction of her own room. "Maha, where is my aunt?" she asked, breathing heavily.

"What is wrong, child?"

Madison shook her head. "Nothing, I just—" She was near to tears. "Maha, I need to see Aunt Kendra."

"Dinner will be served soon, Miss Madison, and there—"

"Madison," Aunt Kendra called from behind a door. "Is that you, dear? Maha, is that Madison you're talking to?"

Maha lifted one finger, asking Madison to wait a moment. "Yes, Miss Kendra, it is," she said opening a set of elaborate double doors that were embellished with shiny brass hardware.

"If Madison needs me, send her in."

"I thought you were resting, Miss Kendra," Maha protested. "I am certain that the miss will not mind—"

"I said send her in!"

Madison hurried through the doors, entering a large chamber elaborately decorated with panels of sheer, jewel-colored cloth hanging from the ceilings to the floor. Her aunt was just rising from a cushioned daybed.

Madison halted, clutching her hands. Aunt Kendra looked pale, and was dressed in only a sheer dressing gown, appeared thinner than Madison recalled. "Aunt Kendra, are you feeling poorly?"

"Of course not." She waved Madison in. "Heavens, what is it, dear? You look flustered."

"Why didn't you tell me?" Madison cried.

Kendra took one look at her niece's face and lowered herself to the daybed again. "Jefford." She sighed. "That didn't take long. One of the servants told you, I suppose."

Madison pressed her lips together, glancing down at the pale polished wood floor. "No, he told me." She made herself look up, tears filling her eyes. "But only after I embarrassed myself profusely by accusing him of taking advantage of you and your hospitality."

"Oh, sweetness." Kendra clasped Madison's hand and brought her down to sit beside her. "You thought he was my lover?" She covered her mouth, stifling a peal of amusement.

"Why didn't you tell me? Why did you let me go on about Jefford all these weeks?" Madison closed her eyes. "I said such stupid things. I made such an utter fool of myself. I—"

"Now, now. None of that," Kendra soothed. "I am not the total coward and deceiver you must believe me to be. I did not introduce Jefford as my son when we arrived in London because he asked that I not do so. We only intended to stay the few weeks and then return home." She shrugged her thin shoulders.

"He thought it would be easier," Madison murmured. "For you." She had a million questions, most of which she wasn't certain would be appropriate to ask. The one that was on the tip of her tongue, though, was, *If he wasn't the late Lord Moran's son, whose was he?*

"Honestly, can you imagine me introducing my thirty-five-year-old illegitimate son to your mother, who never knew I had a child? Or to any in London society?" Kendra chuckled. "If they hadn't tarred and feathered me, I'd have been turned out on my ear." She clasped Madison's hand. "And then I would never have had the chance to know my lovely niece the artist."

"You'd have never been permitted to bring me here," Madison whispered, wiping her tears.

"My only regret is that this matter has caused you pain, my dear. Can you find it in your heart to forgive me?"

"Yes, of course. You have been so..." Madison hugged her, so filled with emotion that she was at a loss for words. "I could never judge you. It was I who reacted so—"

"Now, there's no need to be concerned with anything you've said to Jefford. He deserves whatever you've dished out, and then some, for not telling you the truth sooner."

Madison pulled her hand from her aunt's. "Yes, but I've really muddled things up. I saw him in the garden with that woman and I— Let's just say I misspoke."

"Don't let Chantal deter you, dear." Kendra chuckled. "If he hasn't married her by now, he never will. She's simply a diversion. All men have need of them, you know."

Madison rose from the daybed. "Deter me? What do you mean?"

Aunt Kendra smiled slyly. "The two of you were getting along rather well on the ship, I thought. Perhaps you have more in common than you first thought?"

Madison frowned. "I have no intentions toward that... that...*your son,* I can assure you." She took a step back. "I should dress now, for dinner. I'll see you downstairs?"

"Of course." Lady Moran rose slowly from the edge of the bed and Maha was immediately at her side, offering her arm to support the older woman.

Madison hesitated, her own woes forgotten for the moment. "You're certain you're all right?"

"Right as rain. Now, get dressed. Sashi should have a little something I sent up that I thought you might enjoy wearing on your first night at Windward Bay. Jefford has promised to join us for dinner and we can settle this whole silliness once and for all."

Madison backed out of the room, closing the paneled white doors, and for the first time since she left London, wondered if she would regret the day she had come to Jamaica.

Madison dressed in the lovely flowing garment sewn of nearly transparent turquoise-and-white fabric that her aunt had given her. Constructed much in the same manner as the caftans Lady Moran wore, the gown was loose-fitting and meant to be worn with very little underclothing. At first, Madison had been hesitant to wear the dress, realizing her mother would have been shocked beyond words. But this was not London and Lady Westcott was not present.

She loved the color and the way the soft, filmy fabric felt against her skin. She allowed Sashi to sweep her hair up off her shoulders in a twist of blond curls, and with the addition of a sweet-smelling white bloom, went downstairs to join her aunt…and cousin, for dinner.

Sashi pointed through an open room furnished with floor-to-ceiling bookshelves and large pieces of comfortable-looking dark furniture with cushions. Madison hesitantly walked through the room, into the subdued light of the next.

"There you are, dear," Kendra called from one of several small dining tables.

Jefford, who already sat, his back to Madison, rose. He, too, had changed, but he was not wearing an English-style coat and jacket. Instead, he sported a pair of tan trousers and a black, loose-fitting shirt, open at the neckline, without even a cravat.

"Madison." He nodded, pulling out a chair for her between him and Aunt Kendra.

Madison nodded stiffly. "Jefford."

"Come, come," Kendra called as she patted a bright green cushion on the chair. "Sit and tell me what you think of Windward Bay."

Madison gazed around her, thinking she had never seen such an unusual dining room. With six small tables, some round, some square like the one she sat at now, others rectangular, none were large enough to seat more than six. The walls of the room were a rich walnut wainscoting, lined with gilded mirrors and paintings of exotic birds and plants. The entire outside wall was made of floor-to-ceiling French doors that were pushed open, making the garden appear to be a part of the room. Outside, on a stone patio, torches burned and two men in white cutoff pants and white sleeveless shirts stood guard with rifles in their hands.

Madison's eyes widened at the sight of the guns.

"Just a precaution, lovely. Now, sit before the servants get impatient and burn our dinner."

Madison obediently took her chair and slipped a beaded ring off her rolled magenta silk napkin and lowered it to her lap. "A precaution against what?"

"As I told you, we have serious trouble with the workers on the island," Jefford began.

"With the end of slavery in the thirties, the Brits were forced to pay for labor. There weren't enough Jamaicans willing to work for low wages, so they began shipping workers in." He poured her some sort of drink from a short, brightly painted pitcher and she watched as a piece of fruit fell into the glass and juice splashed onto the table-cloth.

"It's a punch, dear," Kendra explained as she pushed her own glass toward Jefford to be freshened. "Mostly pine-apple juice, a little mango, perhaps some papaya."

Madison lifted her glass. The drink was cool and sweet but also sharp and biting, and burned going down her throat.

Aunt Kendra slapped her on the back good-naturedly. "Oh, and rum. Did I tell you there was rum in the punch? My secret recipe made from cane out of my own fields." She winked.

Madison cleared her throat, setting the glass down, vowing to sip it slowly. "Where did these workers come from?" she asked Jefford.

Servants, dressed in white, began to carry in plates of food, placing them on the table. While Jefford spoke, Kendra spooned assorted unidentifiable dishes onto Madison's plate, then hers and Jefford's. Madison tried to listen, while keeping an eye on the strange foods beginning to pile up in front of her.

"All over, really. The other Caribbean islands. We have a large population of Haitians here. Chantal is Haitian. There are also Indians and Chinese. Many Indians came as indentured servants, but now most workers are free men and women."

"Why are they so upset that you would consider them a threat to you?" Madison asked, eyeing the guards at the door.

"It's complicated. They work very hard and don't feel

they are being compensated fairly. English plantation owners are still trying to adjust to an economy once based on slavery. Like the United States' South, we've struggled to turn a profit with such labor-intensive crops. Another problem is that living and working conditions are not what they should be on the island. Windward Bay cares well for its workers, but not everyone does." He paused to eat a forkful of fluffy white fish.

"Jefford fights hard for workers' rights," Kendra explained.

Madison picked up her fork, unsure where to start.

Kendra pointed with a knife. "Jerk chicken, curried goat, fried plantain, papaya dipping sauce. Careful, it's spicy." She glanced across the candlelit table to her son. "I don't always think Jefford is appreciated for what he does. The workers expect change too quickly."

"Some families have been living in squalor for nearly fifty years. Their basic rights as human beings have been denied." Jefford struck his fist on the table and Madison jumped and her plate rattled.

"No fists at the table, dear." Aunt Kendra slid her hand across the table to cover Jefford's. "Please, it's hard on the china."

"You're not taking this seriously enough, Kendra. I've been telling you that for years."

"And now it's not only working conditions they are up in arms about, it's one another." Kendra tore a piece of bread from a round loaf and began to sop up juices from her plate.

Madison nibbled on a piece of spicy chicken. It was quite good, seasoned with an interesting taste of cinnamon, clove, coriander and a herb she didn't recognize. "Why are they angry with one another?"

"The cultures are too diverse." Jefford chewed thoughtfully as he spoke. "We've got Buddhism, Hinduism, voodooism, and then there are the English and American missionaries trying to push Christianity. Maybe under different circumstances everyone could learn to get along, but tempers are running hot and the incidents are beginning to escalate."

Madison sipped her rum punch, feeling its cool warmth to the tips of her toes. "Incidents?"

"At first, it was just the occasional brawl, mostly workers among themselves. Once in a while an overseer would be attacked. There was some stealing." Jefford helped himself to a piece of bread. "But there's been some rioting, too. So far, the perpetrators have been put down before it's become too serious, but I learned this evening that an Englishman and his family were burned out about two weeks ago."

"Near Windward Bay?" Madison asked.

"On the north side of the island."

"I don't want you to worry about this, Madison." Kendra smiled, patting her hand and pouring her more rum punch. "My only request is that you not go anywhere alone beyond the grounds of this house. Punta is always available to escort you where you might like to go, as are his sons, and I would trust them with my life. With yours."

Madison nodded solemnly, reaching for her glass. Far from being frightened by the danger, she found herself intrigued and wanting to hear more about the labor problems and the varied backgrounds of the workers. Like the spiced food, the conversation aroused and titillated her senses.

For the next hour, they dined, drank more punch and talked, mostly about the unrest on the island. When the platters of food were cleared away, plates of fruit and nuts were served with a dessert wine, which Madison refused. She'd had enough rum, and had already made a big-enough fool of herself for one evening. She needed no fuel for the fire.

"This has been lovely, ladies, but I must go," Jefford said, pushing away from the table as he wiped his mouth with his napkin.

"Go? Wherever are you going?" Kendra asked, obviously annoyed. She bit down on a spear of fresh pineapple. "I thought we were going to have an enjoyable evening together. I wanted to beat you at cards and then perhaps take a walk in the garden later."

"I've got a meeting with some leaders of the Haitian laborers in our district. They've been waiting for my return for weeks."

Realizing that he was looking at something in the garden, Madison turned in her chair. Chantal waited outside the doors, on the stone patio.

Madison turned back, annoyed. As Jefford had pointed out earlier in the evening, Windward Bay was his. As the male of the household, the heir, he had a right to do whatever he pleased, including keeping company with trollops. What did she care?

Kendra ignored the Haitian woman at the door. "Be careful, Jefford."

He rose. "I will. Good night. Get some sleep. The journey home tired you more than you realize." He kissed Kendra's cheek and then walked out through the open doors, disappearing into the darkness of the jungle garden.

Madison met her aunt's gaze and the older woman wrinkled her nose. "Who needs him, anyway? We'll stroll in the garden without him, I'll beat you at cards, and then we will have the most delightful banana and chocolate treat you've ever put in your mouth. What do you say to that?"

Madison smiled. "I think it will make a most perfect first evening in Jamaica."

Lord Thomblin heard a rap on the door and opened it. Light from a single torch burning at the entrance cast a yellow glow over the visitor's face. Carlton recognized the man at the door, but not the one standing in the shadows behind him.

"Lord Thomblin—"

"Who is that?" Carlton demanded with irritation as he closed the door behind him far enough to block the stranger's view inside. "You know the rules, Patterson."

"I know, sir, but—"

"You don't bring anyone here without a formal introduction made in the light of day."

"This is my cousin Henri DuMoine—"

Carlton thrust his cigar between his lips. "I don't care if he's the bloody king of France."

"Monsieur, name your price," he said in heavily accented English.

Carlton eyed the dark-haired Frenchman.

The sound of violin music, punctuated by feminine laughter, filtered through the crack in the door. Carlton glanced over his shoulder and caught the scent of burning hashish on the humid night air. "This is most irregular, Monsieur DuMoine. My *guests* depend on my ability to protect their privacy. You understand—"

The Frenchman removed a money clip from inside his frock coat.

"Perhaps I might make this exception," Carlton confessed, eyeing the English currency. He had returned home to several letters from collectors and it was a most uncomfortable situation.

"My cousin has a particular...*predilection*." Patterson leaned on the doorframe. "I assured him he could be accommodated."

Carlton plucked the bills from the Frenchman's hand and stepped back, opening the door.

The shadow of a young Jamaican woman dancing on a table, a chain around one ankle, fell across Patterson's face and he grinned. "After you, cousin," he said, gesturing grandly.

Carlton allowed the two men to pass into his secret domain and stepped inside behind them, closing the door.

9

"I do not like the way you look at that woman." Chantal pouted.

Jefford scowled, lifting a palm frond back to allow her to pass. In the other hand, he held up a torch that cast a circle of light around them in the dark jungle. "I don't know what you're talking about and, frankly, I'm not in the mood."

She looked at him, her big dark eyes speaking volumes. "You know exactly what I talk of."

Her English was excellent. She was born in Haiti and had grown up on an English plantation on the far side of the island, but still retained that Haitian-Creole accent that sounded part French, part pidgin. Ordinarily, he found her speech pattern beguiling; tonight it only annoyed him.

"Chantal—"

"She is a child," she hissed, following directly behind him on the narrow path that wove through the thick, tangled jungle to the village where most of Windward Bay's West Indian workers lived. "She could never make you happy as I have made you, *amoureux*. She is a *pitit*."

"*Non,* she is not a child. She's twenty-one."

As they moved deeper into the jungle, away from the house and its civilities, Jefford finally felt he was leaving behind the world he had been swept into while in London. He didn't belong there with their elaborate labyrinth of rigid social classes and rules. He wasn't one of them; he never had been.

It was good to be home. He breathed deeply, still feeling the heat of the day in the humid air, smelling the verdant, rotting plant life, his ears filled with insect song. This was his world. Jamaica. Not London. Not Boxwood Manor. He realized he had somehow allowed that spoiled brat Madison to cause him to temporarily lose focus, but he was over that now. He'd been the worse kind of fool to have allowed himself to become attracted to her to begin with. The moment she'd been well enough to navigate the ship's deck on her own, her attention had turned once again to Thomblin.

"I have known you too many years," Chantal went on. "I know you better than *you* know you. And I tell you, she is nothing but bad luck. She will bring you nothing but—"

"What is this?" Jefford snapped, whirling to face her on the path that was walled on both sides by giant ferns and trees. He held the torch high and looked down on her lovely face. "Is this jealousy I hear, Chantal?"

She laid her hand on the open V of his shirt, her warm touch seeming to burn his skin. Chantal's skin was so smooth…so soft.

"Jeal-lousy?" She shook her head, drawing closer. "I do not know this—"

"Jealousy," he repeated with an impatient wave of his hand. "It's convenient the way you sometimes forget the meaning of English words, Chantal."

His homecoming had not been what he had hoped, what he had fantasized those nights alone on the narrow bunk on the ship. Chantal had bombarded him with questions since they'd docked this morning. Most were accusations—all revolving around his mother's niece…who, technically, he supposed was his cousin, except that his mother and her brother, Madison's father, did not share the same maternal blood. *"Jalou,"* he said. "You're jealous of my mother's little niece."

"With that body? She is not as *pitit* as you might think, *chérie*." She ran her hand slowly over his shoulder, up the tense muscles of his neck, her voluptuous breasts pressed against his chest. Even through the fabric of his shirt, he could feel her hard nipples. "I see how she looks at you with those English blue eyes. Do you like her long gold hair?"

Against his will, he could feel himself growing hard, the fabric of his trousers seeming to tighten around him. "I am not going to have this conversation with you," he ground out, turning away to continue on the path. "I cannot keep these men waiting for me. I've been away too long."

"I will not stand for it," Chantal insisted in her liquidy voice. She grabbed his shirt in her fist, forcing him to face her, and sank her teeth into his chin. "Do you hear me?"

Jefford thrust the long, pointed handle of the torch into the soft humus of the jungle floor and grabbed her shoulders with both hands. "You will not tell me what I will and won't do. Who I will and will not have," he grated angrily. Then he clamped his mouth over hers, knowing he was hurting her, not caring.

She wrapped her arms around his shoulders and dug her nails into the flesh of his back. He flinched, but the pain was undistinguishable from pleasure. He thrust his tongue into her mouth, wanting to silence her.

Chantal moaned, clinging to him.

His ardor overcoming his logic, he pushed her up against the rough trunk of a coconut palm and grabbed the hem of her bright green skirt.

She slapped his hand away, but he would not be deterred. He pressed his face into the crook of her neck, pinning her to the tree so that he could leave his hands free to do what he wanted with her. He breathed in her musky scent, trying to will himself to care for her the way he had once, trying to make her what she had once been to him.

"I thought we must hurry. The men—"

"They'll wait," he muttered, sliding his hand up her warm, bare thigh until he found the thick thatch of tight black curls he sought.

She was already slick…ready for him. With his free hand, he jerked down his pants and thrust into her. Chantal cried out, but he knew he wasn't hurting her, not now. Now her cries were thick with passion.

She grasped his shoulder and he grasped both her legs and lifted her up. She wrapped her legs around him and he rammed deep inside her, using the tree trunk to steady them.

Chantal grunted again and again to the rhythm of each thrust. She sank her teeth into the soft flesh of his shoulders and dragged her nails down his back. He came hard and fast, pushing her up against the tree once more. Then, panting heavily, he lowered her until her bare feet touched the ground again.

Pulling out of her, Jefford stepped back, wiping the sweat from his brow.

She shoved her skirt down and leaned against the tree again. "You see," she said, her breath still coming in short gasps. "Your English girl with her blond hair—" she ran her hand over her own dark head "—she cannot do that for you, eh?"

Jefford yanked up his trousers, not knowing what had gotten into him. "Damn it, Chantal, I...you don't deserve to be treated this way. We've been together a long time, you've been too good to me." He ran the fingers of one hand through his hair.

"You all right?" he asked, not making eye contact in the dim light thrown off by the sputtering torch.

She chuckled deep in her throat. "What is chicken with spice? You know me better than that, *amoureux*. Chantal likes it *brital*."

Securing the draw cord of his trousers, he reached out to her, still not looking her in the eyes. "We have to hurry. I don't want to give Ling an excuse not to meet with us again."

She remained against the tree trunk, her hands tucked behind her. "Tell Chantal you love her," she murmured, her accent seeming heavier.

He curled his fingers, beckoning her, growing agitated again. "Chantal, come along."

She sighed and started toward him but made no attempt to take his hand. "I have lost you to her."

Jefford grasped the torch and lifted it high, ignoring her meaning or to whom she referred. She didn't know what she was talking about. "I want you to keep quiet when we go in. But be watchful. You know what kind of bastard Ling can be."

In five minutes they reached the village that was little more than a stand of palm huts. Jefford smelled the women's cook fires, the scent of fried plantain and salted fish heavy in the air, even before the path opened up into the clearing.

Dogs barked and a dark-skinned man, their escort, wearing nothing but a loincloth, materialized out of the night and fell silently in behind them. Torches lit the pathway into the village.

Despite the lateness of the hour, curious children, many naked, peered at them from behind the walls of the open huts as they passed, adults in the shadows behind them. There was a tension in the air that seemed to create a buzz in his ears. Everyone in the village knew the meeting was scheduled to take place; knew the outcome could mean bloodshed.

But the children, not knowing the purpose of the assembly, or not fully understanding the ramifications, chattered among themselves in their colorful language that was a mixture of English and Haitian Creole, with a smattering of Indian, Spanish and even Chinese words thrown it. He eyed a little boy, Napoleon, who he knew well and he waved. Napoleon worked in Kendra's house; he was bright and a hard worker and Jefford had a soft spot for him. The boy waved back shyly. A mangy yellow dog greeted Jefford at the doorless entryway to a large hut that lay near, but not downwind, to one of the communal cook fires. The opening was flanked by two of Ling's men—mean, angry men without interest in diplomacy judging from the hard looks they gave him as he thrust his torch into the sand and walked inside.

Before Chantal could follow him into the light of the hut, one of the Chinese men lowered a cutlass, preventing her entrance.

"I am with Master Jefford," she declared hotly, looking the man in the eye.

"No women."

She thrust her hips against the flat of the blade. "I said, I am with—"

"Chantal," Jefford called over his shoulder. "Do as you're told. Wait there. Keep an eye open."

He turned away before she had the opportunity to argue with him. He knew she was angry, but he didn't care. He needed to be careful with these men. Any sign of weakness they might perceive, real or imagined, could be dangerous, even deadly. Not all cultures believed women had the same duties or rights as men. Thankfully, Chantal fell silent.

Inside, Jefford's gaze circled the men who lined the palm-frond walls of the hut. A lantern, on a stump in the center, filled the room with pale yellow light and the stench of burning kerosene.

Two Haitians sat on the dirt floor side by side as a Haitian guard at the door propped himself on a cut log. The turbaned Indian, Girish, sat across from the Haitians, his legs crossed, his demeanor calm, even relaxed. Only Ling, the Chinese leader, stood, his jaw set, his dark eyes darting from man to man. Behind him stood his second in command, and translator, Jiao.

"Jefford, it is good to see you have returned safe across the ocean," Jean-Claude, the Haitian leader began. "We are fortunate that Ague, God of the sea, has kept you safe." He was a middle-aged man with kind, dark eyes and a jagged red scar that ran from his left ear to the corner of his mouth, a gift from the Chinese laborers during a near riot in the sugarcane fields the year before.

Jefford nodded respectfully. "It is good to be home, sir." He nodded to Girish, and then to Ling.

Girish acknowledged and responded. Ling looked through Jefford as if he were glass.

"I understand there is a disagreement as to who must work which fields on which days," Jefford said, seeing no reason to postpone the cause of tonight's assembly. "As I have stated before, we don't care which fields the Indians, the islanders, the Chinese choose, so long as the work is done."

Jiao translated for his leader in quiet tones.

"That is exactly what I have been saying for many weeks," Girish agreed, but the Chinese will not listen. They will not *ne-go-see-ate*. They want the best fields. Jean-Claude and I, we have—"

Ling burst out in a string of angry words, none of which Jefford could understand, but the leader's meaning was clear. Jefford eyed the translator.

"Mr. Ling say he cannot negotiate with the Indians and the islanders because they cannot be trusted. They lie."

"Lie?" Jean-Claude flared. "I am a man of my word, but you, Ling. Everyone knows you want what is best for Ling." He pointed a long, knotted black finger. "Whatever will make you the most money. You do not even work the fields and yet you put your wife and daughters—"

"Jean-Claude," Jefford interrupted. "Let's stick to the problem at hand."

"This is the problem, Master Jefford." The Haitian, dressed in a white linen English shirt with the sleeves cut off, rose from the ground, still pointing his finger at the Chinese labor representative. "We are here to help our people. To do what is best to preserve our life. But Ling…Ling—"

Jefford felt rather than heard or saw the Chinese men behind him react as Chantal cried out a warning. Jean-Claude lunged at Ling. Girish bounded to his feet, producing a knife from the folds of his clothing. The Chinese guard rushed inside, swinging an ax, and Jefford was just able to step aside in time to avoid being caught in the middle between the Chinese and Haitians.

Chantal, still outside the hut, gave a high-pitched scream as she tried to get through the doorway. Jefford saw the flash of the knife he knew she kept hidden in the creases of her dress, then spun around and lunged forward to protect Jean-Claude's back as the Haitian's secondhand man swung a cutlass over his head at the Chinese guard with a fierce cry.

Jefford hit the Chinese man with the full weight of his body. He was much taller than the guard, but not as broad; the man was like a mountain in Hengduan. Crying out with indignance at being impeded, the Chinese man turned on Jefford, swinging the ax with the fury of a madman.

Jefford ducked, dodged left, then right. The lantern crashed to the dirt floor and the kerosene splashed, igniting instantly, sending flames up one wall of the frond hut as Jefford scanned the immediate area in desperate need of a weapon. Damn it! He *knew* he shouldn't have come without his pistol. His gesture of peace could now cost him his life.

The Chinese man swung his ax again. This time it skimmed Jefford's left shoulder, tearing his sleeve and drawing a thin sheen of blood.

Choking on the black smoke, Jefford threw himself down and forward, catching his attacker around the knees and knocking him to the ground. The two rolled over and over as Jefford tried to pry the ax from the man's hands. Jefford's sleeve caught on fire and he tried to pound it out in the dirt while staying on top of the screaming guard.

Sweat rolled down Jefford's face and he gasped to catch his breath. Larger pieces of the burning roof were beginning to float downward. Sucking in a breath of foul air, he threw every bit of strength he had left and managed to get the ax handle across the Chinese man's neck. "You want to get up and get out of here?" Jefford shouted in his face as he straddled him. "Or you want to burn in hell right here on earth?"

A burning timber crashed down from the ceiling, hitting Jefford's back. By the luck of God, the lightweight bamboo bounced off him and landed in the dirt beside them.

The guard took one look at the burning ceiling overhead and relaxed under Jefford. Jefford leaped up, taking the ax with him, and thrust his hand out to help the man off the ground. The two stumbled through the smoke, which was so thick that only the sound of Chantal, calling to him in Haitian, indicated the direction he should go.

The two stumbled out of the burning hut and Jefford fell to his knees, ax still clutched in his hands, coughing violently.

Chantal threw herself over him. "Jefford." She ran her hands over his hair, then tugged on his shirt. "You are burned," she shrieked.

He felt as if he were coughing out his lungs. He shook his head. "Only my shirt," he managed to say when, at last, his lungs filled with the sweet, warm night air.

Chantal pulled the smoldering shirt from his back and one of the Haitians took the ax. After a couple of more breaths of fresh air, Jefford was able to roll over and sit up.

Young Napoleon appeared beside him, on his knees, carrying a coconut shell full of water to Jefford's lips. The boy looked so frightened that Jefford reached out and tousled his hair before gulping down the water.

Haitians hustled around him, keeping the burning hut from spreading the fire to the other homes in the village. By the second coconut of water, Jefford was able to get to his feet. Chantal tried to help him up, but he pushed her away.

Ling and his men were gone. Jefford looked up to Girish and Jean-Claude, who drew closer, their faces full of concern. "We should postpone our talks for a night or two. Let tempers simmer down," he told the men.

Jean-Claude managed a meager smile. "I thank the gods you live because without you there is no hope." He pumped Jefford's hand up and down. "As for Ling, I have told you he will not be reasonable. It is useless to bring him to talk again. He came to my village and drew a weapon. Once, such an insult would demand—"

"Jean-Claude, you're their leader," Jefford gasped. "No retribution. More fighting, more injuries, even deaths will not settle the difference between you. It will only make them worse." He coughed into his cupped hand. "Girish, tell him."

Chantal slipped her arm through his. "We should go home, *chérie*. The smoke has evil spirits."

He sighed, running his hand over his head, smelling the foul odor of singed hair. "I'll speak with both of you tomorrow. Do nothing until then," he ordered.

Chantal grabbed one of the village torches and led the way to the path to Windward Bay.

Madison, dressed in a sheer pink batiste sleeping gown, sat in a cushioned chair built of woven, hardened vines on her veranda and stared out into the shadowed jungle. She could hear it, smell it and almost taste it on the tip of her tongue. She felt surrounded by the sounds of insects chirping and clicking, night birds calling, their wings fluttering, and the music of tiny tree frogs. Taking in a deep breath of the moist air, she inhaled the overpowering scent of night-blooming jasmine and the rot that she already realized was a large part of the life cycle of the rain forest.

Though it was well after midnight, she still couldn't sleep. It wasn't because she was homesick. Sadly, she realized she did not miss home, her mother or brother, or any of her servants. She couldn't sleep because Jamaica would not allow it. The sounds, the smells, even the humid heat seemed to call to her. She was too full of her thoughts, both hopes and fears, to sleep.

She sipped a cup of tea, realizing she still felt foolish over her encounter in the garden with Jefford earlier in the evening. She was shocked that he was Aunt Kendra's son and even more shocked that she had been so foolish, so self-absorbed in her own life, that she had not figured it out. It all made sense now, of course. How familiar they were with each other, despite their difference in age. How protective Jefford was of her. How much she obviously admired him, cared for him…loved him.

Madison sighed as she propped her chin in her hand and stared down into the lush garden below. Kendra had told her it remained lit by torches at night, guarded by armed men who continued their watch until the master of the household returned home. As far as Madison knew, Jefford had not.

Where in the name of heaven was he so late at night? With that woman? She imagined him kissing Chantal, touching her, but didn't know why she cared. Who Jefford dallied with was none of her business, and since it didn't upset Aunt Kendra, why should it upset her?

But tonight her thoughts kept returning to Jefford's kiss that night in her studio in London. To his gentle touch the day he had come to her cabin on the ship. He had made her hummingbird food to drink, talked to her as if she were an equal, even seemed interested in her ideas of painting those she saw as oppressed or disadvantaged in the world. But the moment she had been on her feet again, he had changed. He'd become cold and distant to the point of rudeness. Had he cared at all? No. Madison knew Aunt Kendra had begged him to check on her when she'd been ill so he hadn't truly been interested in her or her art, only in appeasing his mother.

Movement below caught Madison's attention and she looked over the rail. A dog barked and she could see one of the guards begin to walk in the direction of the jungle.

A light shone in the trees beyond the garden and she rose to get a better look when a male voice called out. Jefford! Recognizing him, the guards returned to their stations and Madison watched as Jefford and Chantal, carrying the torch, walked into the garden through a stone arch.

As they grew closer, she could see he wore no shirt. His muscular shoulders, his flat, lean abdomen and the darker skin that encircled his nipples gleamed in the torchlight. His body was so perfect, so finely fashioned that it seemed to her as if God had formed it from clay, in his own image.

She licked her dry lips, wishing she had her paints and a canvas at hand.

"You must be put to bed, *amoureux*," Chantal said in the voice that sounded so base to Madison.

"I can put myself to bed." His tone was short. He sounded tired…but something more.

"Your burns should be tended to."

Burns? He'd been burned?

"*Amoureux*—"

"Chantal, please." Jefford brushed the dark hair off his forehead, gazing out into the darkness of the overgrown garden. "I cannot do this tonight."

The Haitian woman let her hands fall to her sides. Jefford stood there, then suddenly tilted his head to glance upward.

Caught!

His dark-eyed gaze met hers and she saw a sadness that made her chest tighten. Then he was gone, disappearing into the house.

Madison stood only a moment in indecision, and then ran to find her night robe.

10

She held the oil lamp in front of her, following a long hall-way in search of Jefford's chambers. Though she was still not certain exactly where she was going, she sensed she was headed in the right direction.

At the far end of the hall, light shone from beneath a door, the only light visible in the house, apart from her own. She hesitated, then knocked firmly.

She knocked again, thinking she heard a splash of water…then footsteps.

The door opened suddenly. "Chantal, I told you—"

Startled, Madison took a step back, almost tripping on the hem of her long dressing gown. Jefford stood barefoot in front of her, naked but for a small sheet of fabric around his waist, held in place with his hand.

"Madison!"

His dark hair was slick and wet and the soot she had ob-served from her upper veranda had been wiped clean from his face and bare torso. He'd been bathing…. "I'm sorry… I saw you…overheard you…in the garden." Her eyes strayed to his shoulder, which was red and raw-looking. "Is there something—" She met his gaze. Held it. "Something I can do for you?" She motioned to his burn. "It looks bad."

He tightened his grip on the cloth around his waist. "It's fine. Go to bed, Madison. I don't want you here."

"I'm sorry," she said, taking a step back. She wished she had a pencil and sketch pad...wished that she could sketch his face just as it was right now, raw with emotion, with...vulnerability.

"I didn't mean to intrude on your privacy," she snapped, angered by his rudeness. "I only wanted to—"

"It's all right." His tone softened. "I'll be fine. I've washed it and I have some salve."

"How did it happen?"

"I'll tell you tomorrow." He stepped back inside, beginning to swing the door shut. "Go to bed, Madison. Don't come here again."

He closed the door and she turned and ran, not stopping until she was safely in her room.

"Madison, Madison, where are you, dear?" Aunt Kendra sang, her voice distant in the garden.

"Here," Madison called. She stood up and waved her paintbrush in her aunt's direction.

She'd been in the garden for hours painting the ancient Chinese gardener who sat almost motionless on a cushion, tending a flower bed. Barefoot in cutoff pants and a loose-fitting shirt, he wore a cone-shaped hat made from fronds. His broad, flat feet were encrusted with soil, toes twisted, the nails as thick as horn. He was the ideal subject, sitting perfectly still except for the rapid flick of his gnarled fingers as he sought out and pulled weeds.

"Well, I can see that." Aunt Kendra picked some bright yellow blooming flowers and placed them in a basket she carried. "But I want you inside. We've visitors, including a gentleman!"

Madison set down her paintbrush and pushed back a stray wisp of hair that had escaped her neat chignon beneath her straw bonnet. "Has Lord Thomblin come?" she called excitedly. She'd been in Jamaica nearly a week and Carlton had not yet fulfilled his promise of a social call.

"Certainly not! We're in the library taking tea. Lela has made sweet biscuits, so do hurry."

Curious about Aunt Kendra's guests, Madison hurried along the path, through one of the many open archways of the sprawling house and into the library. A table, complete with a white linen tablecloth and four lovely old mismatched dining chairs, had been set for afternoon tea.

"And here she is," Aunt Kendra cried, as if introducing Queen Victoria. "My niece." She cleared her throat. "The Honorable Madison Anne Westcott."

A young auburn-haired woman in a lovely rose-colored gown of the highest English fashion turned from one of the many bookshelves, her face lighting up.

"This is Alice Rutherford, Madison, one of my dearest neighbors. And her brother, George." She indicated a roguishly handsome young man just coming through the doorway.

"Well, my goodness. I cannot tell you how thrilled I am to make your acquaintance," Alice bubbled, as she set a book down and approached Madison with both hands extended. "There isn't a soul on the island my age, and I am sorely lacking in companionship." She clasped both of Madison's hands and squeezed them affectionately.

"Lacking in companions?" George demanded, only

feigning annoyance. "So what does that make me? Goose liver?"

"I stand corrected," Alice said, nonplussed by her brother. "I am lacking in *female* companions."

George turned to Madison. "I'm charmed to meet you, Miss Westcott." He took her hand and made an event of kissing it.

Madison laughed, stepping back. She liked both of them at once. "You are our neighbors? How far do you live from Windward Bay?"

"To the north only four miles."

"But it seems like forty when the rains begin." Alice rolled her pale green eyes.

"Come, come. Do sit." Aunt Kendra waved them toward the table. "I want you to try my mango pineapple preserves. Magnificent!"

For the next hour, Madison, Alice and George took tea in the library and conversed. Aunt Kendra stayed long enough for her sweet biscuit and tea and then excused herself.

Within minutes Madison felt as if the Rutherfords were the good friends she had never had, even in childhood, but always dreamed of having. After tea, George suggested they adjourn to the well-shaded side lawn to play croquet. He was a bit of a comedian and kept Alice and Madison laughing throughout the afternoon.

The sun had already begun to drift low in the sky when Sashi came down one of the garden's stone paths to find Madison.

The beautiful Indian servant nodded her dark head regally. "Miss Madison, Lady Moran asks if your guests would like to stay for supper," she said, keeping her gaze downcast.

"Sashi," Madison whispered. "Why on earth are you

speaking as if you're a lowly scrub maid from Cheapside in London? And why on earth are you calling me Miss Madison? We agreed days ago that you would address me by my given name. After all, we're already more like companions than servant and mistress."

Madison glanced over her shoulder at George, who was hitting his sister's ball through a hoop. Alice had retreated to a stone bench to sip mango pineapple juice brought to her by one of the many house servants.

"Would you like to stay?" Madison asked. "Please do."

"Oh, let's, Georgie!" Alice clapped her hands together. "We can send a message to Mummy and Daddy. I know they won't object."

George glanced at Madison, then at his sister, his handsome green eyes twinkling. "You two only find Lady Moran's kind invitation appealing because you cannot stand the thought of ending the day with my beating both of you so badly."

"Hah!" Alice cried, tossing a slice of pineapple from her glass at him.

"If you would only stay," Madison begged. "We could have Aunt Kendra join us for cards, and then we would have four players."

"What an excellent idea," Alice agreed. "George?"

Madison glanced at George to realize he was staring in her direction, but not *at* her. She glanced over her shoulder curiously. Sashi had averted her gaze, to study, with great interest, a line of ants marching across the stone path. Madison glanced back at George. Was he looking at Sashi?

"Please, may we?" Alice asked.

"Oh, I'm certain I can spare the time," he said, tearing his gaze from the servant.

"I have no doubt the ladies will rue the day whether you

stay or not, George, but I should love it if you would stay."
Madison rested her mallet against a papaya tree. "You
asked to see one of my paintings. Should you stay, I think
that could be arranged."

"We would have to send a message—"

"I could take a message to the Rutherford plantation,"
Sashi offered before the words were entirely out of
George's mouth. "It isn't far."

Madison frowned, looking back. "You'll do no such
thing, Sashi. My aunt says it's not safe for a lady to travel
the jungle alone. We'll send one of Punta's sons."

"As you wish, Miss Madison." Sashi bobbed her head,
turned away and hurried back up the stone path toward
the house.

"Heaven on earth, who was that?" George asked.

"Sashi. She's my personal maid," Madison said, coming to sit beside Alice on the stone bench. Though it was
late afternoon, the sun was still hot and she needed a re-
prieve from it. "But really, she's a friend."

"Most lovely," he sighed.

Alice giggled. "George, what has gotten into you? Sashi
has been at Windward Bay as long as we've known Lady
Moran."

He lifted one shoulder. Having removed his jacket and
pushed up the long sleeves of his white linen shirt hours
ago, George Rutherford was quite a handsome young man.
Twenty-five and the heir to his father's title and fortune,
he was quite an eligible bachelor, according to Alice's
whispering. She had gone on to explain that upon their father's death, George would inherit his earldom as well as
extensive properties on three continents. Madison immediately realized that Alice was hoping she'd take a liking
to her brother. Even Aunt Kendra had hinted as such, but

though he was handsome, bright and entertaining, and four years her senior, Madison saw him more as a giddy-headed younger brother than a potential suitor.

"Are you certain she's been here all that time?" George demanded, swinging the croquet mallet as he came to join the women under the shade of towering palms. "Surely I would have recalled such an angelic face."

Alice looked to Madison and laughed, slipping her arm through Madison's. "My goodness, I think not only are we staying for supper, but you may have a difficult time getting rid of us now."

Aunt Kendra ordered the evening meal served in the garden after sunset. They dined on simple fare of fresh fish from the sea, vegetables from Windward Bay's own garden and a delightful combination of fruits picked from the surrounding trees and bushes only moments before they were presented on silver and china platters.

Dinner completed, the four diners still sat at the table cracking nuts and sipping one of Lady Moran's famous rum punches as they conversed.

"Come now," George said, stretching out his long, slender legs. "You've piqued my interest, Madison. Bring down one of those famous paintings of yours, or I'll trot right up to your chambers and find one myself."

"George Rutherford, you'll do no such thing," Alice protested. She turned to Lady Moran and Madison. "I honestly don't know what has become of my brother's manners. Mummy says it's all the sun, gone to his head."

"Kendra—" Jefford called from the open windows and Madison almost jumped in her skin. Since the night she had gone to his bedchambers, she'd barely seen more than a glimpse of him.

"In the garden, dear," Aunt Kendra called, waving the pink napkin she had tucked in her gown's bodice.

He stepped through the open doors of the dining room, into the torch-lit garden, and Madison purposely looked away.

"I'm sorry, Kendra." Jefford strode into the garden, removing a battered straw hat. "I hadn't realized you had guests." He nodded. "Miss Rutherford, George. Good to see you."

Alice smiled and sipped her rum punch.

George rose and shook Jefford's hand, then took his seat again.

"Good evening, Madison," Jefford said, barely glancing at her.

She muttered a reply under her breath, averting her gaze.

"Join us," Aunt Kendra declared. "Bobo, another chair." She signaled insistently to one of the young boys who stood in the shadows waiting their mistress's beck and call.

"Thank you, but no." Jefford held up both hands, then lowered them, indicating his attire. "I've been in the cane fields all day. I'm not dressed suitably."

"Since when has that mattered a pence to you?" Aunt Kendra eyed him, speaking firmly this time. "No, sit, dear, and give me that filthy hat. I swear, I'm going to burn it come next Christmas Eve."

To Madison's surprise, Jefford took the chair Bobo carried from the dining room.

"And make a plate in the kitchen and bring it out." Aunt Kendra clapped her hands together, returning her attention to her son. "Did you have a good day?"

Jefford shrugged, reaching for a handful of nuts and

cracking the shells in the palm of his hand. "This incessant bickering is slowing us down." He picked the sweet meat from a nut, then dropped it into his mouth. "The workers complain of low wages, not realizing that their constant arguments, protests and scuffles are hindering production. We cannot afford to raise wages if production goes down, rather than up." He crossed his arms over his chest. "After the trouble the other night the Chinese and the Haitians are staying clear of one another and everyone has been going about their business, but they refuse to meet for any negotiations." He sighed. "I just don't know where this is all going to lead."

Madison ran her hand up and down the smooth surface of her cool glass, studying Jefford's profile in the golden light of a torch just beyond him, nestled in a stand of hibiscus bushes. She thought of the portrait sitting on her veranda above on the second story. She'd tried working on it several times since her arrival, but always ended up setting the brush aside in frustration. Listening to Jefford speak, watching the way his jawline moved and his mouth pursed as he talked, she played with the notion of how easy it would be to paint him in place of Lord Thomblin's.

"Any word of the missing Jamaican woman?" George asked.

Jefford scowled at his neighbor. Obviously he had not wished to share whatever they were speaking of with the ladies present.

"What Jamaican woman?" Aunt Kendra pounced on the conversation at once.

"She's gone missing from Thomblin's place, three days now." Jefford accepted the plate of food Bobo had brought him and tousled the young boy's head as he made a quick departure, grinning broadly at having caught his master's attention. "It's likely she drowned, Thomblin's overseer says."

"Drowned? A Jamaican?" Lady Moran scoffed, fluttering her napkin before replacing it in the bodice of her magenta silk caftan. "Impossible. They swim like pike."

Jefford thrust a forkful of flaky white fish into his mouth and Madison could not take her eyes from him as he drew his lips over the tines. "Anything is possible. She could have gotten lost in the jungle. Fallen from a coconut tree and broken her neck."

His gaze strayed to Madison and she looked away, pretending to watch a fat green lizard climbing lazily up the leg of his chair.

"Or—" Jefford drew out his last word.

"Or she could have met with a worse fate," George finished for him.

"A fate worse than falling from a coconut tree to your death?" Alice cried.

"She could have met up with the wrong kind of man," George said meaningfully, reaching out to pat his sister's hand. "Remember what happened to that young Chinese woman just last winter."

Aunt Kendra turned to her niece. "Raped by a gang of field hands. They carried her off to the coffee fields, keeping her captive nearly a day while they took turns with her," she said pointedly.

Madison blanched. She was aware such atrocities took place, but it was certainly never a subject brought up at the dining table at Boxwood Manor.

"Which is precisely why," Aunt Kendra continued, pointing her finger, "I do not want you wandering into the jungle or the cane fields, unescorted." She looked to Alice. "Either of you."

"I would never!" Alice fluttered a painted fan. "Now, please, may we talk about something else?"

"You're right. I apologize, Miss Rutherford." Jefford pushed his plate away, only half eaten, and rose. "Now, if you'll excuse me, I'm in sore need of a bath and a healthy dose of rum. Good night to you, ladies.

"George, would you join me in my study? I have some information I'd like you to take to your father."

"Certainly." George rose from his seat. "If you'll excuse us, ladies?"

Madison and Alice murmured an affirmation and the men excused themselves to a small, dark paneled room down the hall.

"I wanted to talk to you about Thomblin," Jefford began quietly as he poured a shot of rum into two cut-crystal tumblers and pushed one into George's hand. "I've had my suspicions for some time, but I bumped into a mutual acquaintance of Thomblin's in London and…" He hesitated, throwing back the shot of rum and pouring another before he continued. "It seems that Thomblin is not quite the gentleman he portrays. While he is titled, his once-enormous fortune is all but gone. There is rumor he was forced to leave Bombay a few years back due to debt." Jefford sat on the edge of a leather wing chair. "His properties in London have been confiscated and sold, and I fear it's only time before solicitors do the same with his plantation here in Jamaica."

"Poor bastard." George threw back his shot of rum and allowed Jefford to pour him another. "I never liked him. It's only out of respect for Kendra that he is even welcome in our home."

"I know. I sometimes wonder if my mother's soft heart

puts us all in danger." Jefford paused. "What's troubling me even more about Thomblin than his financial status is the foul nature of the man himself. I hear he's fascinated with every sexual deviance known to man. In London he apparently hosted parties catering to the unnatural sexual desires of aristocrats from some of the best families in the city."

"Where does he get women willing to participate in such foulness?"

Jefford glanced over the rim of his glass. "That's a good question. I have my theories, but without any proof…" He let the sentence go unfinished. "Anyway, I just wanted to make you and your father aware of Thomblin's financial situation should he come to you with any business propositions. He's not fit to be trusted."

"I'll pass the information along to Father." George set his glass on the heavy mahogany desk covered with ledgers. "As for the other, is there anything we should do?"

"Nothing we can do but watch him. Kendra made a promise to Lord Moran on his deathbed that she would keep an eye on his grand-nephew, and I cannot seem to sway her." He shook his head. "I doubt Lord Moran had any idea the kind of man Thomblin would grow up to be."

"I appreciate your concern for my father's interests." George offered his hand. "I'll let him know there's a snake among us."

That night, Madison sat on a chair in her sleeping gown, on her veranda, her bare feet tucked beneath her. The warm wind whistled through the palm trees, tousling her hair, and she arched her neck, allowing the breeze to cool her face. She'd finally uncovered her canvas of Lord Thomblin, wanting to begin completing the portrait. With a piece of slender charcoal, she had outlined Carlton's profile, but when she stepped back she was surprised to realize it was not the face she had intended to draw. She'd given up. Now the unfinished portrait seemed to watch her, to mock her from the darkness, and it was not Lord Thomblin's gentle sloped forehead or slender patrician nose on the canvas, but a stronger silhouette.

Sashi appeared in the bedchamber's open doorway. "Have you need of anything more before I go to sleep?"

Madison looked to her, shaking her head. "No, thank you. Please, do turn in. I know it's late."

She lowered her head and backed into the room.

Madison wanted to ask her about George, knowing very well that a young man from as important an English family as the Rutherfords could never give serious consideration to a lowly Indian servant. "Good night," she called.

"Good night."

Madison stood and walked into her bedchamber, restless. She didn't just want to spend her days playing croquet and drinking lemonade prepared by servants under the shade of the palms. If she was going to live here in Jamaica and truly become a part of the island, she realized, she needed to immerse herself. She admired the passion she had heard in Jefford's voice tonight when he had spoken of the sugarcane field hands and a part of her longed to explore that same passion. And through her painting, she could.

Would Jefford be willing to allow her to accompany him to the fields? She wanted to be able to capture the people of Jamaica as they were, not posed, or stiff with self-consciousness. If Jefford, who seemed to blend in well with them in his cutoff trousers and battered straw hat, took her, perhaps she would be accepted more easily.

She sat at her dressing table and began to brush out her long blond hair. The plan was an excellent one, except for the fact that it would mean having to actually *ask* Jefford to take her. It would mean spending time with him, something he obviously wanted to avoid…as did she. But her painting was important, she thought stubbornly, rising to her feet, and it was worth some self-sacrifice.

So it was final, she decided. She would swallow her pride and ask Jefford tomorrow morning to take her with him when he made his morning rounds in the fields. She would rise early, pack her paints and easel, and join him and Aunt Kendra for breakfast in the garden. How could he deny her, especially with his mother sitting right there? Surely Aunt Kendra would insist, and from past experience, Madison knew he could not say no to her.

A smile on her lips, Madison picked the sailcloth drape off the floor and approached the unfinished canvas.

"What do you think you're looking at?" she snapped.

"Why won't you take me to town?" Chantal sat on the edge of Jefford's rumpled bed, naked, her sensual lower lip thrust out in a pout.

"Because, I told you, I have work to do." He lifted his booted foot to rest it on a chair to tie the lace and winced. The wound on his shoulder was clean and was healing, but in the morning, when he first began to move, it burned like a firebrand. "One of the other men can escort you. I'm certain someone is going to Kingston today. Someone goes every day."

"But I do not wish to go with another man, *amoureux.*" She rose from the bed and walked up behind him. She wrapped her arms around his neck and pressed her bare breasts to his back. "Please? For Chantal?"

"I told you, I have work to do." He put his foot on the floor and lifted the other, wiping the perspiration above his upper lip with his shoulder. It was barely dawn and already it was hot. "I can smell rain in the air. I have several fields to inspect today and I need good weather to do it. I'll have to hurry if I'm going to beat the storm."

"But all work takes the fun from life, *amoureux.*"

"I told you long ago that if you were looking for fun, I was the wrong man."

"Ah, *mi amoureux.*" She nibbled on his earlobe. "But you can be fun when you wish to be. Eh?"

He tied the second boot and dropped it, wincing again as she ran her hand over his shoulder.

"I have to get to work." He started for the door, grabbing her dress as he passed the bed. "Put this on and go. You know how Kendra feels about you being in here to begin with."

She caught the brightly dyed dress in the air. "I will come tonight?"

"We'll see." He pushed one of the tall shuttered doors leading to the garden open, stepped out and closed it behind him. He needed a cup of strong coffee, a little something for his stomach and then he would head out.

He intended to have a look at some fields that lay between his and Thomblin's property. They needed to be inspected. There was concern about a new insect that had appeared in some of the cane, but he was also using the fields as an excuse to talk to some of the men who might know some of Thomblin's workers. This was the third young, pretty woman in the last year to disappear from Thomblin's plantation, and though he had made no mention to George the previous night, something in the pit of his stomach made him question the woman's disappearance.

As Jefford pushed through an elephant-ear plant that was trying to take over the path in the garden, he spotted his mother in one of her favorite oversize bonnets, seated at the table pouring coffee, her back to him. He was glad to see her up so early.

She'd looked overly tired the previous night and he was concerned. He'd tried to discuss the matter with her when he'd escorted her to her chambers to turn in early, but she refused. She insisted it was not her health making her pale and shaky but lack of enough sunshine. She insisted it was London, Lady Westcott and the voyage that had tired her. He knew better but hadn't had the heart to push the matter, maybe because he wasn't ready to talk about it, either.

"Good morning."

"Good morning."

He stopped dead on the path.

"Coffee?" Madison asked sweetly as she turned to face him.

Damn but he was tempted to turn and walk away. He hadn't the time to deal with this chit this morning.

"Bobo brought some toast. He said it was all you liked in the morning, but there's also fruit." Without waiting for his response, she poured a cup of coffee for him.

"Where's Kendra?" He glanced in the direction of the house. "She's not up yet?"

"Still sleeping." She set down the coffeepot and reached for the small bowl of Windward Bay's own sugar to sweeten the dark, thick brew in her cup. "I'm sure she'll be down soon."

He reached for the coffee she had poured for him and sipped it, standing. She glanced up at him and he drew a breath. She was beautiful in the early morning light, her face still marked by sleep and an innocence he found, against his will, to be damned magnetizing.

"Don't you want to sit?" She pointed to the chair across from her.

"No, I…I should go." He glanced in the direction of the jungle. "I've fields to inspect today." He looked up, gesturing with his coffee cup. "Storm coming in."

"Actually, that's why I wanted to talk to you." Madison swallowed the lump in her throat.

He waited but gave her no encouragement.

Madison took a sip of the strong coffee, delaying just long enough to steel her nerve. "I should like to accompany you to the fields today to paint. I won't be any trouble, I can promise you. I—"

Jefford's deep, rumbling, humorless laughter silenced her.

"Won't be trouble?" he scoffed. "You're nothing but." He set down his cup. "No, you're not going to the cane fields with me. It's not safe, and even if it were…" He shook his head as he stalked off. "Talk to Kendra. I'm quite sure a safari can be arranged."

"You insufferable man!" To Madison's surprise, tears stung her eyes. A hundred retorts ran through her head, none of which she could manage to say aloud.

She pressed her lips together, anger stilling her tears. What had made her think for a second that Jefford liked her? He did nothing more than tolerate her for his mother's sake. When would she realize that?

But she wanted to paint today! And if Jefford wouldn't take her—she pushed away from the table—she'd go herself.

11

"Ah, waking, are we?" Carlton stretched his nude body out over the narrow bed and then rolled onto his side to press his groin against the bare brown buttocks of the young woman beside him.

She whimpered, trying to lean away from him, but he slid his hand over her slender, bare hip. "Now, now, we'll not have any of that." Her drew his mouth over her shoulder blade and bit her, not hard, just enough to make her flinch.

Again, she whimpered.

Carlton felt his penis stiffen and he groaned, grinding his groin against her smooth, taut backside. "Play nice," he whispered in her ear, running his hand over her small breast, pinching her nipple. "And we'll have breakfast after, you and I. A nice fruit compote and some bread, hmm?" He squeezed her brown buttocks with his hand, prodding his rigid member savagely between them.

Brigitte sobbed softly as she braced herself, grasping

the edge of the feather tick mattress. The chains around her wrists and ankles rattled and she squeezed her eyes shut against the pain.

Madison followed the path Jefford had taken, a small folding easel in her hand, a cloth pack on her back. In the other hand, she carried a walking stick.

Mosquitoes buzzed around her head, flies hummed, brightly colored finches flitted in the branches overhead and a green parrot called out in protest to the trespasser beneath him. There were giant elephant-ear plants, banana and coconut trees, hibiscus and orchids everywhere in the dense jungle. Enormous black-and-yellow caterpillars crawled over the tree trunks, snakes slithered through the grass, and toads the size of her hand hopped in and out of the plants along the path.

Aunt Kendra had warned her that she should not leave the confines of the clearing around the house without an attendant, preferably more than one. But then, she had spent her entire life in London being warned of dangers that didn't really seem to exist. The intimidation had simply been one more way her mother and father and brother had created to control her and her *obstinate spirit.*

She glanced up at the sky, which was cloudier than it had been when she set out half an hour ago. Jefford had warned her that a storm was coming, but what did he know?

The jungle and the path ended abruptly, and to Madison's delight, a huge field spread out before her. Able to recognize sugarcane plants since her educational journey by wagon from Kingston to Windward Bay, she made a beeline for the shade of a tree that she thought might produce that strange vegetable called breadfruit. There, she set up her easel and opened the cloth bag and spread out her paints. While she drew some curious stares from the dark faces in the field, no one approached her or questioned her presence.

Madison breathed in the heady scent of freedom, taking in the scene spread before her with a practiced eye. The cleared area where the cane had been planted was slightly rolling, the plants only knee-high. From the smell of the dark humus the workers were spreading along the rows, they appeared to be fertilizing with cow dung.

There were both Indians and Jamaicans in the field, but she could see they had divided into two distinct groups according to their ethnicity and did not mix or speak to one another.

Comprised mostly of men, but with a few women, each team had their own mule-pulled wagon of cow dung. They worked on opposite ends of the section of field, shovels in hand, slowly inching toward one another.

A young Jamaican woman with a red head scarf caught Madison's eye, and she dipped her brush into a rich red oil paint in excitement. She always began a painting where the story began. She had already painted the waving green lines of the sugarcane to serve as a background, but what she saw now was not the field, or the cane, but the people who worked it. She saw the young woman, fifteen, sixteen years old at most, toiling in the hot sun. She was dressed like the other Jamaican women, working like the others with her head bent, the shovel moving rhythmically in her hands. But, in Madison's mind, it was the red scarf around her head that made her stand out and separated her from the others. It was the red scarf around her head that made Madison think that this young woman had dreams beyond the sugarcane fields of Windward Bay.

Pressing her lips together in concentration, Madison

began to paint the young woman in the foreground of her canvas. The fact that her subject was moving made the task more difficult, but not impossible, and slowly, as the Jamaicans and Indians grew closer to one another, the woman took form in the painting.

Madison lifted her head, studied her subject, lowered her gaze to add a few strokes of her brush, and then glanced up again. She followed the same process over and over, blocking out the overwhelming heat of the morning. Sweat began to trickle down from her temples, and she wiped at it with the back of her hand as she cleaned her brush on her sleeve.

Time seemed to hang as still as the hot, humid morning; she knew only of its passing because the dark lines of cow dung between the green rows of cane grew longer and the Jamaicans and the Indians drew closer together. When the woman in the red scarf appeared as alive on Madison's canvas as she did in the field, Madison began to add the others, taking care to reflect the differences in the skin tones of the Jamaicans and the Indians.

Madison was dabbing at the brown circle of oil paint she had mixed when a raised voice caught her attention. She glanced up to see an Indian man and a Jamaican man an arm's length apart, the woman in the red scarf between them. The Indian man, bare-chested, with a dirty white turban wrapped around his head, rested one hand on the girl's bare arm. The Jamaican, a short, round man with a bald head, shouted in the Indian's face.

Squinting in the bright sunlight, Madison set down her brush and walked around her easel to get a better look.

"She has crossed row!" the Indian shouted. "She has crossed row. My row."

"Not your row! Not your cane," the Jamaican shouted back, pointing a stubby finger in emphasis.

The young woman tried to twist away from the Indian. "I was trying to help," she spat in the same liquidy voice that all the peoples of the West Indies seemed to have. "The rain is coming." She jutted her chin in the direction of the gathering clouds overhead. "We must finish."

"Let my daughter go," the Jamaican huffed. "If you were not so lazy—" he gestured in the general direction of the other Indian workers "—we would not have to work your rows."

The Indian gave a cry of fury and swung his shovel around in an arc over his head. The Jamaican woman screamed. Her father pushed her aside, out of the way with one hand, and swung his shovel with the other. The sound of clanging metal rent the air and manure flew in every direction. The young woman, shrieking, tried to grab the Indian man's arm and he shoved her back, throwing her to the ground.

Without thinking, Madison grabbed a handful of her skirt in each hand and took off, running along the edge of the field. "Stop that! Stop that fighting at once," she shouted.

Another Indian joined his friend in the fight and two more Jamaicans leaped over rows of green, leafy sugarcane to come to their companion's aide.

"Didn't you hear me?" Madison cried angrily. She cut across the sugarcane, down a row toward the men. "Look at you. Like a bunch of children. Someone is going to be hurt!" Reaching the men, she thrust out both hands to grab the shovel from one of the Jamaicans, who was preparing to swing at another man one row over.

"Missy!" the woman in the red scarf cried. "No! You will be killed."

Madison gritted her teeth, wrenching the shovel out of the man's hand. "If you do not stop this childish fighting this minute," Madison shouted, "so help me, God, I will—"

A gunshot split the air, startling Madison and the field hands, and Madison whipped around in the direction the gunfire had come.

"The next time I pull the trigger one of you goes down," Jefford bellowed, striding through the middle of the sugarcane field straight for Madison. "Indian, Jamaican, I don't care who. Now, put down your shovels and get in the shade and take a break. Get some water. I swear, the June sun is addling your brains!" Still coming straight for Madison, he eyed the Jamaican man, who had dropped his shovel and was now taking his daughter by the hand to lead her out of the field. "Johnny Boy, I didn't expect this of you of all people."

The Jamaican lowered his head in shame. "I am sorry, Mr. Jefford, but my daughter. I could not see her harmed."

"What the hell are you doing out here, Madison?" he demanded, slipping the pistol into the back of his pants and snatching the shovel out of her hand. "You leading the riot?"

Madison ran her hand over her hair. It had come loose from its chignon and she'd lost her aunt's hat somewhere in the cane. "No, I wasn't leading a riot," she snapped. "I couldn't very well let them fight. Someone was going to get hurt." Spotting the bonnet another row over, she took a step and winced as pain shot up from her ankle.

She heard Jefford swear in what she now recognized as Haitian Creole. The language of his paramour. "You're hurt." He threw the shovel down.

She kept going, despite the searing pain. "I'm fine."

"Madison, stop. Wait." He grabbed her wrist. "It could be broken."

"It's not broken," she cried, refusing to look at him. She leaned forward, trying to use her weight to escape him. "It's just twisted. I'll be fine."

With his other arm he grabbed her around the waist and before she knew what he was doing, he had lifted her in his arms. "Put me down," she protested, wiggling. "Put me down this instant."

Ignoring her protests, he stepped over the destroyed cane plants, swept up her hat and headed down between two rows, toward the edge of the jungle where her easel waited.

"You don't have to do this," Madison said, pushing at his shoulders.

"You didn't answer my question. What are you doing here? How the hell did you get out here all alone?"

She smacked him with the heel of her hand. "Painting, not that it's any of your business."

"So I say you can't come with me and you traipse off on your own. What, so you can be kidnapped and murdered like that Jamaican girl?"

Madison ceased struggling. "She was kidnapped and murdered?" she breathed, looking up into his dark eyes.

He glanced down at her, then away. "I don't know, but I have my suspicions. It doesn't matter. There are other dangers. Snakes. Getting lost and dying of sun exhaustion." He strode past her easel, dropping her bonnet on the ground beside it, and continued into the woods.

"Please put me down, Jefford."

He cut off the path Madison had followed to the field, ducking under palm and coconut fronds, circumnavigating bushes and jutting rocks. "There's a stream down here," he said, taking her deeper into the jungle. "The water is cold. If you've broken your ankle—"

"It's not—"

"Jesus, Madison, will you just shut up for once?" He halted, looking down at her, cradled in his arms, her skirts tangled around her knees and showing entirely too much bare calf. "If it is broken, or just sprained, the cold water will hold down the swelling."

As they looked at each other, she could feel the energy crackling between them.

He lowered his head over hers and the jungle seemed to swirl as she felt Jefford's hot mouth, then the tip of his tongue touch her lips. She was horrified…fascinated by the feel of the wetness. The taste of him. Her lips parted, seemingly of their own accord, and she felt his tongue between her lips…then deeper in her mouth.

She suddenly felt a heat in the pit of her stomach, a tingling in her limbs as she slipped her arms around his neck, pulling herself closer to him. All that mattered was the taste of him. The feel of his arms around her.

Madison couldn't breathe. Her fingers found his thick, dark hair. "Please," she panted, pulling away, dizzy from lack of air. "Jefford—"

He took a breath and covered her mouth with his again. The indescribable ache inside her was too great. All she could do was to cling to him, her mouth open, panting as he assaulted her. Made love to her.

It took a third kiss to bring Jefford to his senses, or maybe to render him so breathless that he, too, was in danger of collapsing. "Madison," he breathed, lowering his head until his face was nestled in the crook of her neck, buried in her blond hair.

She kept her eyes closed, brushing her hand across his cheek. He had shaven this morning, but to her surprise she could still feel a roughness. She had never felt a man's cheek before, had always assumed it would be as soft as her own.

"I'm sorry," he murmured after a moment. Then he lifted his head and carried her another hundred feet into the jungle.

There, he stooped by the stream and gently lowered her to the edge. No words passed between them as he pushed up her skirt, spotted the swollen ankle at once and eased her slipper off. She watched, mesmerized by the beauty of his movement as he carefully lowered her ankle into the cold water.

She flinched when the water touched her skin, so cold that it almost hurt.

"Shh," he murmured, his mouth dangerously close to her ear. "Give it a minute. I know it hurts, but—"

"No," she whispered, looking at him. "It's all right."

He released her foot, leaving it in the water, and sat down beside her. "Madison, I don't know what to say."

"You don't have to say anything."

"I—"

She lowered her hand to his knee. "I'm sorry. You're right. I shouldn't have come here alone. It was irresponsible of me. It was only that I wanted—"

"You wanted to paint and I wouldn't take you with me," he interrupted. "Madison, it's not that I don't want you with me, just that—"

"It's her, isn't it?" she said.

His dark brows furrowed. "Who? My mother?"

"Chantal. Your paramour."

He grinned.

Madison didn't know what response she had expected at her mention of Chantal, but that wasn't it. "She doesn't want me with you," she accused.

He glanced out over the stream, no wider than he was tall. "Chantal has no control over what I do or whom I do it with."

"That's not what the servants say. They say Chantal says you're going to marry her."

This time he lifted a dark brow. "Madison, I'm not marrying anyone. Now, how's the ankle?"

She studied his face a moment longer, thinking how handsome he was. Not like Lord Thomblin, but in a different way. His face was broader, brawnier. And his skin, it was the most amazing color. There was no way he could have been sired by an Englishman.

"Who was your father?" Madison blurted suddenly.

"None of your business." He didn't speak the words unkindly. "Now, let's see what we can do about getting you home." He looked overhead at the dark clouds moving in the sky. "We'll be lucky if we make it back before the rain hits."

Late in the afternoon, Madison sat in the garden under a banana tree, her injured ankle propped on a pillow. In front of her, on an easel, was the painting she had begun the day before in the sugarcane field. She had dressed carefully, with the assistance of Sashi, in one of her favorite afternoon gowns, one of the few she had brought with her from London that could possibly be worn in the Jamaican heat. The white pointed bodice was long-sleeved with short basques over a box-pleated, soft-figured leaf green madras. She also wore a pair of dyed-to-match green silk-heeled slippers. A delightful matching parasol and hand-painted Chinese fan were propped up beside her.

When Lord Thomblin arrived she hoped there would be time for them to take a stroll in the garden before dinner.

George and Alice and their parents, Lady and Lord Rutherford, were coming as well, so this would be Madison's first dinner party since her arrival in Jamaica.

Madison dipped the tip of her brush in a paint pot and, taking care with her gown, dabbed at the green leaves that were the rows of immature sugarcane plants in the painting. The piece was almost complete, painted in record time. After Jefford had sent for a wagon to transport her back to Windward Bay, he had sat in the shade of the tree and watched her paint. Usually, someone watching made Madison nervous, but for some reason yesterday had been different. She knew it had something to do with the kisses they had shared, kisses she had tried to rationalize in a hundred ways and, in the end, decided to simply not think about. But something else had been different yesterday…something between her and Jefford. Something frightening yet somehow exciting in a forbidden sort of way.

"Your foot, it is not broken?"

Madison looked up to see Chantal, of all people. Madison could not recall that the Haitian woman had ever spoken directly to her before.

"No." Madison glanced at the still-swollen ankle propped on the cushioned stool. "Just twisted, I think. I'll be fine in a few days." She looked up. "But thank you for asking."

The beautiful woman stared at Madison, her mouth in an unpleasant twist. She wore her hair uncovered and in a mass of tiny braids, each twisted with a different color of thread. Her orange dress, most closely resembling a sarong, bared most of her shoulders as well as her legs from the knees down. "That is good to hear because the sooner your foot is better, the sooner you can go from here."

Madison stared back, brush poised. "Pardon?"

"You heard what Chantal said." She leaned closer, her dark eyes narrowing. "You do not belong here, not at Windward Bay, not in Jamaica." Her accent was thick but perfectly understandable. "You should go back across the great ocean before you are hurt worse." She threw her small, dark hand in the direction of the sea. "Before you hurt others."

Madison set down her brush, not knowing what the woman spoke of, but, just the same, not caring for her tone. "I was invited here by my aunt…by Jefford," she said, thrusting out her chin.

"It is not true." Chantal shook her finger at Madison, her voice rising, her accent becoming thicker. "He does not want you here. He tells me, my *amoureux,* that he wishes you to go back across the ocean, away from him. Away from us."

Madison knew she was lying. Jefford might have thought that, but he never would have said it, not to a servant. Not even to his mistress. A lump rose in her throat. *Would he?*

"Madison," Aunt Kendra called from her balcony overlooking the garden on the far end of the house. "Our guests have arrived."

Madison waved, forcing a smile.

"I'll send Jefford down for you!"

"No," Madison called back. "I'm fine. I can walk. Really." She got up as quickly as possible, leaning on the back of the chair, refusing to let her pain show on her face. Out of the corner of her eye, she saw Chantal hurry away, down a path nearly grown over with vines.

"He's coming down," Aunt Kendra called, ignoring her niece.

Madison began to pack up supplies as carefully as she

could. She was anxious to see Carlton, but if she left any of the paint open to the air, it would not glide as smoothly as she liked. The painting was too good for her to allow that to happen. She had mixed the perfect colors and she would not sacrifice them, even for Lord Thomblin.

"What was she doing here?"

Madison looked up to see Jefford. He had dressed for dinner in long trousers for a change, and a white shirt that showed off the suntanned tone of his skin and the crowing black of his hair entirely too well.

"Who?" Madison asked, though she knew very well whom he spoke of.

"Chantal. I saw her talking to you from Kendra's balcony."

"How would I know what she wanted?" Madison glanced up at him. "Looking for you, I suppose."

He scowled. "She didn't say anything to you?"

She gave a laugh that was without humor and snatched up the paper fan on her easel. "Certainly not. What would your paramour have to say to me?"

Madison limped past him, refusing to take the arm he offered, and when she spotted Lord Thomblin in the open doorway leading into the dining room, she broke into a broad grin. "Lord Thomblin," she cried, waving her fan gaily. "So good to see you at last."

12

"Really now, Lord Rutherford, that can't possibly be true." Madison laughed, covering her mouth with her hand.

Lady Moran's supper party guests were seated at two separate dining tables, and though they had completed their meal more than an hour earlier, they still lounged in the dining room, sipping cool drinks and nibbling on fruit and nuts. Jefford and Lord Thomblin had just excused themselves to go into the garden and have a cigar and the remaining diners now moved to sit together.

Lord Rutherford had been relating a tall tale of his encounter with a lizard the size of a small dog on the Amazon River. His lordship had been quite a traveler in his younger days, and though Madison surmised he had to be close to seventy, he still had the sparkling eyes of a man who enjoyed life to its fullest.

"You're right to not believe a word he says," Lady Rutherford said, sipping her glass of Aunt Kendra's rum punch as her husband took Jefford's vacated seat beside her. "He's a senile old man."

"Senile, indeed," Lord Rutherford harrumphed. "Son, why are you not defending me?"

"Against a pack of Englishwomen?" George lifted a glass of rum in toast. "Because, Father, you haven't a chance."

Alice laughed and fanned her herself rapidly with a lovely fan made of parrot feathers. "Well, my goodness."

"He's a clever young man, my boy," Lord Rutherford told Madison with a wink. "Smarter than I. You should marry him quickly before he's swept up by my wife's cousin twice removed, of Essex, who is drooling for a formal invitation to visit us."

"Father!" George protested. "Please, you're embarrassing me."

"I'm simply telling this charming young woman what a catch you are. Is there any harm in that?" Before George could respond, Lord Rutherford looked to Madison. "When I've passed, Georgie will not only inherit my title and monies, but land here, in England and my vast estates in heathen India."

"India," Madison breathed. "I hadn't realized you'd lived in India."

"Lived there for fifteen years. It's where I met Kendra." He smoothed his balding head. "Kendra, dear, didn't you tell your niece that we met in India? I was utterly infatuated with our enigmatic Kendra until I laid eyes upon my beautiful Portia."

"George, really," Lady Rutherford demurred, tapping him with her silk fan. "You embarrass me."

"You broke my heart, George. You know that, don't you?" Aunt Kendra teased.

"I'll believe that when I believe little green men from Van Diemen's Land distill this fine rum of yours, Kendra."

He lifted his glass in salute. "Besides, by then, someone else had your eye, hadn't he?"

Lady Rutherford, Lord Rutherford and Aunt Kendra all made eye contact and there was a moment of strained silence.

Was Lord Rutherford possibly referring to Jefford's father? Madison was dying to ask, but she knew this wasn't the place or the time. Instead, she turned to her aunt and said, "I hadn't realized you'd lived in India." She was not entirely surprised, though. It seemed her aunt had a great many secrets.

"It was a long time ago, dear." Aunt Kendra patted Madison's hand, obviously wishing to make light of the subject. "Before I married Lord Moran."

Lady Rutherford leaned to whisper something in her husband's ear, and he rose from his chair, bowing formally.

"Well, if you ladies, and gentleman—" he acknowledged his son "—will excuse me, I believe I'll join the other men in the garden for a smoke."

"We'll be out shortly," Kendra called after him. "We can go for a walk and see what we can see."

"If you'll excuse me as well, ladies." George bowed and followed his father through the open doorway.

"Well, my goodness," Alice sighed as she fluttered her fan.

Jefford glanced up to see Lord Rutherford approaching from the house, fumbling with a cigar he had drawn from the inside pocket of his pale umber suit jacket.

"Balmy evening," the balding man remarked.

"That it is." Jefford nodded cordially. He liked old man Rutherford, who went back a long way with Kendra. They

had known each other in Rutherford's wild days in India
when he was an officer in the British army. Those were his
mother's wild days, as well, he supposed.

"So, Thomblin, any word on that missing chit?" Lord
Rutherford clenched the cigar between his teeth and leaned
toward a torch to light it.

Thomblin cleared his throat. "No word, sir. I fear she's
dead, or long gone."

"Gone?" Jefford asked testily. "Where the hell would
she have gone?"

"Slavers, of course." Lord Rutherford drew on the cigar
and exhaled, a cloud of sweet-smelling smoke rising above
his head. "Haven't you heard?"

"Slavers? I've heard nothing of slavers in Jamaica,
George."

"I've heard the same, my lord," Thomblin said, agree-
ing with the older man.

"More than one young woman has disappeared from the
area in the last few months, Jefford." Rutherford hooked
his forefinger around the stout cigar and drew it from his
mouth. "I'm surprised you haven't heard."

"I knew about the missing women." Jefford was only
half listening to the conversation now. A pale green moth
that fluttered over the nearest burning torch had caught his
eye and he watched it with fascination. Surely the moth
must have known that to draw too close would cause its
death; it must have felt the lethal heat. And yet, it was in-
explicably drawn. As he was to Madison, no more than a
helpless insect bemused by destiny? "I…assumed the
women had met some other ill fate," he said, forcing himself to look away, unable to watch the moth die.

"No bodies have been found. Back in the early sixties
in the Sahara, there were slavers stealing young girls right

out of their beds. Barely women yet." Lord Rutherford puffed on his cigar. "Taken from their mothers' bosoms to be sold to sheikhs' harems, they were."

Jefford chuckled, shaking his head. "George, you always have the best stories."

"Not stories, young man. Pure fact."

Jefford smiled. "If you'll both excuse me, I believe I'll check on the ladies. There was some talk of taking a stroll beyond the gardens. If they are still game, I'll need to find some torch bearers."

Sashi, her arm full of soiled towels, turned the corner of the lamp-lit corridor and nearly collided with George Rutherford. "I'm sorry, sir. My excuse, please."

She lifted a hand in embarrassment, turning her head away.

"No, no, it's quite all right, Sashi." The Englishman's voice was hesitant. "May…may I call you Sashi?"

She nodded shyly, still not making eye contact, but unable to resist a smile. "If you like." She lifted her head, daring a peek.

He was smiling at her.

"Truth is," he said, lowering his voice, "I was hoping I might bump into you. All evening I've been trying to come up with an excuse to have Madison call for you, and finally, I just said to myself, 'What the hell, Georgie,' and I came and found you on my own."

Still cradling the towels in one arm, she slid the other hand self-consciously over her jewel-green sari, thankful she had thought to wear it this evening. "You came looking for me, sir?"

"Please, it's George. I want you to call me George. I hope you don't mind, my being so forward as to say so."

He stretched out both arms. "God's bones. How rude of me. Could I carry those for you?"

She chuckled quietly, daring another shy glance at his handsome face. "I am a servant...George. It is my duty to carry my mistress's belongings."

"Where are you going? To the laundry? I'll walk down with you."

Before Sashi could protest, the young English gentleman had taken the towels from her arms and fallen into step beside her. "So tell me how you came to be in Lady Moran's household. I must admit, I'm curious to know everything there is to know about you, Sashi...."

"You certain you can walk, my dear?" Aunt Kendra asked Madison. "I've a litter. Punta's boys could carry you. Strapping young men they are, all of them."

The entire dinner party had gathered at the northeast gate of the garden to take a stroll through the night jungle. Apparently, it was one of Madison's aunt's favorite forms of diversion when she entertained guests.

"I can walk, Aunt Kendra." Madison rubbed the older woman's arm affectionately. "You said yourself, we're only going a short distance."

Aunt Kendra smiled at her, brushing a lock of blond hair that had escaped Madison's neat chignon. "You are such a delight to me, my dear. Proof that we never know what good fortune still lies before us, even in the twilight of our lives."

Madison knitted her brow, not entirely sure what her aunt meant by being *in the twilight of her life*.

"Well, you give a call, should you tire or your ankle begin to ache." Aunt Kendra fluttered her fan as she walked toward the head of the group, waiting on the path for her.

"Is Georgie here? I don't know where that boy has gotten to. Not with your Chantal, is he, Jefford, dear?"

Madison barely suppressed a smile as Jefford shot his mother an angry glance.

"Here I am. Coming," George sang, sprinting through the garden toward them.

With a satisfied nod, Lady Moran turned to her faithful servant who waited patiently at the gate, a burning torch held high. "Punta let the safari begin," she called.

Surrounded by men carrying torches, armed with machetes, the group moved forward.

"You never know what you'll see in the jungle at night," Lady Moran told her audience in a hushed voice as she slid her arm through Jefford's. "Do you remember, that tiger we encountered on the river during the Feast of Shiva, Lord Rutherford?"

"As if it was only yesterday," he said giving his wife's hand a pat as she slipped her arm through his. "It was a moonless night much like tonight...."

Madison fell into step beside Alice, taking her time. Her ankle actually did feel a little better. "Where has your brother been?" she whispered to her companion.

"I can't say for sure." Alice tipped her head toward Madison's. "But if I were to lend a guess, I would say he's been in search of your maid."

"No," Madison breathed, her eyes widening.

Alice nodded rapidly.

Madison gripped her new friend's arm tightly. "You must tell me what you know," she whispered eagerly.

"Now, now, what are you two ladies gossiping about?" George demanded, pushing past Lord Thomblin, who now took up the rear.

"We weren't gossiping, per se," Madison told him.

"I was telling Madison how you're half in love with her Indian maid."

"Alice!" George reached out and pinched his sister's arm. "You weren't supposed to tell anyone."

Alice squealed with laughter and pulled her arm away. "Georgie, stop."

Madison glanced at the handsome young man, intrigued by the whole idea of such an illicit romance. Honorable marriage between an English gentleman and an Indian maid was entirely impossible, even in the remote jungle of Jamaica. "You should have told me, Georgie. I could have made arrangements for you to bump into her."

"Found her on my own," he whispered, obviously quite pleased with himself.

"And was she receptive to your…search?" Madison asked.

He grinned. "Well, a gentleman never kisses and tells, but—"

Madison chatted with George and Alice for another five minutes. Then, glancing up to see that her aunt and Jefford, at the front of the expedition, were engaged in conversation with Lady and Lord Rutherford, she casually slowed her pace, slipping back until Lord Thomblin walked at her side.

"What a lovely evening for a walk," she said. Her ankle was beginning to tire, but she ignored the pain, not wanting him to think she was weak or fussy.

"It is indeed." He smiled, glancing down at her. "I believe Jamaica suits you well, my dear Madison."

The fact that he was forward enough to call her by her given name when they were in private did not go unnoticed by her. "I believe you're right, Carlton. I do hope my aunt will be able to find me a suitable match so that I might stay."

He glanced down at her and smiled, offering his arm. "I imagine every eligible Englishman on the island will be half in love with you. I know I am."

Madison slid her arm through his, her heart giving a little trip. "Sir, you flatter me—"

"Madison, Madison, dear," Lady Moran called from the head of the group.

The entire party had stopped, and those in the front of the line were looking intently at something in the darkness. "Do come here, dear." She waved her fan, beckoning her niece. "I want you to see this giant tree sloth!"

Madison exhaled in frustration and looked up at Lord Thomblin. "If you'll excuse me, sir?"

He nodded grandly, releasing her arm. "By all means."

After observing the giant mammal, the group turned around and started back for Windward Bay. In the garden, the Rutherfords and Lord Thomblin thanked their hostess for the evening and climbed into the waiting carriages.

"What a delightful evening," Aunt Kendra remarked, dropping into a chair one of the servants had brought for her. "Punch," she told the young boy, dressed in nothing but a loincloth. "For you?" She directed her question to Madison.

Madison shook her head. "No, thank you." She dropped in relief into the chair the boy offered.

"You staying for a drink, Jefford?" Lady Moran asked her son.

"I think I've had quite enough socializing for one night." He walked away.

"Good night, dear," Lady Moran called after her son.

Madison watched his back as he retreated through the garden toward his chambers in the far end of the house.

"I suppose he's gone off to be with her," Madison said,

resting her sore ankle on the stool the little boy had carried from the dining room.

"I told you, you needn't worry about Chantal."

"I'm certainly not worried." Madison attempted to keep the emotion out of her voice. "It's his prerogative, isn't it, to have a…a…"

Her aunt chuckled, which Madison did not much appreciate.

"I doubt we'll be seeing much more of Miss Chantal." Aunt Kendra glanced in the direction Jefford had gone. "Something tells me she has nearly outstayed her welcome."

Madison gave no reply but to sigh.

A servant brought Lady Moran a cup of fruited rum punch and she sipped it. "Did you enjoy yourself this evening, my dear?"

"It was quite nice." Madison smiled. "The meal was delightful. I adore the Rutherfords, each and every one of them, and it was so good to see Lord Thomblin again. I do have to say I've missed him."

It was Lady Moran's turn to sigh. "Really, Madison. I'm not one to tell another what to do when it comes to romance. I have certainly made a muddle of my life in that respect over the years, but I must warn you, Carlton Thomblin is not a man appropriate for you."

Madison watched a long green bug that looked remarkably like a blade of grass move slowly up the stalk of a fern. She noticed that her aunt never called Carlton *Lord* Thomblin. "Aunt Kendra, I don't want to hurt your feelings. I adore Georgie Rutherford, but if you're hoping—"

"Oh, by Hindi's teeth, Madison." She slapped her knee. "Lord Rutherford is an old windbag. A dear, beloved man to me, but still a windbag. Pay no attention to what he says.

He's told every unmarried Englishwoman between the ages of twelve and sixty that she should snap up his son before he's wed to that 'buck-toothed cousin of Portia's.' Honestly, I doubt there is a 'buck-toothed cousin from Essex.' I think George uses her as a threat to his son, hoping to encourage him to find a wife." She sipped her punch. "You know, much like a father threatens a boy with barebottomed banshees in the dark, to keep him in bed at night."

Madison burst into laughter at her aunt's colorful illustration. "Well, good. Just so you know, I like George immensely, but he and I would never make a suitable match."

"I understand, my dear. It's all about alchemy, love is. It's about how you feel inside." She pressed her hand to the brightly colored gauze gown, over her heart. "But I must warn you that misdirected infatuation can too easily be misinterpreted at your tender age."

"You're speaking of Lord Thomblin."

"My dear." Aunt Kendra shifted her weight forward, moving stiffly. She took Madison's hand in hers. "Lord Thomblin—"

"Is a gentleman who appreciates a lady. He's articulate and kind and—"

Aunt Kendra released her hand. "I will not give my approval to allow Carlton Thomblin to court you."

Madison glanced eagerly at her aunt. "Has he asked?"

"He has not!"

Madison looked away, trying not to feel disappointed. After all, Carlton was such a gentleman. Perhaps he knew how Lady Moran felt about him and was keeping his distance in respect of that. Of course, maybe this wasn't her aunt's doing at all. "If this has anything to do with Jefford trying to interfere—"

"Madison," Aunt Kendra said sharply. "It is true that Jefford has a great influence over the things I do, but do not think for a moment that he *controls* me in any way. Jefford agrees with me on this subject, but I am the one forbidding you to think of Carlton Thomblin as anything beyond a neighbor. I made a promise to my dying husband that I would not abandon his nephew, but that does not mean I would allow anyone I care for to become too entangled with him. I disagree with Jefford, who thinks he is evil. I think Carlton is simply misguided, but I will not allow my niece to be misguided along with him."

Madison thrust her chin out stubbornly, staring into the darkness. "Misguided with him. I don't know what you mean." She loved her aunt dearly and she would never do anything to hurt her feelings or appear disrespectful, but Lady Moran was older than she. She didn't understand.

"You know exactly what I mean," Lady Moran said tersely. "What you are experiencing with Lord Thomblin is pure infatuation. Most young women experience it, I know I certainly did. Lord Thomblin looks good in a suit, he speaks well, he is flattering, entertaining, but that does not mean he would make a good husband."

"I think I'll go to bed," Madison said, rising. She would not be rude to her aunt, but she had had enough of her advice for one evening. "My ankle is beginning to ache again."

Lady Moran sighed, looking up at her niece. "Now, now. Don't go away angry. I don't say these things to hurt, my dear. Only to protect you. Now, come give an old lady a hug before you turn in." She smiled, opening her arms to Madison.

Madison couldn't deny her. Not when she owed this wonderful turn of events in her life, this exotic adventure, to her.

"Good night," Madison said, leaning over to hug her and press a kiss to her dry cheek. "I'll see you in the morning."

"Yes, yes, I've already made arrangement for Punta to drive us to the distillery so you can paint the workers. I'll have a picnic lunch packed for us."

Jefford waited in the shadows of the house until Madison took the stairs upward to the second story and disappeared inside. He slowly walked back up the path and sat in her vacated seat beside his mother. He took the rum punch from her hand and sipped. "You're drinking too much of this."

She snatched it back. "It makes me feel better."

He studied her face thinking how much she had aged in the last year. "You're feeling worse?"

"Certainly not."

"Are you taking the medicine the doctor gave you for the pain?"

"No. It makes my mind fuzzy."

He slid forward in his seat, clutching his fists in frustration. It was very difficult for him to accept his mother's illness and know that there was nothing he could do about it, just as it was impossible to think of where the illness would eventually lead. "Kendra, we sailed halfway around the world to see the finest physician in—"

"Poppycock! I went to London to attend my niece's coming-out party." She pointed to her empty glass, and the little boy who stood in the shadows, pitcher in hand, hurried forward to refill it. "I knew there was nothing that could be done." She turned, looking at him meaningfully. "You knew nothing could be done."

He leaned back in the chair, folding his arms over his chest, avoiding her gaze.

"Son, we need to talk about this."

He remained quiet, but inside he was screaming. *No! No!* This woman, his beloved mother. She was his world. His reason for existence. He was convinced he'd been placed on this earth to care for her.

"You and I have talked about this before, but I truly think it's time you consider taking a wife."

"No, we have not talked about this. *You've* talked about it."

He got up. He would walk away from her. He didn't have to sit and listen to this.

"Sooner or later I'm going to die and—"

"Kendra—"

"Stop interrupting your mother," she snapped. "Now, hear me out and I'll say no more on this subject."

"At least not tonight," he muttered.

"You can mumble and curse under your breath all you like, in any language you please," she said. "I'm going to have my say. I want you to take a wife. I don't want you to live in this big house all alone when I'm gone. This house should be filled with laughing children. With love. Jefford, I want you to be loved."

Her voice caught in her throat and Jefford felt her emotion in the pit of his stomach. In the lump in his throat.

"My son, I want to die knowing you are loved." She paused, taking a drink. "You, of all people, deserve to be loved. Now, I know how you say you feel about Madison, but—"

"Wait a minute." He halted in front of her. "We are definitely not having this conversation again."

"She's bright, and talented, and she loves it here. She would make a good wife, a good mother. Jefford, if you would just give her a chance, I know she would love you as I do. The way every man and woman deserve to be loved. And you would love her. I think you already do."

"It's late," he said. "Let me help you up to your room."

She sighed, offering him her hand. "You are stubborn."

He eased her out of the chair and let her lean against him, his arm around her waist as they started for the house.

"Stubborn like your father," Kendra said wistfully.

13

Chantal walked into the kitchen adjacent to the main house and reached for a small papaya from the bowl on the center of the worktable.

"Good fine morning to you, *nyes*," Lela, the cook, said, turning chicken legs in a cast-iron spider over glowing coals on the hearth. Beads of sweat rolled down the older woman's cheerful face as her capable brown hands moved gracefully and efficiently to complete this task before moving to another without hesitation.

It was barely past sunup and Chantal's aunt was already hard at work. Her duties not only extended to preparing meals for the mistress and master of the household and their guests, but she was also responsible for feeding those servants in the immediate household. It was Chantal's opinion that Lela worked far too hard.

"Good morning, no," Chantal said, frowning as she reached for a knife in a rack to skin her fruit.

A skinny brown dog ran in through one open door, cut across the middle of the open kitchen and ran out the door on the far side, into the garden. Two naked Jamaican boys, no more than three or four years old, pursued the dog, squealing with laughter. As one went by, he grabbed Chantal's leg to keep from sliding into the table and caught the hem of the turquoise-and-orange dress Jefford had bought her on a trip to Kingston before he left for England.

"Get out!" Chantal cried, dropping the knife on the table and shooing the child angrily, yanking her skirt from his dirty hand. "Out. You do not belong in this kitchen."

The little boy's mouth gaped, and for a second, he looked as though he would burst into tears. Then he stuck his tongue out at her and raced out the door.

Lela eyed Chantal as Chantal retrieved her paring knife and went back to peeling the fruit.

"What?" Chantal snapped at her aunt, after a moment of taut silence. "Stop looking at me that way."

"I am looking at you no way, but you are in a sour mood for so early in the morning." Lela flipped a chicken thigh and the hot fat hissed and sizzled. "A sour mood for a woman who has so many advantages."

Chantal scowled. "I may not have so many advantages as you say much longer."

"Ah, so the gossip is true." The older woman nodded knowingly. "Of course you did not think you would be the master's lover always. You knew he would wed some day. You knew Master Jefford was not a man to keep a woman after he was married."

"Married! My *amoureux* is not getting married! Who would he marry? He loves me." Chantal touched her breast with the tip of the knife. "Only me."

Lela carried a clean wooden bowl to the worktable, saying nothing.

"It is not my *amoureux*, it is that woman," Chantal spat, jerking her chin in the direction of the main house. "She has put a spell upon him. Upon his rod."

Lela picked up a cleaver, and taking a pineapple from the bowl in the middle of the table, she hacked off the stem with one clean chop.

"She has cursed me!" Chantal slid a succulent piece of papaya into her mouth. "Cursed my *amoureux*. Sent *Bossu* to my bed."

"*Bossu*." Lela chuckled. "Chantal, you do not believe in voodoo of your *maman*."

"My mother's voodoo served its purpose." Chantal leaned against the table, crossing her arms over her chest. "Maybe I was wrong. Maybe there are evil spirits. I know there must be. There would be no other reason for my *amoureux* to act this way."

"You should be careful, *nyes*. When the time comes, you must step away quietly. You must take the gifts that are offered, which I know will be generous, and you must find your new *destine*."

"My destiny!" Chantal shouted. "Windward Bay was my *destin*."

Lela reached out and slapped her niece's hand. "Hush your mouth." She glanced around the kitchen. "Someone will hear you, and you will be gone like that girl *Brigitte*." She snapped her fingers beneath Chantal's nose.

Chantal frowned, rubbing her hand, made sticky by the fruit she'd eaten, on her skirt. "What are you doing?" She nodded at the fruit mixture her aunt was making in the bowl.

"Packing a picnic. Mistress Kendra and Miss Madison go to the distillery today."

"Why? She does not even like our rum."

Lela shrugged. "Who knows what a white woman will do? She says she goes to paint pictures of the workers."

"And picnic," Chantal grumbled. "She goes on a picnic and I must tend sick, old women in the villages all day!"

"You once liked your job here, *nyes*. You are good with the old and the sick. Your *men* have a special touch." Lela showed Chantal her palms. "You have a way with the plants and herbs. A gift given to you by my *sé*. May God rest her soul." She crossed herself.

"But I had dreams, *matant*. Such dreams." Chantal eyed the fruit bowl. "If that woman would go back across the ocean…"

"Miss Madison is not going to England, Chantal. And you are a fool to think else." Lela dropped the chunks of fresh pineapple into the bowl and grabbed a papaya. "And if she did, there would be another white woman. He is not for a brown girl, and you be a bigger fool than I think you are, if you believe other."

"But what if Jamaica did not *agree* with her, eh?" Chantal asked, thinking about what her aunt had said about her gift with herbs. The gift did not only extend to healing. There were other things to do with plant extracts, as well. "Would she not go back then?"

Lela looked at Chantal, then at the bowl of fruit. Her dark eyes clouded. "Hush your stupid mouth," she whispered harshly, slapping a hand on the table. "Do not even *say* such a thing."

"I said nothing." Chantal raised both hands, walking haughtily away.

"You poison Miss Madison, and I will go to the master," Lela threatened with the point of her knife. "You will not ruin the life this family has made here. I have children, grandchildren, who eat and sleep and work here. You will not harm them. Do you hear me, you devious hen?"

"I would not do such a thing." Chantal sighed, headed for the door, sashaying her hips. "Chantal knows there are sweeter ways to draw the cock...."

"Thank you so much, Aunt Kendra, for bringing me today." Madison tried not to squirm on the rough wooden seat beside her aunt in the jolting wagon. "I had asked Jefford about seeing how the rum was made, but he said something about women not being allowed near the distillery."

"Oh, poppycock." Lady Moran tilted her parasol painted with colorful parrots, to get a better look at her niece. "There is an old superstition about women not being permitted in the boiler room. Nonsense, of course." She dismissed the thought with one hand. "But, I do find it is easier to abide by certain rules of the native people I live among, wherever I may live."

"Was it the same in India?"

"My! You are curious about my time in India, aren't you?" Lady Moran reached for Madison's gloved hand and took it between hers. "One day soon it may be time for me to tell you of that great adventure."

She smiled, but to Madison it seemed like a sad smile.

"But now is not the time, is it?" Madison asked softly, not wanting to cause her aunt any emotional pain.

"Now is not the time," Lady Moran agreed. "Look, we're here, anyway."

The wagon, pulled by a pair of roan mules and driven by Punta—escorted by one of his strapping young sons—entered a wide clearing. Madison spotted a ramshackle frame building that looked to her as if it had been perched on the rocky incline for a hundred years. A giant black stove of some sort rested precariously on the edge of a stone ledge, a thick pipe leading from it, into the building. Madison wrinkled her noise as she inhaled the tangy aroma of what could only be the cane juices boiling.

"It's an acquired smell, my dear." Lady Moran patted Madison's knee. "Like the taste of rum. It grew on me, as it will on you."

The wagon rolled to a stop on the far side of the clearing, and Lady Moran was on her feet at once, waiting impatiently for Punta's son to help her down.

As Madison rose and waited her turn, she studied Windward Bay's men, busy at work. Two muscular Jamaicans, in their early twenties, stood near the stove, taking turns thrusting armfuls of dry cane husks into the open door of the furnace.

Three more Jamaicans busied themselves loading a wagon with wooden casks, and another wagon with two boys, not more than twelve or fourteen, clinging to the tailgate, rolled into the clearing with more cane husks.

Madison's eye was drawn back to the two men at the stove. They were both bare-chested and barefooted, wearing only a pair of cutoff breeches. Sweat ran down their temples in rivulets, a product of the heat of the stove and the pace at which they fed the fire. The one man who was more slender than the other reminded Madison of Cundo, the dock worker she had painted in London shortly before she came to Jamaica.

This sudden and unbidden thought of England, of Boxwood Manor, drew a sadness over Madison. Not, she realized, because she missed her home, but because she did not.

"I must know exactly what's being done," Madison said

as Punta's son lifted her down from the wagon, England immediately forgotten.

"Over here, Punta," Lady Moran ordered, waving to her manservant. "Right here will be perfect, don't you think, Madison?" Lady Moran chose a shady spot under a banana palm.

"Perfect," Madison insisted with smile, turning to Punta's son. "Yes, the easel can go right there." She leaned over the tailgate of the old mule-driven wagon and reached for the box of paints she used when traveling.

Lady Moran settled in her chair and accepted her parrot parasol from Punta. "Now, didn't you say you had some visiting to do?" she asked the servant.

"My wife's cousin." He bobbed his head. "But I do not need to—"

"Poppycock. I imagine Madison will be hours and I am content to sit here and sip my punch." She looked up at him. "You *did* bring my punch and the basket Lela prepared?"

The son ran from the wagon with a small crockery jug in one hand, the picnic basket in the other. "Mistress," he said bowing as he set the foodstuffs beside her chair.

"Perfect. Now, run along, Punta. You two enjoy the afternoon."

"If you tire, Miss Kendra—"

"I will not tire," she insisted indignantly. "And if I did, I think I am quite capable of driving that contraption the two miles home, don't you think? After all, you are aware, Punta, that I have led a train of elephants across half of India during a monsoon…."

Punta gave a respectful nod, pressing his hands together, making an effort to conceal a smile. "I think you are quite capable." He glanced at Madison.

She was staring at Aunt Kendra but knew better than to ask about the elephants. "We'll be fine, Punta," she said. "A woman who can manage a train of elephants can certainly manage two old mules. Please. Go see your cousin."

Punta and his son hastened into the jungle and Madison set to work. First, she adjusted the height of the easel, then she placed the fresh canvas on it and began to set her paints out on a stump. "Now, I understand that first the cane is cut and run through the pressing mill."

"In the shed beyond the boiler room here." Lady Moran pointed to a building in even worse condition and then proceeded to pour herself a cup of her punch. "The juice goes into a receiver and then into copper cauldrons inside the boiler room. That stove is used to boil the juice," Kendra explained. "Then water is added and the mixture is put into wooden casks to ferment for eight to ten days."

Madison dabbed her brush on the inside of her arm, already knowing the color combination of paint it would take to bring the hue of the Jamaicans' skin to life. "And it's ready to be shipped?"

"Goodness, no." Lady Moran sat back in her chair and reached for the bamboo fan Punta had left for her. "The fermented mixture is then boiled again, and once it reaches a certain temperature, the alcohol is produced and it must be run through copper coils."

Madison pushed up the sleeves of her pale blue, untrained handkerchief dress. As she drew her paintbrush across the canvas, the silver bracelet her father had given her clinked pleasantly. It was very warm and humid, but she didn't mind. She had her paints and her aunt Kendra; it was a perfect day. Nothing could ruin it, except perhaps a run-in with Jefford, but he was said to be busy all day, occupied in Kingston with other English coffee growers on the island.

For the next hour, Madison painted and chatted with her aunt, her painting coming along quite nicely. She had the stove and the side of the rocky hill already fleshed out and was working on the first man, the one with the red handkerchief tied around his head.

Aunt Kendra grew quiet, and when Madison glanced her way, she saw that she had drifted to sleep. Madison smiled tenderly and then went back to her painting.

A wagon rolled in from the road at which the others had come and gone and she noted with interest that there were two Chinese men aboard. The wagon circled the clearing and backed up to the crude loading dock, but this time, the men who came from the boiling shed did not begin loading wooden casks.

One of the Chinese men barked something in his native language, then said something in broken English about loading the casks.

The Jamaican shook his head as if he didn't understand.

The taller of the Chinese men climbed over the wagon seat and impatiently gestured at the stack of casks on the loading dock and then the wagon.

The Jamaican crossed his arms over his bare chest and backed up, seating himself on one of the casks.

Suddenly, the hot humid jungle air seemed thick with tension. Madison set down her brush, wondering if she should wake her aunt. The two Chinese men were now shaking their fists and shouting in a mixture of their own language, English and a little French.

The Jamaican men at the stove ceased feeding the fire and drew closer to the loading dock.

The sound of the men's voices reverberated in the treetops, blocking out the jungle sounds. More Jamaicans were appearing on the loading dock, workers from the boiler room, she surmised.

"Aunt Kendra," Madison whispered. She moved slowly toward her aunt's chair, not wanting anyone to take notice of her.

"Aunt Kendra," she repeated, laying her hand on her aunt's arm.

Lady Moran woke with a start.

Madison spoke softly, keeping an eye on the men on the loading dock. Two more Jamaicans approached from the direction of the press shed and the man with the red handkerchief Madison had been painting jumped up onto the loading dock.

"There seems to be some disagreement going on here," Madison told her aunt quietly.

"What? What, dear?" Lady Moran mumbled, still half asleep.

Madison raised her arm slightly, pointing in the direction of the loading dock. "I think the Chinese men want the Jamaicans to load the casks, but they've refused. I fear there's going to be a fight."

"Oh, heavens," Lady Moran sighed, rising stiffly from her chair. "God save me from men and their never-ending crusade to declare their masculinity." She reached for Madison's arm. "It's really about the package in their breeches, you know."

Madison stared wide-eyed at her aunt, not quite sure how to respond.

"Well, come, come, dear, let's get ourselves to the wagon." Lady Moran tugged on Madison's arm.

"To the wagon? You're not going to step in and settle this matter?"

"Madison, love. Those are machetes those men wear on their belts. Have you a machete?"

"No." Madison walked her aunt slowly to the wagon. The mules were still harnessed and waited patiently.

"Neither have I. And unless I do, I am not stepping between men with machetes. Now, we shall climb into the wagon, draw it around and make haste home. I'll send someone for Jefford."

"But it might be too late," Madison cried, looking in the direction of the men on the dock. The Jamaican had not risen from his cask, but the men behind him were pressing closer.

Lady Moran used Madison's shoulder to push herself up into the wagon. As she did, she closed her eyes, cringing.

"Are you all right?" Madison breathed, still trying not to draw attention to them.

Lady Moran opened her eyes, easing down onto the wagon's bench seat. "I'm fine," she said, taking up the reins from where they'd been tied. "Now, run and get your canvas. I'll come around for you. Just the canvas, dear. I'll send Jefford back for the rest of your belongings."

Madison hurried back to the place beneath the trees where her easel stood. Just as she picked it up, she heard one of the men shout. She turned just in time to see the Jamaican on the cask lift his bare foot and give the closest Chinese man a push.

Like the fight she had seen in the sugarcane field earlier in the week, the men seemed to explode into a fistfight in an instant.

"Madison!" Lady Moran cried, driving the wagon toward her, the thick leather reins in her gloved hands. "Hurry, dear."

A horse and rider burst out of the trees with a shout and Madison pulled her canvas against her chest.

It was Jefford.

"I'm paying you men to work," he shouted above the melee. "Not fight. Now, cut it the hell out, or you'll all be picking pineapples for Thomblin!"

One of the Chinese men, already behind the momentum of a Jamaican fist, flew backward and hit the wagon hard on his bottom, but everyone else froze.

"Johnny Red!" Jefford barked, pointing at Madison's subject. "Get back to the stove. Barkley—"

The Jamaican who had spoken with the Chinese men first clambered to his feet, setting one of the rum casks upright. Miraculously, though several had rolled, none had been broken.

"Mr. Jefford, Chen say we have to load the casks." He pointed at the wagon. "We agreed. Jamaicans don't load Chink rum. Chen loads his own casks." He spat over the side of the dock in distaste.

"Lon, Chen!" Jefford shouted, reining his horse in a circle around the Chinese wagon. "Take your wagon and get out of here."

"Mr. Jefford, sir," the leader of the Chinese said. "We were sent to—"

"Tomorrow," Jefford interrupted. "The Chinese crew is scheduled for tomorrow. You all come tomorrow. You understand? And if Lo Fen has a problem with that, he needs to come see me." He looked around. "Get back to work, all of you!"

The two Chinese men climbed back into the wagon and made a hasty retreat. The men on the loading dock disappeared into the boiler room and the men at the stove returned to their tasks, as well. Only then did Jefford rein his horse around again and ride straight for Madison and the wagon.

And she hadn't even been certain he had realized she and his mother were there.

Jefford rode right up to her. "Inciting riots again, Madison?"

She scowled. "Certainly not. I thought you were in Kingston."

"Something came up. Now, tell me what the two of you were doing here without guards." He looked at his mother. "*You, at least,* ought to know better."

"Don't take that tone with me." Lady Moran glanced at her niece, lifting her nose to her son. "Madison and I were just preparing to return home."

"I would guess you were."

He leaped down off the horse he rode bareback, seeming as comfortable riding without the benefit of a saddle as he had been on the ship's deck. Madison wondered if there was anything this man didn't do well.

Jefford grabbed the canvas from Madison's hands.

"Careful, it's wet," she warned.

"Get in the wagon."

"Don't speak to me as if I'm a child or an imbecile!" she spat. "I want my paints and my easel." She started to march off, but he grabbed her by her arm, stopping her dead.

He drew his mouth near to her ear and suddenly she felt overheated. "Get in the wagon," he intoned.

"Whatever are we in a hurry for now? It's all over." She jerked her arm from his grasp. "This is entirely too much fuss over nothing."

"You'll think it's nothing until Chen and Lo return with twenty cousins with sharpened machetes," he hissed.

"Now, get in the wagon," he repeated, tying his horse to the back of the vehicle, then striding toward the easel.

Madison grabbed the side of the buckboard and managed to heave herself in before he returned to throw her paint box and easel behind the second seat.

Aunt Kendra threw one leg over the front seat with surprising nimbleness. "Sit here beside Madison," she told her son, patting the wooden bench.

"It's not necessary that—"

Jefford landed hard on the narrow seat beside her, his elbow brushing against the bare skin of her arm as he grabbed the reins.

Madison shrank back, completely unsettled, trying to keep any part of his body from touching hers.

The wagon jerked forward and they rolled past the two chairs still sitting beneath the banana palms. Madison spotted the picnic basket under the tree as they rolled away.

"Wait. The lunch basket." She half rose, pointing as he passed it.

He pulled her none too gently back into the seat beside him. "Madison," he grumbled. "I'll make you another damned picnic."

Sashi walked out the rear garden gate, glancing behind her. On her hip, she carried a wide-mouthed gathering basket woven in the traditional Ibo style. If anyone asked her what she was doing, she could easily explain that she'd left the garden to pick some flower blossoms for the house. Daily, she placed fresh flowers in the rooms, and while she often cut flowers from the garden, there were also many species outside the walls that she used to adorn the dining tables as well as her new mistress's and Lady Kendra's bedchambers.

Seeing no one but Madison busy painting up on her veranda, Sashi slipped around a crumbled stone wall that had been here before Windward Bay had been built. Gossip had it that the wall was all that remained of the original plantation house that was sacked and burned by pirates a hundred years earlier.

A hand snaked out and caught Sashi's wrist and she was unable to stifle a squeak of surprise.

"Shh," George murmured, pulling her into his arms.

Sashi dropped the basket, wrapping her arms around his neck. "You came."

"Of course I came. You got my note, didn't you?"

"This is wrong," she whispered. "You must not do this to your parents."

"Wrong?" He kissed her cheek. "How can it be wrong to love, Sashi?"

"You must not disobey your parents," she murmured, squeezing her eyes shut as she pressed her lips to his, unable to stop herself. "To disobey one's parents—"

"I haven't disobeyed them." He brushed the back of the silky black hair off her forehead. "Look at me, Sashi."

She opened her eyes to gaze into his, which were such a pale brown as to be golden in color. She was so afraid, and yet in a matter of two weeks, this white man had become her world. "Yes?"

"Never once has my father said, 'Do not fall in love with that Indian girl, Sashi.' Nor has he said, 'Do not go to Windward Bay and meet her in secret and cover her face with kisses.'" He proceeded to kiss her cheeks, her forehead, her nose.

Sashi giggled. "You know what I mean."

He brushed her cheek with his palm, his thumb caressing her lower lip. "I know what you mean," he said gently. "But I tell you, if my father will not accept you as the woman I want to marry, the woman I love, then I will gladly give up everything, the title, the money, the lands. I would give it all up for you, Sashi, my love. I would become a servant at your side just so that I can see your face each morning beside me in bed," he said passionately.

She covered his mouth with her small hand, frightened someone would hear him. "Shh. Do not say such things. You do not understand what good fortune you possess to have parents who love you, a sister…"

"I'm sorry. You're right." He stroked her shoulder, bared above her sari. "How insensitive of me to say such a thing when you are an orphan."

She shook her head. "It is more than that, my love." She touched his cheek, made dizzy just by the feel of his skin beneath her fingertips. The scent of him. "You have a duty to your father, to your mother and sister. To your ancestors."

He shook his head. "I don't care. I want to be with you. I want to be with you always. I'll tell my father about us and if he is unwilling to accept you, we'll just run away and be married."

"No, do not say that." She pressed her finger to his mouth, silencing him. "Promise me you will not tell him. Not yet."

"Sashi—"

"Promise me," she insisted. "Listen to me. There is something in the air here. Not just at Windward Bay. Change. I feel it." She gazed up into his eyes. "Promise me you will do nothing yet."

She held her breath as she waited.

At last, he gave a nod. "I'll wait, but not forever. I cannot wait forever for you, Sashi."

"Sashi," someone called from the garden.

"I must go." She tore herself from George's arms, leaning over to scoop up the fallen basket.

He caught her hand, pulled her to his chest and kissed her again. "I'll be back tomorrow night, if I can. Watch for me from Madison's balcony."

She shook her head. "The jungle is dangerous at night. You mustn't—"

"Sashi," the voice called from the garden, closer now. It was one of the other servant women.

"Tomorrow night," George insisted. He let her go and ran into the jungle.

Breathless, Sashi hurried for the garden gate. "I'm here," she cried. "Looking for flowers!"

Later that night Jefford stood outside his mother's bedroom door in the darkness, in indecision. He needed to talk to her, but he wasn't certain he was up to it tonight. Wasn't certain she was.

But it couldn't wait. He tapped at the door and it opened at once.

"Is she still awake?" he asked his mother's maid.

Maha glanced into the dimly lit room. "She is in bed, but restless tonight."

"I thought so. I saw her light from the garden."

Maha stepped back, opening the door farther to let him in.

"How was she today?" he asked quietly.

"Tired."

"But the pain?" he asked.

"Jefford!" his mother called, her tone short. "Jefford, is that you?"

He passed through the receiving room, into his mother's main bedchamber. The room was softly lit with candles. Incense burned and the flowing walls of shimmering fabric she had decorated the room with fluttered in the hot evening breeze.

Kendra pulled back the netting on her huge bed that she'd ordered be pushed nearly onto the veranda. "What are the two of you whispering about?"

Jefford leaned over the bed and kissed his mother's cheek. She looked almost emaciated in the thin sleeping gown.

"Oh, a kiss, is it?" she asked. "This must be serious." She looked to Maha. "You can go, dear. Go home to your husband. Jefford can attend to me."

Maha glanced at him. He nodded.

He waited until he heard the door close, then grabbed a low-backed chair his mother used in front of her dressing table and dragged it to the bed, turning it around and straddling it so he could lean forward on the back.

"We missed you at dinner, Madison and I."

He made no comment because he had neither the time nor the energy this evening to argue with his mother over her niece yet again. Besides, he'd already argued with one woman tonight, he didn't need to face another. Chantal had come to his room, cooing and swinging her hips, only to leave after pitching a perfectly good bottle of rum at him.

"I met with some of the men. There's been another uprising. This one north of Port Royal." Jefford leaned forward, pressing the heel of his hand to his forehead.

"So close to home," she murmured, looking away, then back at him. "How bad is it?"

"Bad."

"How bad, Jefford?" she repeated.

He lowered his hand, looking into his mother's eyes.

"Bad enough that I think we need to meet with the Rutherfords and Thomblin. Bad enough that it may be time we
make provisions should we have to escape."

14

Carlton stood barefoot on his veranda in his silk night robe and sipped his coffee, taking in the lovely vista before him. Summer in Jamaica was undeniably hot, but the flowers it produced in those scorching months was worth the inconvenience of high temperatures.

He gazed proudly at the new species of orchids that had begun to bloom in a bed just beyond the stone veranda. The *Ansellia africana* produced the most breathtaking chartreuse flowers with brown spots and a yellow lip. Kendra would most definitely be envious when she saw them.

That thought brought a sour taste to his mouth and he spat out his coffee. There was a growing restlessness, according to Jefford Harris. Carlton paid very little attention to such goings-on; he had too many other concerns these days, mainly bill collectors and unhappy merchants.

Tonight Harris had called a *secret* meeting with his mother and the Rutherfords, and Carlton had been invited. Something about a plan, should the families find it necessary to evacuate the island. Carlton thought the man was paranoid; the natives had been fighting for years, ever since the slaves had gained their independence in the thirties. If the Englishmen would just have the balls to shoot a few coolies, hang a couple of Haitian bucks, they would all quiet down and return to the fields and stop talking of better working conditions and fair pay.

He sighed. Unfortunately, he didn't feel he was in a position to slight Lady Moran. She had too much influence on the island. It was her friendship that kept him afloat some months.

He poured the remainder of his coffee into the grass, taking care not to spill any on the orchids. So, he would dress in his best coat, meet with the neighbors and listen to what Harris had to say. Besides, if the natives did start burning down English homes in earnest, he certainly had no desire to get caught up in the fray. He was not entirely opposed to relocating at this point, as it was possible he had outstayed his welcome in Jamaica, anyway. With talk of seizing his plantation and selling it at the auction block to pay his debts, it might, indeed, be time to move on to a new endeavor.

Carlton stepped back into his bedchamber, his gaze drifting to the bed. "Jonathan," he bellowed with annoyance.

A pretty quadroon youth wearing short, tight breeches and no shirt appeared at once in the doorway. "My lord?" He kept his eyes fixed on the tiled floor.

"Get these sheets off this bed at once. Burn them!"

"Yes, my lord." The boy ran across the room and grabbed a fistful of bloody sheets.

Carlton turned his back. "Put fresh linens on the bed and then draw my bath."

"Yes, my lord," the servant mumbled, backing his way out of the room. "At once, my lord."

* * *

Madison sat in the garden under the shade of a giant elephant-ear palm, dabbing at a painting with the tip of a small paintbrush. Two little girls dressed in colorful dresses, sitting on the upper veranda, bare brown legs dangling, almost came alive as their mothers sat behind them snapping beans.

In the little more than a month since Madison had arrived in Jamaica, she thought she had adapted well. More and more often, she woke in the morning to dress in one of the free-fitting brightly colored gowns that her aunt seemed to own in an endless supply. In the light clothing Madison felt as if she were more a part of the world around her and that world seemed to be accepting her. Everywhere she went to paint, the men and women and children who worked the land, the mills and the warehouse seemed to accept her as easily as they accepted the lizards that crawled across their bedroom floors and the parrots that squawked outside their houses on early mornings.

At the sound of Jefford's voice, Madison shifted her gaze without turning her head. If he knew she was looking at him, it would only increase his already-too-large ego.

Things had been very strange at Windward Bay for the last week, and Madison was curious as to what was going on. The usually lax household seemed to be following schedules and there was a great deal of bustling about, putting rooms in order and reckoning provisions. Aunt Kendra and Jefford had been acting oddly, too, but when Madison questioned them, they both assured her there was nothing to worry about.

That made her worry.

Then, a couple of days ago, her aunt and Jefford rode

off in the carriage in the late afternoon, saying they had an engagement in Kingston. When she had asked her aunt if she could accompany them, Lady Moran had insisted she would only be bored with the tedious meeting with a barrister and promised to take her to the town another day when they could "shop properly." She had the distinct feeling they weren't going to Kingston at all, but, so far, she had not been able to discover where they had gone.

Out of the corner of her eye, Madison saw Jefford start through the garden. Tipping her straw bonnet so that he could not see her face, she watched him. He was barefoot, in breeches, carrying a white shirt over his shoulder.

Sashi had mentioned that there was a small waterfall and pool a short distance from the garden where many of the servants at Windward Bay swam. Watching Jefford walk through the rear gate, she wondered if that was where he was going.

She wiped the perspiration that gathered above her upper lip, musing how pleasant it would be to dip her feet in the water, then rose, grabbing her sketch pad and a small tin of pencils from beneath her stool. She glanced around the garden. No one was paying any attention to her. Aunt Kendra was asleep on a lounge chair under the veranda off the dining room, and the two women snapping beans had disappeared into the house, with their daughters, probably headed for the adjacent kitchen.

Pushing up the sleeves of her white dotted Swiss bodice, Madison casually walked down the stone path toward the rear gate. As she went, she studied the bright blooming flowers and broad-leafed ferns with great interest. At the arched gateway, she took one last look at her sleeping aunt and stepped around the corner.

"Miss Madison?"

Madison stopped short, spinning around. "Punta. Heavens, you startled me." Clutching her sketch pad and pencils, she pressed her hand to her pounding heart.

"You are going somewhere, miss? I should walk you?"

"No…no, you needn't escort me. I was…" She glanced up, her gaze following the path into the jungle. "I was just hurrying to catch up with Jefford." She pulled the sketch pad from her chest. "To…show him this sketch of this plant…he was interested in seeing."

Punta nodded, knitting his dark brows. "Hurry, then, miss." He pointed in the direction Jefford had gone. "I am certain you will catch up. You know you must turn at the fork." He lifted his left hand.

"The left fork, yes." Madison gave a nod as she hurried past Punta. "Thank you!"

Madison could still see the roofline of the house behind her when she took the left fork in the road, and hadn't gone much farther when she began to hear the faint sound of rushing water. The terrain at once became rockier and Madison slowed her pace.

The sound of rushing water grew louder, and she followed an even narrower path to her right that seemed well traveled. Ahead, the trees thinned and she caught a glimpse of a lovely waterfall. Though small, perhaps only as high as the roof of Windward Bay's manor house, the clear, blue-green water cascading off the rock was no less impressive. And at a distance, Madison could feel that the air, filled with mist, was cooler, surprising relief on such a hot day.

Nearing the clearing that must have been the pool Sashi had told her about, Madison ducked off the path and circled. At the sound of a male voice, she froze. Another voice joined in, one definitely female.

Damn him! Jefford was meeting Chantal here. Her face suddenly burned with heat.

Splashes and a feminine giggle filled the air… She reached out to part a large fern to gaze over the pool. To her astonishment, she saw George Rutherford and Sashi.

George leaped in the air, flashing pale white buttocks, and Sashi squealed with glee, turning in a circle to reveal her small bare breasts. Madison released the fern leaves in shock.

"Looks like they beat us here, eh?"

Madison spun around to find Jefford standing right behind her, still bare-chested, his shirt over his shoulder.

"I…" She looked in the direction the sounds were coming from, then back at Jefford, utterly mortified. "I was—"

"Hell, Madison, will you relax? It's hot and we all had the same idea." He grabbed her hand and pulled her back into the jungle. "However, you should not be here alone. Not even this close to the house. I specifically told Punta—"

"It wasn't his fault." She followed him, ducking under a leaf the length of her arm that he held up for her. "I lied and told him I was going with you, to show you one of my sketches," she admitted sheepishly. "Please don't be angry with him."

"You know, once upon time, on this island, English landowners chained their female slaves to the house to keep them from wandering. I know we have some old fetters around the place somewhere. Surely that would keep you homebound where we can keep an eye on you."

To her surprise, she laughed. "Where are you taking me?" She glanced around, seeing that they had not returned to the path but were going deeper into the jungle.

"You wanted to swim, didn't you?"

"No. I—"

"Oh, come on, Madison. I don't have the energy for a fight today. Let's go for a swim. Then we can go back to the manor house and you can infuriate me about one thing or another, and then you can get your pretty hackles up and we can go back to our daily practice."

Still clutching her sketchbook and pencil tin in her arm, her other hand in his, she stared at him, not sure what to say. "You don't think we should—"

"What? Separate those two? The English gentleman and the Indian servant? By the looks of what we saw back there, I'd say it's already too late, wouldn't you?"

"If Lord Rutherford finds out—"

"He'll blow his chimney. Probably send George packing back to London, or maybe a world tour. I know." He shrugged. "But I think they're in love."

Jefford turned away to look in the direction they were going, and Madison studied the back of his dark head. Once again, Jefford Harris had taken her utterly by surprise. A romantic? The man was a romantic? This same man who told his mother he didn't want to marry? The same man who swore he would never bring children into the dreadful world they lived it?

"Here we are. My secret pool, I like to call it." He glanced over his shoulder at her. "I'm sure it's not that big a secret, but it's far enough away from the waterfall that we won't—" he cleared his throat "—*disturb* Georgie and your maid."

He released her hand as they stepped into a clearing, much like the one that had surrounded the other pool and waterfall.

He started to wade into the water. "Now, come on, it feels great."

She set her sketch pad and tin box down in the grass beside his shirt and watched him wade until he was knee deep.

"Come on!"

"I don't know how to swim."

He groaned and flipped onto his stomach, gliding through the water.

"Just where would I swim?" she asked indignantly, walking to the edge to kick off her thin kidskin slippers. She wasn't going in the water; it was completely inappropriate, but there was no reason why she couldn't get her feet wet.

"Fair enough. So take some of those clothes off and get in. I'll teach you."

She clutched her bodice. "Take off my clothes?"

He stood up, water streaming from his dark hair, which touched his shoulders when it was wet. "Not all of them, unless you want to, of course. To that I would not be entirely opposed." He grinned.

She widened her eyes, trying hard to be offended.

"Look, Madison, I know very well you've got twenty-two layers of frilly underthings beneath that skirt. Just pull off the first two layers."

Madison hesitated. She couldn't believe she was actually considering stripping to her undergarments and wading into a pool of water that probably had snakes in it. Her mother wouldn't just faint at hearing such a thing; she'd probably fall over dead of a weakened heart.

"Turn around," she called to Jefford.

"Madison, have you forgotten when you were sick on the ship? I saw you in far less—"

"I said, turn around this instant or I'm going back."

With a heave of his shoulders, he turned away. "You can't find your way back without me."

"You just stay like that." Madison unhooked her pale green dotted Swiss skirt and stepped out of it, and then removed her white bodice. She was already bare-legged, without stockings, and had forgone her corset and any type of bustle weeks ago, but she still wore a thin crinoline under her English dresses and then a combination of single-piece drawers and camisole. It made sense to remove her crinoline, but once she was wet, the pale peach combination would be nearly transparent.

"My skin is beginning to prune," Jefford sang. "For the love of God, Madison, stop being so priggish. You live in the tropics now." He waved one hand. "Get in the water."

Madison stepped out of the crinoline, and before she had a chance to think better of her decision, ran into the water. It was colder than she had expected and she gasped. At just above her knees, she tripped and fell headlong.

She hit the surface and went under, and a hand clasped her arm and pulled her up. "There you go." He patted her back heartily. "You've already learned lesson number one in swimming." Jefford grinned. "Keep your mouth shut."

Madison laughed, coughed and choked again. "I'm all right."

"Of course you are." He let go of her arm. "Now, let's go out a little deeper."

She cautiously waded out with him, covering her breasts with an arm and her hand.

"The whole point here," he explained, "is to stretch out over the water, arms and legs extended, and propel yourself forward." He laid out in front of her and paddled a foot or two. "Or backward," he said, going in the opposite direction.

"Why don't you sink?" she asked skeptically.

"Lots of reasons relating to bone mass and the weight of water in relationship to your weight, but mostly because your lungs are full of air; they act like a balloon." He stood up, water streaming over his bare, suntanned chest. "Now you try it."

"All right." She took a deep breath. "But don't touch me." She raised both hands.

"Wouldn't dream of it. Not even if you sink like a stone."

She scowled. "Maybe you could help me a little in that instance?"

He burst into laughter. "Come on, Madison, show me you can swim."

She took another deep breath, trying to fill her lungs as full of air as possible. Then she squeezed her eyes shut, stretched out her arms and lifted her feet…and promptly began to sink.

Before Madison had time to panic, though, she felt a hand beneath her stomach. He barely lifted her, but the feel of his hand, knowing he was there, made her relax and she felt herself float upward. She gave a kick, throwing her hands outward and was amazed to find that she glided forward.

She did it again, lifting her head, turning it the way she had seen Jefford do it, to get a breath of air. He slid his hand out from under her, but she barely noticed.

"I'm doing it," she cried. "I'm doing it!" With her last word she caught a mouth full of water and sputtered.

"Easy there." He caught her around her waist and she stood up laughing and choking.

"I did it. First time."

"I don't think I've ever seen anyone catch on that quickly," he agreed, pushing a wet hank of blond hair away from her eyes. "Of course, I *am* an excellent instructor."

"Of course you are," she laughed, still trying to get her breath. "Now, show me how to do that on your back. The way you were a minute ago."

"What? This?" He fell back with a great splash and she turned away, laughing.

Jefford then proceeded to float on his back, paddling in a circle around her.

"Yes, that," she said, turning in a circle to watch him. The water felt so good. It was sharp and cool and the sun was warm on her face.

"It's easy enough." He popped up. "Just lie back like this." He wrapped his arm around her and eased her backward. "But you have to relax."

Trusting him utterly, she let go of her weight and fell into his arm, allowing her bare feet to rise up. She closed her eyes, unable to deny how good his secure arm felt around her in the cool, weightless water.

"That's it. Perfect," he said quietly.

He still held her in his arm and when she opened her eyes, he was looking down at her.

"You look like a mermaid, like this, you know," he said quietly. "With that golden blond hair flowing around your head, that serene smile on your face and those luscious breasts."

Madison knew he had crossed the line of propriety, even for the tropics of Jamaica, yet his words sent a surge of heat through her.

"And here we are again," he said.

She lifted her lashes, boldly gazing into his dark eyes. "Here we are again," she whispered, mesmerized.

Jefford lowered his head slowly over hers, her lips parted, and she sighed as his mouth covered hers. *Such a perfect fit,* she marveled.

His tongue touched her wet lip...the edge of her teeth...then the roof of her mouth.

Madison slipped her arms up over his wet shoulders,

around his thick, corded neck, drawing herself closer, molding her wet body to his. The water, the jungle, seemed to swirl around them. He tasted of his morning coffee and some emotion she could not place.

Somehow Jefford's hand found the nub of her wet breast, and she moaned in shock at how good his touch felt through the wet cambric of her underclothing.

She was breathless…needed air. She arched her neck, pulling her head back.

"Madison," he panted, drawing his mouth over her chin, down her throat. Lower.

She knew she had to stop him and yet she couldn't find the words. Her legs, her arms, wouldn't respond.

He dragged his mouth over the wet fabric of the under-garment and she cried out in revelation as his mouth closed over her breast.

Madison panted, threading her fingers through his wet hair. She meant to push him away and yet she only drew his mouth to the other nipple. "Jefford, please," she murmured.

"Madison, I keep dreaming about you," he said, his voice low and husky. He rubbed his warm, rough cheek against her breast sending trills of pleasure through her body. "I keep telling myself—"

"Bastard!" a shriek echoed from the bank.

"Chantal," Jefford shouted. "Don't you dare!"

Madison turned to see the Haitian woman had a fairly good-size rock in her hand.

"Chantal—"

The woman heaved the rock and Jefford leapt in the water, dragging Madison with him. The rock hit with sur-prising accuracy in the swirl of water where she and Jef-ford had just been standing.

"Ou manti!" Chantal shouted from the bank, scrambling to pick up another rock. *"Ou vole!"*

"I didn't lie to you," he called back angrily. "I never made any promises. You know that."

Chantal lifted another rock onto her shoulder and Madison pushed herself away from Jefford, her arms wrapped around her chest, and waded toward the shore.

"Madison, wait."

Chantal heaved the rock. Jefford cursed her and dove in the opposite direction of the missile.

"Chantal, listen to me!" Jefford barked, wading toward the far shore.

Armed with another rock, this one nearly the size of her head, Chantal ran along the shore, toward him.

Madison stumbled onto the dry grass, grabbed her clothes and shoes and darted into the jungle, so upset she was shaking.

"Madison, will you please?" Jefford called after her. "Just wait one—"

Chantal's shriek was followed by another splash, and the last thing Madison heard before she ran down the path was Jefford cursing in a mixture of English, French and Creole.

15

Before Jefford reached the house, he was waylaid by one of the Rutherfords' overseers. The man relayed that two men in a cane field had gotten into a fistfight, which had turned into a knife fight, and when Lord Rutherford had come upon the clash and tried to break it up, they had both turned on him. They knocked him from his horse and the older man had been forced to shoot one of the men to save himself. A riot had nearly ensued and the overseer had barely gotten himself and his lordship away safely.

Jefford had rounded up George, still frolicking in the water with Sashi, and they had ridden immediately to the Rutherford plantation. Once Jefford was convinced the older man was shaken but not harmed, he had left guards behind to keep watch over the family. He had then ridden out, with his own men, to find the instigators. Both perpetrators had gone into hiding; the villages were in turmoil, and Jefford was sorely concerned with what might come of the Haitian's death at Lord Rutherford's hands.

Jefford didn't make it back to Windward Bay until after

dinnertime, only to find his mother already in bed and Madison locked up in her chambers.

"Madison!" Jefford banged impatiently on her bed-chamber door.

Earlier that afternoon it had taken him a while to calm Chantal down and send her home sulking, with nothing settled between them. But he knew now his relationship with the Haitian beauty was over. And not because of Madison. He had simply tired of her, or something like that. He just had to figure out how to tell her gently, assure her that she would always be well cared for, and then get her out of his hair.

He rapped on the door again, then closed his fist, hitting it harder. "Madison, I know you're in there. I saw your lamps from the garden. This is childish, now open the damned door!"

The door opened suddenly.

Sashi lowered her gaze, speaking softly. "Miss Madison says to tell you she is not feeling well, sir."

He gazed over her head. He could see two easels with paintings propped on them in the lamplight. One oil painting, of the rum distillery, was quite good. The other was covered by a colorful drape of fabric. He could also see a chair with the dress Madison had worn today thrown casually over the back. No sign of her, though.

He was half tempted just to tell Sashi to step aside. If he barreled in, Madison would be forced to speak to him. Not that he was really sure what he was going to say. Jefford knew as well as she did that they were ill matched—fire and water. More like fire and fire…

The fact was, he had no need for Madison's kind of woman, and she required a proper husband. A proper English husband. Not a man like him, half one man, half another, belonging to two peoples and yet none. He didn't care what his mother envisioned; he and Madison were not destined to be man and wife. He wasn't sure he could make a marriage work with any woman. He would only end up making Madison unhappy and he couldn't do that to her. He couldn't do it to his mother.

Jefford supposed what he wanted to tell Madison was that he promised to stay away from her. There would be no more interludes like the one that had transpired between them in the water. He pressed his lips together, closing his eyes, trying not to think about the taste of her mouth, the feel of her breast beneath his fingertips.

"Mr. Jefford?" Sashi said softly.

He opened his eyes. "I... Please tell Madison that I'm sorry she's ill. Tell her...tell her I'll talk to her tomorrow."

Sashi dipped her head in deference. "Yes, sir."

Annoyed, worried, Jefford checked on his mother and was relieved to find her sleeping. He dismissed her maid, turned down her lamps and then retired to his own bedchamber.

Alone in his room, he stripped off his sweaty, dirty clothing, half considering returning to the water pool in the dark to bathe, but fearing it might only conjure up more thoughts of Madison naked in his arms, tasting her, touching her... Instead, he settled with a quick washcloth dragged over his body, then poured himself a healthy portion of rum and stretched out on his bed. He sipped his mother's brew and, by lamplight, studied the sketch Madison had made in the garden back at Boxwood Manor in London. It seemed like a long time ago, now, the first time he had seen her...

Jefford groaned, threw back the last of the rum and turned out his lamp. Punching his goose-down pillow, he settled down to sleep.

* * *

In the middle of the night, a sound at the window startled Jefford out of a deep sleep.

"Mr. Jefford! Mr. Jefford!" someone called from the garden.

A torched burned behind the glass and the voice called again, followed by an urgent banging.

Naked, Jefford sprang out of bed, grabbed a knife from beneath the edge of the mattress and ran for the French doors of his bedchamber that opened onto the garden. "Punta?"

Jefford unlatched the door and pushed it open.

"The Rutherford plantation, Mr. Jefford. It has been set on fire. There are men—many men—marching in the jungle. They have guns and knives."

"Where are Lord and Lady Rutherford and their children?" Jefford grunted as he yanked on a pair of breeches he found on the floor.

"In the jungle. I spoke to Lord Rutherford's man. The family is safe, but they flee with nothing but their lives."

Jefford yanked a shirt over his head and sat on the edge of the bed to pull on his hose. Damn! It had come as he had feared it would. Flames of hatred had ignited, and they would not be extinguished until the island soil was drenched in blood. "Do you know where they're going?"

"To the place they are to meet, was all Lord Rutherford's man would say." Punta followed him with his black gaze. "I thought you would know what that meant. Where that was."

"Yes. Good. Were these Haitians?" It was a Haitian man Rutherford killed.

Punta nodded, obviously scared. But he was a brave man and Jefford would see he was rewarded for his loyalty when this was over.

"They were Haitians. But also Chinese. There was fighting among both groups. They want to kill the Englishmen. They want to kill one another."

"How many?" He jerked on his boots and stood.

Punta shook his head. "I don't know. Many. More than a hundred, perhaps twice that. I thought they might see me—kill me. I came to tell you at once."

Jefford cursed beneath his breath as he went to the old sea chest and pulled out a bag he had packed days earlier. It was all he needed.

"Punta, there is a possibility we will have to flee Jamaica. I will send word to Kingston for soldiers, but it may be too late by the time they reach here."

The Indian man's eyes filled with moisture. "Mr. Jefford, I do not understand. Those that set upon the house, killed innocents. They came for the English, but—"

"Punta, listen to me." He grabbed the man by both wrists. "I am going to the Rutherford plantation to see for myself how bad it is—"

"Mr. Jefford, no. You do not—"

"Punta, there isn't time for this. I need you to go wake Lady Kendra and tell her what you have told me. Then I need you to go get your wife and your sons and come back here. We cannot take many with us, only the immediate household. Those of the immediate household who wish to join us." He walked by the nightstand, backed up and grabbed the pad with Madison's Roman ruin sketch and stuffed it in the canvas bag on his shoulder. "If this is as bad as I fear it might be, we'll have to leave the island."

"Leave? Go where?" Punta turned to his master, who was already headed out the door.

"Home, Punta," Jefford called over his shoulder.

* * *

Not yet fully awake, Madison sensed commotion around her before she actually heard it.

"Madison, Miss Madison," Sashi whispered, shaking her. "Please wake."

Madison opened her eyes to find several lamps lit in the room and a pile of canvas and leather bags packed, waiting beside the door to the hall. Beyond her bedchamber, she could hear dogs barking and servants running down the halls. There were voices everywhere, in the hall, below in the garden; people were talking in frightened whispers, others barking orders.

"Sashi, what is it?" Madison scrambled from her bed, still only half awake. "Aunt Kendra isn't—"

"Miss Kendra is well."

The servant turned away and Madison realized she was fully dressed in a sari and open-toed leather shoes. Madison's gaze flitted to the clock on the mantel. It was one in the morning. "What—"

"Miss Kendra says you must dress. Hurry," Sashi interrupted, grabbing up an armful of bed linens from the bed. "We must meet in the garden in half an hour."

"We who?" Madison stood barefoot on the tile floor, slowly turning in a circle. "Sashi, why are you packing? Where are we going?"

Sashi continued to calmly stuff the bed linens into cloth bags. "There has been an uprising of the workers. They have attacked the Rutherford plantation. Set fire and murdered servants."

"No! The Rutherfords?" Her breath caught in her throat. "Sashi—George?"

Tears sprang in Sashi's dark eyes and she looked back at the bag of linens in her hands. "They have all escaped, the family, but many in their household were killed. A fire, out of control, burns there now."

"If the workers have attacked the Rutherfords, why then are we—" Madison stopped short, looking down at Sashi again. "We're in danger? They might come here?" she breathed.

"We go tonight to a place where we will be safe. If the men who have done these evil things do not come here, we will return home," the maid explained.

Madison reached for the skirt she had worn the day before and stepped into it, pulling it up over her short chemiselike sleeping gown. "And if they come here?"

"We will go."

"Go?" Madison pulled the wrinkled white bodice on and fumbled with the buttons. "Go where? There will be no place on this island that we will be safe."

Sashi tossed a pair of thin cotton stockings to her mistress. "There will be no place in Jamaica where we will be safe," she repeated.

Tears filled Madison's eyes as she dropped onto the edge of a chair and pulled on her stockings. "I have to talk to my aunt. I have to talk to Aunt Kendra."

Sashi hustled by, dropping a pair of soft kid-leather boots at Madison's feet. "Put these on. Get a bonnet."

"Yes. Yes, of course." Madison was moving faster now, her mind reeling. "I'll go see Aunt Kendra and I'll meet you downstairs in the garden."

Her boots on her feet, Madison left her chambers and ran down the long corridor. Servants were running up and down the hall, furniture was being carried out, and bags full of clothing were being thrown off the verandas. It sounded as if there were as many people in the garden below as in the house.

The double doors to Lady Moran's suite of rooms were ajar. Madison pushed through. "Aunt Kendra."

"Yes, dear," Lady Moran sang. She sounded remarkably calm.

Madison threw back a curtain of jewel-colored transparent silk draperies to find her aunt fully dressed in one of her caftans, a bright green turban tied around her head. She was dumping a casket of glittering jewels into a pillowcase.

"Ah, you're dressed." Aunt Kendra smiled, looking her up and down. "I'm glad to see that you're not hysterical." She dropped the rosewood jewel box on the bed and carried the pillowcase to Maha, who was on her hands and knees, packing a leather satchel.

"Hysterical, no, of course not," Madison said, trying to pull her tangled hair back with a drooping ribbon she'd worn to bed. "But I don't understand what's happening. Sashi says we might have to leave Jamaica, but everyone is acting like—"

"No need to get one's undergarments in a twist, my dear." Lady Moran splayed a ring encrusted hand. "We've all known for a long time that this day might come." She walked away.

Madison followed her, trying to stay calm. "No, no, I didn't know this day might come."

"This is probably much ado about nothing." Lady Moran began to pick pots of face cream and powder off her dressing table and drop them in a wooden crate left on a chair. "Just a good housecleaning is all that will be the result, most likely. I'm sure Jefford will be home in no time to say that Punta's report was greatly exaggerated. A one-hundred-man mob and the burning Rutherford manor house will become four drunken pineapple pickers and a fire in a garbage receptacle."

"Jefford has gone to the Rutherford plantation?" Madison gripped her aunt's arm. "Sashi said the mob wanted to kill Englishmen. Surely it's not safe—"

"There, there, dear." Lady Moran patted her niece's back. "Have no fear. It would take more than a little riot to harm our Jefford. He'll be back shortly for us, and if he is not, he'll meet us at the predetermined rendezvous point. I would suspect the Rutherfords are already there. As is Carlton. I imagine Carlton was there at the first curl of smoke."

Madison pressed her hand to her chest to still the fluttering there. "That was my next question. Lord Thomblin is coming with us, isn't he?"

"He is, though Jefford is not pleased." Suddenly seeming irritated, Lady Moran lifted the wooden box of toiletries and dropped it into Madison's trembling arms. "I certainly cannot leave him here. Carlton is what he is, but still a friend. Now, carry that to the door on your way out. I'll see you in the garden momentarily. There are wagons to transport us, but it's wise you do have sturdy shoes just in case we have to make a run for it in the jungle."

Madison held the wooden box tightly in her arms. "Make a run for it?" she whispered, her limbs suddenly frozen.

"Do not just stand there, silly girl," Maha ordered, brushing by her. "Take the box to the garden and send one of Punta's lazy boys up for the rest. We must hurry before the mob reaches here!"

Madison took a great gulp of air and hurried out of the room. On the way down the stairs to the garden, she bumped into a little boy, seated crying on one step. By the time she figured out he was one of Lela's grandsons, got him safely to his grandmother and reached the garden,

Aunt Kendra was already there, shouting commands. Besides Sashi and Maha, there was Maha's husband and daughter, Punta and his wife and several of the young Indian maids. There was no sign of Jefford.

Madison dropped her aunt's wooden box into the rear of the closest wagon. "Aunt Kendra, isn't Jefford back?"

"No, but we must press on." The older woman allowed her faithful manservant to help her into one of the mule-drawn wagons.

One of Punta's strapping teenage sons burst out of the darkness, leaping over a bed of Lady Kendra's beloved orchids. "Father, they're coming! We saw them coming. So many men!" He panted. "They are crazy drunk carrying torches. They mean to burn Windward Bay to ashes, as well!"

"Miss Kendra, it is time." Punta looked to his mistress, his dark eyes filled with concern.

"Yes, yes, we're going. Jefford will simply have to catch up. He might already be at the meeting place, for all we know. Madison, load up." She eyed her niece. "And try not to look so frightened, dear. These turns of events are what life is made of."

Madison gripped the side of the wagon, looking up at her aunt. Jamaican and Haitian servants ran everywhere. Now that they had completed the tasks that might be the last they ever performed at Windward Bay, they were in a hurry to return to their villages before the mob fell on the house.

One of Punta's sons climbed into the wagon and took the reins from Lady Moran. Madison, a little dazed, wandered back, passing the four wagons loaded with goods.

"Miss Kendra!" A familiar female voice punctuated the last orders Punta shouted to the servants taking their leave.

Chantal burst through the open rear gate of the garden, running down the path for the wagons. "Miss Kendra."

"Chantal, you should return to your village." Lady Moran slipped on a pair of pale beige kid-leather gloves. "It is not safe to be here when the mob reaches these walls."

"I cannot, miss." Panting hard from running, Chantal threw herself over the wagon wheel. "Please, let me come with you. Those here, they know who Chantal is. What she has done. Please, missy," she begged, clenching her hands together. "They will kill me. Let me come with you."

Lady Moran frowned. "I do suppose you're right. Climb in." She hooked a ringed thumb. "But I swear, you cause an ache in my backside and I'll toss you to the fishes before we clear the harbor."

Chantal was coming with them?

Madison turned away, seething. Frightened. Confused. Where were they going? She couldn't possibly return to London, not to the sheltered life she had led there.

Her paintings! Her paints! Her canvases!

She turned for the outside staircase, grabbing her skirts in both hands, and bounded up the stairs, the sounds of the wagons rolling out of the garden behind her.

Halting at the fork in the road, Jefford rubbed the stinging sweat from his eyes and shifted the rifle strap back on his shoulder. "I want the three of you to go on to the meeting place without me," he told the men who had accompanied him to the Rutherford plantation…what was left of it. One of them was Punta's oldest son, Ojar. Another, an Indian cousin of Punta's, and the last, a Haitian man. None had wives or children and had all chosen to accompany Jefford, wherever he might go.

"I'll go to the house to see that everyone is gone, then meet you at the cave near Port Royal."

"They are on our heels," Ojar panted. "We must hurry."

"You heard me," Jefford grunted, turning away.

"Sir, a light?" Ojar held out one of the torches.

"I'll be safer in the dark. Now, hurry. I don't want you bumping into that mob—none of you would escape with your lives."

Jefford jogged down the familiar path to the house, his mind spinning, knowing he had done everything in his power to aid the laborers' plight. For years now, he'd known the time had come and gone for the English in Jamaica and that there was little chance he and his mother would be able to live out their lives on the island. But he loved this jungle paradise so much that he had hoped...

He jogged through Windward Bay's front gate and then the enormous front door, left ajar, into the house that was dark and silent. Inside the doorway, his fingers found wooden matches in a tin box and he lit an oil lamp. He removed it from its bracket on the wall and walked through the open entrance hall.

The house was filled with ghosts. As he walked down the corridor, gazing at the pale pink walls, he realized he had never been alone in the house before. Even though it had been just he and his mother for as long as he could remember—Lord Moran had died when he was three—the house had always been filled with servants. As a child, he had played with Punta's sons, with sons of neighboring English families. Families smart enough to get out of Jamaica before they were burned out, or killed, he thought wryly.

As he passed the front staircase, a sound from above startled him and he froze. Sliding his rifle down off his shoulder so that he cradled it in his arm, ready to fire, Jefford grabbed the polished English walnut newel and hurried up the stairs, moving soundlessly.

The noise upstairs grew louder. A scrape of furniture, a rattle of tin, someone up there moving hastily. Stealing what they could before the angry laborers reached the house and burned it to the ground.

Jefford eased down the hall, set down the lamp and, raising his rifle, slipped around the corner, into the room.

A flash of color and motion made him lay his finger on the trigger.

Madison, down on her hands and knees, turned in fright. "How dare you sneak up on me like that!"

"Madison!" He jerked the rifle, lifting the muzzle skyward. "What the hell are you doing here?"

16

"You scared me!" she shouted, her heart pounding, her hands shaking. "I...dropped my paints." She reached out to grab a paint pot under the edge of the bed that had been stripped of its linens.

Jefford went down on one knee, pushing his hair from his eyes. "Madison, where's everyone else?"

"They're headed for the meeting place. I was going to catch up. I just came back—"

"My mother doesn't know you're here?" He began to snatch the spilled paint pots and brushes off the floor and throw them into the basket. "Madison, do you even know where the meeting place is?" He was shouting at her now. "Do you know how to get there?"

"I only meant to take a moment!" Her lower lip quivered. "Everything was in such a state of confusion! Lela's grandson got separated from his mother and—"

"Madison, it's all right. Now, listen to me. We have to get out of here. The mob is almost here."

"I understand." She pulled from him and grabbed her

paint basket. Taking an empty silk pillowcase, she dumped the paints and brushes into it, the same way she had seen Kendra dump her jewels. "And just the canvases on the bed. That's all I need."

"We can't carry all this." He walked to the bed, picking up a large canvas with the Chinese gardener painted in the foreground of a patch of pale blue orchids. "These are all excellent, but—"

"I can't leave them behind, not if we can never come back."

"Fine." Jefford groaned. "We can take a few of the small ones, but that's it." He hesitated, another canvas in his hand. "It's me. You painted me…from memory?" He looked at her.

Embarrassed, Madison snatched the portrait from his hand. "I can take the one from the sugarcane field and the one from the distillery." She picked them up, piling them on top of the portrait. "There should be a small one there of the garden, too, with dragonflies in one corner."

Turning her back on him, upset that he had seen the portrait she'd painted of him, the one she had meant to be of Carlton, she laid them down on a curtain and began to wrap them up.

"Here it is. Dragonflies."

She took the canvas without looking at him and wrapped them all up by tying the four corners together. "I can carry these. It's no problem." She reached down to get the pillowcase of paints.

"Give me that," he groaned, taking the bulkier of the canvases. "Anything else? Jewelry, clothes? Other feminine baubles?"

"Just the paints. I think Sashi packed a few other things for me."

"Good." He grabbed the oil lamp off the bedside table

and strode away. "Because we need to get the hell out of here."

Madison followed Jefford down a rear staircase and out a side door. He was headed for the kitchen, adjacent to the main house. There seemed to be a glow of light coming from the northwest and she could have sworn she heard voices.

"Jefford," she whispered.

"I know." He pushed the kitchen door open. "Put some food in the sack." He dropped the lamp onto the work-table in the middle of the open room. "I'll get water."

She grabbed biscuits from a basket and stuffed them into the pillowcase, followed by some mangos and papayas.

He turned a spigot on a wooden barrel and began to fill one of the tin canteens in a bag left on a hook by the door for just this purpose.

The sounds grew closer.

"Jefford!" she whispered.

"Let's go." He pushed the canteen into her sack, slung the rifle on his shoulder, picked up her makeshift bag of paintings and reached for her hand. Clasping it tightly, he led her to the opposite door.

The light was brighter behind them now, the voices louder. They darted out the door, into the garden. Jefford ran through a bed of herbs Lela had so lovingly care for, crushing plants beneath his feet. Shaking from head to toe, Madison ran a step behind him, looking through the garden, toward the front of the house. Figures with torches ran through one of the side-yard arches. Glass shattered.

"Madison, they mustn't see us," Jefford said under his breath.

The garden flared with bright light as the mob spilled

into the yard. Some were in the house, and she heard splintering of wood.

Jefford and Madison darted around an elephant-ear plant, headed for the main rear gate, but instead of following the path, Jefford yanked her to the left.

"Aunt Kendra went that way," Madison cried.

"It's not safe now."

"But, I thought we had to meet everyone. Aunt Kendra—"

"When she realizes we're both missing, she'll assume you're with me. She knows I wouldn't leave here without you."

"But how will she even—"

"Madison, for the love of God, please stop talking." He pushed open a heavy iron gate in the garden wall, one rarely used, and stepped back to let her pass. "Go," he urged.

Her heart pounding, Madison ran as hard as she could, into the jungle, clutching the silk pillowcase with her paints and the food and water. It was still pitch black and there was no path. Branches tore at her hair and vines caught her feet and hands. Panicked birds, disturbed by the humans, took flight, blindly flapping their wings and calling angrily.

"Run," Jefford urged, shoving her ahead and turning back. She heard his rifle boom and she stifled a scream.

A moment later, Jefford was behind her again, breathing hard, pushing her forward.

Madison had no idea where she was going; she just ran. Sweat ran down her face, stinging her eyes, trickling in rivulets down her back. She ran until she felt as if her lungs would burst and her sides would split.

"You have to keep going, Madison," Jefford urged, right behind her.

"I can't."

"You can."

The trek through the dark jungle was too difficult to manage side by side, but he ran behind her, then in front of her, pulling her along when she began to stumble.

"Please," she begged. "I'm...I must catch my breath...."

"Drop your paints. I'll buy you new ones."

"No, I can carry them. I'll be all right."

"Just a little farther. I know a place where we can hide."

"Hide?" Her voice caught in her throat.

"It's all right, Madison." He slowed to a fast walk. "I don't think anyone is following us. But just to be sure, we should sit tight for a few hours. You've reached your limits."

She pushed the hair that had fallen over her face away. Her legs throbbed and her chest ached. "I can go on," she insisted.

"I'm sure you can, but we'll stop, anyway." He pointed. "Just up here." He led her into a clearing by the waterfall. "It's a place to hide. I lived here as a boy, remember?" His voice took on a playful tone. "Who knows better where to hide than a boy who's been naughty?" He reached behind him and took her hand. "Now, when I tell you, you have to do what I say. We linger and your paintings are going to get wet. It's just like a curtain of water. It's strong, but it won't hurt you. Here on the end, it's barely coming down. Ready?"

She barely nodded before he darted under the wall of water, grabbing her hand and yanking her with him. Water splashed her face and she closed her eyes. Another step and she was out of it.

"Where are we?"

"Inside the waterfall, a cave of sorts." He released her

hand and moved slowly away. "Come on, sit down." Again, Jefford's strong hand closed around hers.

She could smell the dampness of the cave, water condensed on rock. There was also the faint green aroma of ferns that she knew grew above and around the waterfall. But mostly she could smell Jefford; the scent of his skin, his hair.

He only held her hand as he guided her to the far wall, but through her fingertips she felt him everywhere, on her face, her lips, her breasts where he had touched her. She trembled.

"Cold?" He sat down, pulling her with him, and put his arm around her.

"No," she breathed, "just—"

"You shouldn't be scared." His arm still around her shoulders, he drew his hand up and down her arm. "It's a lot cooler in here."

Jefford had turned his head and she could feel his breath on her face…her lips.

Madison felt her body sway…lean toward him. She had no intention of kissing Jefford…of allowing him to kiss her, and yet somehow her mouth found his. It was as though they hadn't finished the kiss in the pool the day before. As though it were the same kiss.

Madison felt as if she were floating in the darkness of the cave, in the water that flowed over the falls, in Jefford's strong arms. His mouth on hers, he drew her into his lap and she slid her arms over his broad shoulders, around his neck. She couldn't get enough of the taste of his mouth, of the feel of his arms around her.

Madison's heart pounded, her pulse raced, as she explored the cool cavern of his mouth with her tongue. Never in her lifetime had she imagined this was what a man could taste like. Feel like.

Jefford drew the flat of his hand over her abdomen, upward, over her breast. She moaned as his thumb found the nub of her nipple, gooseflesh rose on her skin; she felt hot and cold at the same time. Gasping for breath, she tore her mouth from his.

Cradling her in his arms, Jefford lowered her to her back and then rested on his side, kissing the soft flesh of her neck, nibbling on her earlobe, as he kneaded one breast and then the other. The thin white fabric of her bodice fell away and he tugged on the drawstring of the neckline of her sleeping gown. The fabric loosened and he slid his bare, cool hand over her warm flesh.

Madison sighed…groaned as, first, his fingers found her nipple, then his mouth. Jefford pressed hot, fleeting kisses in a line, downward, between her breasts. At the same time, he ran his hand over her thigh, found the hem of the skirt and slid his hand beneath it. She groaned in pleasure at the feel of his warm fingers on her inner thigh as the delicious sensations washed over her in waves.

Jefford hooked his fingers in the waistband of her skirt and she lifted it up, fumbling with the button. He pushed her skirt down and she kicked it away when it tangled around her ankles.

"Madison, Madison," he whispered in her ear. "I can't tell you how many times I've dreamed of touching you this way." Holding her in the crook of his arm, he undid the last of the buttons so that the thin nightdress fell open, leaving her body naked to the cool air. "How many times I've dreamed of kissing you this way," he murmured, leaning over to drag his lips across the flat of her belly.

Madison's breath caught in her throat as he moved his mouth lower. She threaded her fingers through his thick, damp hair, intending to pull him away, but the ache inside her was too strong, too commanding. Nothing mattered but the throbbing and her need to satisfy it.

When Jefford's mouth met the bed of soft blond curls at the apex of her thighs, Madison cried out in fear…in wonder.

"Shh," he soothed. "It's all right." He stroked her belly with the palm of his hand. "Relax. Let me love you."

His rough cheek pressed against her sensitive flesh was too much to resist. Against all logic, she felt her body relax, open up. His tongue flicked out to tease, to taunt, and she instinctively lifted her hips to meet each stroke.

Deep inside her body, something was building. She could feel her heart pounding so hard that she feared it might leap from her chest. She panted. She moaned. She lifted her hips again and again to meet his assault. Then suddenly, almost without warning, the pleasure burst into a thousand shards of shimmering delight. Every muscle in her body contracted. Released.

"Oh!" she sighed. "Oh!"

Jefford rolled over on top of her, holding his weight from hers with his arms.

Madison lay there with her eyes closed, the sensations still washing over her. He kissed her neck, her cheek. Her lips.

She could feel his hard, male body pressed against hers. He felt so good, so warm. She lifted her hips, pressing them to his, then felt him unhook his breeches. She knew what he was doing…what she was doing. She knew she should stop him, but the ache was there again…even stronger than before. Her need was greater than reason.

Madison felt his maleness hot and stiff against her bare leg. His mouth found hers and their tongues twisted in a dance only lovers could truly understand.

Her legs parted…seemingly of their own accord. She could feel herself wet, aching for him.

Jefford reached down, using his hand to guide. As he entered her, she threw her head back, not in pain, but in wonder.

"Are you all right?" he whispered, smoothing her hair.

Her eyes squeezed shut, she nodded.

"Do you want me to stop?"

She shook her head, not trusting herself to speak. Stop? No, she didn't want him to stop, didn't want this to stop. She wanted it to go on forever.

After giving her a moment to catch her breath, to adjust to the new sensation, he began to move inside. Somewhere in the back of her mind, Madison thought to herself that this shouldn't feel this good. No one had ever told her it could be this good. And women spoke of this as duty to a husband. She nearly laughed out loud.

But she could feel that building sensation deep inside again. And this time, she knew what it was. She wrapped her arms around Jefford, digging her nails into his back. She lifted her hips again and again to meet his. Faster. The cave swirled. The water rushed. She heard her own cries of ecstasy echo off the ceiling. Again, her world burst and she was racked by waves of intense pleasure.

Madison heard Jefford cry out and felt his final thrust and then they were both still. After a moment, he slipped out of her and rolled onto his side, pulling her into his arms. Not knowing what to say, tired beyond thought, she nestled her head on his shoulder and slept.

17

"Lady Moran."

Kendra glanced up to see Carlton Thomblin standing before her, dressed in a pale yellow suit with a straw boater on his head. He looked more as if he were out on a stroll through Hyde Park than hiding in a cave in Jamaica, fleeing for his life.

"It's beginning to grow light, and I must insist that, if we are to make that ship in harbor without being murdered, we set out before full sunup."

Kendra glanced away, her gaze moving from one clump of refugees to the next. The Rutherfords both rested against a large boulder and Lady Rutherford fussed over her husband, trying to clean a cut on his forehead. Young George leaned against the rock, his sister's head in his lap. They had come a long way with barely their lives.

In the far rear of the cave, where the sun's rays had not yet reached, the servants gathered among the belongings she and Thomblin had managed to bring with them. Chantal was there, too. Kendra had no great love for the woman and knew that bringing her along would only complicate matters, hinder her plan for Jefford and Madison, but she couldn't leave her behind to be killed by a mob. Besides, more than a dozen servants and their families, there were three men with rifles, sent ahead by Jefford, outside guarding the cave.

Lady Moran was so tired she could barely keep her eyes open. Every bone in her body ached and she had a stabbing pain in her backbone. She was worried to death about Jefford and Madison. In her heart, she knew they were safe and together, that they were simply waiting for the right time to meet at the cave. But, as the hours passed, she grew more worried.

"Lady Moran," Carlton said sharply. "Did you hear me?"

She straightened her back in the lovely Queen Anne's chair that had belonged to her mother, one of the few pieces of furniture she had brought from Windward Bay, and stared at him with irritation. "Board the ship and draw attention to ourselves in the daylight? Certainly not," she snapped.

"Which is precisely why we should go *now*." He drew his hand in a grand motion in the direction of the old Port Royal harbor.

"Well, Carlton, that would be a cheeky idea, *if* we had a ship."

"We haven't secured a ship?" he bellowed.

Ojar, standing guard outside the cave, stuck his head inside and frowned. He wore a rifle on each shoulder.

"Keep your voice down," Lady Moran hissed, her gaze returning to Thomblin.

"Sir." Lord Rutherford rose and hobbled toward them, using a makeshift cane of bamboo to aid him. He drew himself up to his full height, looking far older to Lady Moran than he had only a week ago. "I must ask you not to take that tone with Lady Moran."

"I thought we had a ship! Our voyage was supposed to be secured." Thomblin threw his hands in the air, his tone nearly hysterical. "I've been dragged through the jungle in the middle of the night, chased by drunken natives, and now I sit in a damp cave and am told there is no ship to take me from this hell? I thought last week, when we met, we agreed there would be an escape plan!"

"Which there was. We got you here in one piece, with flames on your tail, didn't we?" Lady Moran asked indignantly.

"To a cave filled with cobwebs and bats." He waved his hand in front of his face. "And possibly, with no obvious way to escape. How long will we wait here? Until the mob finds us and burns us out? Tars and feathers us? Worse?"

"Jefford will get us a ship, if need be."

"If need be?" Carlton huffed. "Madam, didn't your lookout, that Indian boy, just say that from the view above, it appears that half of the island is on fire? Did he not say he could see a crowd at the dock torching a warehouse right here in this port? If we had gone to Kingston—"

"I don't care what you say, Carlton. Jefford and Lord Rutherford agreed that leaving from Port Royal was safer. This was closer to home, and fewer people could see us set sail."

"I don't see anyone *setting sail*, do you, madam?"

"Lord Thomblin," Lord Rutherford huffed, throwing his shoulders back like an old rooster. "If you do not control yourself, sir, I will be forced to—"

"George, it's all right, really." Lady Moran raised her

hand to separate the two men. "Please don't get yourself overheated. Go see to your wife. I can handle his lordship."

Rutherford gave the younger man a look of disgust and hobbled back to his wife and children.

Lady Moran crossed her arms over her chest and batted a silk fan Maha had been clever enough to pack. The sun had barely shown itself on the horizon and already it was growing warm. "Now, as I was saying, Carlton, Jefford will be here soon."

"You don't know that."

"I'm quite sure that when Madison became separated from the wagons, she met up with my son and they are traveling in this direction together. Now, here is what we are going to do. We are going to wait here, throughout the day."

"And when darkness comes again, and they are still not here?"

"I'll send Punta to the harbor to secure a ship if we fear we are still in danger and cannot return to our homes."

"I believe it's already quite clear that we will not be returning to our homes." Carlton adjusted his straw hat.

"If you'll excuse me, I'm rather tired." She closed her eyes. "I believe I'll rest." With her eyes still closed, she called to her servant with a wave of her hand. "Punta."

He rose from his knees and hurried toward her. "Some more rum, yes."

Madison woke to find herself alone. It was daylight outside and the sun found its way around the edges of the waterfall to cast light in the cave. Rubbing her eyes, her mind still fuzzy with sleep, she sat up to find herself dressed only in her sleeping gown and her boots, lying on the curtain she had wrapped her portraits in. Hastily buttoning up the thin garment, memories of the night flooded her mind and she felt her cheeks color with shame.

"Ah, you're awake." He appeared at the edge of the waterfall, carrying the canteen. His dark hair was slick and wet; he must have bathed in the pool. "I got some fresh water."

She kept her gaze fixed on the last couple of buttons on her gown, though her fingers seemed to be having some difficulty in finding the buttonholes.

"Need a drink?" He walked over and crouched beside her.

She couldn't look at him. She reached for the canteen, took off the lid and drank.

"Madison—"

"Don't," she interrupted, wiping water that dribbled from the corner of her mouth. "Please. I don't… I'm not ready to talk about…last night."

He turned his head, looking away from her. "Fair enough," he sighed. "I suppose we've got other, more pressing matters, to attend to, haven't we?"

Still avoiding his gaze, she turned on all fours and crawled over the curtain to retrieve her bodice, discarded hours earlier in the heat of passion. Her skirt had been flung in another direction. "We have to get to the meeting place," she said, her voice shaky. "Aunt Kendra will be so worried. Where do we have to go to meet the others?"

"Port Royal."

"That's not far," she said hopefully.

"No, it isn't. There's another cave, larger than this, a cavern, really, near the edge of town. A place pirates used to hide. My mother and the others are waiting for us there now. It's very close to the harbor."

"We're taking a ship?"

"No," he intoned. "We're flying on the wings of a bird."

"You needn't mock me." She grabbed her torn, wrinkled skirt and stood up to step into it. "I'm not the mindless female you think I am."

He got to his feet. "It's just that it sounded like a foolish question. How else would we get off an island?"

"I wasn't sure we *were* leaving Jamaica," she answered curtly. "I don't even know where we are going." She hesitated, stealing a look at him. "London?"

"Good God, no."

Fully dressed, she turned to him, forcing herself to meet his gaze head-on, this time. "Where, then?"

"India."

"India!" she breathed, suddenly feeling light-headed. "That's so far from here."

"It is, indeed. Halfway around the world. We'll gain what passage we can off the island and go to the Americas, a place called Charleston. Once we arrive safely, we'll send word to your family—"

"They don't care where I am," she interjected. "They're just glad to be rid of me." Against her will, she could feel the excitement building inside her. India? She had read stories of India. Accounts of men and women associated with the East India Company who lived there.

Madison was still trying to imagine such a journey. "From Charleston, we will board a steamer for Bombay."

"How long will such a journey take?"

"Anywhere from two to three months, I would guess." He watched her as he spoke, making her self-conscious.

"Depends greatly on how quickly we can book passage," Jefford continued. "Then, how many stops the ship makes. Often the ships take port in Portugal, Gibraltar, then through the Mediterranean, the port in Alexandria, through the Suez Canal, into the Red Sea and then on to Bombay."

"Why India?" she wondered allowed.

"We…my mother had land there, as do the Rutherfords. Thomblin lived there once, as well." He was silent for a moment. "And…I think there is someone there Kendra would like to see again."

There was something in his voice that made her glance up at him. He turned away abruptly. Something was wrong. "Jefford—"

"It's safe for you to go out to take care of your personal needs," he said, his tone short. "Just don't stay out long. I hiked back to Windward Bay before dawn. Part of the house is still standing, but…" He left his last thought unsaid.

Madison studied his broad back and she felt a tightness in her chest. Windward Bay had been his home since he was a child and now it was lost to him.

Madison napped most of the afternoon, mostly so she wouldn't have to suffer the uncomfortable silence between them. Sometime late in the day, he woke her.

"I think it's time we go," he said, shaking her shoulder.

She sat up to find the cave cast in shadows. "It's still light out."

"But things have quieted down a bit. I ran into one of Lela's sons in the jungle. He says two more English plantations were burned last night. Things are pretty peaceful right now, many of the worst offenders are sleeping off their drunks, but there are groups organizing in many of the villages. He expects to see mobs marching with torches again by nightfall. They've placed all the blame for their plights on the English. I think finally we're beyond negotiation."

On her feet, Madison tried to brush her tangled hair with

her fingertips and retie the ribbon. "You think it's safe to go to Port Royal? To join the others?"

"I'll get you to the cave and then I need to procure a ship. Other families are probably trying to get out of here, too, so it could take a day or two."

"You…" She glanced at him. "You don't think they left without us, do you?"

"No. My mother would wait at least a day." The paintings secured, he threw the makeshift sack over his shoulder and reached for his rifle. He was already wearing the canvas bag he had brought with him. "You ready?"

She picked up the pillowcase with what remained of their food and her paints and the canteen filled with fresh water. "I'm ready."

For the next two hours Jefford and Madison walked at a grueling pace through the darkening jungle. Again and again she had to run to catch up with Jefford, but he didn't slow down and she refused to ask him to wait for her. The more time that passed, the more she realized that the smartest thing for her to do about the previous night was pretend it had never happened.

Jefford said nothing about it. He made no apologies, nor any declaration of love. He just kept trudging ahead, his jaw set. And the longer she watched his back, the more convinced she became that she had to wipe out the entire incident from her mind. It had simply never happened.

A moment of human weakness in a night of madness.

Close to sunset, Madison was beginning to tire. Her muscles ached from the hike over rocks and around trees and her arms and face were itching with bug bites. Not once did Jefford ask if she wanted him to take the sack that had not been heavy when they had left the waterfall, but had become increasingly so in the passing hours.

"We're almost there," he said to her over his shoulder, at last.

He halted and she leaned against a tree, heaving a sigh of relief. She watched, her eyes only half open, as he cupped his hands around his mouth and made a sound that was amazingly similar to the ones she had heard in the jungle. To her surprise, something called right back.

She opened her eyes, looking at him.

"They're all there," he said. "Let's go."

She had dragged her feet a short distance farther when Ojar stepped out of the trees.

"My mother?" Jefford asked as he handed the bag of paintings to Punta's oldest son.

"She is good, sir. They are all here, safe. Your mother, the Rutherfords, Lord Thomblin."

Jefford grabbed the pillowcase from Madison's hand without so much as a word to her. "Good. Take Miss Madison inside, see someone gets her some food. I want to speak to my mother and then you and I will set out in search of a ship that will take us out of here."

"The jungle is already beginning to awake. There are fires, again," Ojar warned.

"I know. Which is why we have to get the hell out of here." Jefford walked away, ducking through some vines, and Ojar fell into step behind him, leaving Madison no choice but to follow.

"By Hindi's bare feet, it's about time you got here," Lady Moran's familiar voice called out.

Madison walked through vines Ojar parted for her, to find herself in a cave similar to the one under the falls, only the ceiling of this one was much higher and the opening seemed to tunnel a great distance back.

"Madison, dear!" Lady Moran released her son and

threw her arms around her niece. "I knew you were safe! I told Portia, Jefford would bring you safely back to me."

Madison was so tired, so distraught with emotion, that she could say nothing, do nothing but cling to her aunt.

"Are you all right?" Aunt Kendra demanded, pulling back and taking Madison's chin in her hands to gaze into her eyes.

Madison swallowed the lump in her throat, shifting her gaze downward. "I'm all right," she whispered. "Just very tired. Hungry."

"Well, that we can take care of."

Aunt Kendra released Madison and Alice was right there at her side, along with her brother.

"You made it!" Alice cried, throwing her arms around Madison and hugging her. "You're safe." She began to cry. "I was afraid something terrible—"

"It's all right, Alice, really," Madison assured her.

George put his arm around both of them. "Now, ladies, this is no place for tears," he said, emotion evident in his voice. "We're all safe."

Still comforting Alice, Madison lifted her gaze to George. "Is Sashi—"

George pressed his fingers to his lips and Madison was immediately quiet.

"Georgie doesn't want Mummy and Daddy to know who she is. That she's with us."

Madison frowned but didn't ask. Out of the corner of her eye, she caught sight of Chantal standing near a crate. Jefford had gone to speak to her.

Madison closed her eyes, afraid she might burst into tears. If she was hoping in any part of her foolish head that things had changed between her and Jefford, she was obviously wrong. Like any tomcat, he was obviously back to his old ways. "I think I need to sit down," she whispered.

Jefford extricated himself as quickly from the cave as possible, and taking Ojar with him, began to hike down the side of the hill toward the harbor at Port Royal. Sensing his master's mood, the young man at his side was quiet, leaving Jefford to his thoughts.

Jefford couldn't for the life of him figure out what he was thinking when he had made love to Madison. He hadn't been thinking at all, obviously. At least not with the part of his anatomy he should have been thinking with.

In the hour at dawn, when he lay on the cave floor with Madison asleep in his arms, her breath soft and sweet on his face, he had actually considered asking her to marry him. After all, it had seemed only right after he had taken what rightfully belonged to no man but her husband. And a marriage between them had been what his mother had wanted since the first days they had arrived in London, hadn't it? To give her such a gift would be an honor.

But then, with the coming of light, nothing had seemed to be what it had in the darkness. The way Madison had crooned his name, the way she had touched him with her innocent yet somehow knowing hands had made him think she cared for him. Perhaps even loved him, on some level.

Jefford scowled, wiping his mouth with the back of his hand as if he could wipe away her burning kisses. What a fool he was. If he didn't know better, he would have thought the little English chit had cast a spell on him. But that was really all she was. An English chit. A spoiled little rich girl who had no business in his life, in the life of a man like him.

"Mr. Jefford," Ojar whispered as they reached the main road into the town.

Pushing away all thoughts of Madison, Jefford checked the pistol he had traded back at the cave for his rifle. He'd added a wrinkled broadcloth coat to conceal it, and a long-bladed knife, as well. "Yes, Ojar?"

"Do…do you know who we will go in search of as a captain to take us so far across the sea?"

Spotting a group of five or six rum-soaked Caribs with torches barreling down the center of the street right for them, Jefford slipped behind a building that appeared abandoned and close to caving in on itself. More than a hundred years previously, Port Royal had been one of the busiest ports in the world, but a hurricane had struck, killing hundreds, washing away most of the town and altering the coastline of Jamaica forever. The town had not rebuilt itself to its previous glory, something he somehow thought sad.

"I'm not sure who, but I've got a good idea where."

Standing across the street from a ramshackle dockside bar, Jefford took in his surroundings. The stench of decaying fish and pungent seawater filled his nostrils. A stray cat meowed as it trotted down the alley that ran along the bar. The sounds of drunken laughter, a dog barking, a man and a woman in heated argument filled the hot, humid night air.

"You need to stay outside," Jefford told Ojar. He met the young man's dark gaze. "Not because I don't think you have a right to be in here, but—"

"I understand, *sahib*." The Indian shifted his rifle onto his shoulder. "I will stay in the dark, but keep an eye and an ear open for you."

Jefford clamped his hand on his companion's back. "You're a good man, Ojar. A brave man, like your father."

He looked down at his dirty bare feet, trying hard not to grin. "You honor me greatly, Mr. Jefford, with words this man does not deserve."

"I'll be the judge of that." He checked his pistol again. "All right, Ojar, you stay here and wait for me, unless, of course, you hear gunshots inside. Then feel free to give me a hand."

Ojar nodded his shaggy head.

Confident the Indian had his back, Jefford walked into the Jaded Parrot, which was really more a chicken coop than a bar, and smelled worse, despite the open windows and open doorways. Island music spilled from the windows and light seeped through the cracks in the wallboards. Two chickens scratched in the dirt inside the doorway.

"Evening," Jefford grunted to the one-eyed giant who held vigil at the door.

He had limbs the size of tree trunks and a head as big as a green coconut just fallen from the tree. "Jimbo don't want no trouble here," the Goliath muttered.

Jefford breezed past him. "Not looking for trouble, just a sip a' rum."

The Jaded Parrot was busy, filled with noise and commotion, which was just what Jefford was hoping for. There were a couple of card games going between tar-pigtailed deckhands around barrels topped with slabs of wood for tables. A prostitute in a yellow skirt, her sagging breasts bared, was plying her trade in the far corner amid some shipping merchants. Their nationalities were ambiguous, which, these days, on the island, was the safest way to do business.

Jefford walked up to the bar, leaned against the dirty, rough wood and slapped down a coin.

The bartender, a jagged-toothed, skinny man with a foul apron tied around his waist, brought down a small wooden cup in front of his newest customer and tipped an unmarked bottle of clear liquid.

"This rotgut isn't going to kill me?" Jefford grunted. "Is it?"

"Don't know," the bartended replied. "What you gonna do about it if it does?"

Jefford glanced up, his face stoic.

The bartender stared hard back, then after a moment, broke into foul-breathed laughter. He struck his knee with amusement. "Best one I heard all week."

Jefford tipped his head and threw back the shot of rum. It was foul stuff, nothing like the fine liquor his mother produced. In all likelihood, it *would* kill him. He cleared his throat of the liquid fire and slapped down another coin.

The bartender poured him another portion.

Avoiding eye contact, Jefford took another coin from the purse tied on his belt, this one of far more value, and slid it across the bar top.

"What that for?"

Jefford pulled his hand away. "You."

"Fer what?"

"For a quiet reference."

"Speak some English, French, something I can understand, mate," the bartender said, unable to take his gaze off the glimmering coin.

"I need a ship. Tonight. A name of a captain."

"Fer what?"

"None of your damn business."

"Hmm." The bartender slid his hand slowly toward the coin.

Jefford pulled his knife from his belt and brought it

down hard on the bar top, sinking the blade into the rotting wood between the man's splayed fingers.

"Jesus H. Christ!"

His hand still on the hilt of the knife, Jefford studied the barkeep. "You got a name for me?"

The bartender's eyes were wide, with greed as much as fear, most likely. "Whistlin' Willey!"

Jefford jerked the knife from the wood. "And where might I find him?"

"Right over yonder." The barkeeper pointed to a man seated alone at a barrel top, slumped against the wall. Jefford couldn't see much of his face. His orange whiskers were long and plaited into two thick braids, and a French naval officer's hat was perched atop a head as bald as an onion. The man's patched coat was Spanish, the buttons fashioned from English shillings. One dirty hand, possessing only three fingers, clutched a bottle of rum with a death grip.

Jefford took one look at the purported captain, then back at his newfound friend. "He got a decent ship?"

"No, but what for the like I'm guessin' you need it, ain't no body with a decent ship sailin' you out of this harbor. Not with the Jamaicans beatin' their drums the way they are. Not with them fires they're lightin'. Not be safe helpin' English like you."

"Coin's yours." Jefford walked away, his eye already on his would-be captain.

"Forgot yer *bouse.*"

Jefford didn't look back. At the table near the wall, he dropped onto a smaller barrel that served as a stool and sank his elbow into the ship's captain, who was either passed out or asleep. "Wake up. You're going to want to hear this."

"What? Whasth's that?" Whistlin' Willey lisped, opening his eyes in confusion.

Jefford lowered his voice, sneaking a glance behind him before he spoke. "My name's Harris and I am about to offer you a hell of a lot of money to get me and my family the hell out of here."

Book Three
India

18

Bombay, India
Three months later

"Why, it's just like London!" Madison exclaimed, leaning over the mahogany rail to gaze down into the magnificent marble lobby of the Queen Jasmine Hotel located in the lush countryside just outside of Bombay.

They had steamed into port the evening before and Madison had barely had time to find her land legs, let alone explore the splendid hotel where they would be staying until they set out for Lady Moran's home and properties.

"I suppose it is rather English," Lady Moran agreed, slipping on the pale yellow silk gloves Maha handed her as she took in the view from the second-story balcony. "My father used to bring me here for a proper tea at least twice a year, served just down there." She nodded toward tables covered in elegant white linens set with exquisite silver and bone china. High tea was just commencing and stylishly dressed English men and women were already seated at the scattered tables.

Madison leaned farther over the rail, unable to contain her excitement. She had enjoyed the adventure of sailing on the modern P & O steamship, pulling into port at exotic places she had only read about: Lisbon, Gibraltar, Algiers, Tripoli and then Alexandria, sailing through the amazing Suez Canal, across the Red Sea, and finally to Bombay, but she was thrilled to be in India at last. "I've brought my sketchbook." She fished a pencil from the pale blue embroidered silk purse she carried on her wrist. The purse matched her new silk gown, purchased in one of the many ports the steamship had stopped at, and her eyes, Lord Thomblin had remarked the first time she had worn it to dine at the captain's table on the ship. "No one will think me rude if I make a couple of sketches while we have tea, do you think?"

Lady Moran could only smile and shake her head. "Considering the cost of the rooms at the Jasmine, my dear, I should think not." She gazed down at the dark-skinned natives, dressed in white with lavender trim, silver serving trays in their hands, running at the beck and call of Englishwomen taking tea in the palm-fringed lobby. "One night would pay a man's salary for ten years, I suspect," she snorted. "The Queen Jasmine Hotel, the most elegant on this coast of the continent, consists of three hundred and fifty acres, dedicated solely to the comfort of Englishmen and their ladies. Can you imagine? Beyond the hotel, there are cricket and croquet fields, acres to ride horseback, and, I understand, a small spa has been recently added, complete with Roman baths and authentic Greek statues dredged from the bay of Alexandria."

Madison half listened to her aunt while drawing her

pencil across the paper rapidly, afraid that if she didn't hurry, she might miss a detail, the slight sway of the gracious potted palm trees that set the dining area off from the rest of the grand marble lobby, the sober faces of the young native men, the angle of the feathers on ladies' bonnets. "And we're only staying a week, Aunt Kendra? How will I ever capture it all?"

The journeys of the last three months seemed now to be only a smudge on the pages of one of the many sketchbooks she had filled. As they steamed from continent to continent, her painting had become even more vital; it was now her escape, her life, her passion, and it filled her every waking moment.

"By Hindi's earlobe, Madison," Lady Moran remarked, peering over her niece's shoulder. "What an excellent sketch. I thought your work remarkable the first time I laid eyes on it in Papa's studio, but I must say, your talent has improved these last months, if that's possible. The shadows, there," she pointed with a gloved finger, "are quite extraordinary."

Madison blushed as she drew the pencil over the paper, taking the angle of an elderly woman's nose just so. "Please, Aunt Kendra, you embarrass me with your flattery." She did not take her gaze from the bustling scene below.

"No need for you to be embarrassed, my love. You've worked quite hard these last months, sketching, painting, observing, and, oh, my, the portraits you painted were magnificent. You think I haven't noticed?" She settled her green-eyed gaze on her niece. "When you were not shamelessly flirting with Lord Thomblin, about which you and I shall soon have a conversation."

Madison pressed her lips together but didn't acknowledge her aunt's statement. She hadn't realized her attraction to Lord Thomblin had been so obvious, nor that her aunt was so disapproving.

Once they had safely sailed from Jamaica, her concern had turned to how she would deal with what had happened in the cave with Jefford, but he had quickly made the decision for her by reverting to the cool, disinterested Jefford from their days at Windward Bay. She realized that that night had been a terrible mistake, certainly best forgotten, and never spoke to him of the incident. He never acknowledged it had happened, and once on the steamer, had settled into a private cabin. Gossip among the servants, according to Sashi, was that Chantal had taken up residence with him and that they rarely left the room. It was a thought that galled Madison, not that she cared what that arrogant, self-absorbed rogue of a man did, so long as he stayed out of her path!

"Now, where on earth are Lady Rutherford and Alice?" Lady Moran clicked her tongue between her teeth. "I have my heart set on those tasty cucumber sandwiches and I will not be denied them, my dear Madison. More than thirty years I've waited for one of the Jasmine's sandwiches!"

"Lady Moran," Lady Rutherford, called, gliding down the carpeted hallway toward them, Alice in tow. "Please accept my apologies for our tardiness. My daughter was being obstinate, and I refused to leave the room until she was properly dressed."

"It's just so hot, this bonnet," Alice murmured, tugging on the wide pink grosgrain ribbon tucked under her chin. "I had no idea India would be so hot."

"The bonnet might be hot, but it is very pretty," Madison offered, trying to console her friend as she tucked her sketch pad beneath her arm and took Alice's hand. "Are we ready?"

"Lead the way." Lady Moran gestured grandly.

Madison and Alice walked down the wide curving marble staircase with Lady Moran and Lady Rutherford behind them, and as they made their appearance, ladies and gentleman alike glanced their way. Heads tipped to whisper behind silk fans and gentleman cleared their throats, leaning in to listen.

"Keep your chins high, girls," Lady Moran said. "If they want to stare, we should offer a grand entrance, don't you think?"

Madison tried not to feel self-conscious as she walked down the stairs, taking care not to step on the hem of her new gown. "Why are they all staring?" she whispered.

"New faces. Boredom," her aunt remarked with amusement. "India may be vast, but the English community is small and incredibly self-involved. We know every fault and secret of our neighbor."

Lady Rutherford chuckled. "Lady Moran, I fear your nose is growing. The entire hotel has been abuzz since we arrived last night. Apparently, my dear, you've been a bit of celebrity all these years, practically disappearing in the middle of the night, never to be seen again in polite English society."

Lady Moran smiled and batted her painted Chinese fan as she stepped onto the lobby floor. "I hadn't realized the full impact of my departure until I bumped into Lord Henderson last night, an old friend of my father's. He had heard that I had eloped with my father's butler, murdered Lord Moran and run off to China!"

The two older women burst into laughter.

Madison waited for her aunt and Lady Rutherford. "Thirty years and they're still gossiping?" she asked.

"It's what English society does best, my love." Lady

Moran glided by, greeting the maître d'. "Good afternoon, sir."

"Lady Moran, we are honored to have you with us," the Indian man dressed all in white replied, hands clasped as he bowed. "I have saved you our best table."

The maître d' showed them to an elegant oval table, sparkling with silver and china, and pulled out each cushioned chair to seat the ladies. Servants bustled around them at once, delivering pots of tea and platters of sandwiches and sweets.

"Is Papa joining us?" Alice asked, spreading her napkin on her lap as a turbaned servant poured tea.

"You know your father never cared for tea." Lady Rutherford leaned closer to the table, lowering her voice. "Unless, of course, there was a shot of brandy to accompany it."

All four women laughed, pleased to have at last reached India and safety. After the horrifying last days in Jamaica, they were all too aware of their own mortality, and each looked forward to what life would bring them next in this new country.

"The men are not joining us?" Madison asked, disappointed. While she had dined several times a week with Lord Thomblin on the steamer, she had really not seen much of him in the last three months. He had spent most of his time in the gentlemen's lounge gambling, while Madison had been occupied most days painting and sketching. She had been commissioned by several passengers to paint on-board portraits of their families, and had quickly become the celebrity of the ship.

Lady Moran reached across the table to cover Madison's hand with hers. "To answer the question you are dying to ask, my dear, Lord Thomblin will not be joining us tonight or any other night this week, I suspect. It appears that he has chosen to take up residence at another hotel."

"That was not what I was asking," Madison replied, lowering her gaze as she spread her linen napkin on her lap, "but why in heaven's name would he want to stay elsewhere? This is the most beautiful hotel I've ever seen in my life."

Lady Moran met Lady Rutherford's gaze across the table. "Let us move on to another subject, shall we?" she asked pointedly, pushing a plate across the table. "I want everyone to taste one of these cucumber sandwiches, and tell me, is this not the most delightful sandwich you have ever put in your mouth?"

Lord Thomblin walked along the floating sidewalk, keeping his arms pressed to his sides so that the crowd, foul-smelling, scourge of the earth, did not bump into him and soil his white coat as he made his way along the water. Behind him, two barely dressed native boys trotted, his leather traveling bags in their hands.

The long journey from Jamaica had not been nearly as profitable as he had hoped. Instead of gaining at the gambling tables, now on the shore of India again, he found himself in greater debt than when he had left three years earlier.

Ignoring the stench of the street that ran along the waterside and the wretched natives in the cesspool they had created of their own free will, Carlton turned into a familiar alleyway. Glancing over one shoulder to be certain his bags were still in tow, he quickened his step in anticipation of what awaited. The journey on the steamship had been tedious, with few young women or men available to meet his *refined* tastes.

He kicked at a mangy dog that crossed his path. "This

way! For the love of sweet Christ, don't dally," he called to the boys behind him. His heart was now beating rapidly in his chest. He had nearly reached his destination and could almost smell the scent of her sweet skin. Captain Bartholomew had promised she would be just what he needed, a balm to soothe him.

At the designated building, more a crude shack than a hotel, he counted down the number of doors. "Right here, leave them here," he told the boys, gesturing. He was suddenly hot beneath his starched collar and his palms were sweating.

The boys dropped his bags at his feet and stood staring.

"For the love of Christ," Carlton muttered, reaching into his coat. He pitched them each a copper pence and they caught them in midair, darting off into the fetid crowd.

Carlton licked his lips and, resting his hand on the doorknob, turned and pushed it inward. The door creaked and he heard someone from inside cry out.

She was there waiting for him when he opened the door, her delicate hands and ankles tied together.

Carlton smiled, unable to take his eyes from the frightened dark-skinned face, and he hastily tossed his bags through the door, one after another. "Well, well, well, what have we here?"

She made barely a sound through the cloth that gagged her.

"No need to be afraid, my dear," he chastised. "Come, now. Lord Thomblin appreciates a pretty face." Smiling in adoration, he closed the door behind him.

Jefford hesitated outside his mother's door as he tugged irritably on his silk cravat. He had agreed to escort Kendra to the opera tonight at the Jasmine's grand salon only because he knew how greatly she adored opera and because he knew it could be the very last opera she ever saw, not because he particularly appreciated *Figaro,* or the brilliant composer Mozart. Now that the evening was upon him, he was thinking he'd made a mistake. He had too many things to do before he set out for his mother's properties, too many financial arrangements to make.

Before he could tap on the door, it flew open.

"Aha, there you are," Kendra cried, filling the doorway. She was dressed in an elaborate turquoise silk-and-tulle gown with a feather headdress. "I was just coming for you. You cannot hide from me the rest of my life, you know."

Jefford let his hands fall to his sides, his cravat yet untied. "I'm not hiding from anyone."

"The hell you're not."

"Kendra, I said I would be here and here I am." He checked his gold pocket watch. "Fifteen minutes early, to be precise."

She perched her hands on her hips. "Jefford, just once in a while, I'd like you to call me Mother."

"I've never called you Mother. Not as long as I can remember."

"That was my mistake. I can see that now. You don't respect me the way you should."

"Please, the months of travel have addled your mind. Perhaps we should skip the opera and you should go to bed. I could call Maha for you."

"Don't you tell me what to do, Jefford Harris," she huffed indignantly. "I brought you into this world, I could certainly take you out of it. Now, get inside before you disturb our neighbors."

He chuckled, following her into the elaborately furnished suite. "It's good to see that your ill health has not affected your humor."

"We're not talking about my health right now," she said tartly, taking a seat in front of a silver-gilded mirror at a mahogany dressing table. "We're talking about you."

"No one has brought up the subject of me." He walked to a full-length mirror on the far side of the room and once again attempted to tie the cravat at his neck.

"Not once since we arrived in Bombay almost a week ago have you visited with Madison."

"I'm busy. She's busy with her painting." He stared at the cravat in the mirror, groaned and yanked it free again. "She has no time for callers, and even if she did, I doubt I would be on the guest list."

Kendra slipped an earring dripping with diamonds and sapphires into her ear, eyeing her son in the mirror's reflection. "Would you like to tell me what happened the night we left Windward Bay?"

Jefford steeled his emotions, refusing to allow his mind to take him places he had no desire to go, and gritted his teeth, beginning to retie the cravat again. "Nothing happened. Why are you still harping on this subject? I told you weeks ago, months ago, we waited in the cave until sunset and then met up with you and the others."

"You can't fool me," she harrumphed. "Nothing happened, and the two of you haven't spoken in three months?"

"Kendra, for the love of God, we've been traveling." He motioned with one hand. "The steamship was not set up for socializing. Even if I had wanted to socialize, which I hadn't, it would have been entirely inappropriate on a passenger ship for me to—"

"Since when have you been interested in what anyone thinks about anything you do?"

He fought his irritation, trying to remain calm. "I was simply attempting to protect your niece. Now that we have arrived in India, once we become settled, there will be a great many opportunities for her to find a suitable English husband. I would not want to jeopardize—"

"Oh, poppycock. You can believe all this nonsense if you want, but I refuse to hear it." She thrust her other earring into her earlobe and rose from the dressing table. "Fine. We won't discuss Madison and your marriage now—"

"Kendra—"

She crossed the room to him, pushing his hands aside to tie his cravat for him. "Hush and show me a little of that respect I deserve. Can't you hear me speaking? See my lips moving?"

He looked at the elaborate Turkish carpet beneath his feet, thinking that she never ceased to amaze him. She was such a stubborn, headstrong woman, a match to any man he had ever known. Damn, he loved her. He would miss her so much when she was gone that he could not even bear to contemplate what his life would be like.

"Well then, let's talk about another uncomfortable subject," she said, her capable hands moving quickly at his cravat.

"Let's not."

"Jefford, damn you, look at me."

He lifted his gaze to study her thin face. The feather turquoise headdress she wore covered her lovely red hair, which had greatly thinned in the last few months; obviously she didn't want anyone to know it. "What now?" he said, his tone gentler. He didn't mean to hurt her. She just made life so damned difficult sometimes.

"You agreed months ago that we should return to India, saying it was our best option."

"It is. Even when you're…when you're gone—" the words pained him greatly to speak "—I'll be better here than in England."

Finishing his cravat, she rested her hand on his arm, gazing up into his eyes. "Jefford, in all this time, you've said nothing of the fact that this is your father's birthplace."

He glanced away, his gaze settling on a painting on the far wall that depicted a mountainside in the Himalayas with a trail of pack elephants winding their way through a snow-covered mountain pass. It was a good painting, he thought, but not as good as Madison could have created. "What is there to say?"

"You've never asked me about your father."

"You never offered," he answered dryly. "I considered the information personal."

"Oh, my dear Jefford." She chuckled quietly as she brushed her fingertips across his cheek. "You were not an easy child. What would make me think you would have grown to be otherwise? Now, listen…"

"You know I have never held it against you that you had a child out of wedlock, even if it was me." The truth was, protected as he had been on Jamaica, he had suffered very little, being illegitimate. His mother's wealth and determination had seen to that.

"Would you please stop interrupting and let me speak?" she asked sharply. "Madison is right. You are the rudest man." She removed her hand from his arm and smoothed the silk ripples of the bodice of her gown.

"Now," she continued, "as I was saying." She hesitated and then threw up her hands. "I can't remember what it was I was saying." She lifted her eyes to the heavens. "Just this, I suppose. I'm not even certain your father is still alive, but if he is, if we should cross his path, I would not want you to hold your illegitimate birth against him. I wouldn't want you to hate him."

"Hate him?" Jefford scoffed, crossing his arms over his chest. "In truth, I've never thought much about my father. I don't care who he was or what the circumstances of my…conception were. What has always mattered to me was you and your happiness. Of course—" he smiled "—I suspected the first time you brought up the idea of returning to India that you had a notion to see the man. How can I hate a man I don't know?"

"I want to say that it's my wish, my last dying wish—"

"I thought my marrying your niece was your last wish," he interjected, a slight smile playing on his lips.

She glared threateningly at him and returned to her dressing table. "My *wish* is that you simply give him a chance. As I said, he may not even still be alive, but if he is, it would please me that you get to know him."

Jefford stared at the painting of the elephants, but he was no longer seeing it. Tomorrow his mother and their entourage would be taking a train south and then east to the borders of the jungle where his mother's land lay, thousands of acres, all inherited after Lord Moran died. He would be remaining in Bombay a few days to finish some business and financial transactions, but then he would be joining his mother. If the man she referred to as his father was still alive, still on the property, he would not be able to avoid him forever. "Is that all?" he asked.

Adjusting a feather on her headdress, she rose. "Yes," she said quite cheerfully as she reached for her silk cape on the end of the bed. "At least for tonight. Now, shall we go to the opera? The others are waiting in the lobby."

Jefford stared at Kendra for a moment, then helped her into her cape and offered his elbow. Somehow she had won again.

Thomblin let the weight of his burden in the sack slip to the ground to catch his breath. He ran the back of his hand over his mouth, thinking how badly he needed a drink, some food. He had no idea what time it was except that it was nighttime. He wasn't even certain what day it was; he often lost track in the heat of the moment.

The one thing he did know was that he stank nearly as badly as the alley. He needed to check himself into a decent hotel, get a bath, sleep, eat. Then he would plan his next move.

He grasped the two corners of the rough sack and began to drag it again, thinking it would have been easier to have gotten some help. But he'd been afraid to risk it. After all the time that had passed since he'd last lived in India, he needed to make new connections. He needed to form alliances so that he'd know whom he could trust.

At the end of the alley, panting, he stepped onto the decrepit dock that ran directly along the shore. He dragged the bag the last few feet, then heaved it over the side, watching as it hit the water with a splash. Just as it sank in the darkness, he saw the flash of a slender hand.

He turned away, wondering if once he got to the hotel he would order lamb or beef.

19

~~~~~~~~~~~~~~~~~~~~~~~~~~~~~~~

"Oh, Sashi," Madison said with a sigh. "The train is moving so fast I can't really sketch the scenery." She closed her sketchbook and packed it away, looking to her young maid. "When will we arrive?"

The young Indian woman chuckled and patted her mistress's arm. "Before sunset, I am told. Look out the window at the beauty of my country."

Madison turned to watch the ever-changing countryside roll by. She had not cared much for Bombay. Like any city, it was big and noisy and smelly, though she had been fascinated by the temples, the snake charmers and acrobats plying their trades on the street, the metal workers and shouting vendors. She'd been overwhelmed by the incredibly fascinating features of the men and women on the streets, and charmed by the barefoot children with the faces of copper-colored angels. And while she would have given almost anything to paint the throngs of carts pulled by men wearing little but a loincloth and a turban they'd encountered on their journey from the Queen Jasmine

Hotel to the train station, she'd been relieved when they had reached the elaborate station and boarded the train.

They'd been fortunate enough to gain seats for everyone in their party continuing their travel, though most of the servants had been forced to take less luxurious accommodations than the velvet-seated car Madison presently occupied with Lady Moran and their two personal maids. The Rutherfords were in a different car, and Lord Thomblin had remained in Bombay to attend to business. Jefford, too, had chosen to remain behind with several of his men to settle some financial affairs and see the remainder of their belongings from Jamaica transported. Chantal had remained with him, but Madison cared not a whit. As far as she was concerned, the two deserved each other.

As Madison watched the scenery fly by, she noticed that the landscape was changing. The unfamiliar trees and shrubs were becoming greener and there were fewer open spaces. Pressing her cheek to the dusty glass, she watched in fascination as a herd of black antelope raced across a grass knoll, their long legs flying.

Lady Moran leaned over the seat, settling a hand on her niece's shoulder. "What do you think so far?" she asked, obviously excited to be in India again.

"It's so vast. So much more than I expected," Madison breathed. "And the landscape keeps changing. It's so different now from when we first left Bombay."

"We're traveling east, and nearing the jungle. My properties actually border an area that gradually transforms from this drier deciduous forest and open steppes to the tropical forest."

"And you grow indigo?"

"Along with a few other endeavors, sugarcane and some coffee. I'm sure that once Jefford takes over, we'll be dabbling in all sorts of crops. Farther south some plantation owners are even trying their hand at rice."

"And your home? What is it like, Aunt Kendra? I don't think I ever asked you."

"Only Hindi knows if we will be able to call it a home, my dear. No one has lived there for decades. We have overseers, of course, but it's hard for one to tell how well their property is being cared for ten thousand miles away, isn't it?" Lady Moran replied with good cheer.

Madison smiled at her aunt, whose mood was infectious, and gazed out the window to see more deerlike animals moving in a thunderous herd across the grassland. "It doesn't matter what state the house is in. We'll have a roof over our heads and we'll be together. We'll make it home!"

At the train station that was little more than a platform made of hand-cut wooden slats, Madison and the others disembarked, everyone carting several pieces of hand luggage. The Rutherfords had acquired most of their daily essentials in several ports along their journey. After three months of travel, everyone seemed anxious to go home, even if that home was a mystery, not seen for decades.

After sending Punta and his sons into the small village to seek transportation, Lady Moran turned to the Rutherfords. "Are you certain you won't accept my invitation and come to my home tonight and journey to yours tomorrow?"

"Thank you for the offer," Lady Rutherford replied, stroking her husband's arm. "But I think now that we're so close, George is anxious to return to the home his father built."

"Haven't seen it in almost thirty years," Lord Rutherford said, speaking gruffly to cover the emotion in his voice. "Imagine there's a need to shake out a few rugs."

"Well, you must promise to come and see us the moment you're settled. I'll expect word in the morning, letting me know all is well."

Madison waved to George and Alice and the older Rutherfords. "We'll see you in a day or two, I hope."

"Oh, I do hope so, yes," Alice declared.

Punta soon arrived with several wagons pulled by pairs of some sort of oxen, followed by four men carrying on their shoulders an open box on poles that extended from each corner. The box had two cushioned benches facing each other, and was hung with a luxurious fringed green-and-yellow fabric.

"A palanquin, dear. Come, come, don't stare." Lady Moran held her hand out and led Madison toward the contraption that had now been lowered to the ground. "More wagons coming," she called to the Rutherfords, waving goodbye as Punta helped her into the conveyance.

Madison took Punta's hand next and allowed him to help her inside, then sat next to her aunt, who patted the cushioned bench beside her.

Punta gave a signal to the Indian bearers, and Madison couldn't suppress a squeak of surprise as the men grasped the poles on all four ends and lifted them into the air. The bearers took off at a jog and Madison grabbed her aunt's arm to steady herself.

"Sleep tight. Don't let the pythons bite," Lady Moran sang cheerfully to her neighbors as she departed.

On the seat beside her aunt, Madison waved goodbye, and then turned to take in the sights around her. As Lady Moran had explained, the farther they went, the more junglelike the terrain became. Colorful birds flitted from tree to tree, graceful fernlike plants grew higher than Madison's head, and knee-high grass and tangled vines formed verdant carpets that begged to be sketched. Not yet a half an hour into the ride, Madison had already spotted deer, wild boar and a tree of monkeys. The jungle they had entered seemed less dense, the ceiling higher than the jungle of Jamaica, yet somehow she found it comfortingly familiar.

"Wait until it becomes dark," Lady Moran said, patting Madison's hand. "We have even more nocturnal creatures than those that crawl, creep and slither by day."

Madison couldn't help but smile at the sound of her aunt's voice. It was obvious that there was something here in India that was calling her.

"We're nearly there," Lady Moran whispered after they had been traveling for nearly an hour, slipping her arm through her niece's. "Ah, Madison, I cannot believe I've not been here since before Jefford was born, yet I still remember every turn of this road. Things have changed, of course. There were no train tracks this way then. Lord Moran and I traveled to Bombay by elephant."

"There are elephants right here?" Madison breathed.

"Not like there were once upon a time. A hundred years ago, they roamed a far larger range, as did the tigers. But have no fear, with time, I am quite certain we can acquire an elephant or two."

Nodding, Madison gazed into the jungle, unable to suppress a trickle of delicious fear at the mention of tigers. Darkness was beginning to fall, and the warm night air was filled with the clicking sounds of insects and the rustle of animals in the ground cover. "There are tigers here?" Madison murmured, gazing into the tropical forest.

"Yes, which means when you take your painting excursions, which I know you will, you must take guards with you. Guards with guns. Here, my dear, it is the animals you must fear, not the humans. There are many venomous snakes including our infamous cobra, plus tigers, lions, wild dogs and wild boar."

"I promise to be more careful," Madison insisted, trying to take everything in at once: the soft sway of the palanquin, her aunt's nonchalant talk of cobras and tigers. She could hear the soft voices of the natives who accompanied them, and the wave of the trees overhead in the slight, warm breeze. The air was filled with a strong scent she couldn't quite place and she breathed deeply.

Lady Moran, beside her, inhaled as well. "Jasmine." She smiled. "Heavenly jasmine. And here we are! Jefford's messages must have gotten through! Heavens, look at all the lamps in the windows. How could they possibly have known we would arrive tonight?"

The palanquin bearers followed a lazy curve in the road and Madison had to lean to avoid being hit by a low-lying leafy branch. When she lifted her head again, lights twinkled into view through the trees. More than a dozen. Three dozen, at least!

The palanquin and wagons turned into what appeared to be a drive for carriages, and Madison slid forward to the end of the cushioned bench, staring in awe. "Aunt Kendra," she breathed. "You didn't tell me you lived in a palace!"

"Yes, well, I do still have some decorum." She patted Madison's knee. "It's never proper to brag. Lord Moran's family called it the Palace of the Four Winds."

"You could fit three of Windward Bay into it," Madison breathed. "Four!"

"It was constructed by my late husband's family more than a hundred and fifty years ago, built in the style of the ancient Indian palaces, on a smaller version, of course. You'll see a mixture of architecture, mostly *Rajasthani* and *Mughal*," Aunt Kendra explained matter-of-factly. "Inside and out are some stunning examples of Rajput artistry."

The smooth pale pink stone structure was both simple and magnificent with three square bases, the largest at least three stories high in the center, each with curving, gently swelling domes reaching to the sky and a series of semi-octagonal and delicately honeycombed windows.

The Indian bearers lowered the palanquin in front of a short pavilion that led to a massive white gate, and Punta was there instantly to help Lady Moran to the ground. "It does look quite cheery, doesn't it?" she said, her eyes gleaming as she gazed up at the lights burning in the arched windows.

Madison clasped Punta's hand and stepped from the vehicle, still unable to take her eyes from the palace that seemed to rise from the subtropical jungle like a mirage in the desert.

As with their arrival in Jamaica, the pavilion was suddenly a mass of confusion and people; dogs barked, men ran in the darkness, speaking their native dialects. Both doors of the enormous iron gate at the end of the pavilion, wide enough to drive a carriage through, even two, opened as if by magic, and a procession of Indians dressed in red-and-gold uniforms filed out. Punta ran ahead, speaking to the first man, whose coiled turban was different from the others. A gleaming jewel dangled from the fabric in front of his forehead.

Punta half bowed. The man in the turban bowed lower.

"The caste system can be a little complicated, especially here where we have a mixture of them," Lady Kendra murmured in Madison's ear. "There are the Brahmans at the top, then many non-Brahman castes such as the Andavars, Nadars, Vedhars, all in constant fluctuation, struggling to rise closer to the top. And then of course there is the matter of religion, Hindu, Buddhist, Muslim, Christian."

Madison nodded, not really comprehending but knowing there would be time later to better understand.

Punta and the man in the jeweled turban spoke and then Punta looked up and nodded to Lady Moran. She took her time, walking up the stone walk.

The man in the turban bowed to Lady Moran, his hands pressed together, his gaze focused on the ground in reverence. "My Lady Moran, welcome home," he said in English, his diction nearly perfect.

She smiled, nodding regally.

"I am Eknath, sent by the raja of Darshan for your homecoming," he said, his eyes still downcast. "I hope that you will find your palace suitable to your needs. If there is anything that I or my staff can provide for you, we would be greatly honored." Spotting Madison behind her, he bowed again. "Or for your guests."

"It is very good to meet you," Lady Kendra said. "This is my niece, the Honorable Madison Westcott. I must confess, I am greatly surprised by your welcome. How did the raja know I was arriving?"

"I do not know, *sahiba*. I know only that we have been awaiting your joyous arrival for weeks."

Lady Moran glanced up at the lamps burning in the windows overhead. "Weeks?" she said, her voice filled with amusement. "My, my, my."

"Let us escort you to your chambers. You must be greatly tired from your long journey." Eknath walked in front of Lady Moran, Punta walked beside him, and Madison fell in behind them, turning her head this way and that in awe as they entered the palace. Behind her, at least a dozen Indian servants in matching uniforms followed.

The entrance hall was a round room at least sixty feet in diameter with a soaring ceiling, the pale walls lime-washed and painted with exotic murals of kohl-eyed women in saris and handsome Indian men in robes and turbans. There were elephants, tigers and monkeys and flora Madison didn't recognize. The floor beneath them was tiled in a mosaic, the jungle scene too complicated for her to see it all as she crossed over it.

"Please give the raja my warm regards," Lady Kendra said regally, sweeping through the great hall.

"Yes, *sahiba,* a runner has been sent with word of your arrival."

Lady Moran turned to Madison, raising her eyebrows. Madison couldn't suppress a giggle.

The manservant led them into another round hall, similar to the first but lined with gilded chairs, the murals less exotic. They then walked down a wide, tiled azure corridor, one of the many that spoked from the second hall, each a different color.

"I'll never find my way out," Madison murmured, overwhelmed by the palace's magnificence.

Lady Kendra slowed to hook her arm through her niece's. "Just think, when you first arrived at Windward Bay, you thought you'd never find your way around there, either."

"But, Aunt Kendra, this is a palace!" Her voice echoed overhead on the domed ceiling painted pale blue with stars that seemed to twinkle. She lowered her voice to whisper in her aunt's ear. "Who is this Raja who sent all these servants? They've been here for *weeks?*"

"Just an old friend, my dear. I wasn't even entirely certain he was still alive. We lost touch." She patted Madison's arm. "Now, come see my chambers and then I'll have you escorted to yours. Oh, my dear, you will adore the gardens here once they have been cut back and returned to their previous splendor. There will be so much for you to paint!"

Her aunt's chambers were spectacular, room after room, many round, all draped in silk, the walls painted in soothing colors with exquisite murals everywhere. And Madison's chambers, though smaller in scale, were equally magnificent, and so large it would take her an hour to explore them. By the time Sashi tucked her into a great round bed covered with silken sheets, piled with pillows, and draped in the most transparent of silks, Madison felt as if she were floating in a dream.

"I cannot believe the palace looks like this when Aunt Kendra hasn't lived here in more than thirty years, Sashi." She watched as the young woman quietly moved around the room to turn down the blazing oil lamps.

"I think the raja has been preparing for her return for many weeks."

Madison lay on her silken pillow, gazing up at the silk canopy over her head. She felt wonderful. After a light meal with her aunt, she had retired to her own chambers to find that a warm bath had been drawn and four female servants waited to serve her. They had washed her hair, scrubbed her travel-weary body until it glowed, and then she allowed Sashi to massage her skin with a subtle, fragrant oil. Now she was so drowsy, she could barely keep her eyes open, yet she was afraid to close them, afraid that if she did, the dream might end.

"Sleep well," Sashi whispered as she blew out the last

lamp. I will only be in the next room if you have need of me."

Finally surrendering to her exhaustion and the excitement of the day, Madison closed her eyes in the bed that was big enough for three and slept.

The following morning, Kendra bathed, though she had bathed the night before, and Maha helped to dress her in a gold-trimmed emerald silk sari that her dear friend had made for her on the voyage to India. Kendra then slipped her favorite gold rings on her fingers, emerald earrings in her ears and an emerald-encrusted necklace around her neck. She smiled, fingering the glowing stones. She had not worn these jewels since she had departed India. Only after she had added a gold turban and gold slippers did she walk out of her chambers and through the palace into the garden to have her breakfast.

"By Hindi's eyebrows," she murmured, stopping to stare at the garden. She had expected it, after all these years, to be in near ruin, with plants and vines having taken over the walls and trellises and stepping-stones having been carried off by the natives to make their cook stoves. Instead, the garden looked much like it had the day she and Lord Moran had left it, only lusher, more beautiful if that was possible.

Three fountains, the center one being the largest, bubbled cheerfully, splashing droplets onto the stone pathway nearby. Arched white trellises reaching to the clouds were framed with a profusion of red and white climbing roses. Jasmine, in enormous urns, grew in abundance around the stone patio. Beyond the fountains stretched a maze of well-groomed paths, stone benches and green hedges. "Oh, my!" It was so beautiful that it brought tears to Kendra's eyes.

"Does it please you?"

Kendra gasped. The voice startled her so greatly that for a moment she feared she had died the previous night and ascended into heaven. But the bubbling fountains were so real, the smell of the jasmine so thick and sweet, that she knew she could be nowhere else but the Palace of the Four Winds. Slowly, she turned in the direction she had heard the voice.

And there he was, after thirty-five years. Kendra pressed her lips together, her eyes filling with tears.

"Kendra!" he whispered.

Her painted mouth turned up into a smile. "You're not dead yet? You are an old man!"

He smiled and her heart slammed in her chest. Suddenly she was twenty again and about to enter the raja's bedchamber. Nothing mattered, not her family, not society's rules, only that smile. His smile.

"And you are an old woman," he replied, his dark eyes shining. "Beautiful still, but an old woman."

The Raja of Darshan was a tall slender man with skin a sun-kissed red-brown and black hair, now shot with gray, and nearly black eyes that still haunted her dreams. He was dressed in trousers of gold-shot silk and a long red and white *kurta* with a traditional turban on his head. He opened his arms and Kendra did not hesitate.

"I've waited a long time for this," he whispered, closing his arms around her. "My lifetime."

Kendra laughed and choked back a sob of joy. For years and years she had gone over and over in her mind what this homecoming would be like, if it ever were to happen. Now it was as if no time had passed since she stood in this garden. All the years, the tears and the pain were gone.

"You've been keeping my garden all these years," she

murmured, pressing her face into his shoulder, breathing in the scent of his skin.

"All these years, my love. All these years I prayed to Indra that you would return to me."

Kendra laughed, sniffed, feeling foolish. She was beyond the age of such girlish behavior. "You know, I never had any intention of returning, Tushar. Had it not been for a recent turn of events in Jamaica, I would have lived out my life there."

"And I would have wept a thousand tears for a thousand years," he murmured, stroking her cheek and then kissing it. "Your skin is still as soft as the down of a new-hatched chick."

Kendra laughed and stepped away from him, wiping her eyes. "You were always a man with honey words, Tushar. You think I would have learned by now to pay no attention to such nonsense." She studied him from where she stood, shaking her head in amazement. "I didn't even know that you were still alive."

"I would not die without you, my beloved."

Kendra held his gaze, thinking she would never let him out of her sight again. She didn't care how many blasted wives he had. "Will you join me for breakfast?" she asked. "We have much to talk about and there is someone you must meet."

20

Three days later, dressed in a pale peach sari, her legs curled beneath her, Madison sat in the shade of a large tamarind tree. Exotic birds fluttered and chattered in the branches over her head, and the unseen insects buzzed and chirped in the green foliage. Her drawing pad rested in her lap as she sketched two little girls, the children of servants, playing a game with pebbles tossed on the stone path.

"You are feeling rested?" Sashi asked, approaching Madison, carrying a Jamaican sun hat made of palm fronds.

Madison glanced up, squinting in the bright midday sun. "Yes, finally. Thank you." She gave a little laugh. "I think my body is finally saying enough sleep!" She accepted the bonnet, glancing up at Sashi to see the young woman appearing close to tears. "Sashi, what's wrong?" she asked.

The Indian maid shook her head, looking away.

Madison set down the hat and the sketch pad and rose. Like Sashi, she was barefoot, having taken quickly, not just to the native dress of the women, but many other habits, as well. "Sashi."

"The Rutherfords. They are coming for lunch."

"Yes, I know. They'll be here anytime."

"George, he…" She pressed her lips together, stopping, then starting again. "He thinks that we should go to Bombay and be married, but I think, perhaps, I would be better to leave this place. I could return to my father's village in Bengal. Find work."

"Sashi, listen to me." Madison took hold of both her small, dark hands. "Tell me, do you love George?"

"With all my heart," Sashi whispered.

"And do you wish to be married?"

Again, she nodded. "But among my people, a woman does not choose her husband. It is her father who chooses and she must obey."

"But, Sashi, your father has been dead for years. This is an English household. More important, it is Lady Moran's household, and here women marry who they love. If George is the man you want to spend the rest of your life with, you cannot run away."

"I do not wish to take him from his family. He does not understand the pain of being without those who have loved him and cared for him."

"I understand," Madison said.

"But I do not know what to do," Sashi whispered desperately, her dark eyes filling with tears again. "I've prayed to Devi… My heart is breaking, but I will give him up rather than hurt him."

"Oh, Sashi." Madison threw her arms around the girl. "We'll think of something. I swear we will. Now, no more tears. All right?"

Sashi lifted her head from Madison's shoulder, nodding.

"Good."

Suddenly bells rang out, dogs began to bark, and one of the servants ran by, shouting to another. "I think the Rutherfords are here. Those are the bells on the front gate," Madison said, holding Sashi by her shoulders. "Go to our chambers and stay there. I'll be sure to find an excuse to get George to you. I can't promise you'll have much time to be alone together, but at least—"

"No, that will be enough," Sashi cried passionately. She took Madison's hands in hers and squeezed them. "Thank you. I cannot ever repay you for your kindness."

"Madison!" Aunt Kendra sang from somewhere in the honeycomb of the palace walls. "The Rutherfords have arrived, dear."

"Hurry," Madison whispered to her friend, and then called, "Coming, Aunt Kendra!"

Later, after giving them a short tour of the main house, Madison and Aunt Kendra sat down to lunch in a room that overlooked the gardens with their guests, Lady and Lord Rutherford and George and Alice. Nearly a dozen servants dressed in the raja's colors ran back and forth bringing rich goat-meat curries, plates of fruit, flatbreads and fruity drinks. Madison had yet to meet the raja, though she knew he had been in the palace on more than one occasion and she was beginning to get curious.

"It is so kind of you to have us for lunch, Kendra," Lady Rutherford said as she leaned back to allow a young female servant in a red sari to place her napkin in her lap. "Lord Thomblin sends his regards, of course. He was sorry he could not come."

At the mention of Lord Thomblin, Madison looked up.

"Pity," Lady Moran muttered. "Where is he?"

"He stayed with us last night, but then returned to Bombay, apparently," Lady Rutherford said in a hushed voice, her eyebrows raised.

"Why ever for?" Madison asked. "Doesn't he have a home nearby?"

"We're not actually certain," Lady Rutherford confessed, averting her gaze.

"It seems our Lord Thomblin's debts have caught up to him," George said, leaning back in his chair. "I don't believe I'm speaking out of turn if I say he's apparently in more serious financial trouble than we realized."

Lady Moran lifted a painted eyebrow. "Is he, now?"

Madison didn't know what they were talking about, but she would be sure to ask her aunt later.

"Now, son, this is not appropriate dining conversation," Lord Rutherford interrupted, shifting his gaze to the young women, and back. "Lord Thomblin is our friend. And we do not know, truly, what his circumstances are. I'm sure it's all just a misunderstanding."

"I'm sure it is," George echoed.

Lady Rutherford leaned back to allow a servant to refill her water glass while another offered fruit punch. "Kendra, you have so many servants," she tittered. "We've barely a skeletal staff, and I must admit I'm not dealing well with them. They all look so much alike to me, these Indians. I had forgotten what it was like to have a full staff."

Madison glanced up to look at Alice and George across the table, her eyes sparkling with amusement.

"Such an exquisitely lovely home," Lady Rutherford exclaimed as yet another young female servant offered a platter of traditional *biryani* made with goat's meat. "I had forgotten, Kendra, what a magical place this palace was."

Kendra smiled, passing a bowl of sliced fruit with shredded coconut on top, one of Madison's favorite dishes. "It is lovely, isn't it. Different from Jamaica, but quite nice."

"Mother spoke often of the Palace of the Four Winds," George said, tipping his glass of rum punch. "But truly, I had no idea. I assumed she had exaggerated as Mother sometimes does."

Lady Rutherford's eyes widened in indignation as she glared at her son.

"Now, now." Lord Rutherford chuckled, patting his wife's knee beneath the linen-covered table. "Yes, well, Georgie, all you need to do is find yourself an Indian princess and marry her and perhaps you, too, could live in a palace such as this."

"Madison," Alice asked quickly. "Could you pass the flatbread? It's truly delicious."

Madison passed the bone china platter, decorated with gray elephants, her gaze meeting young George's across the table. "Heavens, Lord Rutherford," she said, choosing her words carefully. "You would allow your son to marry an Indian woman? I thought that wasn't done."

"It is the modern age, my dear. Why, we're almost at the close of the nineteenth century! The old ways are dying out quickly." Lord Rutherford waved his fork. "Should a potential candidate be born into the right family of the Brahman caste, I would certainly give such a union consideration. The Brahmans are, after all, much like the royal family of England."

Again, Madison glanced at George, a smile playing on her lips. She had just had the most ingenious, the most wonderful idea. "George, Alice," she said, grabbing her napkin and wiping her mouth as she slid back in her chair.

"Did I tell you that Aunt Kendra has asked me to paint a mural in one of the receiving halls? You must come and see it."

George was already out of his chair, dropping his napkin to the table. "What a superb opportunity. I must see it." He reached for his sister's hand.

"Now?" Alice rose, patting her rosy mouth. "I hadn't yet finished my—"

"If you'll excuse us, sir," George said, bowing to his father. "Ladies."

"By Hindi's eyelashes, do go," Lady Moran insisted, fluttering her napkin.

Madison linked her arms through George's and Alice's and ushered them out of the dining hall, down a pale green hallway.

"Now, what was that all about?" George whispered in Madison's ear.

"Just wait." Madison led them down the corridor, into the second round entrance hall, then down another corridor, this one painted pale yellow. "If I can just find my way to my rooms, where Sashi waits, I have an idea to share with you."

"Oh, thank you," George murmured. "I cannot tell you how much it means to me that you understand. It's been so hard being so close to her all these months, pretending I don't know her."

"Well, that may have been the most important thing you have ever done in your life, my friend," Madison exclaimed, turning down another corridor. "Ah-hah! This looks familiar."

Madison pushed open a tall, richly carved sandalwood door and Sashi popped off a pile of jewel-colored pillows arranged on a cushioned divan on the floor. At the sight of

George, she pulled her veil over her face. Since her return to India, she had begun wearing a veil again. Sashi had explained to Madison that it was tradition that no man saw a woman without her veil, except male family members and her husband.

"Sashi," George called, throwing his arms open. "Sashi, love."

She rushed into his arms. "Oh, George, I have missed you so much."

"There will be time for this later," Madison insisted, grabbing both their hands and lowering herself to her knees on one of the divans. "Now, listen carefully, because I think I may have just come up with a way for you two to be married and for George to keep his fortune and his family name."

That evening, Madison was still bubbling with excitement over her plan that George, Sashi and Alice thought was so outrageous it might work, but now as the tiger-striped shadows of darkness fell on her chambers, she sobered.

Aunt Kendra had sent word that Jefford had arrived and that she requested their presence for dinner. It had been months since Jefford had said anything more to her than a stiff, polite inquiry as to her health, and now she would have to sit at the dinner table and converse with him. Even worse, the mysterious raja would be in attendance as well.

The journey to India had been so long and so exciting that the last night in Jamaica, in the cave with Jefford, had become just a dim dream, something that had happened to another person, in another lifetime. Now that she knew she would have to face him again, converse with him in front of her aunt as if nothing had ever happened, again, the memories came tumbling back.

As Madison sat on a padded bench in front of an elaborately gilded mirror, allowing Sashi to brush jasmine oil in her hair before plaiting it, she closed her eyes. And when she did, she could still feel Jefford's burning mouth on hers; she could feel his searing touch.

Sashi rested her hand on her mistress's shoulder. "You are ready." She smoothed her blond hair with her hand. "And quite beautiful. The blue of your sari matches the blue of your eyes."

Madison smiled back at her in the mirror. "Thank you."

"No, I must thank you. If you had not come up with this proposal, I do not know—"

"Please," Madison interrupted. "Don't thank me yet. I've still got some planning to do and then I must speak to my aunt. It will only work if she will agree to the ruse."

"I could not blame her if she were to say no."

"She won't say no," Madison assured Sashi as she rose from the bench, her gaze moving to her own reflection. The sari, baring a good deal of her shoulders, was truly beautiful, and her friend had created a lovely coiffure, braiding and winding her long hair until it shone like a golden crown on her head. "I suppose I should go," she murmured.

Sashi leaned over, sliding a pair of jeweled, goatskin sandals toward Madison's feet. "Lady Kendra sent these. They were once hers, and she says they will go perfectly with your sari."

"They're so beautiful," Madison breathed, slipping her bare feet into them. "And they fit as if they were made for me."

"Go now and enjoy the evening."

Sashi gave a wave, and Madison walked out the arched doorway of her chambers and down the corridor, the delicate silk scarf of her sari fluttering over her shoulders. Winding her way through the lamp-lit halls, through the great round dining room, she entered the torch-lit garden. She stepped out onto the stone patio and her heart hammered. Him!

Jefford was there, standing before the largest of the three bubbling fountains, his back to her.

Madison stood frozen. What should she do? Run? No. If she turned and ran she would but delay the inevitable. Pressing her lips together, she pulled in a great breath of perfumed evening air and crossed the stone patio. "Good evening."

He turned to her, dressed in the men's traditional Indian garb of a *kurta* and trousers. He had washed his hair and combed it back, looking quite handsome this evening, if a not a bit roguish with his exotic-colored skin and piercing black eyes.

"Good evening," he replied, making no attempt to pretend he wasn't looking her over. "The sari becomes you." He nodded. "You look lovely, if not a bit thin. You were so busy on the ship, but now you have a radiant glow to your cheeks."

"I'm feeling quite rested and eating as if I've not eaten in months." She came to stand beside him and gaze out on the garden.

"What do you think of India so far?" he asked.

"It's absolutely magnificent, so beautiful and yet so strange at the same time."

"Have you had an opportunity to travel beyond the palace yet? I know there will be a great deal you'll want to see, to paint."

"No, I haven't, everyone's been so busy getting settled in. I didn't want to bother Aunt Kendra with making arrangements for guards, and I only have a few canvases left after all the portraits I painted on the ship." She laughed, remembering the passengers clamoring for a portrait.

"Ah, yes, you were quite the celebrity. Well, you're in luck. Actually, doubly so, as I intend to go to a field tomorrow and have a look at some of our property, *and* I've brought enough canvas and wood from Bombay to keep you painting for the next year." He glanced quickly at her. "You're welcome to come with me tomorrow."

Madison felt her heart flutter. Why was he being so kind?

The bells clanged suddenly, announcing the arrival of guests, and Jefford turned, offering his arm. "Well, shall we go meet this mysterious raja who has my mother tittering like a schoolgirl?"

Madison laughed. "I think we should."

Arm in arm they entered the palace and made their way to a private audience hall, a breathtakingly beautiful room with ornate pillars supporting a high, concave ceiling and walls intricately painted in a delicate red-and-gold paisley design.

Lady Moran waited there, flanked by uniformed servants, dressed in a gold sari and turban, her wrists, neck and ears laden with priceless gems and gold jewelry.

"Kendra," Jefford said, releasing Madison's arm to go to his mother. "You look magnificent!"

Lady Moran threw her arms around her son. "Ah, Jefford, it's good to have you home."

He leaned back, looking closely into her eyes. "How are you feeling?"

"I feel positively radiant!"

He released her, looking back at Madison. "Well, I can see that I need to feed both of you, you're both too thin and your cheeks are wan."

Eknath, the Indian man who managed the household,

entered the hall, bowed to Lady Moran and then turned, standing stiffly at attention. "*Sahiba,* the raja of Darshan," he announced.

A tall, handsome Indian man, in his mid-sixties with graying temples, entered the room. He was dressed in gold trousers and a black-and-gold *kurta* with a gold turban around his head and elegant English-made leather boots on his feet. All the Indian servants bowed deeply. Lady Moran touched her hands to her sides and made a half curtsy and Madison followed suit.

"So good of you to join us, Tushar. Come, you must meet my family." Lady Moran clasped Madison's hand and led her to the raja. "This is my stepbrother's daughter, the Honorable Madison Westcott of London."

The raja reached out and took her hand, bowing and kissing it.

Madison smiled, curtsying again. "It is a pleasure to meet you, sir."

"A pleasure for me, my lady." His English was perfect.

"And this," Lady Moran announced, turning to where Jefford stood, "is my son, Jefford."

Madison was still smiling, her gaze on the raja, but when his face suddenly changed, she looked over her shoulder at Jefford.

"It…is a pleasure to meet you, sir," Jefford said, approaching slowly, his gaze fixed on the raja's.

"A pleasure," the raja murmured stiffly, bowing again.

"Well, now," Lady Moran exclaimed, clasping the raja's arm and turning him around. "Now that all this formal nonsense is complete, let us eat, drink and be merry."

Madison watched her aunt walk away, then turned to Jefford. He walked up beside her and offered his arm.

"What was that?" Madison whispered.

He shook his head, his voice taut when he spoke. "I'm not certain, but I believe my mother and I will be having a conversation as soon as I can get her alone."

For the next three hours, Madison, Jefford, Lady Moran and the raja dined on elegant dishes of spicy curries, exotic steamed vegetables, roasted venison, seared trout and assorted fresh fruits. They then were entertained by a troupe of tumbling acrobats accompanied by adorable monkeys wearing tiny turbans. The diversion was delightful. Madison liked the raja, who had been educated in London, immensely. She was fascinated with his stories of governing the local district, trying to keep both his subjects and the English content. The caste system of India was so complicated, its peoples, religions and landscape so diverse, that Madison hung on every word the well-spoken man had to say. It was only during the lulls in conversation that she became aware of tension, not just between her aunt Kendra and Jefford, but her aunt and the raja, as well.

It was near to midnight and they had moved outside to the patio to have a glass of sherry. The garden was lit with torches, and servants stood quietly waving giant palm fronds to keep mosquitoes and other annoying insects away. The conversation had stopped and started several times and the tension in the air increased with every moment.

Madison was just about to excuse herself when Jefford leaned over and spoke quietly but firmly to his mother. "All right, Kendra, enough is enough." He looked to the raja. "Please excuse me if you find me rude, sir, but I cannot hold my question any longer. I know very well, sir, that the question in my mind also lingers in yours." He glared at his mother.

Madison stared in surprise at the sudden outburst, then started to rise. "I'll just say good-night now," she murmured.

"No. Stay, please, Madison." Jefford eyed Kendra, who suddenly looked as if she was feeling terribly guilty about something. "I think you should hear this."

Lady Moran fluttered her favorite fan with the parrots painted on it. "Jefford, the four of us were having such a pleasant evening! What in the name of heaven is it?"

"*What is it? What is it,* Mother? I think you know."

"Yes, I must agree, Kendra," the raja said.

Kendra pointed to her glass, indicating a servant should refill it with sherry. "Tonight I've hosted a dinner party for my favorite people in the entire world." She drew a breath and smiled at the raja.

Jefford looked to the raja. "Would you like me to say it, or you, sir?"

"I think it would be better if you did." The raja reached for his glass. "I fear I might lose my control and strangle her pretty neck right here in front of all these witnesses. The government does not take kindly to Indian men murdering titled Englishwomen."

Madison would have chuckled at the raja's humor, had the moment not been so tense.

Jefford turned back to his mother, his dark-eyed gaze piercing her. "In all these years you have never said…"

Her eyes sparked with anger. "And you have never asked!"

"As for me, I never had the opportunity to ask," the raja injected.

"Fine. Yes." She threw down her fan. "Jefford, my dear. Tushar, the raja of Darshan, is your father." She looked to the raja. "Jefford is your son. I don't know why the two of you are getting yourselves in such a dither. I was going to tell you, I just thought it would be nice for the two of you to get to know each other first."

Madison stared at Jefford, at her aunt, at the raja and at Jefford again. The raja was his father? She had made the assumption, by the tone of Jefford's skin and his ebony hair and black eyes that an Indian man had fathered him, but it had never occurred to her that his father might be royalty. Madison was so completely flabbergasted, she didn't know what to say.

Jefford rose stiffly from his chair. "I think I'll be excusing myself for the evening."

Lady Moran slapped her hand on the table and the sherry glasses jiggled. "You'll be doing no such thing. Jefford, sit down. Sit down, this instant."

"I believe there has been enough talk for one evening," he intoned, turning to his father. "Sir, if you'll excuse me, I must go, else I will be the one who strangles the life from my mother. Frankly, I think it would be better if you and I spoke at a later time when we have both had time to gather our thoughts."

The raja stood, his gaze on Jefford. "Yes, of course. Please, come to my palace and we will…spend some time together."

Jefford pushed in his chair and walked away.

"Well," Lady Moran exclaimed. "This is precisely why I was not so anxious to tell the two of you. I swear, I don't know which of you is worse."

Madison crumpled her napkin in her hand, rising out of her chair. "It…it was very nice to meet you, sir…Raja." She dipped a quick curtsy. "I think I'll turn in, as well. Good night, Aunt Kendra."

She hurried into the house, through the dining hall, finally catching up with Jefford in the yellow corridor where she fell into step beside him, not knowing what to say, but her heart going out to him.

He glanced at her after a moment of silence. "Did you know about this?"

"Did I…certainly not. I only met him tonight when you did."

He scowled. "You know, this is just like her to let all these years pass and then drop something into my lap like this. His lap." He gestured.

"She never said anything to you about your father?"

He shook his head. "She was living here with her father—they were guests of Lord Moran's. Both men were gone a great deal on military campaigns within the empire and she was here alone with the household staff. I simply gathered…"

"You were the son of one of her servants," she whispered, shocked, but knowing she might have come to the same conclusion, in his position. "I…I understand."

Jefford halted in the corridor, turning to face her. "It never mattered to me who he was. Her father died in the Indian revolt, never knowing his daughter was pregnant. Lord Moran came home, she told him of her situation, and he married her. He retired from the queen's service and they sailed for his lands in Jamaica. All that mattered to me was that Lord Moran was good to her. And he was." He opened his arms. "He was also good to me, but he was never my father. I simply never had one."

"And now?" she asked softly.

He lifted his hand, let it fall, and then brushed back the dark hair that had fallen over his forehead. "And now I do."

He met her gaze and Madison felt a surge of emotion.

She was hurting for him, yet happy for him, as well. Even in the very short time she had spent with the raja, it was obvious to her that he was a good man, as it was also quite obvious that, in many ways, his son took after him.

"You should go to bed," Jefford said. He reached up to brush her cheek with the back of his hand. "I'm worried about you. You look tired."

She closed her hand over his, so confused by her emotions that she didn't know where to start trying to understand them. "You mustn't hold this against the raja. I imagine he never knew she was going to have his child."

"Oh, it's not the raja I'm angry with," he called over his shoulder as he walked away. "It's Kendra who has some explaining to do."

"Well, what have you to say for yourself?"

Kendra didn't meet Tushar's dark-eyed gaze in the mirror in front of her, even when he rested his hand on her shoulder.

"I don't understand why everyone is so upset. There was no need to tell the droll details before." She removed her turban and smoothed back the thinning red hair she had left. Even now that she was in India again, she refused to wear a woman's veil. A man's turban better suited her disposition. "And then we came back to India, so there was."

"That is not a good-enough explanation," he said sternly.

She rose, slipping her white silk dressing gown off her shoulders and tossing it on the bed. She had dismissed all her servants and they were alone in the glowing light of her round bedchamber, hung with the jewel-colored silk draperies of her past. "Well, it's the only explanation I have and I am sorry if it does not please you. I did what I thought best at the time."

She slipped her feet out of her kidskin slippers and stepped up on the platform to her silk-curtained bed. "Lord Moran knew before he married me that I was with child. He wasn't cheated out of anything. In return for marrying me and taking away my shame, I was a good wife to him." She turned to face him, meeting his gaze with defiance. "In every sense of the word, despite the terrible injuries he'd received in the war, injuries that prevented him from ever fathering an heir. From ever consummating…oh, it was so long ago!"

She turned her back to him and lifted her thin sleeping gown over her head, naked beneath it. "So now—" she faced him "—are you going to pout about this all night or are you going to come to my bed and make love to me? Neither of us are getting any younger, you know."

The raja smiled as he removed his *kurta*. "You're not going to get away with this so easily, I warn you. Yes, tonight I will make love to you, but tomorrow—"

She dropped onto the bed, stretching out to look up at him. "Oh, Tushar, forget about tomorrow. Who knows if we'll even still be here." She raised her hand up to him in a peace offering.

The raja hesitated, then took it and lowered his head, pressing a kiss to the soft skin of her bare shoulder. "You are still as magnificent as you ever were… If we do live to see the dawn, there is only one way you can make this up to me."

"How?" she asked, smiling up to him. "I still think I know a few tricks." She winked.

He laughed. "Marry me, Kendra. Make an old raja happy."

21

Madison rested her head on her pillow, watching Sashi pull back the silk drapes on her bed. Sashi had been acting oddly for days, watching her, behaving as if she needed to talk about something but wouldn't say it, and it was beginning to worry Madison. "All right, out with it," Madison said suddenly, unable to stand it any longer. "What is it?"

"What is what?" Sashi asked innocently.

Madison eyed her companion. "You know what. Why do you keep looking at me that way? Is there something wrong? Have I done something wrong?"

Sashi came to the side of the bed and sat down on the edge, something she had never done before, and suddenly Madison was concerned.

"I would ask that you not take offense," the young woman said, "but I must ask you a question."

Now Madison almost wished she hadn't asked. "And what is that?"

"The servants, the girls in the laundry, have been whispering as servants do." Sashi halted and started again. "And they say your sheets always come to be washed unstained. Is there…" She hesitated. "Is it possible that you could be with child? I have noticed that you have not had your monthlies since we were in Jamaica."

Madison's eyes flew open and she covered her mouth with her hand. "No! Of course not. Certainly not. I—" Her voice trembled and she closed her eyes.

The same thought had crossed her mind more than once, especially in the last two weeks. The very thought was almost more than she could bear, which was precisely why she had not allowed herself to consider it. "I couldn't be," she murmured.

Sashi sat there quietly until Madison opened her eyes again. "Oh, Sashi," she whispered, knowing in her heart of hearts it was true. "What am I going to do?" Tears slipped from the corners of her eyes. The idea was even too horrible to consider, and yet she knew she finally had to. In the three months since she left Jamaica, her courses had not come. She had told herself it was due to the commotion of her life, all the travel. She'd made one excuse after another, but now it seemed as if she could longer do so.

"Madison—"

"Yes," she cried, sitting upright and throwing her bare feet over the side of the bed. "Yes, all right," she said, suddenly on the verge of hysteria. "I could be…there could be a baby."

Sashi calmly folded her hands in her lap. She was wearing a bright yellow sari this morning and looked simply radiant. "Then you must tell Lady Kendra at once."

"No." Madison threw herself back in the bed and closed her eyes again. She shook her head vehemently. "I can't tell Aunt Kendra. She'll be so hurt, so angry. I can't tell anyone."

"How long?" Sashi asked calmly.

Sashi waited a moment and then went on. "You must tell me so that I can help you. Has it been since the night before we left Jamaica?"

"How did you know?" Madison opened her eyes, staring up at her silky bed curtains. "Do others really know?"

Sashi shook her head. "I do not think anyone else suspects." She looked down at her hands. "I only thought that you were different after that night. That Mr. Jefford—"

"Please, I cannot even bear to hear his name," Madison moaned miserably.

"You know that that is not true," Sashi said. "You are only upset. Let me get you some tea and a bit of sweet biscuit. I will bring your aunt here."

"No. No, Sashi, I can't tell her. I really can't." She squeezed her eyes shut, tears running down her cheeks. "I'm so ashamed."

Sashi patted her hand. "Do not cry. It is bad for the baby. Will make him sad. I will get Lady Kendra. She will know what to do."

All too quickly, Sashi returned with Lady Moran in tow.

"Come, come, come, you cannot lie in bed all day," Lady Moran declared. "Sashi, open all the draperies, let some morning sunlight and air in and then fetch us some tea."

Sashi nodded, backing out of the room.

Lady Kendra came to Madison's bed and plopped herself down on the edge. "Madison, look at me."

Madison slowly opened her teary eyes.

"This is not the end of the world, my darling. Now, sit

up and wipe those lovely blue eyes." She snatched a handkerchief off the table beside the bed and dabbed at Madison's eyes. "Not only is this not the end of the world, but it might very well be the beginning of an exciting adventure. I can tell you that my unexpected pregnancy with Jefford certainly was!"

Madison took the handkerchief from her aunt's hand, wiped her eyes and then lowered it to her lap. "I'm so sorry," she whispered miserably. "I never meant for this to happen. I never thought—"

"There, there, you needn't feel you must give me the details, sweet. Let's move on, shall we?"

Madison stared at her aunt, sniffed and wiped her nose with the cloth. "You're not upset with me?"

"Certainly not. How in the name of Hindi's coffin could I be upset with you? In fact, I must admit, I'm quite delighted." Lady Moran rose from the bed and went to a large elaborately carved sandalwood chifforobe where Madison kept much of her clothing. "Now, get up, get yourself dressed." She chose a lavender sari and tossed it on the bed. "Have Sashi comb your hair and then meet me in my chambers where we can discuss this matter sensibly."

"Is that all?" Madison asked, sliding her bare feet over the side of the bed. "You…you're not going to tell me how terribly wrong this was of me. How—"

"Madison, love, did you not hear what I said? I'm delighted, dear." She floated toward the door. "I'm going to be a grandmother!"

An hour later, dressed and groomed and with tea in her stomach, Madison bravely walked down the corridor to her aunt's chambers. To her shock, the raja was just leaving, wearing the same clothing he had worn to dinner the previous night….

He gave a slight bow and smiled. "Good morning."

Madison could feel herself blushing as she realized the implications of seeing the raja this morning under these circumstances. "Good…morning," Madison stammered.

"I must leave to attend to daily matters at my palace," he said as he passed her. "But I hope that I will see you this evening for dinner."

"Yes. I'll…I'll see you this evening," she said, turning in a circle to watch him go, then walking through Lady Moran's open doors.

"You may enter," Maha said, in the first chamber. She pointed to a small room off Lady Moran's main bedchamber.

Madison walked in to find her aunt seated at a table signing documents, with Jefford standing at the floor-to-ceiling windows that opened onto the garden.

Madison stopped short. She hadn't expected to find Jefford here. Why, she wasn't sure. Of course he would be here. But she wasn't certain she was ready to see him yet. Not certain she was ever—

"Come, come, now, young lady. No need to be shy with him, is there?" Lady Moran didn't look up from the document she was signing. "Now, children, this is quite a simple matter to solve. I wish all my problems were this uncomplicated."

Madison rested her hand on the arched doorway, wishing she were anywhere else, even London.

Jefford turned from the window, not even bothering to speak to Madison.

"You will be married at once," Lady Moran commanded, laying aside her pen.

"Of course, I accept full responsibility. I'll marry her," Jefford said.

"I'm not…I'm not marrying him!"

Both Jefford and Lady Moran looked at Madison.

"I'm not!" she said, wrapping her arms around her waist.

Jefford glared at her. "Is the baby mine?"

"How dare you, you insufferable lout of a—"

He waited, his dark-eyed gaze on her face.

"Yes," she confessed after a long moment of silence, tears filling her eyes. She wiped at them impatiently. "Of course the baby is yours. I have never been with another man. Only…only with you." She looked down at the pale green tiled floor. "Just that once."

"All it takes, my dear!" Lady Moran rose from her chair. "Now, I'm going to bathe and dress. Why don't the two of you have a little chat? Kiss and make up and then, Madison, you can join me on my veranda. We have a great deal of work to do in a very short time. By my calculation you're already more than three months gone, so we've no time to waste."

Madison stepped back to let her aunt pass, staring at her in utter shock. It was almost more than she could grasp. Pregnant. Going to be married? To Jefford?

Lady Moran took her leave and Madison just stood there in the doorway, not knowing what to say. Jefford had turned back to the window.

"I'm sorry," she whispered after a long moment of silence.

He lifted one shoulder in a shrug. "I'm a grown man. I know the risks involved."

His words were so cold. Madison didn't know what she expected, but that wasn't it. "You don't want to marry me,

Jefford, and I certainly don't want to marry you." She took a step toward him. "We'll just tell your mother no, we won't do it."

"That's out of the question. This is not little isolated Jamaica. This is India, the crown jewel of the British Empire. There is no place for English girls with bastard babies except in dark establishments on the streets of Bombay, and I am certain your friend Lord Thomblin can tell you about them."

She pressed her lips together, gazing down at the floor. His words stung and she wanted to hurt him back.

He just stood there at the window, watching as a snake slithered across the grass. "Tell me something," he said quietly, after a moment, turning toward her. "Do you not want to marry me because I am half Indian? Because the child will be a mudblood?"

She stared at him, horrified he would think she'd think such a thing. "Certainly not!"

He watched her for a moment as if he didn't believe her, then glanced away. "This week has certainly been full of surprises." His tone was undeniably cynical. "I learned that my father, whom I never knew, is an exalted raja. And now I learn that I am to be both a father and a husband." He turned back to her. "So, I think I will go now to see to this land we'll be working. Would you like to go with me?"

Madison felt her ire rising until it burned on her cheeks. "No, damn you, I am not going with you! I won't be manipulated like a wooden doll by your mother or you! I wouldn't go with you if you were the last living man on this earth," she shouted. Then she spun on the heels of her silk slippers and left the room.

Carlton picked his way along the dark, narrow street, taking care to avoid other pedestrians as well as the foul-smelling puddles. He heard the whine of a child and looked down to see one of the filthy creatures thrust out its hand. Bloody beggars! They were everywhere in Bombay. This one was particularly repulsive with its hare lip and drooling mouth. He despised this degenerate city and could not for the life of him remember why he had agreed to return.

He kicked the child out of his way with his boot, snatching his cloak from its grimy fingertips. With a yelp, the foul little beast tucked itself into a ball and rolled into the gutter where it belonged.

Thomblin continued along the street. He did not have to look at the address; he knew where the opium den was.

His meeting at the Bombay Gentlemen's Club had not gone well. While he insistently told the banker that the monies he owed had been transferred from London, the man was threatening to take his Indian holdings. Then where would he go? When last he had been in London, what was left of the family estate in Essex was being auctioned off and divided among a dozen creditors. It wasn't his fault if the coffee trade was down! The damned Caribs in Jamaica had ruined the crop. One of his shipments had been lost at sea. Then he'd had to evacuate the island or be burned at the stake by the bastards. These things took time, he had tried to tell the banker.

Time was apparently what he did not have. And now the gambling debts he had racked up on the steamship on the journey here were coming to haunt him already. And he was barely two weeks in the country. Damn, he was the seventeenth earl of Thomblin, did no one have respect for the title anymore?

Thomblin passed a young, barefoot, pale-skinned girl in a dirty sari standing in a doorway. It was difficult to tell how old she was, but certainly past the age of bleeding.

"Sahib?" she called out to him, swaying her hips suggestively. It was obvious she was half Indian, half white, a by-blow of a passing English soldier, and she appealed to him. Cleaned up, deloused, she might be rather entertaining. Women like her were eager to please. It was amazing what humans would do for food. Water.

He stopped, looking back, and raised a coin in the air. "Do you speak English?" he asked.

She raised her hand in the air, eager to snatch the coin from his.

"Take this, get something to eat. Then come back. There's more where that came from. Do you understand?"

The girl nodded, her pale brown eyes wide with hunger.

Thomblin tossed the coin in the air, not wanting to touch her until she was clean. She snatched it in midair and ran off. He continued another half block and then halted at an unmarked door. He knocked and the door swung open.

The cloying, sweet scent of opium filled his nostrils. It was a habit he knew enough not to succumb to. It made men weak. Dull. "Captain Bartholomew," he told the doorkeeper, slipping him a coin. This was what these bankers did not seem to understand. It took money to make money.

"In the back," the doorkeeper said. "Red door."

Thomblin walked through a dim room where some men sat at small round tables, while others lounged prostrate on cushions and smoked from elaborate opium pipes, their eyes glazed. A naked boy of no more than five or six lay on the floor at the feet of one of them, crying softly, gripping his belly.

Thomblin scowled and cut down the hallway. He knocked on the red door and walked in. A group of English officers were playing cards. Captain Bartholomew glanced up, a thick cigar in his mouth. He was a painfully thin man with a fat man's face; Thomblin theorized that there was a reason why his headquarters was at the rear of an opium den, but it was none of his concern what ghastly habits the queen's magistrate possessed.

"You wanted to see me?" he said, smoke curling around his head.

Thomblin glanced at the other men and back at Bartholomew.

"For Christ's sake," the captain muttered, shaking his head. "All right." He slapped down his cards. "Get the hell out of here," he told the men at the table.

With some grumbling, they all rose and walked out the red door, closing it behind them.

"Heard you were back in town. Jamaicans run you out as well?" Bartholomew chuckled at his own joke and rocked back in his chair to pull a bottle from a desk drawer. He gathered two small glasses from the table and poured two shots. He pushed one glass to Thomblin, pulled his cigar from his mouth, lifted his glass in toast and threw it back.

Thomblin preferred clean, unused glasses, but he drank the whiskey. "Come to see what you're in need of. Back in business, are you?"

"Don't know that I ever was *in business*. I provided what was requested by a few friends."

"And took the gold offered, didn't you?" The captain slapped his glass down. "Trade changed since you were last here. Two years is a long time to be gone."

"Changed how? Men will be men won't they?" Thomblin cracked a smile.

"What you're talking about is in abundance on the street. Anyone can walk out and buy it, steal it on his own.

No, my new clients are more, *particular,* shall we say?" He puffed on the cigar.

Thomblin glanced away. He despised having to deal with filth like Bartholomew, but had little choice. "Look, are you interested in making purchases or not?"

"Oh, I'm interested and paying top price." The captain rose. "But I don't want that trash you used to bring me." He grabbed an oil lamp off the desk and indicated with a jerk of his head that Thomblin should follow him.

They went out a different door than Thomblin had come in and down a narrow hallway that smelled of human urine. He stopped halfway down, and for a moment Thomblin feared the man might be intending to strike him over the head and take what he had in his coin purse. Instead, the captain lifted his chin in the direction of a narrow door. "Open it and have a look-see."

Thomblin hesitated, hating to even lay his hand on the filthy brass knob, but he reached out and turned it. The battered wooden door creaked as he pulled it open.

Bartholomew lifted the lamp high and Thomblin looked inside.

A young woman, blue eyes distorted in terror, gagged and hands bound behind her, shrank back in the corner of what appeared to be an old linen closet. She was filthy, naturally, and reeked, but that was not unusual. What was extraordinary was that she was a white woman. And not a white woman off the streets, either. Her light brown hair was thick and full and she appeared well fed. This was some Englishman's daughter…wife.

"Can you provide this?" Bartholomew asked, closing the door. "No light-skinned natives. No Eurasians."

Thomblin glanced up at him. "Name your price and perhaps we can do business."

* * *

Several days later, Jefford paced in the small but lavish private audience hall of the raja's palace. He paused and studied the murals on the walls, hunting scenes and lush gardens, and thought to himself that they were not as good as the paintings Madison had produced. He shook his head and almost smiled, the idea that such a thought would occur to him struck him as odd. He'd been thinking a lot about her this past week. On the one hand, he was angry that he was being forced to marry her this way, but a part of him was glad to have the matter settled, glad to see Kendra so pleased. She had been feeling well since they arrived in India, but he knew her health was still deteriorating and to give her this one joy pleased him. Of course, Madison continued to swear she would not marry him, and he knew she would be nothing but trouble, but everyone in the household seemed to be ignoring her wishes, especially Kendra. She was going about her merry way, making plans for the greatest wedding the Palace of the Four Winds had ever seen. Madison would come around, she had assured him. Jefford sure as hell hoped so, because he would not have his child born a bastard, even if he had to tie Madison up and carry her to the altar bound foot, hand and mouth.

"Mr. Harris, sir." An English-speaking Indian servant appeared in one of the arched doorways and bowed formally. "The raja will see you in his private chambers."

Jefford followed the servant down one corridor after another, weaving his way deeper into the old palace that was actually not as large as the Four Winds, though much older.

At a set of intricately carved, gold-leaf doors, the servant halted, opened the door and stepped back. Jefford walked in to find the raja seated at a walnut desk. He was surprised to see that the small room, obviously an office, resembled an Englishman's library with dark, wainscoted walls and floor-to-ceiling bookcases. It even smelled of English tobacco.

"Raja." Jefford pressed his hands to his sides and lowered his head, surprised to find that he was this nervous.

"Please," the raja said, rising. "I prefer no formality between us." He was wearing a pair of tiny wire-framed reading glasses; his dark eyes studied Jefford's as he came around the desk. "I cannot tell you how pleased I am that you have come."

"I apologize for not coming sooner, sir." Jefford glanced away, uncomfortable under the man's scrutiny. He was who he was and he made no excuses to any man. "There is so much to do. So much I have to learn if I am to oversee Kendra's properties. This land is altogether different from Jamaica."

The raja leaned against his desk. He was dressed in Western clothes: straight English trousers and a white shirt with a stylish cravat. A jacket lay on the back of his chair. Jefford, on the other hand, had chosen the native dress with baggier trousers and a loose-fitting shirt.

"Please. No apology is necessary." The raja held up his hand. "I know it must have taken a few days for you to get used to the idea."

"Me?" Jefford chuckled. "At least I was aware I had a father. You had no idea you had a son!"

"Yes." The raja folded his arms over his chest. "I wanted to be very angry with Kendra. She broke my heart when she left. If she had only given me a chance, I could have made her my first wife."

"But she should have told you she was carrying your child."

The raja nodded. "I never knew what happened. She even lived a short time here in the palace with me while her father and Lord Moran were gone."

"In your harem," Jefford ground out, his words harsh.

The raja glanced up, removing his English glasses. He set them on the desk. "Life has changed a great deal in the last thirty-five years. Then, my father had only recently died. I was young, trying to learn his duties thrust suddenly upon me in a world I barely knew any longer. After years in England I was suddenly home again, attempting to manage the needs of my people while meeting the demands of the British. I had only recently returned from school in England, and I missed the way of life; in some ways I looked down upon my father's life. Your mother, Kendra..." He looked away, as if looking back into the past. "She was a part of the world I wanted to belong to. She was so bright, so beautiful, and so headstrong."

Jefford chuckled. "I suppose she hasn't changed much, then."

"No, she has not. She is as stubborn a woman now as she was at twenty years old." He smiled fondly. "You know, I have asked her to marry me again and again but she refuses. My wives are all dead. I never had any sons and my daughters are all gone, married and living with their husbands' families. I want Kendra to be my one true wife as she should have been all those years ago. I want her to live out her last days in the joy she deserves."

It was Jefford's turn to glance away as he fought the emotion that tightened in his chest, threatening to embarrass him in front of the man he could not quite bring himself to see as his father. "She told you of her illness."

The raja nodded. "We agreed no secrets. The last time she left me, she simply walked out of my chambers and did not return." He took a deep breath and turned his head slightly to look out a window toward mountains far in the distance. "I had promised to marry her, but when my father died, I was forced to make the decision to make a political marriage first." He looked up again. "That was not, apparently, satisfactory to Kendra." He half smiled. "I heard from servants later that she had married Lord Moran and sailed for Jamaica."

Jefford smiled inwardly. So that was why his mother had not stayed in India, why she had married Moran. Because she would be second to no one, not even in name. Jefford smiled inwardly. It was so like her. "Well, I wanted to come and pay my respects." He raised his hand. "I will not keep you."

"Please, come again. Anytime, you are welcome in my home. If you would like to discuss indigo or coffee or any of your crops with one of my district overseers, they are at your disposal. They might have knowledge of weather patterns and growing conditions that would be of value to you."

"Thank you." Jefford nodded. "I'm not certain how much time I will have for calling. It seems I have a great deal to occupy my days."

"Yes, yes, your wedding." The raja clasped his hands. "Kendra is so pleased."

"She seems to be. I believe I was drawn into another of my mother's spiderwebs in this matter and I suspect that the day we set foot in London, she intended for me to marry Madison."

"Your wife-to-be is a very beautiful and very intelligent woman, full of love of life. That was quite obvious the night we dined. A rare woman, indeed, and Kendra tells me she is an excellent artist."

Jefford nodded. "Well, sir." He started to back his way out of the office. The meeting had gone better than he expected, but he was not yet prepared to become a son to this man. A moment of conception could not make up for thirty-five years.

"Please." The raja approached him. "I know that it would not be right for you to address me as *Appa*... Father, but—" He halted, looking Jefford squarely in the eyes. "It would honor me if you would call me Tushar, as my friends do." He hesitated. "Because I would like for us to be friends."

"Until we meet again, Tushar," Jefford said. "Invitations for my wedding should arrive shortly. I hope that you will come."

"I would not miss your wedding, Jefford. And I understand that you and your bride wish for elephants as wedding gifts?"

Jefford chuckled. "If you are trying to endear yourself to my wife-to-be, I believe an elephant would certainly make an excellent impression."

We wanted elephants? Kendra had to be at the bottom of this notion. Jefford was still chuckling when he emerged from his father's palace into the hot Indian sun. He had one more visit to make, one he suspected would not have such a pleasant outcome.

"Jefford, my *amoureux*." Chantal put her arms out to him as he walked through the doorway of the small room she shared with several other servants in the palace. "You should have sent for me," she said, her voice sultry. "Chantal would have come at once." She ran her palms over his chest, slipping her hands up over his shoulders.

Jefford kept his gaze downcast, as he caught both her

wrists and stepped out of her reach. "Chantal, please. I need to talk with you."

"The other girls, they work now. Busy. Come lie with me." She grasped his hand and tried to draw him toward one of the simple pallets made up along the walls of the servants' quarters.

"Chantal, damn it, will you listen to me?"

She released his hand, staring up at him, her dark eyes flashing with anger. "Tell me it is not true," she whispered harshly. *"Souplé!"*

Jefford looked into her eyes, which had filled with tears, then glanced away. He knew it had been a mistake to sleep with her on the steamship. He felt guilty as hell about it, now that he knew Madison had been pregnant then. But he hadn't known. If he had, he would never have done it.

"Chantal, I'm marrying Madison—"

"Non!" she cried, flinging herself into him.

He instinctively put his arms out and she instantly molded her body to his, slipping her leg between his, pressing her groin to him.

"Jefford, *amoureux, souplé.*" She rested her cheek against his chest.

Once, this young woman had stirred his blood as no woman ever had before, but he felt nothing for her now, not even a ripple of desire.

"Non," she sobbed. "You must marry me. You promised me!"

He grabbed her shoulders, pushing her away from him. "No, Chantal," he said firmly. He was angry now, ready to be done with this, done with her. "I never said I would marry you. *Never.*"

"Liar!" she shrieked. *"Ou manti!"*

"Chantal, you knew what we had between us. You always knew what it was."

"Non!" She flew at him again, nails bared.

He flung his arm upward to block her attack. "Chantal, listen to me and listen carefully. You and I are done." He wiped his mouth with the back of his hand. "Been done for some time."

"For her? For that cold English fish? What of me?"

"I want to be certain that you're taken care of, that I did promise you. But you'll have to leave the palace."

"Non," she screamed angrily, kicking him. "Never."

He silenced her tantrum with a withering glare. "Either you'll move into the village," he said quietly, "or I'll send you to Bombay to work in the raja's house there. You might prefer living farther—"

"Non, please!" she murmured, lowering her talons, suddenly contrite. She stared at him with those big dark eyes of hers that he had once been so fond of, her cheeks shiny with tears. "Do not send Chantal so far away," she begged, clutching her hands. "Chantal could not bear to be so far from you, my *amoureux!"*

He started to back toward the door. Kendra had offered to take care of Chantal for him, but he had thought he owed it to the young woman to at least tell her himself. Now he almost wished he had let Kendra deal with her.

"Pack your things," he said, suddenly realizing that he should have done this long ago. "Someone will come for you in the morning."

She wiped at her eyes, following him as he stepped into the narrow corridor that connected the servants' quarters in the palace.

"You make a mistake, *amoureux.* You will never be happy with that white woman bitch."

Without thinking, Jefford drew back his hand, catching himself an instant before he struck her.

Chantal flinched, her eyes suddenly filled with fear.

"Do not let me ever, *ever* hear you say that again, do you understand me?" he demanded between clenched teeth.

She wrapped her arms around her waist, staring at him. "You make a mistake," she whispered as he walked away. "You make a terrible mistake and she will see...."

22

"Madison, please, you must stand still," Aunt Kendra clucked from the divan where she rested. Beside her, amid the silk, tasseled pillows, a full-grown white tigress stretched languidly and yawned.

Madison clenched her fists to her sides, seething. She wanted to be out and about, not cooped up with all these women. She had a portrait of one of the kitchen maids to complete and there was her mural in the receiving hall that she'd barely begun! It frustrated her that she had been in India six weeks and had not left the elaborate compound of courtyards, gardens and buildings of the Palace of the Four Winds. Six weeks, and she had not seen anything of the jungle, but for what she could see when she peeked out of the gates. There was not a tiger, not an elephant, not a python to be seen in the inner walls of the palace. With the exception of her aunt's new pet, Nanda, a gift from the raja, she hadn't seen a single wild creature!

Bribery, Aunt Kendra called it, shameless bribery. Nanda was a rare white tigress that one of the raja's men had found wounded in the jungle, shot by English rifles and left to die. He'd ordered that the tigress be brought to his palace and ministered back to health. Now the white animal with her dark stripes was bright-eyed and well fed, her belly rounded with the cubs that would be born any time. Nanda had taken so easily to the humans that the raja was certain she had been someone's pet who had escaped or been stolen for sport. She seemed so used to being fed by hand she would never have had a chance of survival in the wild jungle.

"Only a bit longer, *sahiba*," the Indian dressmaker assured Madison, her mouth full of pins.

Madison couldn't resist a sardonic smile. "You know, Aunt Kendra, some things are no different, no matter where in the world you live. In my mother's home in London I've stood on a stool and served as a pincushion until I was hot and irritable too many times to recall. Now in India, more than ten thousand miles away, here I stand, arms outstretched, enduring this endless torture again. And for a wedding ensemble, no less!"

"Ah, Madison, but the dress suits you so well!"

Madison could not deny that the wedding gown Lady Kendra had designed was beautiful. A *farshee* gown, patterned after a Mogul design that was more than three centuries old, it was lavish teal-and-white silk with glimmering jewels sewn along the neckline, over the delicate cap sleeves, and down the folds of the shimmering garment.

Of course, Madison had no intention of wearing it. She was not marrying Jefford. She'd told her aunt she would not marry him, again and again. She told Jefford each time he saw her; she told anyone in the immediate household willing to listen to her. Yet preparations for the festivities of the three-day wedding celebration, only a week away, continued. Wedding gifts had begun to arrive and they were so many, so grand, that one of the vast public halls in the palace had been set aside to display them.

"Please," Madison groaned. "I must get down, Aunt Kendra. I can't breathe, I can't think!"

She turned to her aunt, who was feeding the tigress bits of goat cheese from her plate. Her aunt had not been eating well and the kitchen and servants dedicated many hours to trying to tempt their mistress with appetizing morsels.

"Aunt Kendra, did you hear me? I fear I'm going to faint."

"You most certainly are not going to *faint,*" Lady Moran cried drolly. "For lavish parties, sumptuous gifts, a wedding celebration, this is the price a bride must pay."

The Indian girls, servants from the household and the dressmaker's shop, giggled. India, Madison had learned, was no different from England in that a woman's wedding day was supposed to be the greatest day of her life. Looking ahead, the day fast approaching, Madison saw it as the worst. How could she marry Jefford? He didn't love her. He didn't even like her, but that argument had gotten Madison nowhere with her aunt. *Poppycock* was the only response she had gotten.

Out of the corner of her eye, Madison saw Sashi enter the room and walk over to Lady Moran. The young woman leaned over and whispered in her ear.

"No!" Lady Moran explained excitedly. "He hasn't!"

Sashi grinned and nodded her head.

"Madison, love, another gift has arrived for you." Lady Moran rose from the divan with Sashi's assistance.

"I suppose it must be placed in the audience chamber,"

Madison said sarcastically. "I do hope someone is keeping an inventory of these gifts, because they will all have to be returned."

"I do not believe this gift can be placed in the audience hall." Lady Moran clapped her hands and the dressmaker stepped back and lowered her head. "That will be enough for now. Our bride-to-be has grown quite contrary. Shall we all adjourn for refreshment and meet again later?"

"As you wish, *sahiba*," the dressmaker agreed, bowing her head repeatedly, while shooing her servants in Madison's direction.

"I don't want to see any gifts," Madison protested as the young women helped her down from the stool, removed the gown and helped her step into a brightly colored two-piece sari with a separate skirt and a bodice that barely reached her midriff. The first time Madison had worn this particular style of sari, she'd been terribly self-conscious. But after seeing her aunt parade about, her fifty-five-year-old abdomen bared, Madison realized that it was time she began to adapt to her new surroundings, just as she had done in Jamaica. Unlike Alice Rutherford, who still wore her stifling high-necked, long-sleeved English gowns, Madison saw a definite practicality to the Indian styles in the infernal heat and humidity of the climate.

Fully clothed, sandals on her feet, she reluctantly followed her aunt out of the commotion of the room. She had no desire to see this wondrous gift, but she would do anything to get away from the dress fitting.

"Where is this gift?" Madison asked as they cut through a rectangular open chamber, down another hall to an area of the palace they rarely frequented.

"In the west courtyard," Sashi said, unable to hide her delight on her face.

Madison had talked several times with Sashi about her situation with George, and Madison wanted to talk to her aunt, but Sashi and George both insisted that presently, it was Madison and Jefford's wedding that had to take precedence. They understood the need for Lady Moran to be a part of the plot, but thought it prudent to delay a little longer. It was important to Madison that she keep her promise to her maid and to George, but she gave in and agreed to wait to set their plot in motion.

They reached a room with open doors leading to the courtyard, and Madison glanced out the windows to see several servants' children laughing and racing across the tiled pavilion, obviously intent on seeing something.

"What are you up to, Aunt Kendra?" Madison asked.

Lady Moran looked to Sashi, who was raising her veil before they stepped outside, and they both giggled.

"I'm not up to a thing," Lady Moran declared. "It's the raja who is responsible."

"Responsible for—" Madison stepped out of the room, into the walled courtyard, and her mouth fell open. "Oh, my," she breathed. "An elephant!"

Several servants gathered around, watching while the children darted forward to rub the rough skin of the giant creature.

Madison lifted her hand to her forehead to shade her eyes. A square box covered in red-and-yellow silk, much like the palanquin in which they had ridden to the palace, sat securely on the elephant's back.

"*Sahiba.*" A short, slender young man dressed in the raja's colors bowed formally, first to Lady Moran, then to Madison. He was carrying a short stick with a bright red tassel on the end of it. "The raja sends his congratulations on the glorious wedding to take place and offers this elephant as a gift to the lady."

"It's for me?" Madison breathed, approaching the giant beast.

"Her name is Bina," the man explained, "and I am Vijay, her *mahout*."

"Kendra, what in God's name do you—" Jefford walked out the door, into the courtyard and stopped short.

Lady Moran turned to him. "A wedding gift from the raja." She lifted her arms upward. "I thought you would like to see it."

Madison looked away from him, back at the elephant. They had barely spoken since the day her aunt had declared they would marry, and when they did talk, it was only to argue.

"I'll be damned," Jefford chuckled.

Madison stroked the rough, wrinkled hide of the elephant, staring up at its tiny eyes. Bina swung her trunk back and forth gently, then reached for a tall, umbrella-shaped rain tree and snatched some leaves. Madison watched with delight as she tucked them into her mouth and chewed.

"I think you should take a ride," Lady Moran suggested. "You've been saying you wanted to escape the palace grounds."

"She's beautiful," Madison breathed. "I can't believe how big she is."

Madison watched Jefford walk over with a handful of leaves he had pulled from a bush and offer them to the elephant. "So, the raja sent me an elephant," he mused aloud.

"It's for both of you." Lady Moran patted her son on his back. "And I think you should both take a ride. The motion is quite comfortable. You'll be surprised." She signaled to Vijay, who tapped the elephant's leg with the stick.

The elephant immediately began to go down on its front legs and Madison stepped back fascinated, yet still a little wary. Vijay reached up into the box secured to the elephant and pulled out a short ladder.

"Go ahead," Lady Kendra urged, laying her hand on Madison's shoulder. "Climb into the howdah and try her out. Jefford, you should go with her."

Madison stood hesitantly in front of the ladder. She didn't want to be alone with Jefford, but she desperately wanted to ride the elephant. Of course, she couldn't accept the elephant from the raja, but perhaps one ride wouldn't hurt....

"Up you go." Jefford walked up behind her and before she could protest, he grasped her waist and lifted her up into the howdah, climbing in right behind her.

Madison dropped onto one of the red-and-gold divans, piled high with pillows, and scrambled to get out of Jefford's way. He stepped over the side and Madison grabbed a wooden pole as the whole howdah swayed and rose in the air as the elephant got to his feet.

"Oh, my goodness, we're up so high," she said as she gazed out the back.

Jefford laughed, taking a seat on the divan. "You sound like Alice now."

She glanced at him, unable to suppress a half smile.

Lady Moran, Sashi and some of the other servants stood at the pavilion waving as the elephant followed his handler out of the courtyard and through the massive gates, beyond the walls of the palace.

"Comfortable ride, though," Jefford remarked. "Beats the hell out of a camel, I hear."

Sliding down into the pillows on the divan, she looked at him, then out over the side of the howdah again.

"You look well," he said. "I'm glad to see that my mother's excessive wedding preparations haven't worn you out." He sighed. "Madison, look, I know this isn't exactly what you might have wanted but—"

"Might have wanted!" She turned on him, her blue eyes flashing. "Of course I didn't want to marry you. I didn't want to have a baby, either. Not with you, at least, damn you!"

He looked away and when he glanced back, his tone had changed. Any warmth, any courtesy she had heard previously, was gone. "My point is," he ground out, "that you are going to have *my* baby. Since I'm responsible for your condition, it's my duty to you, to this child, to marry you."

Madison rose up on her knees to get a better look at the jungle around them and tucked a lock of blond hair behind her ear. "Once again, you say nothing of caring for me, or even the baby. This is all about the *responsibility* you think you have, but I don't give a damn about your *responsibility!*" She stared at him for a moment, then threw up her hands. "But you're not listening to me. No one is listening to me. I don't want to go through with this!" she said, grabbing up a pillow and throwing it at him.

"You don't have a choice." He threw the pillow back.

"I'll run away."

"That's a mature response. Run away where? How? Are you going to take this elephant yourself?"

She whipped around. "I hear Lord Thomblin is staying with the Rutherfords. I could go to him. He would help me."

"Help you how?" he demanded.

"Perhaps he would marry me."

"Marry you? Thomblin? Please." Jefford threw his head back and laughed.

"It's not funny," she cried. "Carlton cares for me."

"Listen to me." He grabbed her wrist, and though she tried to twist away, he held her tight. "Thomblin cares for no one but himself and he's a dangerous man. A very dangerous man. I don't want you anywhere near him. Do you understand me?"

Madison felt tears sting the backs of her eyelids, but she refused to let Jefford see her cry.

"Do you understand?" he repeated, pulling her close.

Madison pressed her lips together stubbornly.

Jefford stared into her eyes, then suddenly pulled her against him. She tried to fight him. She shoved her hands against his chest, using all her strength, but he was much bigger than she was. Much stronger.

Jefford closed his mouth over hers, forcing his tongue into her mouth. She choked back tears and tried to pull away, but somewhere, deep inside, she was enjoying his kiss. She liked the feel of his arms around her and the taste of him. She liked the feel of his body pressed against hers. All these months she'd gone without a single kiss, and one brush of his lips and the heat of her loins seemed to flood her entire body. She was shaking all over with anger…with desire.

Jefford eased her onto her back on the divan, below the sides of the howdah, so that no one could see them. "Madison, please," he murmured, covering her face with kisses, caressing her breast with his hand. "Please stop fighting me. Please see that this is the best solution to the situation."

He kissed her again and she couldn't help herself. She kissed him back, running her hand over his chest, remembering the feel of his bare skin beneath her fingertips. Remembering the feel of him deep inside her, filling that ache that was there again now, throbbing, pulsing.

But, somewhere in the recesses of her mind, somewhere beyond her desire, her heart cried out. She didn't want this to be about her *situation*. She wanted Jefford to love her. She wanted him to *want* to marry her.

He spoke of duty. She wanted desire. She wanted him to want and love her more than any other woman on earth. She would never settle for less. She couldn't…

Madison tore her mouth from his, pushing away from him, both hands on his chest. "Get off me!" she cried, as angry with herself as with him. "Just leave me alone." Pushing her hair from her face, she leaned over the howdah and called down to the mahout. "Vijay. Take me back. Please." She wiped at her eyes as she fell back on the divan, scooting as far from Jefford as she could.

Vijay guided the elephant around in a slow circle and then headed back toward the palace courtyard. Madison ignored Jefford for the return journey. She didn't care what anyone said. She wasn't marrying him and no one could make her.

"Please," Sashi begged, a pile of fluffy white towels cradled in her arms. "You will feel better, dear Madison. I promise you."

Madison sat cross-legged on the stone patio outside her bedchambers packing up her box of paints. Her work had not gone well today. The light was poor as a thunderstorm threatened, but the day had proved to be hot and humid, anyway. All day she had worked on a simple still life, a basic study, the mastery of which was one of the very first techniques a fledgling artist needed to accomplish, and she'd made a total a mess of it. Her painting portrayed the objects, but it was wooden, lifeless. The light was all wrong, the colors muddy and dull. Had impending motherhood robbed her of every spark of creativity? Or did her unhappiness flow from her brushes and break the bond between eye, heart and canvas?

She scratched behind her ear with the wooden handle of a paintbrush. "A bath, Sashi! I don't have time for a leisurely bath! I've this mess to clean up, I've yet to choose my gown and jewels for the evening, and the raja will soon be here with the diplomat he wished me to meet."

Sashi plucked the paintbrush from her mistress's hand. "I will clean up your paints and lay out a sari and jewels. You will feel better if you bathe and take a few moments to relax. You spend too much time painting and not enough time preparing for your wedding day."

Madison pulled the pile of towels from her friend's arms. "Sashi, I told you. I am not marrying him!" She whipped around. "I'm going to bathe, but not because you or anyone else wishes me to! I won't be…be managed."

"Of course." Sashi smiled as she watched her mistress step into the shade of the bedchambers. "As you wish, my friend."

Chantal crouched behind a lounging chair at the edge of the small pool and opened the basket, taking care to step back. She was rewarded with a sinister hiss and watched with excitement as the cobra slithered out of the basket and across the tile floor to disappear behind a small table used for massages.

"I won't be long!" Chantal heard Madison call from elsewhere in the chambers. "Come for me if I fall asleep!"

Chantal hastily gathered the basket and ran barefoot across the cool tile floor for the door leading to the outside. Behind her, the door to the bathing room opened as she slipped between the silk draperies, into the garden.

Madison dropped the towels and kicked off her sandals inside the doorway to her private bathing room adjacent to her sleeping chambers. A circular chamber with smooth, pale green-and-white tiles on the floor and walls, it always seemed to be the coolest place in the palace. The only furniture it contained was a small stool to rest on while dressing or undressing and a narrow table for massages; the rest of the room was filled by a bathing pool large enough to easily accommodate three people and deep enough to submerge in entirely if she wished. Around the bathing pool were green-and-white glazed jars overflowing with thick green ferns and blossoming jungle flowers.

Madison sighed as she slipped off her sari, letting it fall to the tile floor around her ankles and stepping over it. The room was dim, the open door and windows to the garden covered with dark green silk drapes, and refreshingly cool after the heat of the day on the patio.

She stepped into the cool water and glided down the steps, unable to suppress another sigh of pleasure. Madison walked down into the center of the pool until the water covered her breasts, then back up to lean against the side and stretch her arms out. The water smelled heavenly, like the garden just after a morning rain.

Madison let her eyes drift shut and listened to the trickle of the tiny waterfall on the far edge of the pool, wanting to rest a few moments before gathering the soaps and lotions to begin bathing in earnest.

Her mind raced, filled with a hundred images and thoughts. She turned her head, easing the muscles of her neck and forcing herself to take slow, deep breaths.

Uneasiness pricked at her. The bathing room usually lifted her spirits, but today, nothing seemed right. She closed her eyes again and tried to clear her mind.

But her mind would not still.

The wedding was approaching at an alarming speed and she hadn't yet formed a plan. How would she avoid marrying Jefford while still protecting the child in her womb? Her child. Instinctively, Madison slipped her hand over her bare belly that was just beginning to grow round. How was she—

Her eyes flew open, but she remained perfectly still, knowing what she had heard, praying she had been mistaken.

The fountain trickled….

Hssssssss…

Every muscle in her body tensed. A snake! It was right behind her!

Madison's heart drummed in her chest. There were many snakes in India; she saw them daily in the garden. But the sound of this snake was ominous and instinctively she knew she should be afraid.

Slowly, ever so slowly, she turned her head around to gaze behind her.

In reaction to her movement, the king cobra raised up off the tile floor, flattening its hood and stared at her with cold, black eyes. The snake swayed, relaxed, slithering closer, then hissed at her, flicking out its deadly tongue.

Hurrying down one of the garden paths toward his room, Jefford froze at the shriek of terror that echoed from the house and tore through the garden.

"Madison!" Jefford shouted, springing over a hedge, drawing his machete from his belt as he raced down the path. While the distance was no more than two hundred feet to the doors of Madison's chambers, it seemed to Jefford as if it took a lifetime for him to reach them. "Madison," he called.

"A snake!" she screamed. "In my bath. Jefford!"

Reaching the palace wall, he eased himself through the green draperies that covered the open door and windows to Madison's bathing room and froze at once, unable to take his gaze off the cobra, seeing how close the snake hovered over her shoulder.

"Don't move," he whispered. "For the love of God, don't move."

She stiffened, staring straight ahead, her bare breasts glistening with bath water.

Jefford slid one foot closer, his fingers tensing on the machete. He would never reach the snake in time to cut off its head. It would strike at Madison the moment it spotted Jefford's movement.

"Kill it," Madison moaned. "Please."

"Shh," he murmured, his voice low and full of constraint. "It's all right, *chérie,* don't fret. My mother has spent a great deal of my inheritance on my wedding. I will not be cheated of my bride."

Madison's lower lip trembled and his breath caught in his throat. If he thought he could throw his own body in front of hers, shield her and his child she carried from the deadly strike, he would have done it, but he was too far away. There was no way he could get close enough.

"Easy," he whispered, sliding his foot inches closer as he calculated the distance between him and the cobra and the spin the blade in his hand would create as it cut through the air.

He had only one chance. And if he failed, he would regret it every hour of the rest of his life.

The cobra raised half its body off the tile floor, flattening its hood again, filling the steamy air with the ominous hiss.

"Hold still," Jefford murmured. "Very still." He slowly drew back his arm, muscles tensed.

The cobra rose up higher and drew back to strike. In one clean motion, Jefford set the machete in his hand free. It sliced through the air, seeming to take an eternity to reach the cobra.

Madison screamed.

The blade Jefford had sharpened only hours before sliced the cobra's head off cleanly and the thick body and hideous head fell to the tile floor. The body coiled and squirmed, slapping the tiles with heavy thuds, spraying jets of blood across the room.

Madison threw herself forward, scrambling to get through the water. Jefford jumped into the bathing pool and reached out for her. "Are you all right?" he demanded, pulling her into his arms. "It didn't strike you, did it?"

She shook her head, opening her arms to him, pressing her wet, naked body to his fully clothed one. "Oh, Jefford," she breathed, resting her cheek on his shoulder. "I thought it was going to bite me. All I could think of was the baby, how—"

"Shh," he whispered, smoothing her silky wet hair with his hand as he held her in his arms. "It's all right. The baby is fine. You're fine."

"A cobra. It was immense. Bigger than any snake I've ever seen. How…how did it get in here?" she asked, her whole body now trembling.

"I don't know, sweetheart." He kissed the top of her damp, sweet-smelling head, realizing just how close he had come to losing her…his child. Realizing how much he wanted them both.

"Madison!" Sashi threw open the bathing room door, her gaze falling to the twitching body of the dead snake.

"Sashi, she's shivering." Jefford lifted Madison into his arms and waded through the pool and up the steps. "The fright chilled her."

"Yes, Mr. Jefford." Sashi lowered her gaze, obviously uncomfortable in front of him without her veil. She grabbed one of the large, clean towels and opened it for her mistress.

Jefford eased Madison to the tile floor and reached out to draw the towel Sashi offered, around her wet, nude body. "Are you all right?" he whispered in her ear. "Do you need to lie down?"

"No." Madison's voice grew stronger as she took a step back from him, out of his arms. "Of course I don't need to lie down. I...I'm fine." She turned away from him, clutching the towel, trying to cover her nakedness from him. "I...I suppose a thank-you is in order." She started for the door, her tone taking on the coolness he was more used to. "Thank you. Now, if you'll excuse me, I should dress for dinner."

He watched her disappear into her bedchamber with her maid and leaned over to retrieve his machete, giving the still body of the cobra a kick. What the hell had he done to make her angry with him this time?

"Madison, dear, there is something I have been meaning to discuss with you for some time." Lady Moran lay back on the cushions a servant had brought from inside and turned her attention to her niece.

They sat in a small private courtyard off Lady Moran's rooms, alone, without any servants, which was a rarity since the wedding preparations had begun. It seemed that someone was always there, needing Lady Moran's attention: cooks, gardeners, the servants who were preparing bedchambers for guests. The bells in a tower in the garden had just rung, as they did five times each day to call those who were Muslim into the house, to prayer. Soon it would be dinnertime.

The idea of having to face the guests, who had filled the palace almost overnight until it seemed more like a grand hotel than a home, was almost more than Madison could tolerate. The British and Indian aristocracy had come from the far reaches of the country—Bombay, Calcutta and Delhi—in honor of her marriage, out of respect to the raja and just out of plain curiosity, she suspected. The wedding, which still seemed unreal to her, was the following day; in the meantime Lady Moran's entire staff and a good deal of the raja's ran at the beck and call of the guests, serving elaborate meals, providing recreation on the palace's lawns by day and entertainment in the numerous receiving halls by night. Every room in the palace was adorned with urns of fresh flowers and yards of colorful silk, the doors and windows thrown open until one didn't know where the gardens ended and the walls of the palace began.

Madness, it was all madness, Madison thought as she took her time tucking away her sketch pad. She had a feeling she knew what Aunt Kendra wanted to talk to her about and she wasn't certain she was ready for it. She knew her aunt was ill, had probably been so for some time. The symptoms were all there, her loss of weight, her thinning hair, the days when she was unable to get out of bed in the morning. The flickers of pain Madison saw on her lovely face.

Madison told herself that she had not asked her aunt directly about her health out of politeness. She told herself

Lady Moran's health was private and that if and when her aunt wished to inform her of the details, she would. The truth was, Madison didn't want to know what was wrong with her aunt, or the prognosis. She simply couldn't bear the possibility of the answer.

"Madison, look at me," Lady Moran commanded.

Madison, sitting on pillows under the shade of a breadfruit tree, glanced up. "Yes, Aunt Kendra," she said, trying to keep the fear out of her voice.

"I've been meaning, for some time, to talk to you about this, but simply haven't found the time or place. However, the situation has reached the point where I believe something must be done."

Madison's brow furrowed. "Done?"

"This situation, as it is, simply cannot continue any longer."

Madison was confused. "What situation?"

Lady Kendra leaned over, looked left, then right, as if someone might be eavesdropping. Then she whispered. "The situation with that maid of yours and young George Rutherford. It's shameful."

Madison's eyes widened.

"Now, don't you tell me that you know nothing of it. I suspect you knew from the very beginning. Why didn't you come to me concerning the matter the moment you realized there was a problem?"

"Aunt Kendra, while I understand your concerns, I can't help but think that what is most important is their love. Sashi and George love each other and—"

"Well, of course nothing is more important than love," Lady Moran said indignantly. "Which is why I don't understand why you didn't come to me sooner."

Madison burst into relieved laughter. "Oh, Aunt Kendra,

how I love you! How much I admire you and how full of surprises you are!" She couldn't stop smiling. "I wanted to come to you, but I just wasn't sure what you would think and I hoped maybe I could help on my own. Lord Rutherford would never allow his son to marry an Indian serving girl."

"No, he would not."

"George just wants to run away and be married and give up his family name and inheritance."

"Preposterous! And you were going to allow him to do that?"

"No. Of course not. Not if I could help it." Madison looked to her aunt. "Actually, I had an idea. It's crazy, I know. I doubt it would ever work, but…"

"Come, come, spit it out, dear. We're all growing older by the moment."

Lady Moran listened to Madison's inspiration, interrupting several times to ask questions or clarify something. Finally, she clasped her hands together and rose. "Well, all in all, I think you have an excellent plan! And what better place to launch it than your wedding tomorrow?"

"The wedding," Madison breathed.

"Yes, of course. By tomorrow, with the palace overflowing with guests, we will have nearly reached the limit of confusion. What better time to introduce the princess to everyone?"

Madison's head spun. All these weeks, she had been so certain she would find a way out of the marriage. The wedding was tomorrow!

"We have so much to do if we're to be ready." Lady Moran started for the open doors. "I have trunks packed somewhere in this house that might be useful. Now, I'm going to send for Georgie on some pretense or another. You gather Sashi and we shall meet in my chambers, shortly. A little rum punch, a quick lesson on proper tradition and etiquette and I believe we just might pull this off." She stopped halfway up the tiled path. "Well, Madison, what are you doing sitting there, dear? Get up." She flapped her arms. "Get up, stop feeling sorry for yourself and let's see what we can do for these two love doves."

23

"I can't go through with this!" Madison declared fervently, reaching out to grab Alice's hand.

"Lift arms," the dressmaker ordered, whipping her thread and needle in the air.

Madison raised her arms because it was easier than arguing. She felt as if she was hurling forward at the speed of a steam locomotive, unable to steer or slow down as she approached a turn in the tracks.

The receiving room off her bedchamber had been filled with women since dawn: the seamstress and her three assistants, the milliner, a jeweler's wife, a shoemaker, two maids, an under maid, and too many other servants coming and going. The entire palace was in chaos, bursting with old friends of Lady Moran's and local dignitaries and military officers and their wives, both English and Indian.

"Alice, do you hear me?" she demanded under her breath. "You have to help me. I cannot go through with this! I can't marry Jefford. Do you know that I saw Chantal just yesterday in the garden, strutting shamelessly down the path in a new sari? Jefford said he sent her to the village, but how do I know it's true?"

"Oh, Madison," Alice breathed, averting her eyes. "You're only flustered, brides always are. Everything will be fine. You'll see."

"But, Alice, he doesn't love me." She grabbed her companion's hand. "He isn't the kind of man I want to marry."

"I say, arms out," the dressmaker ordered sternly.

Madison groaned and lifted her arms in the air again. "You have to help me."

Alice fiddled with her white silk gloves; she was dressed in a pale pink watered-silk gown with long, fitted sleeves and a lace neckline that had to be stifling in the November heat. "I…I can't. There's nothing to be done." She glanced around to be certain no one was listening. "And truly, Madison, in your—*condition,* you really have no choice. You cannot give birth to a *bastard.*" She went on faster than before as if she might, somehow, be tainted personally by the word. "My goodness, you'll be ruined. No one in polite society will receive you, not even in this godforsaken India. Your family will be ruined. Word will reach London and—"

Madison pressed her hand to her forehead, suddenly feeling light-headed. She was beginning to wonder if she had been wise to tell Alice about the baby. She had done it to get her help, but the young woman seemed to be unable to get beyond the fact that Madison had had sex with a man she was not married to. Truthfully, Madison suspected that Alice couldn't get beyond the fact that her friend had had sex at all.

Madison felt her knees weaken and she swayed precariously on the dressmaker's stool. Several maids squealed and reached out to steady her.

"By Hindi's elbows," Lady Moran swore, entering the

chambers with an entourage, including Maha and the tiger. Madison's aunt was dressed in a traditional sari of gold and green, bedecked in emeralds with an emerald-green turban on her head. "The guests are all assembled. We've but need of a blushing bride."

"Lady faint," one of the Indian maids declared excitedly. "Must wait."

"Faint!" Lady Moran cried. "Women in my family do not faint. We have greater fortitude than to succumb to such nonsense." She marched up to Madison, surrounded by the tittering servants. "Young lady, gather your wits. We've three hundred guests, an elephant, a powerful raja and a tiger come to see you wed my son. There will be no postponement." She turned away. "Bring her here. Have her sit." She waved the servants to a pile of pillows on a low silk divan.

Madison was barely able to walk to the divan. Her knees shaking, she sank down into the soft pillows in a cloud of jeweled silk. "I can't do this, Aunt Kendra," she declared, her voice trembling. She lowered her face to her hands, the gold crown on her head heavy with jewels. "He doesn't want to marry me."

"Oh, poppycock." With the assistance of one of the maids, Lady Moran eased down, in all her regalia, onto her knees on a silk pillow, to look into Madison's kohl-lined eyes. "Now, listen to me. Don't think, for one moment, that Jefford Harris does anything he does not want to do. He pretends to want to please me, but the truth is, ultimately, he pleases no one but himself. He loves you, Madison, as I think you love him. Like you, he's stubborn. He simply has not been willing to express his true feelings."

Madison stared at her hands, which had been adorned with floral henna designs, as was the fashion for a bride in India. She wanted to believe her aunt, but she knew it wasn't true.

"Now, I don't know what childish thoughts you might have that your affection might lay elsewhere, or that affection for you might exist from another source." Lady Moran eyed her shrewdly. "It's time to lift your chin, walk out of these chambers in this priceless gown and marry the man destined to be your husband." She turned. "Maha."

The middle-aged servant handed Lady Moran a jeweled, gold goblet, and Lady Moran, in turn, pushed it into Madison's hands. "Drink this. It will calm your nerves."

Madison clasped the goblet, her adorned hands trembling, and drank obediently, feeling almost as if she were preparing for her execution as she swallowed the sweet, unfamiliar-tasting juice.

Lady Moran rose with the aid of a servant on each arm and began to order people about. The chamber was quickly returned to its former pristine state. Two wide-eyed maids drew Madison to her feet and placed a transparent silk veil over her head, while a third slipped sapphire rings on her fingers. Yet another clasped a heavy gold necklace laden with glittering sapphires and diamonds around her neck.

"A gift from the raja many years ago," Lady Moran murmured in her ear. "And now it's yours."

"Thank you," Madison breathed, brushing her fingers over the cool, faceted stones.

As everyone bustled about the room, Madison felt herself begin to relax. Her morose thoughts drifted away and she began to take notice of things she had been too overwrought to notice before: the weight of the jewels in her ears and around her neck, the smooth feel of the silk wedding gown against her skin and the scent of the jasmine that adorned her hair.

"There, feeling better now?" Lady Moran inquired, drawing very close to gaze into Madison's eyes.

Her aunt's face was familiar, yet looked different, somehow. The lines around her kohl-adorned eyes were softer, her pert, red-painted lips seemingly less demanding. Madison felt her mouth turn up in a smile. "Yes, much better, thank you."

Somewhere in the distance, Madison heard music. Trumpets blared and musicians beat on their *dholaks*.

Time seemed to slow until it stood still. Everyone was hurrying about, but she was no longer in the least bit anxious.

"Time to go, my love," Lady Moran whispered in her ear.

Someone drew Madison's white silk veil down over her face and led her forward. She was vaguely aware of walking out of her chambers, down the long, now-familiar pink corridor.

"I am very happy for you and for Jefford," a voice said in her ear.

Madison turned her head to find that she was in the dining room and the raja stood beside her. She remembered that he was to escort her into the garden where she would marry. Marry Jefford… *Jefford, whom she loved,* she thought languorously.

The next thing she knew, she was in the lush, fragrant palace garden. The ceremony was being performed by an English vicar from Bombay, but everywhere were symbols of the culture she now lived in.

Madison turned her head to look at the raja and realized it was not the raja who now held fast to her arm. It was Jefford. Jefford looking quite handsome in a traditional white *kurta,* trimmed in gold and a gold wedding *saffa.*

"Madison, say yes," he told her under his breath, squeezing her hand.

Madison could feel a thousand eyes watching her, but none mattered but Jefford's. His dark eyes seemed to pierce her soul. "Yes," she murmured, unable to take her gaze from his.

The vicar spoke. Jefford tugged on her hand and she knelt beside him on a white satin pillow. More words were spoken and Madison could feel the warmth of Jefford's skin against hers where their fingertips touched.

The next thing she knew, the old vicar was no longer standing before them in his black robes; it was the raja. He lowered a gilded mirror before them and Madison gazed at the blond woman with a sapphire dangling from her headdress, against her forehead. Her eyes were lined with kohl and she was staring at the dark-haired man wearing the gold turban beside her. Jefford. Her husband.

There was a great roar of cheering and Madison felt herself being lifted to her feet. Music began to play and she was surrounded by people, most she didn't know, offering their congratulations.

The garden seemed to spin around her, congratulatory voices rising up into the darkening sky. The aroma of the jasmine and gardenias was almost overwhelming. Jefford, holding tightly to her arm, responded to the well-wishers for her, his voice formal but warmly pleasant.

"Are you all right?" he whispered in her ear as he escorted her across the garden to a dais that had been built above the newly erected dance platform, much like the one her aunt had had constructed in the garden at Boxwood Manor for her coming-out ball.

She nodded, smiling up at him through her veil.

Jefford settled on the low divan, covered with pillows, and she slid down beside him, reveling in the feel of his strong arm around her waist. Strains of music grew louder.

Food appeared on platters before her. There were people dancing, laughing.

"You're certain you're all right," Jefford repeated, looking very closely into her eyes.

She nodded dreamily. "I'm happy."

His brow furrowed. "Are you, now?"

She nodded.

"Well, good." He rubbed her hand, which glistened with a heavy sapphire ring he had slipped on her finger at some point in the wedding ceremony. "I'm glad. I told you it was all for the best."

"The best," she murmured.

Still looking at her oddly, he took a gold charger from a servant's hand and offered it to her. "I think you should have something to eat."

She smiled up at him and reached for a slice of fruit. "If you want me to, I will."

Jefford chuckled and brushed his lips across her cheek. "I don't know what's gotten into you, Madison, but I must admit I am pleasantly surprised by what a submissive bride you are."

Madison bit off a piece of papaya and offered the other half to him. She watched as he took it in his mouth from her fingertips and thoughts of his mouth on hers danced dreamily in her head.

Lady Moran hung on the raja's arm, smiling with contentment as he led her through the crowd of wedding guests to one of the many silk divans brought into the garden for guests.

"You look tired," he whispered, his breath warm in her ear.

"Leave me alone." She gave him a push, smiling up at his handsome face. "Let me enjoy the day."

"I only speak because I am concerned for you." He helped her sit down and then lowered himself beside her. In an instant, there were a dozen servants before them offering goblets of wedding wine and platters of exotic foods from all over the realm. There were curried dishes of goat and fowl, platters of fresh fruit picked that very morning and delicate honeyed cakes and candied rose petals.

"Keep your concerns to yourself or sleep alone tonight," Kendra told him as she accepted a goblet of wine, her gaze searching the crowd. Her face lit up in a smile. "Ah, Tushar, help me up, quickly, please." She pushed her goblet into a servant's hands.

The raja rose, offered his hands and raised her to her feet. With her most gracious smile, she glided across the tiled courtyard. "Princess Sashi, I am so pleased you saw fit to accept our invitation."

Sashi, dressed in a gold-and-violet sari, laden with antique amethyst jewels, offered a gracious hand. "Lady Moran, I must thank you for the kind invitation." She spoke so regally that no one could possibly have guessed, by her speech, that she had been born into a family of humble servants rather than revered royalty.

A group of English officers, in full dress uniform, with their wives on their arms, turned with sudden interest to Lady Moran's *royal* guest, just as she had anticipated they would. Many had been officers under her father's command and she knew them well. Most were more than pleased to see and be seen by those of greater rank and importance. Usually, Kendra had little time for such petty games, but today, the practice suited her plans perfectly.

Lady Moran closed her hand over Sashi's and leaned forward to kiss her cheek through the transparent purple veil.

"I'm frightened," Sashi whispered.

"Don't be. You had them the moment you entered the garden." Kendra stepped back. As she had hoped, quite an inquisitive crowd was beginning to gather around the *princess,* including George Rutherford and his sister.

"Princess Sashi, please allow me the pleasure of introducing you to a few of my very dear friends," Kendra said with a regal sweep of her hand. "This is the Honorable George Rutherford, son of Lord Rutherford, and his sister, the Honorable Alice Rutherford."

"Oh, my goodness, I'm so pleased to make your acquaintance," Alice said solemnly as she curtsied.

Young George stared boldly, his eyes on Sashi as he bowed. "Your Royal Highness, what an unexpected pleasure."

"Your Royal Highness, what an honor it is to have you with us," Lady Rutherford declared, pushing her way through the officers and their wives to be the first to be introduced after her son and daughter. In her wake, she dragged Lord Rutherford, who was trying not to spill the wine from his gold goblet. "Lady Moran hadn't informed us you would be here," Lady Rutherford gushed.

Sashi lowered her gaze for a moment, but then lifted her lashes, like any true princess. "I...was uncertain I would be able to accept Lady Moran's gracious invitation," she said, her diction impeccable. "Royal duties, you understand. But I was able to come with my aunt and uncle."

"Have you, now? Well, I should certainly like to meet them," Lady Rutherford replied. She grasped her husband's arm. "Mr. Rutherford, did you hear? We've a princess with us today."

"By all means, Your Royal Highness, do make yourself at home," Kendra insisted. "Tell me if there is anything we can bring you to make your stay more comfortable, or your aunt and uncle." She nodded in the direction of the palace's ancient, toothless gardener, Japar, whom she had dressed in one of the raja's best *kurtas*. His wife, Indiri, the head laundress, wore one of Lady Moran's own saris, diamonds sparkling from her ears, gold bracelets jingling on her wrists.

"I can't believe my eyes," Alice bubbled.

George courteously offered one elbow to the princess and she gave a regal nod, accepting. On the other arm, he escorted his sister. The threesome moved through the garden in the direction of Sashi's *royal family,* who were occupied eating as much lamb with roasted garlic and rosemary and cucumber salad as they could possibly consume.

"Princess Seghal?" the raja whispered in Kendra's ear. "I do not recall a Princess Seghal in our region."

Kendra turned to him, doing her best to appear surprised. "No? Heavens, she must be from elsewhere." She gestured. "From the north, I believe. The Himalayas, perhaps. Oh, I'm not quite certain where. You know I'm not good with geography, and this is such a vast country."

The raja looked down into her eyes, his mouth twitching with amusement. "I do not know what you are up to, my love, but I will hear the entire story when you and I have retired for the night."

Kendra offered her hand to him. "I know it is not your tradition that men dance with women, but I believe this is a waltz. Do you care to dance, my love?"

"I would not miss it for the world," he whispered, gazing into her eyes.

Kendra felt a lump rise in her throat. She had all here today she could possibly ask for. Her son married. Her dear niece married with a wonderful life full of excitement before her. And finally, finally, after so many years, she had Tushar—Tushar, whom she thought was long lost to her. If she died in her sleep tonight, she could not complain to Gabriel.

The raja led her onto the dance floor and she let her eyes drift shut as they began to waltz.

She swayed slowly to the music, held in Tushar's arms, and sighed, realizing she had just a few more months. If only she could live long enough to see Jefford and Madison's child, her grandchild. It was her dying wish….

"Lord Thomblin, good evening." Alice Rutherford smiled, patting her mouth with a silk handkerchief before slipping it into the cuff of her sleeve.

"Miss Rutherford." He bowed. "Your gown is truly lovely this evening, my dear. It is so good to see that some Englishwomen have not taken to the native dress."

"No, I could never." She ran her hands over her silk gown. "I would never be so brave as to wear a sari. I'm not like Madison." She dared a look at his handsome face. "I could never be so bold."

"Boldness is not necessarily a trait a man admires in a woman, Miss Rutherford." He met her gaze. "Would you give me the honor of this dance? I believe they are playing another waltz. An *English* waltz."

Alice fluttered her fan, overwhelmed by Lord Thomblin's attention. She had always thought him quite refined, quite handsome, but he'd never paid any mind to her, beyond cordial greetings.

She was twenty-three and fast approaching an age where marriage would no longer be an option. A man like Lord Thomblin for a husband… Alice was no fool. She knew she was plain. She knew she was a dull stone when compared with Madison's jeweled character, but now that her friend was wed, Alice could see no harm in exploring where Lord Thomblin's affection might lie.

Alice lifted her pale lashes, shaking with a mixture of fear and excitement. "I...I should be honored to dance this waltz with you, my lord."

"Madison," Jefford murmured in her ear. "I think it's time we retire to the bridal chambers." He gazed out over the crowd of wedding guests, who had been celebrating and dancing for hours.

Laughing and clapping with the other women, Madison shifted her gaze from the circle of men dancing a traditional Indian celebratory dance, the raja in the very center.

"Do you think so?" she asked, still feeling as if she were floating on a cloud.

"You look tired." He reached up beneath her veil to brush a smudge of kohl paint at the corner of her eye.

She laughed. "But I'm not."

"It's expected that we leave, my love," he murmured in her ear.

Her eyes widened, and then she laughed, slipping her hand into his. When he said it was time to retire to the bridal chambers, he meant the bridal *bed,* a thought Madison was not at all opposed to. Every time Jefford had touched her tonight, either to point out an important dignitary or to feed her a tidbit of curried lamb, the pleasant shock of his skin against hers had reverberated through her entire body. Suddenly, she was anxious to be alone with him, to be alone with him as his wedded wife.

Jefford signaled to his mother, who was seated to the

right. The garden was again full of dancing, laughter and the whistling beat of the *dholaks*.

Madison walked through a gauntlet of well-wishers on Jefford's arm. Someone threw rose petals, women approached to kiss her, and men offered Jefford their congratulations.

He led her, surrounded by servants, through the palace and into her bedchambers, which had been transformed at some point during the day to a lavish bridal chamber. The walls had been hung with jeweled silks like those in Lady Moran's chambers. Persian carpets had been added to the floors and incense burned in silver stands, filling the room with the aroma of sandalwood.

"Out, out," Jefford declared, clapping his hands.

"But, *sahib*," one of the more daring female servants said, her veiled face bowed. "It is tradition that a bride's maids prepare her for her bridal bed."

Jefford ushered the giggling, veiled women to the double doors. "It is this bridegroom's tradition that he prepare his bride for her bridal bed himself. Now, out, all of you, and if anyone so much as knocks on this door again tonight," he warned, "heads will roll."

Madison lowered herself to the edge of her bed, which had been covered in gold-shot silk, piled with new jewel-colored pillows. She pulled the veil from her head and watched it float slowly from her hand to the Persian carpet beneath her feet.

Jefford poured something in two gold goblets and came to her. "Something to drink, to steel yourself for your wedding night?" he said, his tone teasing.

She accepted the goblet, letting her fingertips brush his. "I do not think I need to *steel* myself for anything," she murmured huskily.

He chuckled and brought his mouth down to hers. Madison parted her lips, allowing her eyes to drift shut. She eased her tongue out to meet his; he tasted of wine and desire for her and she felt her pulse quicken. He took another sip of the wine and then set both goblets on a teak and ivory table beside the bed.

"I cannot tell you what a pleasant surprise this has been," Jefford whispered, plucking the jeweled crown that had secured her veil and the pins from her head. "You have been so congenial today. I thought, for certain, I would have to drag you to the altar."

Her blond hair fell over her shoulders in a lush curtain and he brushed his fingertips across her neck, sending shivers of pleasure through her.

Jefford kissed her again and she responded hungrily, leaning back, allowing him to lower her onto the bed. His warm hand slipped through the layers of teal-and-white silk and she gasped when his bare hand, at last, cupped her breast.

"You smell so sweet, like a jungle flower," he breathed in her ear.

Madison felt as if the bed was spinning, the room turning around her in the opposite direction. The weight of Jefford's warm body pressed against hers, the feel of his hand on her breast, his thumb stroking her nipple, brought her breath in short gasps. She ran her hands over his chest, his back, sighing, groaning with pleasure. Again and again his mouth found hers; their tongues twisted.

Madison pushed the wedding *kurta* off his back and skimmed both hands over the taut muscles of his shoulders and chest. She hesitantly touched his nipple with her fingertip, and when she heard his breath catch in his throat, she smiled. Stroking his nipple with an unpracticed touch, she rose up in the bed and covered it with her mouth.

Jefford groaned loudly. "Madison…"

She lathed the nub until it grew hard, and then, fascinated by his response to her touch, she boldly slid her hand over his flat abdomen. Lower...

Her fingertips barely brushed the velvety skin of his engorged member when he caught her hand and pushed it away. "Not yet," he whispered in her ear. "Not yet, my love. I want the opportunity to see you, first. See all of you and not in the darkness of a cave."

While the oil lamps burned brightly, Jefford drew her to her feet on the floor, then sat on the edge of the bed, his gaze locked with hers, and he slowly removed her jeweled sandals and then the layers of her wedding dress.

Madison was not in the least embarrassed, reveling in the way he looked at her. She felt as if it were she who was the princess. The most beloved.

Before she knew what had happened, she was standing in front him, in the bright lamplight, completely unclothed. He took his time, gazing at her, drawing his hand over her arms, her waist, her thighs, the curve of her hips. With each passing moment, Madison's desire for him increased until her entire body was trembling with that ache that she knew only he could fulfill.

At last, he stood and, still holding her gaze, removed his white trousers. He sprang from the fabric, brushing her thigh, hot and tumescent, against her skin.

"Please," Madison begged, her eyes half closed. "Please."

He wrapped his arms around her waist, pulling her against him so the crisp hair of his groin and the hardness of his member rubbed against the sensitive flesh at the apex of her thighs. She slid her arms up and around his shoulders, clinging to him, grinding her hips against his.

"Please love me," she breathed.

He kissed behind her ear. "But I *am* loving you, Madison." His hand glanced over her bare buttocks.

"You know what I mean," she managed.

"Such an anxious bride," he teased hoarsely. "We have the whole night." He started to lower himself to his knees. "There's no need to hurry."

Madison tried to step back, away from him, but he caught her around her knees, trapping her. Her hands fell to his head as he lowered it, her fingers threading through his thick, dark hair.

Jefford's hot, wet tongue darted out to tease that place that only he knew and she groaned as a sweet wave of pleasure washed over her. He licked again. She swayed. Two more short, quick flicks of his tongue and she could feel the heat in her belly fanning out. She could hear her own breath as she panted, her heart thumping in her chest.

He delved his tongue deep into the soft, moist folds of her flesh and she cried out, throwing her head back. Jefford massaged the smooth skin of her buttocks and the backs of her legs, and when she caught her breath, he began to lick again.

"No," she moaned, trying to push his head away. Now, despite the release, an even deeper pressure was building inside her. Her skin was on fire, every nerve in her body was thrumming.

His tongue flicked out again and again and she was powerless to fight off her own desire. Again, she cried out in ecstasy as waves of pleasure racked her body. Now her knees were so weak that she could not stand. She leaned over, holding on to his shoulders, panting.

"Jefford," she whispered. "Please."

Slowly he rose, gazing down into her eyes. "I just want your wedding night to be one you will always remember," he said softly.

She swallowed the lump of emotion in her throat and closed her eyes. "Husband, if you don't do your duty quickly, I shall—"

"You shall what?" he teased, sitting down on the bed and drawing her into his lap. "Will you torture me with your tongue the way you did there on the bed?"

She opened her eyes, holding on to his shoulders. "If you do not fulfill your husbandly obligation, the torture with my tongue will be even far greater, *sahib.*"

Jefford laughed heartily and then lowered her onto her back, stretching out over her. He caught her hands with his, threading their fingers together. Then, holding her gaze, he thrust into her.

Madison cried out in relief…in sweet fulfillment. He began to move at once and she writhed beneath him, lifting her hips again and again to take him more deeply. Harder.

Madison's body shattered in ecstasy again, and then, when she thought she could not stand another ripple of pleasure, he began to move inside her again. Hot and damp with perspiration, near to exhaustion, Madison clung to him, allowing him to lift her higher, closer to that pinnacle once more. Then at last, she gave a cry. Jefford thrust one last time, groaned and fell still over her.

Madison couldn't catch her breath. She rolled her head, trying to take in the sandalwood-infused air that now was thick with the scent of their lovemaking. Jefford slid off her and reached up to a small bowl left discreetly on the bedside table.

With a soft, wet cloth, he first mopped her brow, then he drew it down between her thighs. Madison sighed at the feel of the damp wetness, groaned as the last ripples of pleasure flowed through her, then lay her head on a pillow, smiling. The room seemed to have stopped spinning, at last, and her mind was less clouded. But she was so tired…so tired.

"Madison," Jefford whispered in her ear.

"Yes?"

"I have a wedding gift for you."

"I don't have to go to the courtyard to see it, do I?" she asked, her eyes still closed.

He chuckled. "No, I have not brought you an elephant, although, if you asked me for one right now, I would dress and fetch one. Fetch two and bring them here to you."

She smiled.

He got out of the bed and came back a moment later. She heard the musical sound of the clink of silver and felt him lift her bare foot and place something around her ankle. She opened her eyes to see his gift. He had put out all of the lamps but for the one beside the bed so that the darkness encircled them like a silken veil.

"Oh," she breathed, staring at the delicate chain-link anklet. "It's beautiful."

"A rare, precious metal, white gold," he murmured, releasing her ankle. Then he lifted his wrist to show her an identical piece of jewelry. "And now we are bound to each other, forever," he whispered, touching his lips to hers. "Here," he said, touching her belly, which was just beginning to swell. "And here." He jingled the bracelet on his wrist.

Smiling, happy beyond words or thought, Madison closed her eyes. Jefford lay down beside her and slipped his arm around her. She nestled her head on his shoulder, still too hot even for a thin sheet, and drifted off to sleep in that lovely haze that had enveloped her all day.

24

Madison woke slowly from the dream that was as vivid as a painting brushed with her own strokes. Images flashed through her head as the sweet, fragrant scent of freshly brewed chai crept at the edges of the canvas.

She had dreamed she married Jefford, and in that place, she had wanted to marry him. There had been music, dancing and laughter. And then they had gone to bed. She sighed as she remembered the way he had touched her in the fantasy. The way he had made her feel. They had made love twice, no, three times on her bed, which had floated on a cloud, and each time he had brought her to fulfillment, again and again.

Madison vaguely heard sounds in the room. Two hushed voices. The clink of a serving tray. Not Sashi, though. Where was Sashi? She always served Madison in the morning, and had been especially attentive the last few weeks.

In Madison's dream, Sashi had been the Royal Princess Seghal and been introduced to the Rutherfords. The serving girl had truly looked, sounded and moved like a princess. In her dream, Sashi was no longer a lady's maid, but a lady herself and an honored guest at the Palace of the Four Winds.

The scent of fresh *puttu,* a breakfast stew Madison adored, crept into her mind. She felt her stomach grumble with hunger. Sashi had to be there; she had brought breakfast.

Madison stirred in her bed and stretched. She felt the cool satin sheets against her bare skin and smiled to herself, taking pleasure in the erotic sensation.

Her bare skin?

Madison's eyes flew open as she came fully awake and bolted upright to find herself in her own bed, completely unclothed, the sheets tangled around her bare limbs, pillows strewn haplessly. She heard a sound and snapped her head around to see Jefford standing stark naked at the open windows to the courtyard, sipping coffee.

"Good morning." He turned and greeted her with the languid smile of a man well satisfied.

Madison's mouth fell open in shock as she realized that her dream had not been a dream at all. She'd married Jefford yesterday! She had done those things with him in this bed. Worse, she had enjoyed them.

Swallowing hard, she grabbed two handfuls of sheet and yanked them over her bare breasts. How could this have happened? How was it possible?

"Would you like something to eat? I have hot—"

"You son of a bitch," she shouted, rearing up on her knees in the bed. It was all coming back to her now—no wonder she had felt so strange yesterday. No wonder she had thought she was dreaming.

He stared at her for a moment, as if he was unclear what he was seeing. What he had heard.

"You son of a bitch, you drugged me," she accused. "You made me marry you. You made me—" Her face grew hot with the memory of what she had done with him last night in this bed. It hadn't been a dream!

His brow furrowed as he walked toward her, making no attempt to cover the evidence of his well-endowed maleness. "What are you talking about, Madison?"

"Yesterday!" Holding the sheet across her breasts with one hand, she pushed the tangled hair from her face, trying not to look at him. At his nakedness. Trying not to think about last night. But she could smell him on her, everywhere. She could still feel his mouth. "You gave me something to confuse me. It was in the drink someone brought me—"

She halted in midsentence, lowering her gaze as she tried to recall exactly what *had* happened the previous day. It was all so fuzzy that she was uncertain what had actually transpired and what she might have dreamed…or even hallucinated. Madison thought she recalled talking with Alice in her bedchamber, telling her friend she couldn't marry Jefford. Then Aunt Kendra had arrived and they had sat together on the divan…and Maha had passed the goblet….

Madison climbed out of the bed, dragging the sheet behind her. "Get out," she shouted. "Get out of my rooms."

"Madison, what's wrong?"

He came closer and she backed away, not trusting herself yet to let him get too near.

"What are you talking about someone drugging you? I didn't—"

"Aunt Kendra. I was very upset yesterday before the—" She couldn't bring herself to even say it. "*Before,* and she gave me a drink. She said it would settle my nerves." She thought for a moment and then struck out in anger, knocking a delicate ivory figurine of an elephant off a table to send it shattering across the floor.

Jefford cursed, bringing his coffee cup down so hard on a teak table that coffee splashed out of it, and the silver stand that had apparently burned sandalwood incense the night before toppled over. "I was wondering why you were so damned pleasant all evening," he muttered. "And here I thought it was—" He swore again foully and yanked his wedding trousers off the floor where they had fallen the night before.

Madison's wedding gown was in pieces all over the floor, as well. One heeled sandal stuck out from under the bed; the magnificent jewelry that had been a gift from Lady Moran lay piled on the teak table beside the bed as if it were a child's baubles. All discarded in the heat of passion.

Pulling on his trousers as he went, Jefford strode for the double doors. "I'll kill her," he mumbled.

Madison dropped the sheet and ran for her chifforobe. "Don't you dare touch her," she screamed. "I want to do it."

Madison thrust her arms into a white silk dressing gown and ran after Jefford. She caught up to him in the pink corridor. "How could you have let her do this to me?" she demanded angrily. "How could you have married me in that state?"

"That state? How was I supposed to know?" He made no attempt to slow down and she had to run every few steps to keep up.

"How were you supposed to know? Didn't you notice that simple look on my face? That dazed look in my eyes? Didn't you think it odd that suddenly I'm fawning over you, yes-dearing you this and yes-dearing you that?"

He scowled. "You're right. I should have known something was wrong. You've never been that pleasant in your life."

Madison stared hard at him.

"Stop looking at me like that. I didn't physically force you into anything. And I asked you if you were all right."

"How was I supposed to know I wasn't?" She threw up her arms. "I was drugged for sweet Hindi's sake!"

They reached the doors to Lady Moran's chambers and Jefford only paused long enough to bang with his fist before ripping a door open. "Kendra Westcott Harris Moran," he bellowed.

The inner door to Lady Moran's private bedchamber opened and the raja stepped out, closing a red silk dressing gown around him.

Embarrassed, Madison halted behind Jefford, lowering her gaze.

"I want to speak to her," Jefford said through gritted teeth.

The raja shook his head; he looked tired, as if he hadn't slept all night, and at once Madison knew there was something wrong.

"Not now," the raja said quietly.

"Oh, no," Jefford bellowed. "She is not going to hide behind—"

"Jefford." The raja said his name so quietly, so gently, that Jefford fell silent at once.

"She's ill?"

The raja nodded. "The pain began shortly after you retired last night. She's just now fallen asleep after my physician gave her a strong medicine to cut the pain and allow her to sleep."

Jefford stared at the tiled floor.

"She was worried about today. She wanted to know who would see to the wedding guests."

Jefford brushed his hair over the crown of his head. "We'll see to our guests."

Madison turned to Jefford. "If you think—"

"Madison, not now."

Jefford's words were so harsh that tears filled her eyes.

"Will you stay with her?" Jefford asked the raja.

"Of course."

"And send someone for me when she wakes?"

"I will."

Without another word, Jefford grabbed Madison's hand and led her out of his mother's chambers.

"Jefford, Aunt Kendra?"

"Would you please be quiet long enough to get back to our rooms?" he intoned. "The whole palace is full of people, and I am not a man who enjoys sharing his personal life with others."

Madison tried to pull her hand from his, but he held fast, leading her, in silence, back to her rooms and only letting her go when they were behind the closed double doors.

"What is happening here?" Madison demanded, jerking her hand from his and taking a step back.

"How can you be such a...*woman* one moment and such a child the next?"

She stared at him, her hands resting on her hips as she waited for his explanation.

"Damn it," he said. "Don't you understand? My mother is ill. She's dying. She's been dying as long as you've known her!"

Madison stared at him, horrified. "No," she whispered, taking a step back. She shook her head. "She can't be dying."

"Well, she is. So, as soon she wakes from the drugs they

had to give her to take away the pain so she could sleep, you may certainly go in and complain to her about how she forced you to marry me. To marry me so that *your child* would have a name."

Madison's eyes clouded with tears as she took another step back, wrapping her arms around her belly as if she could somehow protect her baby from him. The baby he obviously didn't want. "I…"

"Madison—" Jefford turned away, not finishing what he was going to say.

She just stood there, staring at his bare back, her shoulders shaking as she fought her tears.

"Look," he began after a moment, "the fact of the matter is that you and I are married." He turned to face her, his face stoic. "We have a house full of wedding guests and my mother is too ill to see to them. We owe this to her, you and I. So, you are going to get dressed." He walked to her chifforobe and opened it. "You are going to join me and our guests in the garden." He yanked a sari from the closet, one that was a soft green with pink embroidered veins and flowers, one of her favorites from Kendra. "And you are going to smile and pretend your life is now complete." He threw the dress at her. "Do you understand me?"

Madison caught the sari, her lower lip trembling. She was heartsick, angry, hurt that he would talk to her this way when only last night…

"I said," he repeated louder, "do you understand me?"

"Don't speak to me as if I'm a child or a simpleton! Yes, I understand you," she snapped, and then turned away. "I'll need a maid."

"No maid. The *Princess Seghal* is occupied with her new beau, I believe."

Madison met his gaze.

"Yes, I know about George Rutherford and Sashi and the whole charade. It sounds just like something my mother would do to amuse herself, so it surprised me when she told me the whole thing was your idea." He lifted his brow haughtily. "Until we can find you a suitable new maid, I suppose I'll be helping you dress."

"I'd rather have a jackal help me," she muttered, stepping behind a carved sandalwood screen.

Madison spent the day in the gardens with her guests, where there was more food, more wine and entertainers the raja had summoned from all over the province. There were games to play, both English and Indian, and the elephant handler gave rides on Bina to the English guests.

All afternoon, Madison mingled among her guests, laughing and pretending to be the happy bride. She and Jefford mostly avoided each other, but several times in the course of the day, he came to her and put his arm around her and she was forced to play the role of the blushing bride.

Madison spoke privately with Sashi midday. The young woman was so grateful to Madison that she was in tears. The Rutherfords had fallen for the Princess Seghal story, and Lord Rutherford had already twice suggested to *the princess* that his son would make an excellent catch as a husband. George was already swearing he would name his first daughter after Madison. Leaving Sashi to join George and some of the other younger guests for a game of croquet on one of the lawns in the gardens, Madison had found herself musing that at least someone would have a happily ever after.

At sunset another great feast, equal to the wedding feast, was served and Madison was, once again, compelled to sit beside Jefford in the garden on the divan and listen as others offered toasts in their honor. She was obligated to share the same plate with him and accept tidbits of food from his fingertips, when all the while, all she wanted to do was strike him. She wanted to hurt him for the things he had said to her. Perhaps for the things he had not said.

The last hours dragged by as Madison waited for it to grow late enough that she could excuse herself to her bridal chamber. She didn't want to give Jefford the pleasure of appearing to be anxious to crawl back into the bed they had shared the night before, but she was desperate to escape from the public eye.

Around nine in the evening, the raja appeared, dressed handsomely in a red *kurta*. He gradually moved through the brightly lit garden speaking to Lady Moran's guests, making apologies for her and encouraging the guests to eat and drink. Eventually, he made his way to the marriage dais.

Jefford looked up anxiously at his father. "Is she awake?"

The raja nodded, glancing around to be sure no one was close enough to overhear them. Jefford had simply told the wedding guests that his mother suffered a headache—too much wedding punch—and everyone had laughed. He had promised that as soon as she was feeling better, she would join them. After such an elaborate celebration the day before, no one thought it odd that Lady Moran would not make herself available the next day.

"She is awake," the raja said. "But she is very weak."

"The pain?"

"Better."

Madison had to gaze beyond the raja's face to keep her emotions under control. He appeared to be in pain, loving Aunt Kendra so much, Madison supposed, that when Kendra felt pain, he felt it, as well. It was the most touching demonstration of love Madison thought she had ever witnessed.

"I'd like to see her if you think she's up to it," Jefford murmured, rising to his feet.

The raja nodded.

Madison started to get up. "I'll go, too."

Jefford grabbed her hand and smiled broadly as he lowered his head to speak privately to her. "No, you will not. You will go to our chambers and you will wait for me there," he whispered from between clenched teeth.

Madison tried to break away without making it obvious.

Jefford leaned forward to whisper in her ear again as the raja took his leave and headed back into the palace. "I will not have you upsetting her with your childish accusations of her drugging you and forcing you to marry me."

"Childish accusations?" she flared.

Madison barely got the words out when Jefford clamped his mouth over hers.

There was a roar of applause.

"I believe we will now be retiring, my bride and I," Jefford announced jovially to more applause and shouting. "Please," Jefford continued, laughing with his guests. "Eat our food, drink our wine, and we will see you all on the morrow."

Jefford then led Madison into the palace and down the corridor toward the family's private rooms. "Go now to our chambers and wait," he ordered.

"I—"

"Madison, this is not negotiable." He met her gaze, his face hard.

She pressed her lips together, looking down at the floor. "Please tell her I was asking for her and I hope that she feels better."

"I will." He halted at her bedchamber door, the chambers they would now share. "You should get ready for bed. It's been a long day and I know you must be tired."

"I'm not—"

"Madison, it's time you stop thinking about yourself. You're carrying a child. For the baby's sake, you must get proper sleep and food." He pushed the door open for her but did not step in.

Madison walked into her room, fighting her tears as the doors closed behind her.

Jefford closed his eyes for a moment, preparing himself before he walked into his mother's private bedchamber. Most of the lamps had been turned down to a soft glow, and someone softly played a sitar from the corner of the room. Incense burned, filling the air with the sweet, pungent aroma of sandalwood. There was no one with her except Maha and the raja.

Maha rose from her chair and lowered her veil the moment Jefford stepped into the darkened room. He met the faithful servant's gaze. "Thank you for being here with her all day. You go to your chamber, be with your husband," Jefford said quietly. "We have others who can sit with her while she sleeps."

Maha nodded and walked out of the inner room as Jefford strode toward the bed.

"Who needs anyone to sit with her?" Kendra demanded weakly from the bed. "Jefford," she added, "what are you and Maha whispering about? Come here this instant."

Jefford met his father's gaze across the wide expanse of the great bed. Both smiled knowingly.

"Here I am, so stop bellowing like a sacred cow." Jefford approached her bed, drawing back the pale yellow silk curtain that shielded her from anyone who entered the room. "We were talking about what a disagreeable witch you could be." His gaze fell on his mother and he had to check himself to be sure she saw no reaction on his face.

In one day, Lady Moran appeared to have aged ten years. Her face was thin and haggard, and without the usual turban on her head, the wisps of red hair remaining on her ivory skull made her appear like a caricature of herself.

Lady Moran smiled up him. "You were always a difficult child, son." She patted the bed beside her. "He was always a difficult child." She turned to the raja, who sat in a chair on the other side of the bed, reading documents he must have had sent over from his palace.

Jefford eased carefully onto the bed, trying not to respond as his mother winced at the slight movement. "How are you?" he asked, taking her bony hand in his.

"Who cares?" She gave a feeble wave with the other hand. "I've just been too busy. Exceeded my limit. I'll be fine in a day or two." She clasped his hand between hers. "Now, tell me, how are you? And our new bride?"

"I'm good. We are good."

She eyed him shrewdly. "Was she angry when she woke up this morning and realized I had given her a little something to calm her?"

"You shouldn't have done that without asking me, Kendra."

"You would have said no," she scoffed. "Sometimes mothers know best and they must do what is best for their children with or without their approval."

He couldn't help smiling.

"So was she…angry?" she prodded with a chuckle.

"You could put it that way."

"Hah!" Lady Moran grinned. "Spitting fire, I bet she was. Throwing things?"

Jefford didn't answer as he thought of the ivory elephant shattered on the floor.

"I told you she would be angry, but the anger will pass," she told the raja. "In the end, she'll realize this was best for everyone."

He glanced up from his papers, over the rims of his glasses. "I have already told you, do not draw me into your webs of deceit, my love. I am already concerned for your soul."

Lady Moran laughed weakly.

"Yes, I must admit, when *Princess Seghal* arrived with her *aunt and uncle,* I was surprised," Jefford told his mother, yet unwilling to release her hand. "It's remarkable how closely she resembles my wife's maid."

"And how is the princess getting along with our neighbor, that nice George Rutherford?" she asked, grinning wickedly.

"Quite well, from what I observed today. Lord and Lady Rutherford seem quite taken with her."

"And I know Alice must adore her."

Jefford thought for a moment. "Actually, I didn't see Alice today, but with every room in the palace full of guests, she could have been anywhere."

Lady Kendra rested her head back on her pillow.

"Tired?" Jefford asked gently.

She closed her eyes. "Mostly just relieved that you and Madison are wed."

He was quiet.

"Jefford, I know this may not have been what you thought you wanted or what Madison thought she wanted, but honestly, mothers truly do know best sometimes. She is a woman who will love you as fiercely as I have loved you."

"Kendra, please—"

She opened her eyes, still holding on to his hand. "Can you not hear that I am speaking? Hush." She closed her eyes again. "Now, it may take some time to adjust to this new arrangement. When a woman is carrying her first child, her emotions can be— Well…let's just say it is a difficult time for a woman. She doesn't know what she feels. But give her a chance."

Jefford said nothing.

"Did you hear me?" She squeezed his hand.

"I heard you." He leaned over and pressed a kiss to her forehead. "And now I want you to listen to me. I want you to take the medicine the doctor has left—"

"Morphine. I hate it. It muddles my mind."

"And get some sleep," Jefford continued. "In a few months your granddaughter or grandson will be arriving and you will need your strength to chase him or her in the garden."

His mother loosened her grip in his hand and smiled, her eyes remaining closed. "Come tomorrow," she whispered, "and we will play Parcheesi."

Jefford lifted her delicate hand to his lips, pressed a kiss to it, then lowered it to the bed, looking up at the raja, who nodded.

"I'll be back in the morning," Jefford said quietly, rising to his feet. "But if she grows worse in the night—"

"For heaven's sake, Jefford, don't speak as if I have already gone to my grave!"

The raja flashed a grin in his son's direction. Jefford chuckled quietly and left the room.

* * *

Dressed in a sleeping gown and robe with as high a neck as she could possibly find, Madison waited apprehensively on the bed, desperately worried about Aunt Kendra. While she had been gone during the day, maids had come in and cleaned the room. The bed had been made freshly, the broken elephant swept up, there were freshly cut flowers in vases on the tables and food and drink had been left in case the bride and groom became hungry in the night.

The moment the doorknob turned in the outer chamber, Madison was up on her knees. "How is she?" she asked, clasping her hands together.

He dropped into a chair that was draped in a jewel-blue fabric and lowered his face to his hands. "Conscious. In pain, but still able to be the pain in my ass she's been as long as I can remember."

Madison fought back a little sob and smiled.

"Did you eat?" he asked, lifting his head to look at her. "You ate nothing all day."

"I ate."

"Madison—"

A knock on the door interrupted what he was about to say. "Yes?" he called, glancing through the bedchamber doorway, to the double doors in the outside chamber.

The door opened. "Sorry to disturb, *sahib,*" one of the servants said, keeping his head down as he backed up, holding the door open. "Mr. Rutherford insists he must see Mr. Harris."

"Georgie?" Madison climbed off the bed, taking care to be sure she was well covered with her robe.

Jefford rose as George came through the door. It was obvious by the look on his face that something was wrong.

"What is it?" Jefford walked toward him.

"I'm sorry to disturb you." George gestured. "I just didn't know who else—"

"What's wrong?" Madison rushed forward. "Sashi—"

"It's not Sashi." George lifted his troubled gaze. "It's my sister. She's missing."

25

Jefford left at once with George to search for Alice, insisting Madison remain in her bedchambers. Jefford had assured Madison that Alice was certainly not lost. In all the confusion of the past two days, including the arrival of *Princess Seghal,* the Rutherfords had merely lost track of where Alice told them she was going.

So Madison reluctantly remained behind. She lay in bed and read, determined to stay awake until Jefford returned to tell her that the fuss had been for nothing and Alice had been located safe and sound, laughing at all the effort on her behalf. But at some point, Madison fell asleep.

She opened her eyes at the sound of someone moving in the room. The single lamp beside her bed was still burning, but she saw the first streaks of sunrise around the edges of the closed draperies.

"I'm sorry," Jefford said, sitting on a chair to remove his boots. "I didn't mean to wake you."

Madison blinked the sleep from her eyes and sat up. "You found her?"

He was leaning over to remove his second boot. He shook his head.

"No? But what could have happened to her? Where could she have gone?"

"I don't know," he answered tiredly.

She watched him stand and pull off his linen shirt that was stained with perspiration and streaks of green. A bit of leaf fell from his hair to the Persian carpet beneath his bare feet. "You've been in the jungle looking for her?" Madison gripped the sheet in both fists. "I don't understand. How could she have just disappeared? She was there at the wedding. I remember seeing her."

"Everyone remembers seeing her." He dropped his shirt over the chair and walked to the washbasin.

Madison watched him pour water from a silver pitcher into the basin and take a fresh, clean linen cloth and begin to wash. First he rinsed off his face and then he began to draw the cloth over his chest, under his arms. She glanced away, annoyed with herself that she would be so fascinated by his body.

"How can she be *gone?*"

"I don't know, Madison." He was irritable, his voice taut with concern, drained by lack of sleep. "We're not even certain *when* she was last seen. She had been invited by one of the other young Englishwomen her age to stay the night here at the palace. Mary something—her father is some sort of diplomat. George and his mother and father went back to Palm Hall after the wedding. Mary says that Alice did not sleep in her chambers with her, and she assumed she had gone home with her family."

Madison stared at her hands in her lap. "How could no one know where she is?"

"Madison, we still have more than a hundred guests between this palace and the raja's. She could be anywhere."

She glanced up, willing to grasp at any spark of hope. "You haven't checked the raja's palace?"

"As best we could, considering the time of night it was by the time it occurred to us that we should look there." He picked up a silver-handled toothbrush left by a maid and began to brush his teeth.

Again, Madison looked away, feeling strange to be alone in a room with Jefford, observing such intimacies as bathing and brushing his teeth. "But you'll search there again when everyone is awake?"

"Of course." He spat into the washbowl and wiped his mouth with a clean linen towel before turning to face her. "We searched the nearby jungle, as well. A tiger has been seen prowling the area west of here where a child was taken from a village a few weeks ago."

"Taken?"

"Eaten."

He walked toward the bed and she sat back. As he drew closer, she could see both of his arms were scratched and he had a small cut across his cheek.

"What happened?" she asked, brushing her fingertips across her own cheek.

He ran his hand over his stubbled chin. "Nothing, a few scratches. We beat around the bushes a little, just in case—"

"In case she'd been carried off by a tiger," she said softly, the notion too horrendous to even consider.

"I don't think she was. I think Alice is here somewhere." He halted at the edge of the bed and grabbed a thin sheet that had been left neatly folded on the end.

Madison lifted her lashes to look at him. He was obviously exhausted. Upset. About Alice, and his mother. A part of her wanted to reach out and take him in her arms, smooth back his damp hair and hold him until he slept.

With the sheet in his hand, he turned away and she felt her stomach fall. She had assumed he would sleep in her bed.

"You…you don't want to sleep here?" she asked, taking care to keep the emotion from her voice.

"I think you made it pretty clear this morning how you feel about that." He walked past the table with the lighted lamp and turned down the wick. The room was instantly dark. "It will be light soon. Try to go back to sleep. I told George to catch a couple of hours and then we'll launch a more organized search party."

Madison lay back in the bed and listened to him cross the room to a low divan against the wall. She heard him sit, punch a silk pillow and lie down.

She was hurt that he didn't want to sleep with her, but angry with herself that she would care. They had married for the sake of the baby, to keep her from being disgraced; no one had ever suggested any differently. So now that they had consummated their union and made it legal, what had made her think he would sleep with her?

Madison lay in the great bed, piled with silk pillows, and listened to Jefford settle on the cushions on the divan. Within minutes, he was breathing rhythmically, sound asleep, leaving her alone in the darkness.

Midmorning, Jefford and Madison arose. He had ordered breakfast to the chambers, including pots of hot coffee and chai and began to dress at once, impatient to leave the palace to search for Alice.

Madison sat on a chair sipping her chai and glanced at Jefford.

"I might be gone most of the day," he told her, sitting on the edge of the bed to pull on his boots.

A young serving girl, her face veiled, moved quietly around the room, tidying it. A manservant who had brought Jefford's clothes to him gathered the dirty ones, as well as his muddy boots from the night before.

"In light of what has happened, I imagine most of the guests will be taking their leave today. I know we promised three days of celebration but—"

"Everyone will understand. With your mother ill…" Madison didn't complete the sentence. "I'll dress and see that our guests have all they need to make their journeys home. I—"

"That's not necessary. I can make excuses for Kendra and—"

"Jefford," Madison said, rising from her chair. "Your mother went to a great deal of trouble and spent an enormous amount of money to see me properly wed. A wedding she would have liked, but never had, I should guess," she said softly, turning away to go to her wardrobe. "The least I can do for her is to play hostess for a few hours."

Jefford stood, dressed, and strapped on a belt. "Well, don't tax yourself too greatly." The servant handed him a scabbard with a cutlass and a pistol. "With the baby—"

"Jefford, I'm fine." She pulled a sari from the clothing closet, a pale ivory silk with tiny pearls embroidered into one shoulder. "I know you think me incapable, but I can do this." She glanced at him. "After all, I *was* trained in my father's house to be the mistress of my own home, to be a wife and mother some day." She met his gaze, wanting to say something more. Wanting *him* to say something.

And for a moment, she thought he might. The look in his eyes told her that he was thinking as she was, how awkward this was between them. Man and wife now and yet not.

"Look, Madison."

She waited, suddenly feeling slightly light-headed. If he opened his arms at that moment, she thought to herself that she would go to him. She didn't know what it was to love a man, not really, but this feeling in her chest right now, this longing to make things right between them was so strong that she thought maybe it was love, or some early form of it.

But he didn't open his arms. He just looked at her, then shook his head and turned away. "If we find her, if we know anything, I'll send word."

Madison didn't allow herself to cry as he walked out of the room, she didn't even allow a tear. There was no time for that, not now, not when she was the mistress of the palace. "You," she said to the young serving girl. "What is your name?"

The young woman, no more than fourteen or fifteen, bowed her head, freezing where she was beside the bed, arranging the pillows. "I am called Chura, *sahiba*."

"And you speak English?"

She nodded.

"Good, and I am learning a little of your language, so between the two of us, we should be able to communicate." She carried the sari to the bed. "I am in need of a new personal maid. Mine has apparently returned to her village in the north. Would you like to be my new maid?"

"Yes, *sahiba*." Again the girl nodded. "I would be greatly honorable...*honored*."

"Excellent." Madison walked to the washbowl and poured fresh water from the same silver pitcher Jefford had used a few hours earlier. When she breathed deeply, she thought she could still catch the scent of his skin in the warm morning air. "You'll need to help me dress so I can greet my guests. You can clean up here later."

"Yes, *sahiba.*"

Madison leaned forward to gaze into the oval gilded mirror on the washstand and she picked up a clean linen cloth. Strange, she thought, she looked the same as she had before she married two days ago, yet she also looked different.

"Please, Lady Rutherford," Madison cajoled, patting the older woman's hand from across the table. "You really must eat something. Have a little tea or chai. Perhaps some sherry?"

The quiet room where Madison had just secluded the Rutherfords was away from the hubbub of the palace and had just recently been redecorated to look like a London drawing room, another gift from the raja to her Aunt Kendra. "I can't." She shook her head, sniffed and reached for a fresh handkerchief, and wiped her nose. "I simply can't."

Madison's gaze shifted to Lord Rutherford, who had been out searching for his daughter all day and into the evening and had only recently returned at Jefford's insistence that he join his wife. Lord Rutherford's face was smudged with sweat and dirt and his clothes were rumpled. As he removed his pith helmet to rub his nearly bald head, Madison couldn't help but think that he, too, was aging before her eyes.

Apparently, when Alice had not been located in the Palace of the Four Winds, at Palm Hall or at the raja's palace, the men had begun searching the surrounding jungle in earnest. The tiger had not been seen in the area in days, but some evidence in the jungle had suggested that a large creature had been attacked and dragged off. Blood evidence, Madison guessed, although Lord Rutherford was too much a gentleman to say. She would ask Jefford when he returned.

There was a knock on the door and a very young boy, barefoot in a loincloth and turban, who had been operating the overhead fan, ran to open it.

Lord Thomblin walked in, dressed in a white linen suit with a pale blue handkerchief tucked in his breast pocket, carrying a white straw boater beneath one arm. "My Lord and Lady Rutherford, Mrs. Harris." He bowed. "I was on my return to Bombay when I heard the news at the train station." He went to Lady Rutherford and took her hand. "Is there anything I can do?"

Lord Rutherford slumped back on the settee and reached for the whiskey Madison had ordered for him. "There is nothing to be done, I'm afraid, young man," he said gallantly. "She's lost to us."

Lady Rutherford began to cry softly again.

Madison rose from her chair. "It was good of you to return, Lord Thomblin."

"After all our families have been through," he said, "I could not have continued my journey, despite my pressing business. Are you certain there is nothing I can do?" He looked to Madison.

She studied his face for a moment, thinking that he was, perhaps, not as handsome as she had once believed. He was really more pretty in a soft way than anything else. "I imagine the best thing would be to join one of the search parties. I suspect they will be out all night." She leaned over to speak to the boy propelling the overhead fan and sent him in search of Maha.

After Jefford had left this morning, Madison had commandeered Maha's assistance since she had been with Lady Moran here in the palace more than thirty years ago and knew how the household was to be run. She also knew most of the guests and all of the servants, and could speak to those who did not speak English, translating for Madison. So far, she'd been a great deal of help.

As the boy slipped out the door, Madison heard Jefford's voice outside in the corridor and her heart gave a little trip as she walked to the doorway to see him approaching. His face was impassive, but she knew by the way that he walked that they had not found Alice.

George walked beside him, his head hanging in defeat. "My mother and father?"

Madison rested her hand on his shoulder and kissed his cheek before pointing inside. She waited for Jefford, who had fallen a step behind him. "You didn't find her?" she asked softly.

He glanced at the open door, then backed down the corridor a few steps. She followed him.

"We found no body, but there was a trail of blood. A lot of blood. Also, we found—" He cleared his throat and swept his hair off his forehead, glancing away. "A blood-stained lady's glove. George says it was hers and he fears the worst."

A lump rose in Madison's throat, but she swallowed it. There would be time to grieve later. "But she might not be dead, so you'll keep looking?" she asked softly.

"Certainly. We'll send word out to some of the outlying villages, too. I have some fields to attend to in the next few days, overseers to meet with. I'll make them all aware that she's missing—those who haven't already heard. Word of this kind of incident moves pretty fast, even in the jungle."

Madison nodded, reaching out to brush her fingertips along his arm. "You need to eat. Wash, get some sleep."

He nodded. "I should see Kendra, too."

"I checked in with her about two hours ago," Madison continued, keeping her voice down. She was not saying anything now that the Rutherfords should not hear, but it lent a certain intimacy to the conversation between her and her new husband. "She says she's much better."

"Yes, well." He wiped his mouth with the back of his hand, still avoiding her gaze. "She lies."

Madison chuckled, but a silence hung between them.

"Listen, Madison," Jefford said, after a moment. "I've been thinking about…this…our marriage."

Madison held her breath. She'd been thinking about him all day, too. At least when she wasn't occupied having chambers cleaned, ordering food hampers packed for travelers, seeing that servants were fed and put to work, and ensuring Lady Moran and her seemingly permanent guest, the raja, were attended to.

"Yes?" she managed quietly.

"This…" He sighed and started again. "It was important to my mother that she see me married. She thought, for some strange reason, that we were well suited." He continued to stare at the intricately arranged tiles on the floor. "She loves you and…she has very little time left. A few months, perhaps. I know that you didn't want this, but—" He cleared his throat. "It won't hurt either of us to keep certain appearances for a few months…perhaps weeks."

Madison felt her lip tremble. This was not what she was hoping he was going to say, but she knew what he was getting at. He was saying he didn't want to be married to her, either, that he had been forced as much as she had. He was asking for the sake of his dying mother that they pretend they were now happily married.

Pretend! He was almost coming out and saying it. He had no intention of attempting to make their marriage a real one.

"I know—" he continued.

"Jefford." Madison closed her eyes for a moment. If he didn't stop. If he said *another word,* she was going to crumble. "We have guests. I should get back to them. Lord Thomblin—"

"Thomblin?" He glanced up, making no attempt to hide his dislike of the man. "I thought he was gone."

"He was." She drew herself up, annoyed by his tone of voice. "He was departing for business in Bombay but returned at once when he heard Alice was missing."

Jefford made a derisive sound in his throat. "Business? I wonder what kind of business he's up to now."

"Go to our chambers. I'll have a bath and food sent," she told her husband, turning away. "Once you've cleaned up and eaten, you should look in on your mother and then go to bed. You've had a long day." She caught sight of Maha approaching. "Now, if you'll excuse me, I've things I need to do."

Lifting her chin, Madison walked away and did not look back. She never saw the sadness etched on Jefford's face.

A dirty-faced manservant in a ragged turban bowed low to Lord Thomblin, his hands pressed together fingertip to fingertip. *"Sahib."*

Carlton looked up from the shot of foul liquor made from rice that had been poured for him at the dockside bar. He was glad to be back in Bombay, away from the dull country life with the Rutherfords, but he required better accommodations than what he presently had. Fortunately, his financial situation was about to change. "Christ, what is it now?"

The manservant lowered his head farther. "The shipment, *sahib,* there is a problem."

"Problem? What kind of problem?" Carlton threw back the shot and slammed the dirty glass on the bar, signaling for another.

"It…it makes noise, *sahib.*"

"Goddamn you natives, must I do everything myself?" He pitched a coin onto the bar top and slid off the stool.

The manservant scurried out the door. "This way, *sahib.*"

Carlton followed the man through the darkness along the plank dock and then out toward a small steamer being loaded with cargo before setting sail for Singapore. The air was foul with the stench of fish and sweaty bodies and he drew a white handkerchief from his pocket to cover his mouth and nose.

Ahead, by the light of several burning torches, he could see four dockworkers crowded around a large wooden crate that had just been unloaded from a wagon. "What the hell is going on here? I'll skin you alive if any harm has come to my cargo," Carlton threatened.

The manservant halted in front of the crate, keeping his gaze downcast. "It makes noise," he repeated. "The men are frightened."

Carlton took one look at him and sighed irritably as he tucked his handkerchief back into his pocket and grabbed a crowbar from one of the other dockworker's hands. "Then shut it up!" He thrust the crowbar into a crack, jerked it, and the wood creaked and the fresh nails groaned as the side came loose.

Carlton took one quick look over his shoulder and then leaned forward, pulling back the wooden slats to peer inside. He drew back instantly as the stench of vomit assaulted his nostrils. "Jesus," he muttered, waving his hand in front of his nose as he leaned forward again.

By the dim light of the torch, he saw the three sweat-drenched white women crowded together in the far corner of the crate. One of the brunettes was unconscious, but the other two trembled, staring at him with wide, terrified eyes. Whimpering cries, much like those an injured dog might make, spilled from Alice Rutherford's swollen mouth. When she caught sight of him, she groaned and thrust her delicate hands out in a wordless plea for help. The drugs they had been given to keep them quiet were beginning to wear off.

"You must be silent," he threatened, "if you don't want this box dropped into the harbor." He forced patience into his voice. "You need only be still for a few more moments, my dear, and I promise you will be released. No one here will harm a hair on your head, I swear it on my mother's grave."

Carlton turned to the manservant and whispered. "She makes another squeak, gag her and tie her hands behind her back. I want that lid back on before anyone see them and I want them aboard ship before they suffocate in there. Must I do everything? The crate is to be delivered to the section of the hold reserved for precious cargo. Do it now!"

Thrusting the crowbar into the manservant's hand, he walked away. The annoying whine became muffled and then ceased altogether, drowned by the sounds of hammering. Carlton hated leaving his precious cargo in the hands of others, but it had to be done. The contract would be sealed tonight and he would get an advance on his money, but if Alice and the other two died before they reached the client in Singapore, Captain Bartholomew would never pay the second half and he certainly would buy no more women from him.

He plucked his handkerchief from his pocket, wiped his mouth and then pulled his new watch from his vest pocket. It was twenty-four-karat gold, Italian, and new…or nearly so. He'd seen it in a shop window that afternoon and couldn't resist. He checked the time, wondering how long the final transaction with Captain Bartholomew's agent would take, and when he would be free to seek entertainment for the evening. He knew the six-thousand-pound deposit he would get for the women would be best spent to pay off his most urgent debts, but instead, he thought he might check himself into the Queen Jasmine Hotel for the night and seek some feminine companionship. What was left over could be sent on to his most adamant creditors. After all, all work and no play…

Carlton was only sorry he hadn't sampled the Rutherford bitch's charms before making the bargain, but taking her virginity would have badly lowered her price. Besides, he had always preferred women with more meat on their bones. Still… Carlton sighed with regret; her wails did ignite a hunger in him that wouldn't be stilled until properly fed.

An hour later, Carlton watched through a peephole in a wall in the hold of the ship as a mute Indian woman offered a slightly soiled towel to the naked Rutherford girl. An area in the ship's hold had been specifically altered by a clever captain out to make a couple of hundred extra pounds. A room had been built with crude bunks and a toilet facility. The mute servant, who could tell no tales, was provided to care for the shipment on its journey; there would be adequate food and water to ensure the cargo reached its destination in good health.

Through the peephole, Carlton watched as Alice stood,

shivering in a tub of cold water while the servant scrubbed her pale skin until it reddened.

"You can see that they are in excellent health," Carlton murmured to the agent sent to him by Captain Bartholomew. The captain, concerned about appearances, no longer liked dealing directly with his suppliers. "Young and vigorous."

"All virgins?" the dark-skinned man of unidentifiable heritage questioned.

"Of course." Carlton moistened his lips, still watching as the servant on the other side of the wall ran the rag over Alice's bare back, down her pale buttocks. "And most important, all white women." He glanced at the man. "I am told you will guarantee their safe arrival in Singapore?"

"Nothing is a guarantee." The man chuckled. "But I can promise the best care will be taken." He took a peek through the crack in the wall. "The juice they drink has been laced with a drug that will not harm them, but will render them unable to do anything but sleep, and perhaps mew."

Carlton smiled. He liked the idea of Alice Rutherford mewing, wishing it could be under his tutelage... But alas, it was not to be.

Clean, Alice stepped out of the tub as the servant motioned and she reached for the tin cup offered. She was so thirsty that she didn't even attempt to cover her nakedness with the towel as she drank greedily, juice dripping from the corner of her mouth.

"Have you the money?" Carlton asked, thrusting out his hand.

The agent hesitated. "These women will do, but they are not the quality we look for."

"Not of quality!" Carlton snorted. "What the hell are you talking about?"

"Our man in Singapore, he likes the stock lively, strong. These women—" he spat on the wooden floor at Carlton's feet "—they are skinny. Docile. Top price is paid only for the strong."

"Lively," Carlton repeated, still holding out his hand. "I can get 'lively,' but my price increases."

The man slapped a leather wallet of money into Carlton's hand and smiled. "Then we can do business again." He tipped his imaginary hat and walked away.

Carlton slipped the money into his coat and leaned forward to catch one last glimpse of the naked women before he took his leave.

~~~
⋘⋙⋗⋐⋑⋙
~~~

26

Madison sat cross-legged on a sturdy platform that raised her six feet above the floor. Dabbing at a circle of blue paint on her palette, she reached up to draw a streak of sky. Her painting was almost complete and she was very pleased with it.

Four months had passed since her marriage to Jefford. In the first days after the wedding, after all the guests had finally left and she had settled into the daily routine of overseeing the palace and caring for Aunt Kendra, Madison had thought she might go mad.

Even after Alice had been given up for lost, though her body was never found, and Kendra's health had stabilized, Jefford had not returned to their marriage bed. For the first few weeks, Madison had continually told herself that he would return. She thought that the subject would come up and she would invite him, or he would simply decide to collect on his husbandly rights. But as more time passed, it seemed as if they moved farther apart.

Jefford was busy each day tending to the vast fields and

plantations his mother owned. He had begun organizing the labor forces and seeing to improvements in the villages of the workers, bringing medicines in for the ill, and had started two schools with classes for both boys and girls. He was so busy that he was rarely in the palace, and then he was either sleeping or spending time with his mother and the raja.

Jefford did not speak of the raja and never referred to him alone or in his presence as his father, but Madison could tell that they were getting to know each other. And though Jefford would not admit it, he admired the raja. Admired him and liked him. Despite their vastly different backgrounds, they found much to talk about, so much that there were times when Madison and her aunt could barely get a word in the conversation.

Lady Moran was rarely out of bed now, but when she was well enough to sit up, Madison and Jefford would join his parents for an evening of dining, and even a game of Parcheesi. Madison began to look forward to those special evenings because in his mother's presence, Jefford pretended to be a loving, attentive husband. Madison found herself pretending, too. She and Jefford laughed together, teased each other, and occasionally even shared a caress or a kiss. He was so adept at pretending to be a good husband that there were some nights Madison forgot everything would change once they left his mother's bedroom.

The minute they walked out, headed for their own chambers, Jefford grew distant. They no longer fought; he was simply indifferent, and it was that which she found the most maddening of all. A screaming, shouting, glass-breaking argument would have been more preferable than his cool distance.

Madison sighed and dabbed at the palette beside her and

then glanced up at her creation on the wall. Her aunt had asked her to paint a mural in the second receiving chamber, which guests walked through upon entering the palace. She'd designed a jungle scene with a green rain forest and bright blue sky, which surrounded visitors when they entered the grand hall, then painted in bright tropical birds, tigers peeking from behind fronds and tortoises crawling along the grassy jungle floor. Her favorite part of the painting, though, was the addition of Bina, her elephant. She had painted Bina on the west side of the wall, added a brightly colored howdah on her back, and in the very top, if one looked carefully, one could see a blond Englishwoman.

As Madison gazed at the painting in the round, she found herself very satisfied with the end result. Especially when she considered the fact that she had barely been beyond the palace walls since she had arrived and had very little knowledge to draw upon. After the wedding, Jefford had refused to allow her to leave, insisting the jungle was too dangerous for a woman, let alone a pregnant one.

He used Alice as the perfect example after it was determined that the young woman had strayed from the palace walls, encountered the tiger, and been attacked and devoured.

No amount of begging, cajoling or shouting had convinced Jefford to allow her to leave the palace. He refused to escort her himself and he had ordered servants to stand at every palace gate. If any of them allowed her to pass, he swore to them that he would personally feed them to the tiger.

So Madison found herself a prisoner in the Palace of the Four Winds. And with every day that passed, the huge palace seemed to grow smaller, the walls around her seemed to draw closer. She had little to occupy her free time, excepting painting these walls, thinking about the baby she was carrying, who suddenly seemed so real to her, and caring for her new kitten.

As promised, when her aunt's white tiger had given birth, Madison had received a kitten. She chose the only white tiger born of the litter of four and named her Rani, which meant *queen* in Hindi. Now nearly weaned, it was Rani who slept in her bed with her and kept her warm on cool nights, rather than Jefford.

The sound of familiar footsteps caught her attention and she turned to see Jefford coming down the pink corridor.

"How is she?" Madison called down the hallway, her voice echoing in the domed ceiling over her head.

"I don't know." He scowled. "Maha wouldn't let me in."

"Do you think she's worse again? She's really seemed better the last few days, we've even been able to walk a little in the garden."

"Maha swears not, saying my mother will *send for me* momentarily." He entered the round chamber and walked to the scaffold. "I thought you told me this painting was done two weeks ago. You should not be up on this scaffold."

He offered his hand to her and she accepted it. She rose slowly, encumbered by her growing abdomen, and grasped the railing to the wooden steps that had been built to reach the top of the scaffold so that she would not have to climb up and down a ladder.

"It's almost done." She allowed him to help her down the stairs. "I'm just adding a little dimension to the sky."

His gaze strayed to the elephant on the wall. "Just you in the howdah?" he asked.

She shrugged. "Perhaps when the baby is born, I will add him." Her swollen bare feet touched the cool tile, but she did not move away because Jefford remained directly in front of her.

"And what if the baby is a girl?" He lifted an eyebrow.

Madison smiled, her heart swelling with an emptiness, an ache. "Then I suppose I will place her in the howdah, or perhaps on Bina's head, right between her ears, the way the native children like to ride."

He gazed down at her, his face so serious. "You look good." He rubbed her cheek.

"Paint?"

He nodded.

She chuckled and rubbed at her face.

"You know, this is how I remember you the first time I saw you in London," he said, his tone distant. "Do you remember?" He rubbed at the stubborn streak of paint on her cheek with his thumb. "Your hair was pulled in a mass of tumbling, uncombed curls, and you were wearing some sort of smock covered in paint and the strangest little shoes."

"You came in through the window, shouting at me, accusing me of putting my subject in jeopardy with my brother's dogs."

"Do you miss them?"

She kept her face impassive. "The dogs? Certainly not. They were stupid little creatures. I much prefer tigers like Rani."

Hearing her name, Rani, who had been sleeping under the scaffold, meowed and stretched her legs before curling into a ball again.

"She's growing," he remarked.

"She is always hungry! She eats her share of *puttu* in the morning and mine, as well."

"You should not be letting that cat have your breakfast. It's important that you eat."

"Yes," she chuckled, reveling in the feel of him still standing so close. "And look at me." She drew her hand over her round belly covered by the thin pink silk of her sari. "I look as if I'm starving, don't I?"

When he placed his hand on her belly, something he rarely did, and then only in his mother's chambers, Madison felt her breath catch in her throat.

Every nerve in her body seemed to quiver. She was shocked that despite her advanced pregnancy, her body still ached for him. She ached to feel his hands on her bare breasts. His mouth…

She moistened her dry lips, lifting her lashes to look at him. He was staring at his hand on her belly.

"What was that?" he whispered.

She smiled. "The baby."

His brow burrowed. "It kicks like that?"

She couldn't stop smiling. She wanted to put her hand over his, to feel the baby move with him, but she was afraid to do anything that might shatter the moment.

"Does it hurt?" he asked.

She shook her head, still smiling. "He's very strong."

"Perhaps *she's* very strong."

She studied his face as he continued to stare at her belly in obvious fascination as the baby kicked and rolled in her belly. "Would you mind?"

"Would I mind what?"

"If the baby were a girl."

He shook his head. "Not if she were blond like you." He glanced up, his hand still on her abdomen. "Not if her eyes were the color of yours, the color of the Caribbean ocean on a sunny day."

Madison's heart was suddenly pounding in her chest; she wanted so badly to find the feelings they shared at their wedding. It hadn't been a dream. It had been a perfect night. And even though he had never uttered the words, he had made her feel loved. That was what she needed right now, with the baby coming and all the fears she had of becoming of mother. With the pain of knowing that Aunt Kendra could take a turn for the worse at any time, Madison desperately needed to think that there was at least the chance that Jefford might love her.

He lifted his hand from her rounded belly to her cheek and drew his thumb over her mouth. She felt her lips tremble. Her eyelids suddenly grew heavy, but she refused to close them.

She lifted up on her bare toes as he leaned over her and she met him halfway. Their lips touched and she drew in her breath. She felt his arms go around her and she sighed, parting her lips. His tongue touched hers tentatively, as if they had never made the child she carried in her womb, as if it was the very first kiss they had shared.

A soft moan rose in her throat as he delved into her mouth and she felt herself sway in his arms. She slipped her hands over his shoulders, clinging to him, needing to breathe but unwilling to tear her mouth from his.

Fast female footsteps echoed in the corridor. "Madison, Mr. Jefford?"

It was Maha.

Jefford had barely lifted his mouth from Madison's when Maha halted just inside the rotunda. She cleared her throat, but it was obvious she was pleased. No doubt the servants suspected that not all was as well with the newlyweds as they let on.

"Lady Moran will now see you," she said, being oddly formal.

"I have to go," Jefford whispered, seeming unwilling to release her.

"Lady Moran will see you *both*."

Madison looked up at Jefford.

At once, a trickle of fear eased down her spine. What if her aunt had taken a turn for the worse and she had been hiding it from them?

"It's all right," Jefford whispered, taking her hand in his. "We'll go together."

"Kendra?" Jefford called, leading Madison through her receiving chamber toward the main bedchamber divided by open doors draped with floor-to-ceiling multicolored silk panels.

"Come, come, the vicar and the mullah cannot wait forever on you two," Lady Moran called, sounding more like her old self than she had in months.

"Vicar?" Still holding Madison's hand, Jefford pushed through the silken drapes to find his mother on her feet, dressed splendidly in a red sari with a gold turban and ruby jewels around her neck, her wrists, even her bare ankles. The raja stood beside her smiling, in a traditional coat and *saffa* that looked much like the one Jefford had worn on his and Madison's wedding day.

"Don't just stand there with your mouth gaping open, son." She waved him closer. "Give me a kiss and let's get this nonsense over with."

"What nonsense?" Jefford asked, releasing Madison's hand to kiss his mother.

"The nonsense of marrying me," the raja explained. "Shall we, Kendra?" He motioned toward the two holy men standing by the open windows, appearing rather comfortable in each other's presence.

"They're getting married?" Madison murmured as Jefford returned to her side.

He nodded his head. "Apparently."

The only other people in the room were Maha and the raja's closest confidant and personal assistant, Zafar.

"Would you two cease the whispering?" Lady Moran quipped. "I'm trying to get married!"

Madison looked at Jefford wide-eyed and had to bite back a chuckle.

So Madison, still barefoot, stood witness to her aunt's and the raja's wedding ceremony, performed twice, once in Christian ritual and then Hindu. It was the most beautiful wedding she had ever attended. As the raja leaned forward to kiss his new wife tenderly on the lips in front of the mirror placed before them by Zafar, tears filled Madison's eyes.

At the end of the ceremony, the raja led Kendra to a chair piled with pillows and the room began to fill with servants bearing the wedding feast. The raja's personal musicians had arrived from his palace and set up just outside the windows in the garden and began to play.

Jefford pushed a goblet of fruit juice into Madison's hand while he chose something a little stronger as they approached the newlyweds.

"So this is why I could not meet the train to pick up the new vats for the indigo?"

Despite her illness, Lady Moran's thin face glowed. "This was why. I finally gave in to Tushar, mostly because I didn't have the energy to fight him any longer, but I wanted no fuss."

"She would not even accept an elephant as a gift," the raja explained, feigning annoyance. He reached out and took her hand in his, lifting it to his lips. "She has agreed, however, to accept the title of Princess of Darshan."

Madison wasn't certain what pleased her more, the grin on Aunt Kendra's face, or her husband's. "I'm so happy for you," Madison murmured, leaning over to put her arms around Lady Moran's neck and kiss her cheek. "If there was ever a match made in heaven, it is yours."

Madison stepped back to let Jefford kiss his mother.

"You're not upset with me?" she asked, her tone surprisingly hesitant.

Jefford drew back to look into her eyes, still holding her shoulders. "Of course I'm not. The raja is a good man. You deserve to be happy, Mother."

Tears filled Lady Moran's eyes and Madison had to look away. Maha appeared at her side, pressing a silk handkerchief into her hand.

"I wanted to speak with you beforehand," the raja told Jefford. "But she insisted the decision was not yours."

Jefford stepped back, coming to stand beside Madison again. "And she is right, sir."

"I only did it for you," Lady Moran declared. "Is that punch, boy?" she called to a passing servant. She waved him closer. "I cannot tell you how greatly I miss my Jamaican rum, although what we've been making here is not half bad."

Jefford chuckled and raised his goblet in toast. "I cannot say how greatly I admire you both. This took a great deal of courage. To your happiness."

They all raised their glass in English tradition. "Here, here," cried the raja. The others echoed.

"Jefford, I have been meaning to ask you some questions concerning your new indigo operation," the raja said. "Have you a minute?"

"Certainly."

"If you'll excuse me, my love." The raja kissed his princess's hand and rose. "Please take my chair, dear. You should sit," he told Madison.

"I feel fine."

"Sit," Jefford murmured from behind her, his breath warm in her ear.

Her aunt patted the cushioned chair beside her. "Come, make your old auntie happy."

Madison sat down and tried to pull her bare feet beneath her sari, but too much fabric was needed higher up due to the expansion of figure. "Really, Aunt Kendra, you could have told us we were coming to a wedding. I would have, at least, put on shoes."

She chuckled, nibbling on a piece of fresh pineapple. "Ah, my dear Madison, it was a rather sudden decision. Our opportunity to have the life I had dreamed is long passed. I wed him only out of practicality, not any romantic notions. The thought of leaving Tushar a widower so quickly does not sit well with me."

"You shouldn't say that," Madison choked, looking away so that her aunt could not see her tears.

"It's time for us to stop pussyfooting around this subject, my dear," Kendra insisted, taking her hand.

Madison couldn't meet her gaze.

"Come, now, you mustn't be sad for me. I have lived a long, happy life. I am ready to go when the good Lord calls me."

"I cannot bear the thought," Madison murmured.

"Listen to me! No woman in England, Jamaica or India has been as fortunate as I. All these years I have had a son who loves me, many lovers whom I have greatly cared for, and now I've come home to die in my beloved's arms. What more could any woman ask for?" She sipped her rum punch. "Except, perhaps, a grandchild?"

"It won't be much longer. Less than a month." Madison had to smile, in spite of her tears.

"Well, I promise you I shall remain at least long enough to see his or her tiny face," Lady Moran assured her. "After that…" She shrugged. "We shall see."

"Princess, your guests have arrived," Maha announced. "Lord and Lady Rutherford, Lord Thomblin, the Honorable George Rutherford and Princess Seghal."

Madison couldn't help but smile at the mention of Sashi and George. He had recently asked for her hand in marriage and her *father* had sent word from the north that he would be honored to give *his daughter's* hand in marriage to the young Englishman. Though the wedding would not take place for months, her dowry had already arrived, thanks to Lady Moran's generosity.

"Thomblin's here, too? George said the other day that he thought Carlton might be back. Apparently he has indeed lost his plantation north of here." Lady Moran made a clicking sound between her teeth. "I was afraid it would eventually come to this." She looked to Maha. "I'm sorry, dear. Send them in, send them in." She offered her goblet. "And do get me some more punch."

That evening, Madison and Jefford walked side by side down the corridor to their chambers. He had taken her arm to help her from a chair in his mother's room and had not released it, so they walked hand in hand.

Madison was so happy, she thought she might burst. After all this time, Jefford seemed to be relaxing, seemed less angry with her. Would he join her in her lonely bed tonight?

Alone in their chambers, Jefford helped Madison out of her sari and into a whisper-thin white sleeping gown. He removed his boots and shirt and stood at the end of the bed, telling her about a man in his thirties in one of the villages who had asked to be taught to read, despite his age. Jefford thought he might make an excellent overseer of the new indigo factory he was building.

Madison sat and listened, thrilled by the excitement she heard in Jefford's voice. She knew how hard it had been for him to leave Jamaica, where he had worked his whole life to improve the lives of the workers. Now, here in India, he seemed to have found his calling yet again, and even the raja was coming to him seeking consultation.

"I just look in this man's eyes," Jefford continued, drawing up his fist. "And I see a man who wants a better life for himself and his family."

"He is lucky to have a man like you take an interest in him," she said, reaching out hesitantly to touch his bare chest.

Jefford moved in front of her, taking her hands in his. "You looked so beautiful dancing tonight."

She laughed, gazing down. "I should be ashamed of myself carrying on like that with this big belly."

"No. I mean it. You were so beautiful. I was watching you and thinking about something the raja said to me tonight about how fortunate he felt to have my mother as a wife. I…" He halted in started again. "I was thinking that I should feel the same way about you."

When he raised his hand to stroke her cheek, she heard the bracelet around his wrist jingle, and realized that all these months, despite their differences, she had not once thought of removing her ankle bracelet.

Madison lifted her chin to gaze up into his eyes. Slowly, he lowered his head and drew his mouth across hers. "I… I want to ask you…" he started awkwardly. "And if the answer is no, I'll understand. You're very close to your time and—"

Madison pressed her finger to his lips. "Yes," she murmured.

"Yes?"

"Yes, you can come to my bed. Our bed."

The corner of his mouth curled into a smile and he leaned over to kiss her again. This time, however, it was a more intimate kiss. His tongue flickered out to tease hers and she felt the first finger of desire curl in her belly.

A tap on the outer chamber door brought a curse from Jefford's lips as he lifted his head. "Yes?" he barked.

The tap came again and he shook his head. "I'll be right back."

Madison watched Jefford walk through the open doorway into the outer chamber and turn the doorknob. It was a young man she didn't recognize who spoke too softly for Madison to hear. Jefford responded, obviously annoyed. When he walked back into the bedchamber, the stranger remained in the open doorway.

"I'm sorry," he said. "I have to go to one of the villages."

"Why? What's wrong?"

"It's Chantal."

"She wants you to come to her?"

"It's not like it sounds."

"I'll come with you, then."

"No. Absolutely not." He walked away to grab his boots and discarded shirt. "I won't be long."

Madison fought the anger that curled in the pit of her stomach. One call and he runs to his whore's side! She crossed her arms over her chest.

"I'll be right back." He grabbed her arm to lean over and kiss her. "I have to go."

"You don't have to go!"

His lips brushed her cheek rather than her mouth. "I don't want to argue about this. Wait up for me."

Madison watched him walk out the door, unsure whether she wanted to cry or break something.

27

Madison waited and waited, and the more time that passed, the later it became, the angrier she became. First she paced her chambers, then when she grew too tired to take another step, she climbed into bed and stewed there. The hands on the old gilded clock on the shelf near her chifforobe slowly turned as night became the wee hours of the next morning and still there was no sign of Jefford.

As Madison lay on her silken pillows in the massive bed, her hand on her swollen abdomen, she remembered the times over the last few months that Jefford had been called from their room at night. It was always under the excuse that he was needed by a foreman or overseer, that there was a fire, or an injury, or a dispute that required the master's hand, but Madison could see now that it was all lies. All these months it had been Chantal sending for him; this was simply the first night she'd been bold enough to give her name. Or Jefford had been bold enough to tell her the truth….

Madison was too hurt for tears now. Too angry. So what

if Jefford had gone to Chantal's bed? He had never tried to hide his mistress from her, not from the first day they had set foot on Jamaica. Even after the wedding, though Madison had not seen Chantal, she had known she was somewhere nearby. She'd known it all along and just wanted to deny the fact.

She rose, rubbing the small of her back, which ached this morning, probably because she'd barely slept, only nodding off once or twice while waiting for her philandering husband.

At the windows, she drew back the drapes and the room was filled with bright September sunlight. It was hard to believe that a year ago she had lived in foggy, rainy London at Boxwood Manor, never dreaming what was in store for her in the coming months: Jamaica, India, a husband, a baby. She smiled, thinking what a bittersweet cup it was.

What to do now? she wondered. She would not stand here and feel sorry for herself any longer. When Jefford returned, she would put him out of her bedchambers. She didn't care what the servants thought, or even Aunt Kendra. She had done what she could to make her aunt happy in these last few months of her life, but she would not sacrifice herself in the process. Lady Moran...the Princess Kendra would understand that.

Yes, Jefford would have to go. If he wanted to continue to live the life he had had before they were married, that was fine, but he would not do it so blatantly in front of her. She wouldn't allow it.

Madison pushed open the floor-to-ceiling windows that led onto the gardens. The palace was beginning to stir. She heard the rhythmic tick-tick of the windlass as someone drew water from the well near the kitchen. A barefoot native boy ran through the garden, his arms burdened with a heavy basket of fresh fruit for the morning meal.

Pacing in front of the window, Madison realized she could not stay here all day waiting for Jefford. She just couldn't. Her gaze fell to the canvas bag she used to carry her paints into the gardens or one of the courtyards. That was what she needed to do today to keep her mind else-where. She needed to start a new painting. Something fresh.

She picked up the bag and opened the flap, breathing deeply the scent of the oil paints. To her, it was an aroma sweeter than the sweetest flowers in the jungle. Paint. That's what she would do today. And not here. Not in the palace. She was going to take Bina and go into the jungle, and no one was going to stop her.

Jefford stretched his neck to one side and then the other, rubbing it where the muscles had grown sore from sitting up in the chair all night. The tiny hut was beginning to fill with morning light. His gaze shifted to Chantal lying on the narrow bamboo platform bed, her eyes closed. Her face peaceful, at last.

He shut his eyes for a moment, running his hand over his face to ease the ache of sleeplessness behind his eye-lids. Thank God she was at last still. Watching the pain she must have felt as the poison spread through her body had been almost more than he'd been able to stand. Some-times, he knew, people killed family members rather than allow them to suffer the excruciating chest and head pain, then paralysis before inevitable death.

According to the villagers, she'd just been walking through an open field; grassland was often where the king cobra lived in India. Her companion had run to the village for help, but it had been too late.

"*Sahib.*" The young man who had come for him at the palace stood in the doorway staring at the bed. "She is dead?"

Jefford nodded but made no attempt to rise. He felt guilty, realizing he should have found her a husband as soon as they reached India, whether she wanted one or not. Perhaps if he had married her off to one of his overseers, her life would have taken a different turn.

He rose, leaned over Chantal's bed, caught the filmy gauze sheet and drew it over her body, covering her face. "Rest in peace," he murmured.

He turned away. "I'll send someone for the body," he told the villager, then walked out into the morning air, thankful to be able to breathe again. It had been hot in the little hut and the aura of death had been suffocating. "I appreciate you coming for me." He offered him a coin from his pocket.

"Will call for palanquin?" he asked, fingering the coin in amazement.

"No. I'll walk. It's not so far." He started through the village, ignoring the curious onlookers. Those who already knew him bowed. A little boy he recognized from the village school waved shyly from a doorway.

Jefford just wanted to go home now. Home to Madison. He wanted to sleep in her bed and hold her in his arms, hold her and the child that would soon be theirs.

Madison sat back on the cushions on the howdah and closed her eyes. Bina's slow gait was so comfortable, the jungle so warm in the late-day sun that she found herself drifting off to sleep. After going without much sleep all night and then painting for hours, she was tired.

When she had sought out Vijay he had been hesitant to agree to take her beyond the palace gates, but when she had ordered him directly, he had obeyed. He had placed the howdah on Bina, and they had made their escape through one of the unguarded gates, with him carrying an American-made repeating rifle.

Vijay had taken her to a picturesque place in the jungle where, beneath a tangle of vines as thick as her wrists, lay a fallen statue of the Buddha. The place was an ancient temple, long left abandoned, the elephant handler had explained to her as he helped her down from the howdah. He had set up her easel and camp stool and then sat patiently in the shade of a great palm tree while she painted. Bina stood nearby, content to pick the most succulent leaves off the tree.

Even in the state of ruin, the stone Buddha and its craggy, cracked features had fascinated Madison. Inspired by the serenity the fallen statue had seemed to emote, her hand had flown over the canvas. The Buddha had quickly come to life amid the vines and wildflower blossoms. At home, in the shade of the pavilion near one of the many trickling fountains on the palace grounds, she would fill in the background of the jungle, beneath the canopy of the endless blue sky.

Now she was just eager to return home to her chambers, to get a cool drink and, perhaps, even take a short nap before she joined her aunt and the raja for the evening meal.

Madison's head had just dipped drowsily when she heard a strange sound. She felt the howdah shudder and her eyes flew open as she gripped the sides of the flimsy contrivance. "Vijay," she called, sitting up to look out through the silk curtains.

Again, the elephant shuddered. This time, she made a quick side step and the howdah swayed precariously.

"Vijay," she called, gripping the howdah to look down at the elephant's keeper. "What's wrong—"

As the screeching sound tore the air again she realized

what it was, though she had never heard it in the jungle, only in the garden or at the foot of her bed. It was the growl of a tiger, but not the playful growl of a mother tiger playing with her kitten or the baby cry of her half-grown pet, Rani. This was a tiger that dragged children from their villages at night. A tiger that could take a full-grown Englishwoman by surprise.

"It is all right," Vijay called up, his voice filled with fright. "Do not be afraid, *sahiba*."

The tiger growled again and Bina reared up on her hind legs. Madison screamed and caught the frame of the howdah.

Bina came down on both front feet, roaring in distress. Vijay was shouting up to the elephant, trying to calm her.

The tiger screamed again and Madison heard Vijay give a strangled cry. Gunfire exploded and the elephant reared up again. This time Madison held fast to the side of the howdah. Her canvas bag of paints hit her across the stomach and she sucked in a great breath, crying out more in surprise than pain. Her freshly painted canvas and a water skin flew over the side.

The tiger growled again; it was much closer. Vijay fired his rifle and Bina took off at a run, crashing through the jungle.

"*Sahiba!*" Madison heard Vijay's voice growing fainter by the moment. "*Sahiba…*"

At least he wasn't dead, but Bina still raced through the jungle, her feet pounding the earth. The giant animal must have run for more than five minutes and Madison just hung on, too stunned really to even be afraid. Twice she lifted her head to try to see where Bina was taking her, but from that height in the trees, everything looked the same. All she knew was that they were not headed back in the direction of the palace.

At last, Bina began to slow and finally came to a stop. Madison rose above the edge of the howdah to gaze at the elephant, who still seemed nervous but was comforting herself with snatches of fresh bamboo leaves she stuffed in her mouth.

With a groan Madison sat back on the cushions and surveyed the mess around her. Her paints and brushes had spilled out all over the silk divans and her beautiful painting of the Buddha was gone. At least she was unharmed and she prayed Vijay was, as well.

She rubbed the small of her back, which seemed worse now. Nature was calling as it did with increasing frequency these days, and she rubbed her back again, gazing over the side of the elephant. How was she going to get down? There was a little rope ladder Vijay drew down in the jungle to allow her to enter and exit the howdah, but that was with Bina kneeling.

She peered over the side of the howdah, then grabbed the rope ladder and dropped it down, but it fell rather short. From the end of the ladder to the ground was probably the distance of her full height, more than she dared to drop so large with child, but she *really* needed to relieve herself.

After a moment's debate, which included the very brief consideration to just remain in the howdah and do what must be done, she began to throw what pillows remained, over the side of the howdah, letting them fall just under the ladder. When she had tossed the last pillow down, she dropped a water skin, as well. She knew there would be no returning to the howdah unless she could convince Bina to drop to her knees, something she saw as unlikely.

Taking a breath, her discomfort increasing by the moment, Madison turned around and climbed over the side of the howdah. The rope ladder swayed precariously, but she hung on, and thankfully, Bina didn't move, content to munch on the bamboo leaves.

When Madison's feet reached the lowest rung, she pulled them away, groaning at the strain on her arms and the pain that shot through her palms. She managed to lower herself another rung, then one more and then another until her hands could support her weight no longer and she closed her eyes and let go.

Her landing was surprisingly gentle. She met the ground feet first, her knees buckled, and then she fell over on her side, onto the magenta pillows. Laughing with relief, she scrambled up and walked to a tree so she would have something to steady herself.

Feeling much better once she had answered nature's call, she carried the pillows to an umbrella tree that offered shade, retrieved her water skin and sat down to wait for Vijay or someone from the palace.

"Gone?" Jefford bellowed. "What do you mean, she's gone?"

Chura cowered in the corner of the room, her eyes downcast. "Gone, sir, Mr. Jefford. To paint."

"She walked?"

"Elephant."

Jefford slammed his fist down on a table and a small wooden box flipped over the side, hitting the tile floor with a splintering of wood. Madison's ivory and silver hairpins scattered on the floor like long grains of jeweled rice.

His chest tightened. He knew very well she had taken off because of Chantal. He realized now that he should have sent word to Madison, but it hadn't occurred to him back at the village when Chantal was in the last throes of death.

"Damn it, Madison," Jefford muttered under his breath as he strode out of the room. "Couldn't you have a little faith in me?"

Never once since their wedding had he so much as turned his head to Chantal or any of the pretty, young, willing women he saw every day.

He wiped his mouth in bitter anger. If only she could have given him the benefit of the doubt, it could have made such a difference between them. And now…

Jefford entered his mother's chambers without knocking, pushing through the silk drapes into her private bedchamber. Kendra sat alone in her bed, reading from a book the raja had brought his bride. The author was Bombay-born, but an Englishman, by the name of Rudyard Kipling.

"Did you know Madison had left the palace?" Jefford exploded.

Kendra laid her book on her lap, her face immediately lined with concern. "Of course I didn't know she had left. You had a quarrel?"

Jefford ran his hand through his hair. "No, we didn't quarrel," he snapped. "She didn't give me that opportunity."

"I don't understand."

He shook his head. "Don't concern yourself. I'll find her." He leaned over and kissed her cheek. "Where is the raja?"

"Jefford, I wish you would call him your father. At least refer to him as your father. It would mean a lot to me."

"I'm not getting into this conversation with you right now. I'm going out to look for her." He strode away. "And when I find her—" He crushed his hand into a fist.

"Now, now. She's carrying your child. She's overwrought with emotion," Kendra called after him as he walked out of the room. "You should have seen what a witch I was when I was carrying you!"

Jefford slammed her chamber's doors.

Madison woke to a sharp pain in her abdomen, a pain that swelled…then eased. She looked around in confusion, then realized she must have fallen asleep on the pillows under the umbrella tree.

Gasping for breath, shocked by the intensity of the sensation, she cradled her belly with her arms. Panting, she grasped the tree trunk beside her and slowly rose, hoping that standing would ease the ache in her back.

On her feet, she looked up, realizing something was different. Bina! Bina had left her while she slept. Tears filled her eyes and she wiped at them.

Going out today to paint had been foolish. She knew that now, she had known it when she had made the decision. Her belly began to tighten and she felt the pain wash over her, then something warm gushed from between her legs.

She grasped the tree trunk and panted.

28

"Which way, Vijay?" Jefford asked quietly, kneeling in front of the wounded elephant keeper.

Not ten feet away lay the body of a Bengal tiger that had to be seven feet long and the weight of two men. It had taken Jefford hours of wandering in the jungle to find the mahout; so far, there had been no sign of the elephant or Madison.

When Jefford and his men had come upon the Indian man, he had been drifting in and out of consciousness from loss of blood. The tiger had attacked him, he related, but he had been able to beat it off with his rifle and then shoot it. He was now seated upright, leaning against a tree, his arm bandaged and placed in a sling.

With his good arm, Vijay lifted Jefford's canteen to his lips. "I am much sorry for this to happen, *sahib*."

"It's all right," Jefford said, keeping his voice calm. "You didn't know she wasn't supposed to leave the palace."

"The raja, he tell Vijay, the miss is his new master. Obey her. Protect her."

"And you did protect, didn't you?" Jefford lifted his chin in the direction of the dead tiger. "You didn't panic and you didn't abandon my wife. You will be greatly rewarded for your bravery."

"That is not necessary, *sahib*. Only to see the miss safe."

"We found this," Ojar, said as he approached.

Jefford rose to accept the painting she must have done this morning of the Buddha from a ruin not far from where they stood. He shook his head. It was utterly captivating, not only in the details of the finely formed face with its cracks in the granite, but in the serenity the painting emoted.

"Which way?" Jefford asked Vijay.

He raised his hand, pointing north into the dense jungle.

Jefford nodded. "Ojar, I want you to send two men for a palanquin to take Vijay back to the palace. We're going to need more men with torches if we don't find her soon." He gazed up at the failing light.

"Yes, *sahib*."

"I'm going to follow Bina's path. It can't be too hard to track an elephant."

"You go alone?"

"I want this wounded man guarded, and someone also needs to remain here in case my wife finds her way back."

"Yes, *sahib*."

Jefford picked up his rifle and jogged off in the direction the elephant had gone. As he suspected, Bina's tracks weren't hard to follow and it didn't take long for him to find the place where the elephant had finally stopped.

Bina was gone, but in an area of trampled grass and chewed vines, bright pink and blue silk pillows under a tree caught his eye at once.

Jefford fought the fear that tightened in his chest. Vijay had killed a tiger. But it was not the only tiger in this part of the jungle, and there were so many other dangers.... He forced himself to push his fears aside and survey the area again, looking for clues. The pillows and the water skin on the grass made him realize she had been able to get down from Bina's back, but not able to return to the howdah.

Why didn't she wait? Why would she leave? Surely she would have known they would come looking for her!

Spying a dark spot on one of the pillows, he knelt to get a closer look. Had she spilt water?

No…it was blood.

Madison heard women whispering. She couldn't understand most of what was being said but she knew that the villagers were trying to help her.

She gritted her teeth, refusing to cry out as the next birthing pain racked her body. She squeezed her eyes shut, clutching the rags tied to each side of the cot and counted away the seconds until she knew the spasm would subside.

The pain waned and she exhaled with relief. Someone laid a cool, damp cloth on her head. Another pressed a piece of papaya to her lips and she sucked on it.

Her back throbbed and she had to consciously make an effort to relax, knowing the pain would return in a moment, knowing she had to conserve her energy.

Madison's belly began to contract again and she bit down on her inner lip, swearing to herself if she got through this, if her baby was born alive and well, she would change. She would think before she acted.

The pain washed over her like a tidal wave and she strained against the cloths tied to the bed. Tears filled her eyes. She wanted him here; she wanted to hear his calm voice, feel his touch. If Jefford were here, she knew he would make sure the baby was born alive. He would keep them safe.

Jefford jogged through the darkness, following a narrow path that had to lead to a village. He could see a glow of cook fires in the distance, smell goat meat roasting. There had been no sign of struggle where he had found the pillows, no more blood but the few smears he found amid the wetness.

He had discovered Bina less than half a mile away, munching contentedly on new bamboo shoots, the howdah still attached to her back. There was no sign of Madison, but he knew she had to be nearby. How far could a woman close to giving birth go?

Logic told him to follow the path to the village. A boy met him near the first hut he encountered and in broken Hindi he asked about his missing wife.

The boy led him to another hut and called inside. An elderly native woman smelling of incense appeared. The boy talked to her and she looked to Jefford, nodding.

"She's inside?" Jefford asked, his heart pounding in his chest. "Is she hurt?" He took a step forward and the boy put out his hand.

"No! Shea say…" The boy struggled for the right words. "No go. Baby come."

"Baby?" Jefford murmured. "She's having the baby?" Ignoring the shrieks of the woman, Jefford pushed his way past her into the dimly lit hut.

Madison gasped and tried to catch her breath as the contraction passed. She was feeling as though she were floating between the pains. Nothing seemed real anymore. The sounds, the presence of the women around her, had faded.

All that seemed to exist now was this baby inside her and its urgency to enter the world.

"I want some light in here," she heard someone demand.

A male voice.

Then she thought she heard a growl. The tiger?

No, that didn't make any sense. But neither did the voice. It was Jefford's voice. She wondered if she had dreamed about the children who had found her. About the men and the old woman who had carried her to a hut on a makeshift palanquin.

"Don't touch her. I want warm water to wash my hands. Water!"

Why did he want water?

Madison felt her muscles begin to contract again and she steeled herself for the onslaught. The pressure was so great in her belly now that she actually welcomed the pains.

She felt hands touch her bare legs.

"Madison." Jefford's voice invaded the fog of pain and determination to push the baby from her body.

"Madison." He grasped her hand. "I don't know what the hell I'm doing here, but I can see the head. You need to push."

The urge to push became overwhelming and she screamed against the searing pain, then suddenly the pain was gone. In an instant it was over she heard Jefford laughing.

Crying?

She heard the baby's shrill wail and smiled, too exhausted to open her eyes.

The next thing Madison knew, the bed was swaying rhythmically. She was lying on her back and the pain was gone. There was nothing but a dull ache in her belly now. She heard something mew and she realized it was tucked in her arm beside her on the bed.

She opened her eyes to see light all around her in the darkness. Torches. Trees were passing by. She was being carried in a palanquin, the baby in her arms, fussing. She lifted her head, which seemed as heavy as a leaded weight.

"Hey."

Madison lifted her lashes to see Jefford leaning over her. "You're awake."

She smiled, still feeling a little dreamy. "Boy or girl," she whispered.

"Boy."

She smiled, her eyelids almost too heavy to keep open. "Disappointed?"

"No." He leaned over and kissed her, than kissed the tiny head in the crook of her arm. "Just thankful you're both all right."

"Vijay?"

"He'll be fine. Some bad scratches, but he'll recover."

"He shot the tiger," she murmured, beginning to feel as if she was drifting away again. "Bina ran."

"We found her. Someone is leading her back to the palace now."

"Home," she sighed.

"Yes, my love. We're going home."

The next morning Madison awoke amid the soft pillows of her own bed. Chura brought her the baby, who nursed greedily, then Madison enjoyed a large breakfast of goat stew and fresh fruit.

After Madison and the baby had eaten, Chura helped

her to her feet so she could wash up and dress in a clean sleeping gown. She had just returned to her bed where the baby lay asleep when Jefford appeared in the doorway.

"He's beautiful, isn't he?" Madison smiled.

Jefford approached the bed and Chura took the breakfast tray and backed out of the room. Madison rose on her knees to look over the sleeping baby. She felt as if she'd taken a fall; every muscle in her body ached, but she felt surprisingly strong.

"He ate well," she told Jefford, running her hand over the pale fuzz on his tiny head, fascinated by the fact that he was here and he was hers, fascinated by the intense love she felt for this child she had only known a few hours.

Jefford eased down on the bed.

"You want to hold him?"

He shook his head, looking startled. "No. That's not necessary. He's sleeping."

Madison laughed. "I think that's all babies do at first. Sleep. Eat." She picked him up and he barely stirred. "Here. Hold him."

Madison lowered the sleeping baby into his arms, a strange sense of contentment coming over her as she looked at Jefford holding their son as if he were made of porcelain and might shatter at any moment.

"He needs a name," she murmured, brushing her fingertip across his rosebud mouth.

In his sleep, the baby's lips moved as if to suckle.

"Any thoughts?"

She shook her head. "He's a boy. His father should name him."

Jefford held the baby against his chest and rocked him. "So we'll think about it for a few days." He lifted his head to look at her. "Madison, I'm sorry—"

"Don't," she interrupted. "I should be the one apologizing." She looked down at her hands on her lap. "I was jealous of Chantal, of the fact that you had loved her for so long and—"

"Madison, I never loved Chantal. If I had loved her, I would have married her."

Madison searched his dark eyes. "Really?"

"The young man came for me because Chantal was dying."

"Dying?"

"She died early yesterday morning from a cobra bite." His voice was flat. He looked down at the baby in his arms again.

They were both quiet for a moment and then he looked at her. "What I wanted to say was that I think we need to start all over again. The fact is that we're married and we have a child. I…" He seemed to search for the right words. "I want to do right by you both. I don't want you to be unhappy because of me."

He didn't speak of loving her, but Madison wondered if perhaps that could come with time. "I want the same," she said.

"So let's take some time to get used to the idea of this." He moved his arms; the baby slept on, oblivious to his parents' conversation. "Fair enough?"

She smiled, looking into his eyes, seeing a kindness she yearned for. "Fair enough."

29

Six weeks after the birth of the baby, Madison stood on the scaffold and added the finishing touches to the mural she had begun in the domed receiving chamber of the palace months before. In the howdah on Bina's back, she had painted in her son, William, named after Kendra's father. She depicted Wills as a little boy with his father's sun-kissed skin and her own pale blond hair and intense blue eyes.

Smiling, she took a step back to view the completed scene. It was good; she'd captured the light perfectly, and a leaf that she'd added falling from Bina's mouth was the best she'd ever done. But something was not quite right; something was missing.

She had always preferred odd numbers when grouping objects in her paintings, whether it was flowers in a vase, or tiger kittens beneath a coconut palm tree. The howdah needed a third person, someone besides herself and little Wills, and though she seriously considered adding her dark-haired hus-band…she wasn't quite ready to make that concession.

In the last weeks, Jefford had been true to his word. He had been amazingly pleasant, attentive, but not forceful. He continued to sleep on the divan in her room, making no attempt to join her in bed, but in the last week he had begun flirting with her, and she had found herself enjoying his interest. She was physically well recovered from Will's birth, and her thoughts were returning to Jefford and their marriage.

Madison just didn't know how to bridge the gap between them. He had suggested weeks ago that they begin their marriage anew, and while it was very obvious he was trying to accommodate her, she didn't know how to take that next step. She didn't know how to invite him into her bed and begin to establish a relationship that would last the length of years the raja and Kendra's love had endured.

Madison heard the sound of the front gates opening in the distance and one of the servants inviting a visitor inside. A few minutes later, footsteps approached and she turned on the scaffold to see Lord Thomblin dressed as if he was prepared for a Sunday stroll in a London garden.

"Lord Thomblin, how good to see you." She grasped the ladder and climbed down from the scaffold, pleased to see her aunt's old friend, but feeling none of the attraction to him she had once known. After the months of being married, of having Wills, of seeing the raja and Kendra together, she realized that her infatuation with Carlton had been juvenile, based on girlish romantic notions. Lord Thomblin was not the kind of man she could have ever been happy with, certainly had children with. Jefford was so good with Wills, so attentive, so loving. Right now, she could not imagine having children with anyone else but him. She couldn't imagine allowing any man to touch her the way a husband did, except Jefford.

"Mrs. Harris, how good to see you." Carlton took her hand and bowed to kiss it, looking up at her in apparent amazement. "I must tell you, you are absolutely radiant."

She ignored his compliment. Both Jefford and Kendra swore she was even lovelier since she gave birth to Wills, but Carlton's praise meant little to her, perhaps because his opinion no longer mattered that much.

She smiled pleasantly as she withdrew her hand. "I'm surprised to see you, Lord Thomblin. I had heard you remained in Bombay and were unsure as to whether you would be able to attend George Rutherford's wedding."

In two weeks, George Rutherford would be marrying Princess Seghal here in the Palace of the Four Winds. Lady Moran had offered her hospitality because the *princess's* family lived such a great distance. Once married, the new couple would be joining their household and taking a suite of chambers on the east side of the palace.

Jefford's indigo production was growing so quickly that George Rutherford was taking over a good deal of the business of selling and shipping the commodity. While he would, someday, inherit from his father's title and monies, he was a young man who, like Jefford, did not enjoy the sometimes tedious life of a gentleman, and was proving to have an exceptional mind when it came to financial transactions.

"Why, yes." Lord Thomblin cleared his throat. "I had thought business would keep me in Bombay, but when I found myself able to get away, I welcomed the opportunity. I only hope I will be able to remain long enough to attend the wedding."

Spotting a smear of brown paint on her hand, Madison wiped it on the paint smock she wore over her sari. He continued to stare at her, to the point that he was beginning to make her uncomfortable. "You're staying with the Ruther-fords, then?"

Lord Thomblin had never provided an explanation to what had become of the lands he supposedly once owned nearby but everyone speculated that he had lost the property to debt.

"Yes, yes, indeed." Thomblin shook his head, adjusting his pith helmet, most fashionable among Englishmen in India this year, beneath his arm. "I must say again, Madison, after producing such a short time ago, you are looking remarkably beautiful."

She frowned, not caring for his term. She had not *produced,* as if making some commodity. She'd given birth. She'd brought a beautiful baby boy into the world. "Well, it's good to see you, Lord Thomblin." Her smile was now forced. "But I must excuse myself to check on my son. You're here to see Lady Moran, I assume?"

"Yes, of course. I know she has been feeling poorly, and I thought I might pay my respects."

"Why don't you have a seat?" She directed him to one of the many upholstered benches that now lined the round room. In the last months, visitors came more and more frequently: men to see the raja, who was almost never at his own palace, old friends of Lady Moran's, and also guests to see Jefford. In the time he had been in India he had made quite an impression upon both Indian and English businessmen, as well as those who governed the empire. It seemed as if they were always entertaining one dignitary or another.

Madison walked away from Carlton. "I'll send word to Lady Moran to see if she's receiving. Someone will come for you."

Madison left word with Maha in the hallway outside her aunt's chambers and then made her way to her own rooms.

Wills was just waking from his nap, well-cared-for by his new nanny, Sevti, a granddaughter of Maha. Dismissing Sevti, Madison settled on the bed to nurse her son, and after he drifted off to sleep again, she picked up a book and began to read.

At the sound of the door, she glanced up with surprise. At Jefford's order, no one entered their chambers without knocking and gaining permission to enter. It had to be Jefford.

Madison rolled over onto her back to see him walk through the arched doorway into the bedchamber. She smiled, thinking what a pleasant surprise it was to see him in the middle of the day. Usually, he was so busy that he left the palace early and came home late, not always joining her and his mother and father for the evening meal.

"Hello," she said, smiling.

He smiled back. "What are you two doing? A little nap?"

She rested her head back on a silk pillow as he leaned over to kiss her. He usually greeted her with a kiss on her cheek, but he kissed her mouth. Pleased, she slipped her hand around his neck to keep him from moving away.

"I was reading. Your son has eaten and gone back to sleep again. I'm certain he will have plenty of strength to remain awake tonight and exercise his lungs when his mother and father wish to sleep."

Jefford sat on the edge of the bed and reached over to brush the blond fuzz that was growing in on his son's tiny, round head. "You could ask Sevti to take him to her chambers at night so that you can sleep."

"Certainly not," Madison admonished. "Look at how quickly he's growing. Before I know it, he'll be old enough to be asking to go with his father to the villages or the fields and he'll be gone from me forever."

"I saw the addition to the painting in the reception chamber."

"You like it?"

"It's quite good." He reached out to toy with a lock of her long blond hair that fell over a creamy-white breast barely covered by the loose silk fabric of her sari. "I wondered what a person had to do to get included into one of your paintings."

"I go afar to get most of my ideas. I thought you had no time for such nonsense as elephant rides in the jungle," she teased.

Madison had just begun taking short painting safaris into the area surrounding the palace. After the scare with the tiger, Jefford had been very hesitant to allow her to go, but when she had promised to take several of the raja's soldiers with her each time, he had reluctantly agreed. But he had never accompanied her, though she'd invited him several times.

"It would depend on who invited me and what the elephant ride entailed," he said in a teasing voice, leaning over to kiss her neck.

Madison giggled. "What the ride would entail? Why, it would entail going to a site, painting and then returning. What did you think it would entail?"

"I was thinking more along the line of a picnic lunch, a nap in the grass and perhaps a little afternoon…" The last words were whispered in her ear.

She blushed and laughed huskily, enjoying the shiver of pleasure that went through her. "We would certainly have to leave your son home for such an adventure as that. And then there is the matter of the raja's soldiers who usually escort me."

He nuzzled her neck. "You wouldn't need the soldiers

with me. I can handle one elephant, one wife and a couple of ferocious tigers."

"Are you certain?"

"Well, the tigers and the elephant, most definitely. The wife?" He lifted one shoulder. "But I'm a man willing to give my best shot."

Madison brushed her hand across his cheek. "Your offer is tempting."

"I could give you a little taste right now of what such an afternoon could be," he murmured against her lips, his fingers brushing her breast.

Madison gasped. Giving birth had made her even more aware of her own body. Aware of Jefford's and the way her body reacted to him.

She glanced at her sleeping infant, sorely tempted, then back at Jefford. "But the baby," she whispered, slipping her hand around Jefford's neck, fingering the hair at his nape.

"He's sound asleep. I could tuck him into his cradle." He kissed her cheek and then drew his lips over her jaw, down her neck, to the V of skin between her breasts, sending delicious tingles of pleasure through her.

"It's not that I don't want to, Jefford, but I…" She looked up into his dark eyes. "A little privacy would—"

"I understand." He sat back, releasing her. "You're right."

Madison continued to hold his gaze. He was saying the right thing, but she wasn't convinced he *did* understand.

"I'm really not trying to put you off, Jefford." She grasped his arm. "I want this, too. I just—"

"It really hasn't been long enough since you gave birth," he said. His tone was without emotion as if he were reciting the words by rote. "You need to regain your strength."

"Jefford, are you listening to me?" She sat up, trying not

to lose her patience with him. "I'm fine. I'm healthy." She opened her arms wide. "I feel better than I've felt in my life. I just want to be alone with you without fear of interruption."

"I need to go, anyway." He rose from the bed and walked away. "I only came for a clean shirt." He stripped of the white one he wore and pulled an identical one from a chest against the wall. "Don't forget that tonight the raja's cousin is coming, Prince Omparkash. His connections to merchants in Bombay could become vital to our indigo operation. He's heard you're an artist and is particularly interested in meeting you. We'll be eating in the main dining hall and the raja will be joining us."

Madison got up from the bed. "Do you think your mother would feel well enough to—" The look on his face made her halt in midsentence. The anguish she saw there made her want to run to him and gather him in her arms, made her want to hold him and cover his face with kisses.

"No, I don't suppose she will be joining us," she finished softly. Then she glanced up again, trying to sound cheerful. "But I think she's having a good day. Lord Thomblin came by and she wanted to see him."

"Thomblin has resurfaced again?" Jefford pulled the shirt over his head. "Haven't seen him in months."

"He's been in Bombay."

"Yes, well, you'd know better than I."

Madison held her tongue, tired of fighting with him. "I'll see you tonight," she called as he went out the door.

He raised his hand and was gone.

After seeing Jefford, Madison found herself restless. When Sevti reappeared, she turned her sleeping son over to her and gathered a canvas bag of paints. She hadn't intended to start a new painting today, but she didn't want to go to her aunt's chambers where Lord Thomblin might still be visiting.

She decided she would go into the series of rooms George and Sashi would be occupying after their wedding. Perhaps she would begin painting a mural in one of the chambers and present it as a gift. She had already promised Sashi that once she was married, they would redecorate the rooms together.

"I'll be back in time for the evening meal," Madison told Chura as she pulled on her paint-covered smock and slipped into an old pair of worn leather slippers. "Mr. Jefford has an important guest joining us. I'll need to bathe when I return. Pick out something nice for me to wear."

"And jewels, *sahiba?*" the young girl asked.

"Yes, jewelry. Lots of it. It pleases my husband when I wear his gifts."

In the last few weeks Jefford had given her priceless jewels: pearls, rubies, sapphires, emeralds and diamonds. Many of the antique bracelets and necklaces belonged to his mother, but there was a spectacular ruby necklace, earrings and bangle bracelets that he'd bought for her in Bombay.

There were also anklets in the collection, which Indian women wore in abundance, but Madison wore no anklet except the one her husband had given her on their wedding night. The anklet represented, to her, her optimism that their marriage could be more than it was. It was silly, but she checked regularly to be sure Jefford was still wearing the matching bracelet. Even in the months before Wills had been born and she feared Jefford had all but forgotten her, the fact that he continued to wear the white-gold bracelet gave her hope.

"I think I should like to wear the rubies," Madison told her servant as she went out the door after kissing her sleeping son's forehead.

Jefford, dressed in a blue traditional *kurta,* lifted his glass to his mouth, his gaze straying to the double-arched door. He had escorted the raja and his cousin, Prince Omparkash, from his father's palace, where he had dressed for the evening an hour earlier.

They had walked in the garden and discussed business. His father's cousin had also been educated in England and spoke English quite well, as well as French, Hindi, classical Sanskrit, Arabic and German. When Madison did not appear half an hour after the designated dinner hour, he sent word to their chambers that they were expecting her and ordered the servants to begin the meal by bringing a course of fruit, nuts and wine.

At first he'd accepted Madison's tardiness as a woman's prerogative; dressing always took longer for a woman than he could fathom possible. And his son was sometimes fussy in the evenings; she could have been feeding him and settling him down for the night.

"Tell me," Prince Omparkash said, addressing Jefford as he allowed a servant to pour more wine. "You said your wife would be joining us?"

"Yes," Jefford said, now both embarrassed and angry, "I'm quite certain she'll be here momentarily."

"Women!" the raja joined in.

The men chuckled and Jefford's gaze again moved to the door. The servants had begun carrying in the next courses on silver and gold platters. Musicians, set up just outside the open doors to the garden, played the *pakhawa, santoor,* flute and sitar. It was a perfect evening, except for the fact that his wife had not bothered to show up.

Jefford folded his silk napkin and laid it beside his plate. "If you'll excuse me, gentlemen, I believe I'll look in on my wife. I cannot imagine what is keeping her so long, short of a stray tiger consuming servants or fire in the palace."

The raja and his cousin chuckled and Jefford signaled for more wine for both men as he left the dining room.

As Jefford strode through the palace, servants, seeming to sense his mood, gave him wide berth, turning down halls to take alternate routes to avoid him all together, or lowering their gaze and hurrying past him, as far from him as the passageway would allow.

Jefford entered the first room to their chambers to find Sevti lying beside Wills on a divan on the floor, talking to the infant. She sat up at once, raising her veil before he saw her face.

"Where's my wife?" he demanded, walking through the room to look in the bedchamber.

"I do not know, *sahib,*" Sevti answered, her eyes downcast.

"What do you mean, you don't know?"

"She is somewhere in palace, *sahib,*" the young girl said, sounding as if she were about to burst into tears. "But I not know where."

He stepped back into the first chamber, looking down at Wills, who was kicking his little bare feet with great enthusiasm.

"I don't understand. She knew we had dinner guests."

"Yes, *sahib.*" The servant picked up the baby, holding him against her as if she feared his own father might injure him in his anger. "She ask for bath, clothes and jewels, but she not come for the dressing yet."

He scowled. What the hell was she up to?

Thomblin had come today, after they hadn't seen him in months. Jefford knew she had thought herself in love with him before their marriage, and he had hoped that the infatuation would pass, with time, but now he couldn't help wondering if that scoundrel had anything to do with his wife putting him off when he had interpreted previous indications to mean she was willing to sleep with him again. Even desiring to. And now she was missing.

Jefford looked down at the baby's nanny, who now sat up on her knees, cradling Wills in her tiny arms. "You said my wife must be somewhere in the palace. How do you know that?"

"She come, feed baby."

"When?"

Sevti shook her head. "Time, I do not know. When he hungry. Mothers know when baby hungry."

Jefford groaned. "Fine. If she appears, tell her we're waiting in the dining hall for her."

She lowered her head. "Yes, *sahib.*"

Outside the chambers, Jefford halted, looking one way and then the other. He knew he should rejoin his father and their guest, but he wanted to know where the hell Madison was and he wanted to know now.

He turned away from the direction of the dining room and started down the corridor, asking every servant he met where his wife was, but no one seemed to know. Then he bumped into a little boy carrying an armful of large paint-spattered cloths. "You, boy! Where are you going with those?"

"Miss Madison." He grinned. "She say bring and she will paint me in picture."

"Did she, now? Well, let me take those to her and I will remind her. How would you like to be painted?" He took the drop clothes. "As a fierce warrior, or a humble priest?"

"I want to be tea-cher."

"All right, a teacher it is." He tousled the boy's jet-black hair. "Now, where is Miss Madison?"

He pointed. "East sleeping chambers."

Jefford wasn't halfway down the next corridor when he heard his father's voice.

"There he is."

Jefford halted stiffly, waiting for his father and the prince to catch up. "I apologize for taking so long. It appears my wife is at work and has possibly lost track of time," he told them, trying to keep his anger out of his voice.

He was a private man, and though he and his father had grown close in the last few months, he had no desire to share his marital problems, especially not when the raja and his mother seemed so happy together.

Perhaps that was what galled him most about Madison. Like his father with Kendra, Jefford had so much to offer Madison if only she would allow him to be a part of her life. He loved her so much, but she made it so hard to show her, and impossible to tell her.

"I thought I would retrieve the wayward artist and we could join you," Jefford explained. "You should eat without us."

"Nonsense!" Prince Omparkash declared. Unlike the raja and Jefford, he was dressed in western clothes and sporting a silver-tipped walking cane. "I should like to see more of her work. The mural in the entry hall was quite exquisite. One would think an artist who could depict our jungles so extraordinarily would have been born in our country."

Jefford smiled stiffly. "This way, sir," he said, indicating with a sweep of his hand.

Jefford and the two men followed the lavender corridor,

then the yellow, to the chambers that would become Sashi and George's after the wedding.

Jefford was actually pleased that George would be joining the household. In the last few months, he had become indispensable in the flourishing Four Winds Indigo Company. Jefford also liked the idea that Sashi would be in the household to provide companionship for Madison when his mother was gone. He had a feeling Madison did not yet comprehend how greatly she would miss Kendra.

When Jefford pushed open a set of ancient double doors that he had learned had been taken from the ruins of a nearby Hindu palace, the smell of oil paint immediately assailed his nostrils and he knew he had found his errant wife.

Jefford had fully intended to remain calm in front of his father and their guest, but when he spotted her, balanced precariously on a ladder, clad in a filthy, paint-streaked smock, her hair tangled and fallen from a none-too-neat-to-begin-with chignon, his good intentions flew out of his head.

"What the hell are you doing here? You're late," he barked, throwing the drop clothes at her feet.

Madison turned in surprise. She took one look at him and he could almost see her hackles go up. A fire lit in her blue eyes and her mouth twitched in annoyance. "Late?" she demanded from between clenched teeth. "Late for what?"

30

"You're late to attend to our guests," Jefford snapped.

Madison lifted her gaze to see the raja and an Indian man dressed in a bright green suit jacket.

"You remember, dear, the raja and his cousin Prince Omparkash," Jefford said, continuing to use that hateful tone of his. He offered his hand to help her down.

"Raja." She nodded to their guest as she descended the ladder, plopping her paintbrush in Jefford's outstretched hand.

"Prince Omparkash, how good to see you, Your Highness," she said, speaking to him as if he were the emperor himself. "Please accept my profuse apologies for being tardy. I started this project earlier today and," she laughed, "time simply got away from me."

The two older men laughed with her.

"Please, do not apologize, Mrs. Harris." The prince bowed deeply. "It is a profuse honor to meet an artist such as yourself, and so beautiful as well."

When the prince took her filthy, paint-streaked hand and kissed it, Jefford thought he might explode.

"Well, let me show you what I have done so far and then I'll change and we can adjourn to the dining room." Pointedly ignoring Jefford, Madison led the raja and the prince to the wall she'd just prepared for a new mural. "Are you familiar with the fallen Buddha statue a few miles southeast of here?"

"I am," the prince exclaimed. "And this will be the Buddha. I see the outline." He looked up at the nearly life-size form she had begun. "I must say, Mrs. Harris, I have been to Paris and seen some of the works of the great masters, but your work, it holds such depth, such—"

"If you'll excuse me, gentlemen," Jefford interrupted stiffly. "I have a quick matter to attend to and I'll join you in the dining room in a moment."

"What do you think, Prince Omparkash, of this shade of paint? There are so many greens that it is impossible to capture them all in anything like their natural beauty," Madison said, ignoring her sulking husband. "It needs to show more reflection, don't you think?"

"How dare you bring them into my studio without my prior agreement?" Madison flared the moment Jefford walked into their private chambers after the evening meal with the raja and the prince. Though hours had passed, her temper had not cooled. "It was rude, inconsiderate and boorish."

"How dare you ignore my request to attend a dinner party? Have you any idea how important Prince Omparkash's influence could be to our indigo plantations?"

Madison jerked the red veil that had been secured with ruby hairpins from her head. "I didn't ignore your request. I merely lost track of the time."

"If I hadn't come looking for you, you'd still be there

now." Jefford strode through the first room, into their bed-chamber.

Sevti hurried out, bowing. "*Sahiba,* the young master be sleeping." She pressed her hands together, nodding her head.

"Thank you, Sevti. Would you mind taking Wills with you? Just put him in the cradle in your room and I'll come for him later."

"Yes, *sahiba.*"

Madison waited in the receiving chamber until Sevti had retrieved her son and exited through a small door to her own room. Only then did she enter her bedchamber.

Jefford sat on a chair. He pulled off one shoe and tossed it.

So now he was going to be a child and throw things because she was late for his silly dinner party? She kicked the shoe as she made her way to her chifforobe. "All you had to do was send someone for me."

"I tried. No one knew where you were."

"Jefford." She whipped around. "I was painting."

"Perhaps you should have been seeing to your duty as a wife and mother, instead."

"How dare you?" she shouted, beside herself with anger. "Of all my faults, being a poor mother is not one of them."

"You weren't with Wills."

"He was asleep with his nanny! Do you expect me to sit here all day on a silk divan and wait to see if Wills fusses? Do you want me to sit here in case you have need of me?" She stood in front of him. "Wait, perhaps you'd like me to take to wearing a veil, as well. No man may ever see my face again, but you?"

"Exactly who is it that you are so anxious to have see your face?"

"And what is that supposed to mean?" Despite the fact that she had little time to dress, she had taken great care in her appearance tonight. She had hastily bathed and put on Jefford's favorite red-and-gold sari and the ruby jewels he had given her, just to please him. Not that he had noticed. "Who are you talking about?"

He walked away, pulling his *kurta* over his head.

"I asked you what you were talking about," Madison repeated, tears burning the backs of her eyelids. "Just what were you inferring? I'm tired of these word games of yours. Your constant sulking."

"I don't sulk!"

"Jefford, it's time you come out and say what it is that you want to say."

He threw his *kurta* on the bed, whipping around to face her, bare-chested. "Fine. You want me to speak? To come right out and say what I mean? What I want to say is that if you want me to release you from our wedding vows, all you have to do is ask."

"Released from our vows?" she sputtered, turning to him so that her back was to the open doors to the garden. "When did I ever say—"

"Remove the gold anklet I gave to you as my gift, as my promise to you, and you'll be released," he exploded. "You can go back to England if you want. Divorce me, marry Thomblin, whatever it is that you want, Madison. Whatever will make you happy, because above all else I want to make you happy!"

She stared at him for a moment, so horrified that she couldn't react. He wanted to divorce her? What was he talking about, marrying Lord Thomblin? A sob rose in her throat and she turned away, so devastated that she felt sick to her stomach.

Someone tapped on the outside door, and when they did not respond right away, the knock came again, louder. "*Sahib.*"

It was Maha, and Madison's throat constricted in fear. Maha never came to their chambers; she always sent lesser servants.

"Yes?" Jefford called, hurrying for the door.

"*Sahib,* Mr. Jefford," she said softly. "You must come. Your mother is—" She gave a soft cry of anguish.

Madison, still standing in the bedchamber, closed her eyes, fat tears rolling down her cheeks.

"It's all right, Maha," Jefford said gently, laying his hand on her shoulder. "Just let me get a shirt."

He walked back into the bedchamber that was lit with only a couple of oil lamps. Madison turned to him to find his back to her as he dug for a clean shirt in his trunk. His mother was dying....

He had been so mean... Said such terrible things to her.

Finding his shirt, he strode toward the door, barefoot, pulling it over his head. "You coming?" he grunted.

"Yes." She took a shuddering breath, on the verge of breaking down. "I'll be there in a moment. Go without me."

He walked out the door, closing it behind him, and Madison sank to her knees as a sob racked her body. She felt as if her world was coming to an end. Her husband, whom she wanted so desperately to love her, had told her he wanted to divorce her, and now her aunt—the one person in the world who seemed to love her as she was, for whom she was—was about to die. Where did that leave her now? She buried her head in her hands and felt the wetness of her tears.

A hand on her shoulder startled her.

She whipped around to see a large, dark-skinned man she did not know.

"What—"

Falling to his knees behind her, he closed his hand around her mouth, gathering her up into his arms.

Madison tried to scream. Tried to kick. As he tried to rise to his feet, she kicked him hard and he grunted and fell back. Madison threw herself forward and hit the hard, smooth tile floor. She tried to scream but couldn't catch her breath. Grabbing for the edge of the bed, she pulled herself up and tried to climb over it, but the man grabbed her ankle. She kicked with the other foot, but he was too strong for her.

"Get her! Get her at once," a voice ordered softly but firmly from the garden doors. "I told you there would not be much time."

She knew that voice…

Her attacker flipped her over onto her back and dragged her toward him, and Madison gave another hard kick. He caught her ankle and twisted it. In the process, her anklet broke and fell to the bed.

"No," Madison screamed, trying to grab it as he turned her around and clamped a piece of fabric over her mouth. He yanked the gag tightly and then pulled a dark cloth bag over her head. "Please…" she muttered against the stale-tasting cloth.

Jefford held tightly to his mother's hand and glanced at the doorway for the one-hundredth time. "I don't know what is keeping her," he murmured. He was embarrassed that his wife had not come to his mother's deathbed. Embarrassed that she would allow his father and the servants to see her disrespect him in this way. But worse, he was hurt. Her refusal to come to his mother's chambers as she breathed her last, because of some petty argument, hurt so badly that he could feel a physical ache in his chest.

All he wanted was for Madison to love him just a little. Just a sliver of her heart, and he would devote himself to her forever. But she really was just the spoiled child he had thought she was a year ago in London, wasn't she?

Jefford's eyes felt scratchy and he shifted his gaze to a pale burning oil lamp. His father sat beside him reading from a Hindu prayer book. He was such a strong man with such a good heart. He had actually told Jefford an hour ago that he was relieved Kendra was dying. He was pleased that she would soon be joining their Creator. His only regret was that it was not yet his time to go, as well.

"Perhaps you should go see if she is all right?" the raja said gently, laying his hand on Jefford's forearm.

Jefford looked at his mother.

"She is asleep," the raja said, smiling lovingly down at the woman who had been Jefford's world until Madison and then Wills had come to him. "She is not quite yet ready to leave us. Go," he urged.

He rose slowly from the hard wooden chair. He would just go to her, apologize for his mostly unfounded anger… his jealousy, really. And he knew that was what it was. He wasn't just jealous of that jackass Thomblin, either; he was jealous, perhaps even more so, of her painting. Of her extraordinary ability, and of the fact that she had something beyond him and Wills, and that he, soon, would have nothing. Madison and the child she had given him would soon be his reason to exist.

At the door, Jefford looked back once more. The raja had moved to his chair and now leaned over Kendra, his arm around her wasting body. He spoke softly to her…words meant to be shared only by lovers.

With a heavy heart, Jefford entered the hallway and made his way to his chambers. The palace was frighteningly quiet and the sounds that he did hear were hushed, as if the household were already in mourning.

He walked through the double doors into his rooms. "Madison," he called. "Madison, please, I need you—" He halted in the doorway to their private bedchamber. Nothing had changed since he'd left nearly two hours ago. The same lamps still burned, the lid to his clothing chest still sat open, the curtains still drifted in the warm breeze in the open doors to the garden. Even the bed was still made, Madison's colorful silk and satin pillows piled high. Then his gaze fell on Madison's anklet. She had removed it. Left it on the bed. Left him.

"Let me go, you son of a bitch!" Madison struggled against the ties that bound her wrists and ankles. It was pitch dark, but, at least, the gag and the cloth bag had been removed from her face. She was inside a swaying palanquin, conveyed by four runners. Occasionally, she heard Thomblin's voice as he gave orders.

Madison twisted her head until her neck ached. "Did you hear me, Thomblin? You won't get away with this. My husband will come for me."

She was petrified. She had heard Thomblin talking about "the sale" and "the white woman" to the big man who had taken her from her rooms. Thomblin was selling her! From the way he talked, this was not the first time he had kidnapped a woman, either. Madison realized in horror that Alice had probably been kidnapped by Thomblin.

"Jefford will come for me," Madison shouted, "and

he'll kill you! There will be no trial with my husband, you know that, don't you? This is the raja's district. Jefford will see you tied spread-eagled on the ground in the jungle and left for tiger bait!"

"Someone shut her up," Thomblin muttered from very near by.

There was another voice, but Madison couldn't make out what he said.

"I don't care!" Thomblin snapped. "So long as she's still alive when we get to the transfer station. Just shut her up!"

Jefford made himself walk to the bed and pick up the anklet, fighting the lump that rose in his throat. So this was her answer. She hadn't even had the decency to open the clasp. In her eagerness to get away from him, she had ripped the anklet off and thrown it down.

He turned away from the bed and strode to the door that led to Sevti's small room. He opened it and peeked in to see the maid asleep with Wills still in his cradle. At least his wife had had the good sense to leave the baby behind. She had known he would never let his son go.

He tightened his grip on the doorknob, looking down at his sleeping child. But how could she have done this? How could she have left Wills? He could understand Madison leaving *him*, but her baby?

She must have known she was leaving when they had entered the bedchamber earlier in the evening. That had to be why she had asked Sevti to take the baby, something she'd never done before.

The maid stirred and opened her eyes, looking startled when she saw Jefford.

"Have you seen my wife?" he asked.

She shook her head.

Jefford shut the door behind him, closed his eyes and leaned against it, still holding the anklet. The weight of his matching bracelet was suddenly almost overwhelming. He felt as if his chest were splitting in two. Splintering. To lose them both on the same day.

His mother, at least, would go to God, but his wife? Had she run off into the arms of Lord Carlton Thomblin? Had they planned this all along? She would stay with him until the baby was born and then go with Thomblin?

Jefford left his chambers and returned to his mother's room, in a daze. Maha greeted him at the door.

"She is awake, *sahib*. She asks for you." The faithful servant laid her hand comfortingly on Jefford's forearm.

"Thank you," he whispered.

The raja sat beside the bed but moved to the other chair when he saw Jefford.

"There you are," his mother said when he drew close enough for her to see him.

Jefford leaned over and kissed her cheek, which was as dry as an oak leaf on a November day back in England. "Mother."

"Oh, please," she groaned. Her voice was very soft, but it still possessed the spirit by which she had always lived. "You never called me *Mother* in my life. Don't start now. It's insulting."

He chuckled and lowered himself to the chair.

She closed her eyes, but held on to his hand. "I have my two men…now, where is my Madison?"

Jefford could not look at her.

Lady Moran opened her eyes. "Jefford?"

He didn't want to tell her, didn't want to hurt her. But they had always been so honest with each other that he could not bring himself to lie, not even when she was dying.

"She's gone," he whispered. "Gone from us." His voice caught in his throat and he looked down at the rich Turkish carpet on the floor. "Gone from me."

"Gone? By Hindi's nostrils, what are you blabbering about?"

The raja slid forward in his chair.

"Madison has left me. Left Wills." Jefford paused to get his breath. "I think…I think she went with Thomblin."

"Oh, poppycock," Lady Moran cried. "Why would she go with that perverted blackguard? She loves you."

"She doesn't."

Lady Moran fixed her gaze on Jefford and he couldn't look away. "And she told you this?"

"Not in so many words."

She sighed heavily, closing her eyes. "Jefford, Jefford, you really must work on listening to what those around you say. What makes you think she left you?"

He raised his hand and let her anklet dangle from his thumb and forefinger. "She took off the anklet I gave her that matched my bracelet. It was…a symbol of our union."

The raja put on his glasses and leaned forward to look more closely. "It was broken," he observed, "not removed."

"Yes." Jefford closed his hand over the piece of jewelry, no longer able to look at it. "I suppose she broke it and threw it on the bed."

The raja looked down at his wife. "Would she do this, leave her husband?"

"Never," Lady Moran said firmly.

"Where is the child?" the raja asked.

"Asleep with his nanny."

"Madison would never leave Wills," Lady Kendra said, trying to sit up. "My son, perhaps he might make her so angry that—" She looked at the raja. "Tushar, I'm afraid something terrible has happened to my niece." Her last words were gasps and then she broke into a coughing fit.

Jefford was on his feet at once, his hands on his mother's painfully thin shoulders. "Kendra, please. You'll make yourself sick."

"Sick?" she muttered, closing her eyes. "Can't you see I'm past sick? Tushar." She reached for the raja's hand.

"Here, my love." He clasped her hand, leaning over her so that she would not have to struggle to find her voice.

"Please, if my son does not realize something has happened to my Madison and that he must go for her, will you, at least—"

"Of course, my love." The raja squeezed her hand and kissed her dry lips. "I will find her and bring her home to you."

Lady Moran nodded slightly and then seemed to relax, drifting off to sleep. The raja tugged on his son's sleeve and walked away from the bed, bidding Jefford to follow him.

"I do not know the truth of what has happened tonight," the raja said.

"Sir, she despises me. I know that you must know we were married so quickly—"

The raja held up his hand, silencing him. "You need not say anymore." He met Jefford's gaze with eyes that matched Jefford's own.

"It is not my place to come between you and your wife. Your path to happiness must be found on your own, but I agree with Kendra. Madison would not depart this way. Not knowing how close her aunt was to leaving this world."

Jefford looked away. They were right. It didn't make sense. Why would she leave tonight, even if she had already planned it, knowing Kendra might not live until dawn? And the idea that she would abandon Wills gnawed at him. The hair rose on the back of his neck. In the last four months, two more Englishwomen, besides Alice Rutherford, had vanished in the area.

He thought about the missing women in Jamaica, his mind churning. They were not Englishwomen, but nothing had ever been heard of them, either. They were just gone.

What did all these women have in common?

Thomblin?

Jefford knew what kind of depraved sexual interests Lord Thomblin possessed. Were the missing women and his sexual exploits somehow connected?

"My son," the raja said gently. "We must go in search of her. I will send a runner to bring soldiers from my palace."

"Yes," Jefford murmured, suddenly dizzy with fear. "We have to find her."

31

A clap of thunder brought Madison back to consciousness. Someone had hit her hard on the back of the head; there had been a sharp spear of pain, then blackness. She didn't know how much time had passed since then.

It was still dark, but the palanquin was no longer moving. Her hands and ankles were still tied. She leaned to one side and tried to part the curtains of the palanquin with her chin. There were two torches that cast feeble light in the dark jungle.

Thomblin's voice was a harsh whisper. "Jesus Christ, Abdul. You'll get your money. Now, tell those men to pick her up and pick her up now. We cannot sit here like this any longer. Do you know what the raja's soldiers will do to you if they find you here with her?"

The Indian man said something.

"No! I'm an English citizen, bound by English laws. I would have to be tried in court," Thomblin said haughtily. "And what do you think the chances are that will happen in this godforsaken land, hmm?"

Madison began to slide her feet back and forth. By shifting her bare feet back and forth and pointing her toes like a dancer, she was able to slide the fabric bindings down over her feet.

"What was that?" Thomblin snapped. "Cock your rifles. See what that was. You see anything, *anyone,* you shoot. You hear me?"

One of the men responded in Hindi.

"Jesus, Abdul. Tell them to move," Thomblin snapped. "Tell them before I blow all your brains out."

Madison parted the curtain again. Something was behind him, just beyond the ring of light from a burning torch. She thought she recognized something. A silhouette.

Her breath caught in her throat. She knew where she was! They were at the site of the Buddha ruin. If she could just get loose, she could run home, barefoot or not.

She rubbed her feet back and forth even faster. It hurt, but she just wanted to get away. Wills needed her. Her aunt was dying. She couldn't let Aunt Kendra go without saying goodbye.

The sound of gunfire cracked in the night.

"Get the woman!" Thomblin ordered. "Get her!"

Drawing her shoulders together, Madison rocked back to gain momentum and then rolled sideways through the ragged curtain of the palanquin, onto the ground. She hit hard with a bump, but the bindings at her ankles slipped free. She bounced up and began to sprint—streaking through the darkness.

"She's gone!"

"Gone! She's tied up," Thomblin snarled. "She can't be gone."

Her hands still tied, Madison cut in front of the stone Buddha. "There she is! Jesus, get her, Abdul!"

* * *

Jefford crouched down to reload his repeating Winchester rifle as shots rang out over his head. Two more shots rang over his head, tearing the tranquillity of the Buddha asunder.

"Madison," he shouted.

"Jefford!"

She was still alive!

"Jefford, help me," she called. "It's Thomblin! He took Alice, too."

"Get her," he heard Thomblin shout from somewhere in the darkness.

"Madison, get down. I'm going to shoot," Jefford cried.

Madison screamed as a shadow lunged out of the tangled vines and Jefford felt his heart leap in his chest. He turned his head, catching Ojar's gaze.

Ojar nodded solemnly. He would cover Jefford as long as he lived.

Jefford sprang out from beneath a giant elephant-ear fern. Even in the darkness, he could make out Madison. Her long blond hair whirled around her as she fought a tall, dark-skinned man.

"Let me go!" she screamed, kicking him violently. "Let me go!"

"Release her," Jefford ordered. "Release her and I'll give you a chance to run before I shoot you down. You don't let her go, and I'll blow your head off."

"And risk killing her?" Thomblin shouted from where he hid.

A shot ricocheted off a tree trunk only a hand's span from Jefford's head. Another glanced off the granite Buddha. They were coming from somewhere behind him or to his side, probably from one of the men Thomblin had sent into the jungle.

Jefford ducked. "I'd rather kill her than see her go where the likes of you would sell her."

"They pay a good price for white women. You're a businessman, Harris. Surely you understand business."

Jefford scanned the dark line of the jungle, which was only broken by huge leaves and tree trunks that seemed to climb into the heavens above his head.

Another shot rang out behind Jefford. This time, Ojar had pulled the trigger. That was three men dead. Another, already wounded by Ojar, had run off into the jungle. The only ones left, by his calculation, were Thomblin and the man holding Madison.

The man was trying to wrestle her into his arms so that he could throw her over his shoulder, but Madison was putting up a hell of a fight. Jefford's heart swelled with pride as he looked down the sight of his rifle. Alice might have been an easy target, but not his Madison. Not his stubborn wife.

Sweat trickled down the sides of his face as he beaded in on the man. If he missed…

He wouldn't miss.

The man tried to spin Madison around, and she grabbed a vine that hung down in front of the huge Buddha's face, pulling her body in the opposite direction he was attempting to take her. At that instant, the man's head became visible in the dim moonlight. Jefford didn't hesitate.

He felt the rifle kick in his arms, heard the shot, smelled the burning powder. He heard the bullet strike, and flesh and bone splinter.

Madison screamed, but he knew his aim had been true and it was not his wife's blood that spattered across the face of the stone Buddha.

Jefford flew through the flowering shrubs and giant ferns toward her.

"Jefford!" she cried, falling to the left, away from the dead man.

"Madison. Are you all right?"

"Yes," she cried as she stumbled forward and ran into his arms. "Thomblin. Get him! He took Alice!"

Jefford heard someone running blindly through the bushes. It had to be Thomblin. "Ojar!" he called.

"Yes, *sahib*." Ojar burst out of the darkness, flying by them.

"I want him alive," Jefford barked, pulling Madison against his chest. Still holding her close, he used a knife to cut her hands free from their bindings.

Ojar had just disappeared into the dark behind the statue when a pistol shot rang out.

"Ojar?" Jefford called. Madison was trembling all over, panting hard, but he knew she was all right.

"It was not me, *sahib*," Ojar called from the darkness.

"No, it was me." Thomblin stepped out of the dark, into the torchlight, a pistol raised.

Jefford swung Madison into one arm and lifted his rifle. "I'm a better shot than you, Thomblin. Put it down."

"I'll shoot you, I swear I will," Thomblin threatened, his voice trembling with fear. "Or her." He swung the pistol around to take aim on Madison.

"You still won't live." Jefford's voice was stony. "This is my father's jurisdiction."

"He has no authority over me," Thomblin cried, his face pale in the feeble torchlight. Above his eyebrow, a wound oozed blood. "I am an English citizen, I have rights!" He shook his head, frenzied, spittle flying from his mouth. "These heathens can make no judgment over me!"

Jefford realized he had to get Madison down on the ground where she would be safer, but he knew the look in

Thomblin's eyes, a look of desperation he had seen in men before. Any slight movement by Jefford, and Thomblin might fire. Right now, talking him into lowering the firearm was the safest bet. "You think laws will stop these soldiers from stringing a rope up over that branch? Put the gun down and I'll protect you. I'll see you stand a fair trial."

"No," Thomblin muttered, not seeming to hear Jefford's words. "They won't hang me. They can't."

Thomblin made a sudden movement and Jefford was ready. He shoved Madison to the ground, dodging in the opposite direction. He didn't pull the trigger because he knew it was pointless; he was out of ammunition.

Thomblin's pistol exploded with sound and Madison screamed. As Jefford went down, out of the corner of his eye, he saw Thomblin fall.

Ojar burst through the bushes, his rifle drawn, and came to a sudden halt. "He took his own life," the young Indian man spat. "Coward."

Madison rose on her knees, covering her face with her hands, and Jefford crawled to her and pulled her into his arms.

Suddenly they were surrounded by the sounds of men approaching from every direction.

Madison tensed in his arms. "Who—"

"It's all right," he soothed, getting to his feet and bringing her with him. "It's my father's soldiers. They heard the gunshots."

Madison nodded her head, her face buried in his shirt. She lifted her head suddenly. "Your mother?" she whispered.

He grasped both her arms to pull her away so that he could look into her eyes. They were filled with tears and a lump rose in his throat as he struggled to remain in control of his emotions. "We need to get back in a hurry if we want to see her still alive."

Lady Moran's passing was not at all what Madison had expected. After nursing Wills, she had joined Jefford and the raja beside her aunt Kendra's bed. There were no tears, no wailing. For the first time in many months, the woman Madison had come to love so greatly did not seem to be in pain.

Lady Moran opened her eyes several times and smiled. She seemed to understand that Madison had been found, though by the time they returned it was too late to explain what had happened. She kissed her grandson good-night before he was returned to his cradle by his nanny and then reached out to her loved ones.

"Madison," she whispered.

Madison took Aunt Kendra's hand and pressed it to her lips, fighting her tears. "I'm here."

"Quite an adventure we've had this last year, you and I, eh?" Lady Moran murmured, too weak to open her eyes.

Madison chuckled, choking back a sob. "Quite an adventure."

"You were a gift to me," Lady Moran continued. "You brought such light into my life. Into my son's life."

"Aunt Kendra—"

"Shh," Lady Moran murmured. "I know. I know." She took a shuddering breath. "Jefford?"

"Here." He took her hand from Madison. "I want you to know that I love you," he said, his voice filled with emotion.

"I know." Again she smiled, tears slipping from her closed eyes. "Just promise me that you will take care of her, of my Madison."

"Please, you don't have to say these things."

"And babies. I want many grandbabies."

Jefford smoothed her wrinkled hand in his, kissed it. "You always did like giving me orders."

"Of course, what else is a woman for in a man's life? You must also promise me that you'll be good to your father. It's not his fault I ran away and you never got to know him the way you should have."

Jefford nodded.

"Now, give me a kiss and leave me with my Tushar," Lady Moran murmured.

He kissed her dry cheek one last time and then drew back with Madison on his arm to give his father and mother some privacy.

Madison and Jefford stood in the shadows of the bed-chamber, not touching each other, and with each passing moment she felt as if he was drawing away from her.

A few moments later, the raja's words echoed in the large, airy room and in Madison's mind. "She is gone."

Tears ran down Madison's cheeks as she stood behind the colorful silk curtains of her aunt's bedchamber. When she looked at Jefford, he was not crying, but the sadness on his face was even harder to bear than the loss of the precious life in the bed behind.

"I'm sorry," she whispered, wanting to reach out to him but feeling as if her attention was unwelcome.

He just stood there, arms at his sides. "Thank you," he said stiffly. "And now that she is gone, I want you to know that I release you from the marriage."

"What?" she cried, looking up at him in the darkness, his words taking her completely by surprise.

"I know that you did not want to marry me, and even if Thomblin was not your goal, that does not mean I was."

Madison felt dizzy. He was sending her away... Now that his mother was gone, now that he had fulfilled his duty to her, he no longer wanted her. "Jefford—"

He held up his hand. "Let me say this. I would not take Wills from you. I know how much you love him. We can live however it is you choose. I can join my father in his palace now that my mother is gone. That way I can see Wills every day. I will give this palace to you in Wills's name, to be passed on, someday, to him."

Madison's heart was broken by her aunt's death, and now the shattered pieces were falling to the smooth tile floor. Jefford was crushing them beneath his dirty boots. He didn't love her. He had never loved her. He married her for his mother's sake, and now that Aunt Kendra was gone, he wanted no part of her.

Madison heard thunder behind her. Lady Moran had ordered the windows to the garden opened so that she could smell the rain. Now drops were falling faster, harder.

"Yes," she heard herself whisper, her chest tight with anger that he would treat her this way. "You can divorce me. Whatever you want." Unable to bear to look at him, she walked away, out of the bedchamber, through the receiving chamber.

If Jefford had taken one step toward her. Just one step...said one word. But he did not.

In the pink corridor, Madison looked up at the blue sky painted on the domed ceiling. She was too broken to cry. Too angry to break something. In her bedchambers, she fell on her bed and turned her face to listen to the falling rain. The monsoon rains.

Jefford stumbled past his mother's bed, where his father again sat peacefully beside her, reading from his prayer book. Jefford knew a time would come when he would comfort his father, but this was not it. Not yet. His mother's death was still too raw.

Jefford pushed through the bright curtains, leaving behind his mother, who had been his world for thirty-five years, and walked out into the stone courtyard. He was immediately drenched by the pouring rain, but he didn't care. If he stayed inside, he would go mad.

He walked past a terra-cotta urn of his mother's orchids, now drooping in the rain. It was almost dawn, and he could not keep his own pain much longer. He would soon have to announce the death of Lady Moran.

Jefford wandered down a stone path, past a fountain, past the roses and jasmine that thickened the air with their perfume. At a stone bench, his knees buckled and he sat. He stared at the palace. There were almost no lamps lit yet. Only those in his mother's rooms and…his gaze shifted.

A lamp burned in his own chambers. The chambers he had shared with Madison. Even sleeping on the divan, these had been the best months he had ever experienced. Just being near her, smelling her hair, her skin, even the oil paint on his fingertips.

Jefford lowered his face into his hands, fearing he might cry.

Madison rolled on her side to look out at the rain falling in sheets from the sky. It was almost dawn, and somehow, even in the pouring rain, Aunt Kendra's garden seemed beautiful.

Movement outside caught her attention and she recognized the silhouette at once.

She bit back a sob as she watched Jefford crumble onto

a stone bench. Then, when she saw him lower his face to his hands, her tears began anew, her heart breaking not for herself, but for him. He didn't have to be alone.

The words in her head tightened in the pit of her stomach, taking her breath.

Jefford didn't have to be alone.

Didn't he realize that? Didn't he realize she loved him? Didn't he realize that if he would only give just a little, she could give him so much?

She sat up suddenly, thinking back to the conversation they had shared less than twelve hours ago. It was as if someone had lit an oil lamp inside her head. Earlier, she had accused Jefford of not saying what he meant. What he believed. What he felt.

But what if he didn't know how *she* felt? When had *she* ever told Jefford how *she* felt?

Hastily wiping away her tears, Madison climbed off the bed and walked to the open doors that led to the garden. She had to tell him, even if he turned her away. Even if he said he didn't love her, that he would never love her, she still had to speak the words.

Madison pushed one foot in front of the other and stepped out into the pouring rain. "Jefford!"

He rose from the bench.

She took another step toward him, her tears mixing with the raindrops, her hair plastered to her back, her torn, dirty sari transparent. She was running now, and he was running toward her. Halfway between the palace and the bench in the garden, they met.

"Jefford, I love you," she cried, throwing her arms around him. "And even if you don't love me, please don't divorce me, don't send me away."

He crushed her in his arms. "If I don't love you? How

could I not love you? I've loved you since the day I stepped through your window in your studio!"

The warmth of his arms penetrated the cold of the rain and the fog in her mind. She leaned back to look into his eyes. "You do? You did?" She almost laughed aloud she was suddenly so giddy, so happy. "Why didn't you tell me?"

"I don't know." His laugh came from his lips as almost a cry. "I was afraid. I knew you could never love me. No one as beautiful, as smart—" he laughed again, his voice stronger now "—as stubborn, could love me."

He spun Madison around in a circle and she lifted her feet, laughing. "He loves me!" she shouted, tipping her head back to let the rain wash over her.

"I've been a fool." Jefford leaned over her. "I'm sorry."

She brushed her hand across his cheek as he set her feet on the ground again, and she gazed into the eyes she loved. His hair was soaked and stuck to his face; rain ran in rivulets down his forehead, over his nose. The forehead she loved. The nose she loved.

"I've been as big a fool," she told him. "Please forgive me."

"We'll forgive each other," Jefford said, pressing her against him. "I love you, Madison," he crooned. "I'll love you forever. Be true to you forever. I swear to you."

"You don't have to make those promises," she murmured, pushing his wet hair from his face. "Just love me now, Jefford."

He swept her into his arms and walked out of the pouring rain, through the silk curtains, and into their bedchamber and their new life together.

Epilogue

～◌◌◌◌◌～

Three years later

"Wills!" Madison called, following the garden path, picking up first a sandal, then a second one, and finally a trail of silk clothes, like brightly colored cookie crumbs left behind on the grass. "Wills, where are you?"

The tigress Rani growled playfully and Madison followed the sound off the path, ducking palm fronds. "If we are playing hide-and-go-seek," she called to her son as she balled his clothes in her arm, "I told you that you must inform me first."

She heard a little boy's giggle. The white tiger growled again, then purred. She was very close to the hiding place in the garden now.

"Hmm," she said aloud. "Now, if I was a little boy and a big tiger, where would I hide from my mother so I wouldn't have to take my nap?"

Another giggle.

Then she heard the rumble of a deep male voice.

Yet another giggle.

A nearby white flowering tree swayed unnaturally and Madison looked up. There in the tree above her head was Wills seated on a branch, naked, his bare legs and small feet swinging back and forth. His hair was soaking wet and his body glimmered with water. He'd obviously been playing in one of the stone fountains in the garden again.

"Wills!" she cried, trying to keep the fear from her voice. "How did you get up there?"

The tiger stalked languidly out of the bushes behind the tree and stretched out in a sunny spot on the warm stone path.

Wills covered his mouth and giggled as he glanced up over his head.

Madison's eyes widened as she followed her son's line of vision. Several feet above the boy, Jefford sat on a branch, wearing nothing but a pair of breeches. His hair was also soaking wet, as were his pants.

"Jefford!" she cried indignantly. "You ought to know better than this even if he doesn't!" She pointed to the ground with one finger. "Get down out of that tree, the both of you."

Wills broke into a peal of laughter as Jefford swung down out of the tree, landing on his bare feet beside Madison. Jefford motioned and Wills jumped fearlessly into his father's waiting arms.

"Sevti has been looking everywhere for you," Madison admonished, dropping Will's little silk *kurta* over his naked body.

"We was playing, Dada and I," Wills explained.

"I can see that." Madison cut her eyes at Jefford. "I swear, I don't know which of you two is worse."

"Princess?" Sevti called, hurrying down the path toward them.

"Yes, Sevti," Madison answered, turning to her son's nanny. "I have found your wayward charge. Apparently he and his father have been swimming in the fountains again."

Sevti smiled shyly, taking the clothing from Madison, then offered her hand to the little boy.

"Go with Sevti now," Madison ordered in her best mother's voice. "You must have a nap if you're going to stay up for the party tonight."

"Will there be monkeys?" Wills asked, his eyes wide with excitement.

Madison looked at Jefford, trying to keep from laughing. "I believe your father has hired several monkeys."

"Have you, Papa?"

"I have. Now, do as your mother says. You may take him, Sevti."

"Yes, Raja." The maid nodded respectfully.

The little boy laughed and clapped and danced away, holding on to his nanny's hand.

Madison watched them go, thinking how strange it still felt to hear herself addressed as Princess and Jefford as Raja. So much had happened in the four years since she had left London that her life there no longer seemed real.

After Aunt Kendra's death, the raja had begun grooming his son to serve in his palace when he was gone. It had been difficult at first for Jefford; he had wanted to think his father would live forever, or at least long enough for them to feel they had truly gotten to know each other. But the raja had seemed to somehow know that his days on the earth were limited, and with some convincing on his part and Madison's support, Jefford had stepped easily into his father's position. When the raja died in his sleep only a year after his wife's passing, some thought from a forlorn heart, Madison was certain he had died knowing his people would be well governed and well-cared-for by his son.

Though Jefford had inherited his father's position as the raja, he and Madison had decided to remain in the Palace of the Four Winds, because it was less pretentious and reminded them both of Kendra. The raja's palace now held government offices as well as a school and a small hospital. Jefford had turned over most of the business of the indigo plantations to George, and he and Sashi still lived with them in their wing of the palace. As new parents of Alice, named after George's sister, who was lost to them, they insisted they didn't need privacy as much as they needed to know that Jefford and Madison were there to help them learn to be good parents. With George overseeing the plantations, Jefford now spent most of the hours of each day attending to his position as lord and raja over the district.

Lord Thomblin had been dead three years and the district had lived in peace, without the fear of their daughters being kidnapped. After Thomblin's death, Jefford and the raja had organized an investigation into Thomblin's foul enterprises. Sadly, Alice was never found, but the slave-trade ring was broken and there were more than a dozen men, including high-ranking British officers, now rotting in jails for their part in the abhorrent partnership.

Madison turned to her husband, unable to resist a smile when she looked into his eyes. She felt so truly blessed to have found a man to share her life with, a man who loved her as deeply as she loved him. "Really, now," she admonished lightheartedly. "Didn't I tell the two of you to stay out of the fountains? How does it look, a great raja and his son, the prince, playing in a birdbath?"

"I suppose you'll have to let me build that stone pool

for swimming." He reached out and drew her into his arms. "Then we would stay out of your fountains."

Madison slipped her arms around his neck. "I doubt that."

He laughed and kissed her. "Mmm. You taste good." He ran his finger over her nose.

"Paint?" she asked, reveling in the feel of his arms around her.

Jefford gently wiped the smudge of paint from Madison's nose. "What have you been doing today?"

"Want to come and see?"

He nibbled at her earlobe. "I'd rather do this."

She brushed her mouth across his, teasing his lower lip with the tip of her tongue. "Come see and then let's go to our chambers. Wills will be asleep for at least two hours."

"I think you have a deal, wife." He kissed her soundly and then slipped her hand in his. "I'm all yours. Lead me where you will."

Barely able to contain her excitement, Madison led Jefford out of the gardens, around the palace and inside, by way of the front pavilion.

"Where are we going?" he asked.

They walked through the round entrance hall Madison had painted the first year they were married. "I was just doing a couple of touch-ups and I thought you might want to see them."

"Madison, you know how much I like this painting, especially now that I'm in it. I'd rather you didn't change it one bit."

She led him past a ladder, past a drop cloth where her paints still lay out. "Oh, I think you'll like this change." He halted in front of the elephant with the howdah on the wall.

Jefford stared at the painting for a moment. "What change? I don't—"

Madison laughed and grinned. The howdah in the painting contained her and Jefford and Wills, with one addition. Tucked in her arms in the family portrait was a tiny bundle.

Jefford looked at Madison. "A baby?" he murmured.

Madison couldn't stop smiling. "Are you pleased?"

"Pleased?" He threw his arms around her and lifted her off the floor. "I'm thrilled. Elated. I—"

"All right. All right," she laughed, kissing him.

"When?" He lowered her to her feet, gazing into her eyes.

"Not for at least six months."

His face was immediately lined with concern. "Are you feeling all right? You haven't been sick, have you?"

She shook her head. "Not a bit."

"A baby," he breathed. "I can't believe we're going to have another baby."

Hand in hand, they walked down the corridor toward the larger bedchambers that had once been Kendra's. "Why are you so shocked? You *do* know how babies are made, do you not?"

He laughed again. "I'm just so happy." He pushed open the door for her. Inside, the drapes were pulled to block the hot noonday sun and the rooms were dark, cool and inviting.

"I'm glad."

"Have you thought of a name for this new prince or princess?"

"I have. Her Royal Highness, Princess Kendra the Second."

"And if it's another boy?"

"Prince Kendar has a lovely ring. Unless you don't like—"

"Give me another child like our Wills and you can name him whatever you like."

"Her." Madison chuckled. "Name *her.* And she is a girl."

"You know that for certain?"

"Mother's intuition." In the privacy of their chamber, she looped her arms around his neck and pressed her mouth passionately to his.

Jefford pulled back. "Are you certain we should—"

"By Hindi's teeth," she whispered, molding her hips provocatively to his. "I'm pregnant, not ill." She rubbed her nose against his, looking up into his eyes. "Besides, some say this is just the thing to keep a woman's stomach settled during pregnancy."

"Do they, now?" Jefford lifted a dark brow devilishly. "Well then, I shall certainly do my duty."

Madison threw her head back with laughter as he lifted her into his arms and carried her to the bed. "Say it," she told him.

"I love you."

"Say it again." It was a game they played, but it was important to them both. After Kendra's death, they had promised each other that no matter how angry or frustrated they became with each other, they would repeat those words every day for the rest of their lives.

He eased her onto the green-silk-covered bed and lowered his head over hers, drawing her into his dark-eyed gaze. "I love you, Princess Madison. I will love you for all my days and then beyond."

Madison let her eyes drift shut as his mouth brushed hers. "I love you, Raja," she murmured against his lips. "I'll love you, forever and beyond."

MILLS & BOON

Historical

On sale 7th September 2007

Regency

THE LADY'S HAZARD
by Miranda Jarrett

Major Callaway returned from war a damaged but determined man. Thrown together with copper-haired beauty Bethany, he must uncover a mystery that involves them both. They are in grave danger…and the truth could tear them apart.

TAMED BY THE BARBARIAN
by June Francis

Cicely Milburn has no intention of marrying a Scottish barbarian! But when Lord Rory Mackillin rescues her from a treacherous attack she reluctantly accepts his help – even though his kisses trouble her dreams.

THE TRAPPER
by Jenna Kernan

Wealthy socialite Eleanor Hart finds forbidden pleasure in the arms of the rugged, passionate Troy Price. How can Eleanor return to the privileged prison of a world she's left behind?

Medieval
LORDS & LADIES
COLLECTION

*When courageous knights risked all
to win the hand of their lady!*

Volume 1: Conquest Brides – July 2007
Gentle Conqueror by Julia Byrne
Madselin's Choice by Elizabeth Henshall

Volume 2: Blackmail & Betrayal – August 2007
A Knight in Waiting by Juliet Landon
Betrayed Hearts by Elizabeth Henshall

Volume 3: The War of the Roses – September 2007
Loyal Hearts by Sarah Westleigh
The Traitor's Daughter by Joanna Makepeace

6 volumes in all to collect!

Medieval
LORDS & LADIES
COLLECTION

VOLUME THREE
THE WAR OF THE ROSES
Bold fighters, courtly lovers

Loyal Hearts by Sarah Westleigh

Lady Pippa d'Alban was in turmoil. Her betrothed
had returned to England with Henry Bolingbroke. Sir
Giles d'Evreux had been in no hurry to wed her five
years ago, so how could the contract be honoured now?
Especially when her family supported the rightful king!
Astounded at her blossoming, Giles meant to wed her,
with or without her consent!

The Traitor's Daughter by Joanna Makepeace

Lady Philippa is tainted by her father's politics. Sir
Rhys Griffiths has the power of life and death over her
family. Yet he seems a man of honour, a man who has
appointed himself her protector. Could it be that he
seeks her father for quite a different reason – to ask
for her hand in marriage?

Available 7th September 2007

www.millsandboon.co.uk

M&B

*Victorian London is brought to life in
the stunning sequel to Mesmerised*

London, 1876

Though Kyria Moreland is beautiful and rich enough to
attract London's most sought-after gentlemen, she has yet to
find love and refuses to marry without it. When she receives a
mysterious package, she is confronted with danger, murder and
a handsome American whose destiny is entwined with hers...

Rafe McIntyre has enough charm to seduce any woman, but
his smooth façade hides a bitter past. Still, he realises Kyria is in
danger, and he refuses to let her solve the riddle of this package
alone. Who sent her this treasure steeped in legend? And who
is willing to murder to claim its secrets for themselves?

Available 17th August 2007